I0650120

Tillers of the Soil

— MARK CLAVIER —

Sacristy
Press

Sacristy Press
PO Box 612, Durham, DH1 9HT

www.sacristy.co.uk

First published in 2025 by Sacristy Press, Durham

Sacristy Limited, registered in England & Wales, number 7565667

British Library Cataloguing-in-Publication Data
A catalogue record for the book is available from the British Library

ISBN 978-1-78959-404-1

To the memory of my father, Tony Clavier (1940–2025).

His boundless love of history has been a guiding light in my life, inspiring every page I write. I carry his stories, his wisdom, and his impish humour with me always.

"People come—they stay for a while, they flourish, they build—and they go. It is their way. But we remain."
The Wind in the Willows, *Kenneth Grahame*

Dramatis Personae

The Rusticelii

Gaius Rusticelius Armoricus: the *paterfamilias*

Corotica: the materfamilias and daughter of Theodwald, who owns a neighbouring estate

Marcus Rusticelius Quercus: Armoricus's father. His cognomen Quercus means "oak"

Aurelius Rusticelius: eldest child of Armoricus and Corotica, studying in the Corinium

Publius Rusticelius: the younger son of Armoricus and Corotica

Rusticella: Armoricus and Corotica's only daughter

Lupus and Flox: the family dogs

The Villa household

Cadfan (*Cad-van*): the villa's steward, husband of Ancarat, and foster-father of Ria

Ancarat: the villa's headmistress, wife of Cadfan, and Ria's foster-mother

Ria: foster-daughter of Cadfan and Ancarat and handmaid to Corotica

Baglan: the villa's shepherd

Awen (*Ah-wen*): Baglan's wife

Brochfael (*Brock-vile*): Baglan's son

Ceridwen (*Care-ID-wen*): Baglan's daughter

Riderch (*Ree-dairch*): the villa's master carpenter

Gwen: Riderch's daughter and Ria's best friend

Owain (*O-wine*): the villa's blacksmith

Rhodri: Owain's son

Drichan (*Dricken*): a young priest from Isca Augusta with ambitions to become a monk

Corotica's family

Theodwald: a veteran Frankish auxiliary, Corotica's father, and master of a nearby estate

Tewdrig: Corotica's younger brother. ("Tewdrig" is the British version of "Theoderic")

Gwladys (*Glad-iss*): Tewdrig's wife and Corotica's sister-in-law

Cunicatus: Meurig's twin brother and Corotica's cousin

Meurig (*May-rig*): Cunicatus's twin brother and Corotica's cousin

Bonaven Taberniae

Potitus: a magistrate in a small mining town and grandfather of Patricius

Patricius: a small boy who is the grandson of Potitus and son of Calpurnius

Calpurnius: Potitus's son and Patricius's father

Vibiana: Calpurnius's wife and Patricius's mother

Other characters

Gwas: a strange man who lives near a standing stone in the wilderness

The Bishop: the Bishop of Isca Augusta

Crassula: a tax collector

Muconius: a Roman veteran and refugee

Prince Cormac mac Urb: a prince of the Irish Déiri, who now govern the tribal lands of Demetia in modern-day Pembrokeshire

Aongus: an Irish bard and advisor to Prince Cormac

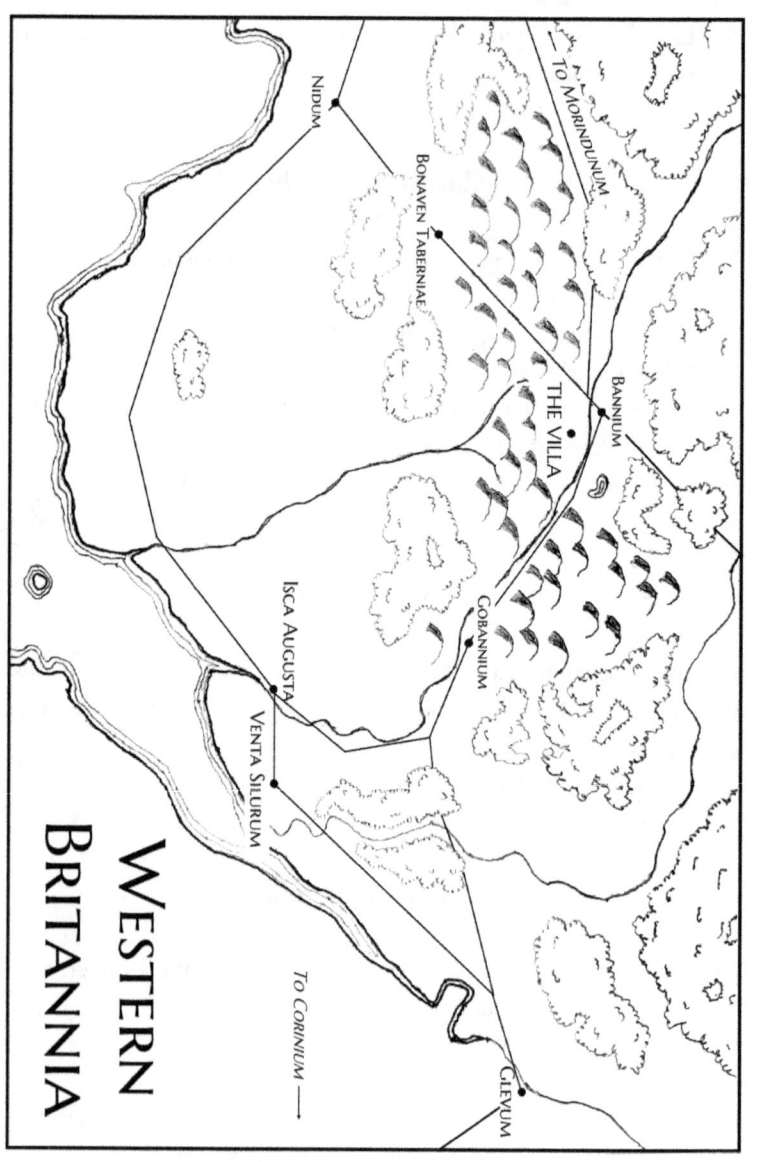

WESTERN BRITANNIA

NIDUM

BONAVEN TABERNIAE

THE VILLA

BANNIUM

— TO MORINDUNUM

ISCA AUGUSTA

GOBANNIUM

VENTA SILURUM

To Corinium —

GLEVUM

Place names

Glevum (Gloucester): a major Roman colony and trading centre

Londinium (London): the capital of Roman Britain

Garthmadrun: roughly equivalent to the old county of Breconshire

Bonaven Taberniae (Banwen): a small mining town and home of Potitus's family

Isca Augusta (Caerleon): a city that was a base for the II Legio Augusta, but now in a state of decline

Venta Silurum (Caerwent): provincial capital of the Silures, the British tribes occupying modern-day Monmouthshire, Gwent and parts of south Powys

Corinium Dobunnorum (Cirencester): the capital of the Roman province Britannia Prima

Moridunum (Carmarthen): originally a Roman fort but now a town and capital of Demetiae

Nidum (Neath): a Roman fort

Gobannium (Abergavenny): a Roman mining settlement at the head of the Usk Valley

Bannium (Y Gaer Roman fort): an abandoned Roman auxiliary fort a couple of miles west of modern-day Brecon

Armorica (Brittany): the ancestral homeland of Armoricus's branch of the Rusticelii

Burdigala (Bordeaux): a major Roman city in Gallia that was a centre of both learning and early Christianity

Isca/Wysg (River Usk): a river running through the north-eastern territory of the Silures

For you were a remnant, a common folk that knew nothing of the ways of war, who were employed in other business: tillers of the soil . . . Thus, when foemen from foreign nations fell upon you, they drove you out of your sheepfolds into the wilderness. You were like sheep straying without a shepherd . . . if you are men, behave yourselves like men: call upon the name of Christ, that he may embolden you to defend your liberty.

Geoffrey of Monmouth, History of the Kings of Britain 6:4

—

His winnowing fork is in his hand, and he will clear his threshing floor and will gather his wheat into the granary; but the chaff he will burn with unquenchable fire.

Matthew 3:12

—

No act of kindness, no matter how small, is ever wasted.

Aesop

De rerum humanarum et divinarum

AD 396

I

"Admire the thrift of the ancients more than the luxury of the moderns."
The old man might have added, "Our own forefathers, it seems, never read much Varro", but Publius and Rusticella knew their grandfather's sentiment in the same way they knew the gravel of his voice. Nor did they have to look at the object of his gaze: the bathhouse that lay at the northeastern corner of their villa.

The three of them sat at the edge of a wood of beech and ash that defined the western boundaries of the family's ancient estate. Their grandfather leaned against the trunk of an old fallen beech, cradling his heavy-headed walking stick with Publius and his younger sister perched by his side. The villa's lands unfolded below them: fields marked with hedgerows, the stream vanishing into the woods to the east, and thin smoke rising from the adjoining village. Beyond all this loomed the mountains, their hazy form a constant presence against the eastern sky. The spot was one of Grandpa's favourites, especially when he could amble there with his grandchildren to watch the swallows flitting to and fro in the late summer's air. He had sat many times there with their father when he was a small boy, just as he had with his own father before him. "It has become our family throne," Grandpa once remarked. And so it had.

Publius followed his grandfather's gaze towards the bathhouse, the estate's grandest building. "Grandpa," he asked, "why do you hate the bathhouse so much?"

The old man snorted. "Why do you think, lad?"

Publius shrugged. "I don't know. Because it doesn't work anymore?"

In a cold, damp place like western Britannia, it was hard to think kindly about a nonfunctioning bathhouse. Publius often dreamt of soaking in hot water on a cold, rainy afternoon or lying down on a bed while a slave massaged his muscles with scented oils. Now, though, he couldn't do anything more than imagine it, which didn't bring much relief when the cold settled into his bones. No hot water had touched its brightly coloured mosaic floors since long before he'd been born. To Publius, it had only ever been a place of shadows, acrid odours, and of men busy in their workshops and by their blazing hearths.

"No," replied his grandfather as he tousled Publius's hair. "I disliked it long before that happened. In fact, I like it better now as a workshop."

Publius had guessed as much. He had often seen his grandfather enjoying himself in the bathhouse, chewing the fat with the workmen or discussing the price of corn with the steward or debating with his father about how best to farm the villa. "That makes no sense, Grandpa."

His grandfather laughed again. "That's because you don't pay attention. What is it I always say up here? Come on. You've heard it enough times."

"Admire the thrift of the ancients more than the luxury of the moderns," quoted Publius.

"That's it. Now, what does that mean?"

Publius furrowed his brow, his young mind wrestling with the words. The baths were a marvel, everyone said so. Built by his ancestors to impress, they had once hummed with heat and laughter, the finest baths this side of Isca Augusta. His grandfather had told him as much—how the steam had risen like clouds and how the polished floors had shone. He had known those baths for many years before the legions marched away and the evil days of the marauding Irish arrived. But he was sure that even back then he had disliked the bathhouse. Publius couldn't imagine such a place as anything but wonderful.

Before he could give Varro any further thought, Rusticella suddenly squealed, "Oh, look!"

Not twenty yards away, a stag emerged from the trees, its red coat shining and its antlers a crown of fierce beauty. It stood as though surveying the land, as silent and self-possessed as the woods themselves. Publius was transfixed. It made him powerfully conscious of the wood and the wild, and of an alien world governed by fear and forage and the thrill of the race.

He glanced back at the bathhouse. Unlike the stag, it stood out from everything else. For all their shared splendour, the stag belonged to the landscape in a way the bathhouse never could. In that respect, the creature was more like his grandfather—they were the kindred spirits in this scene. His grandfather's abiding love for the land, tested by all Publius knew he had endured for it, made him worthy of the stag's company. He could imagine them almost as friends.

With that thought, Publius finally understood his grandfather's antipathy towards the old bathhouse. It wasn't its purpose that upset him, but its *out-of-placeness*. It had been imposed where it didn't belong. Erecting it in the middle of nowhere had been a way of showing off. *Grandpa hates it because* ... Publius searched for the right word. *Ostentatious.* That was it. *Grandpa hates things that are ostentatious, and that's exactly what the bathhouse once was.*

The stag remained indifferent to their presence for a few more moments before it sniffed, flicked an ear and swung its head slowly in their direction. Its eyes met Publius's and held him in their dark gaze for a few heartbeats. Then the stag turned casually around and stepped back into the gloom. It could not have declared its unperturbed majesty more effectively than in that elegant movement.

Grandpa barked with laughter. "Well, blow me down! Not so long ago, we'd have said that the god Silvanus or Cernunnos himself had just paid us a visit. I suppose we can't say that anymore, leastways not after our new priest arrives. Still, I think these woods have given us a gift. Treasure it, my dears. Treasure it."

Rusticella hopped off the trunk, pirouetted and clapped as though the moment had transformed her into a wood nymph. Grandpa took her hand and twirled her around. Both had been animated by the stag's presence, which seemed to possess them with the wild spirit of that late summer countryside, heavy with the cooling heat of the day.

But Publius remained spellbound. His grandfather was the wisest person he knew, but this time he was mistaken. For a moment, Publius had felt seen—not as a child but as part of something vast and unknowable. He couldn't explain what that even meant. But he understood enough to know that the stag had not offered a gift; it had issued a summons. And somehow, Publius knew he must answer.

—

Ria's face always seemed on the verge of laughter. She did not, in fact, chuckle or giggle more than anyone else, but there was something in the twinkle of her lively dark turquoise eyes and the rows of dimples beside her slightly upturned lips that usually made others want to. She had realized this about herself when she was still a girl and had come to shoulder that responsibility with a detached attitude, as though the delight she gave others was no more remarkable than the colour of her hair or the length of her fingers.

Her demeanour disguised a difficult start to life. Her mother, barely more than a girl herself, had died in childbirth. Her father had been an old scoundrel interested only in slaking his carnal appetite with no thought for its natural consequences. He had almost entirely ignored his daughter before having the good grace to be carried off by fever. And so Ria found herself, at the age of three, with no family to look after her.

For the next couple of years, she moved from house to house as the womenfolk joined in an undeclared yet fierce competition to mother her. Fortunately, Cadfan, the villa's steward, perceived the danger and so set himself up as her father.

"You were a wild little thing when I took you in," he was fond of telling her. "In fact, I used to call you my little polecat. Remember?"

But what Ria mostly recalled was being loved. Cadfan and his wife Ancarat were childless, so they had taken her in as their daughter, and she almost straightaway embraced them as her parents. Only much later did she work out that her adoption had saved them too. Before she arrived, they had yielded half-consciously to an estrangement of feeling. Each bore the frustration of their barren marriage alone and so came to possess their pain personally, even competitively.

"It's a hard thing for a woman to be without a child," her mother would say from time to time. "Hard not to deal with an empty womb by filling yourself up with shame."

"What of Dad?" Ria would ask when they sat alone by the brazier on a long winter's evening. "He must have found it difficult, too."

"He did," her mother replied. "But he was better at hiding it. He thought himself a failure, I think. Hard for a man who devotes his life to the fertility of the land to be shackled to a barren wife. But I think he blamed himself more than me."

Conversations like this made Ria realize that her arrival had been a kind of manumission for her parents. Where they'd each borne the pain of their childlessness alone, now they could love their adopted daughter together.

"Your arrival saved your parents," remarked the master carpenter's wife once, while they were sowing seeds. "Probably saved the farm as well."

"How so?"

"Your mother was no longer bound to her shame and your father to his resentment. That freed them both up to be good stewards of the villa. As simple as that."

Observations like that burdened Ria with a sense of responsibility towards her adopted parents. The *feeling* of that obligation manifested itself in the paradoxical way she mothered them by being the daughter they so desperately wanted. Such was their need that they never once suspected it. In giving them the love they longed for, she, too, was nurtured—each of them quietly building the other up in love.

But all that had now changed. Ria was in love with someone else. And the object of her passion was not the man her parents wanted her to wed.

As she followed this path upstream in the dappled light of the wood, she gave way to her unhappy frustration. The love she felt for her parents was one she had always known—rooted, dependable, the kind of love that shaped the seasons of her life. But the love for him—the young man—was different, unsettling in its urgency, in its pull. There was no reconciling those two loves. She tried to distinguish them by naming the one *sensible* and the other *silly,* hoping that the first would extinguish the second.

But no matter how she turned it, no matter what names she gave to the feelings that rose and fell within her, she could not change the truth: it was the boy's gaze, the way he had looked at her that day, that made her heart quicken. The memory of his shy grin, which had sent a tremor through her, lingered like a secret she didn't want to keep. And try as she might, she couldn't deny that this love—wild, unmeasured—seemed to count more than all the reasons her mind could offer in favour of her parents' wishes. It was a foolishness she couldn't untangle, and yet, there it was, beating relentlessly against all she had been taught to honour.

With an exasperated sigh, she sank down into her skirts beneath a towering beech. She came to the spot regularly, especially in the spring when the wood anemone, bluebells or wild garlic carpeted the woodland floor and made the air thick with scent. But now she was too preoccupied to appreciate any of the late summer beauty that lay around her.

Rhodri, the man her parents wished her to marry, was neither ugly nor unkind. The thought of being his wife did not, in itself, upset her. She had known him all her life—had played with him as a child, and in the passing years watched him become a young man of quiet strength. He was the son of Owain the blacksmith, Cadfan's oldest and dearest friend, and so was like a brother to her. Therein lay the problem, she thought. For in every other way, he was a sensible choice for a husband. The hammering of iron had shaped his body into something that seemed carved from the earth itself, a form so solid and sure it could have been sculpted in stone. And yet, despite a physique that had been hardened by fire and sweat, he possessed a quiet shyness that made him, in his own way, soft. So when her father Cadfan and her mother Ancarat had first proposed the match, she had not found the prospect disagreeable. Rhodri was a good and steady man. His skill at the anvil was already near that of his father's, and his future seemed as sure as the work he produced with his hands. Despite not knowing if she could ever see him as anything more than the boy who had once played at her side, she had obediently accepted her parents' intention.

That was before the Midsummer festival.

Ria had been eagerly anticipating Midsummer. It would be her first as a young woman, the first when she could join fully in the dancing, feasting and merry-making, and the first when she would pray with the other women for hearth and home. In the old days, mothers had made offerings to the goddess Vesta, but now that they were all supposed to be good Christians, the gifts went instead to Iesu. Still, the rituals remained largely unchanged—it was these rather than their divine object that held value.

Ria had risen early with Ancarat to help bake a loaf of bread, which they would leave at the wooden altar in the room where the household gods had formerly presided. Iesu's table had been festooned with freshly picked flowers that stained the altar linen and obstructed the silver candlesticks Ria had carefully polished for the priest. Piled around it were loaves of every shape and size offered by the womenfolk for their families. As the old priest sat snoozing in his dotage and declining health, Ancarat and Ria made their prayers—Ancarat for protection and prosperity and Ria for fertility and abundance.

It was as they were leaving that Ria had first seen Brochfael, the shepherd's son, in a new light. She had long known him, of course, but there was something in his demeanour, in the mood of the day or perhaps in her own prayers that had made her notice him in a different way. He had crossed Ancarat and Ria's path as they emerged from the gloom of the chapel. Although he was carrying wood for the evening's bonfire, he had too enthusiastically gestured a greeting, and the kindling in his arms did not so much fall as scatter like a disturbed flock of birds. He shot Ria a sheepish grin before quickly gathering up the wood and scurrying away faster than a whipped dog.

That grin was all it had taken. It caused her heart to do something it had never done before. She found herself thinking that she would like to see it again. In fact, she fancied getting to know its owner better and on different terms from when they were children. That smile intimated something about Brochfael she had never noticed before and couldn't articulate. But she liked it. His grin looked to her as if it belonged closer to her own cheerful face.

"My child," remarked Ancarat as they walked back to their home, "you look a little flushed. Are you feeling well?" All Ria could do in reply was to turn an even darker shade of red.

How magical that Midsummer festival had been! Ria and Brochfael gradually and bashfully gravitated towards each other as conscious of each other as they were of the gaze of those around them. Their awkward banter became their eloquence as they each groped clumsily after words of love neither knew how to express.

They danced instead. Movement, laughter, song and merriment served as their initial courtship. But as the evening settled into night and the drink continued to flow down the receptive throats of the merrymakers, Ria and Brochfael had withdrawn into their own world as they whirled around the burning bonfire. They eventually drew closer together until finally they nestled into each other's arms in a dark corner by the old bathhouse and spoke falteringly yet sweetly to each other. Brochfael never tried even to kiss her. She recognized his restraint for what it was: not so much self-control as bashfulness, and she accepted it for the gentleness it implied.

He was gone the next day, back to the high pastures with his parents Baglan and Awen to tend the villa's flocks. Since then, he'd returned only on occasional errands for his father. But each time he had devised a way to spend time with her. Ria had even once or twice risked a proper scolding by neglecting her chores in the villa just to walk a little way along the stream with Brochfael as he made his way home. It was during the last of these, in a narrow glade by a low waterfall, that he had finally kissed her, sealing with his lips the devotion that his words and attention had promised.

That was two weeks ago. Ria probably wouldn't see Brochfael again for another week or so. But she knew that soon his family would lead the flocks back down to their winter pastures, and then they would have all winter to enjoy each other's caresses and see how far their love could grow. That thought both thrilled and dismayed her. She would not willingly disappoint or defy her parents for all the money in the world. But for Brochfael she just might.

She was suddenly stirred from her sad reflections by the sound of a distant wail followed by a caustic chorus of crows. It had come from somewhere up towards the old forest in the direction of Empress Oak, too far for her to investigate further. Somewhere high up on the slope, someone was in anguish. She listened carefully for further sound, but none came except for the endless gurgle of the stream. She began to tremble. Only a great tragedy could provoke such a cry. It seemed to her to augur the approach of some great evil, as though it were the baying of a hound from the underworld. The wail had been unmistakably human, but to Ria it felt like the forest itself had given a cry of warning.

Fear banished all thoughts of Brochfael or her parents. Gathering up her skirts, she fled back to the safety of the villa.

II

The gods were growing silent. Baglan sensed that as he stepped across the threshold into the moss-carpeted space that lay beneath the towering boughs of a venerable oak. Whereas all the other oaks were stunted, this tree alone had withstood the gales that assailed the mountain slopes to grow to a great height. Its long boughs reached out over the other trees like a hen protecting her chicks. Its trunk was thick and scarred, bulging with old wounds and armoured with deep, furrowed bark. Moss and lichen cloaked its branches, bending them with their weight. The villagers called it Empress Oak, seeing in its gnarled form the shape of a woman, round and powerful. But for Baglan, the tree was less the queen of the old wood than his oldest and truest friend.

"I need you now more than ever," he whispered as he approached the old Empress.

Even in his grief, Baglan couldn't help recalling when his father had taken him and his family there when he was a child. During the summer, they had lived above the wood in the same hut—called a *hafod* in their own tongue—where now he dwelt with his own family in the summertime. On many an evening, they'd take a loaf of bread, a bit of ewe's cheese and a handkerchief of berries and wade through the bracken to go and sit beneath the old oak and listen to his father tell tales.

In those days, the wood was inhabited by old stories that clung to the slopes as stubbornly as the trees themselves. Some were ancient myths and legends that had come to dwell there as they had done in woodland spaces throughout Britannia—stories about the horned god Cernunnos, the wild dogs of Nodens or the healing waters of Nemetona. At other times, Baglan's father brought the Ancestors back to life with epic stories of ancient battles or of their people's stalwart defence against the Romans. But Baglan's favourite stories were those of his father's youth, when the village gathered beneath the Empress Oak to honour the woodland gods. When the wind rose and the seasons turned, their music and dancing swelled until it seemed the gods themselves had possessed them. They felt more animal than man, like hares running free or dogs chasing the scent.

The oak was also a place of love. His own mother and father and their parents and their parents had pledged their fidelity to each other there, as Baglan had with his wife Awen. Generations of lovers had been crowned with mistletoe and had touched the gods by placing their entwined hands into the oak's hollow during their nuptials. His son would have been mortified to know that he had been conceived on the carpet of thick moss that lay between two of the oak's roots. They were not the only ones who used it so. Empress Oak blessed her people with fertility.

Such reflections now brought a stabbing pain to Baglan's chest, snapping him rudely back to the here and now. He had not come to Empress Oak to recall old memories or to think on love. His was a sterner business that demanded his full attention. Only the aid of the horned god and the fierce spirits of his battle-hardened Ancestors could give him the wherewithal to accomplish what he knew he must do. For that, they demanded a sacrifice.

Baglan dropped his leather bag at the foot of the oak where a crop of milkcaps would soon appear. He hadn't prepared himself for the effect of his arrival. He felt his emotions well up and his fingers grow clumsy as he fumbled with his bag's leather cord. Swallowing hard, he wiped the tears from his eyes as he breathed deeply until he regained his composure. He needed to be brave. The horned god didn't respect weakness.

He carefully pulled a red, slimy object from his bag: the heart of a sheep that had been killed the day before. He knew that Cernunnos expected a living sacrifice—a healthy ram or calf—and not the cold heart of a dead ewe. But it was the best he could do. Even in his desperation, he daren't sacrifice one of his master's remaining sheep; they weren't his to offer, and theft was no basis for beseeching the divine. The heart would have to suffice.

But would the dead heart of a worthless carcass offered to a god growing silent be sufficient for his task? Though Baglan remained loyal to the old gods, even he could sense their diminishing power with the advent of Iesu, whom the Romans called Christ. The crucified god ruled a world far wider than any of their own gods and was said to have power over death itself. He had some vague recollection that he was honoured for rescuing people from bondage, which would make him an appropriate god to listen to Baglan's entreaty. Had he known what to do, he would have brought a sacrifice for Iesu too, just to be safe. But the new god seemed only to ask for people to consume his body and blood. That required a priest. But he was dead, so Baglan had to settle for the ewe's heart.

He retrieved his knife and made a long incision in the cold organ. Congealed blood oozed over his hands, which he smeared with outstretched fingers on the oak in the vague shape of antlers. Then he reverently placed the heart inside the hollow of the tree. Leaning back, he dropped to his knees and lifted his hands to the oak in a gesture of supplication. Now, the emotions poured out of him freely as he faced squarely the catastrophe that had befallen his family.

He had returned home the previous afternoon to find his *hafod* ransacked, his wife and daughter missing, and the broken body of his son lying in a pool of blood.

"My darling boy," he wailed loudly. "My own precious Brochfael. How can you be dead?" The crows perched among the branches of Empress Oak added their raucous cry to his own before taking flight like dark prayers ascending.

"My Brochfael," were the only words of supplication he could find to say. But that was more plaint than prayer. Defeated, he gradually, inch by inch, allowed his weary arms to drop against the oak. His posture of prayer became an embrace as he wrapped his arms around the trunk and rested his head against the rough bark. It would have looked to an onlooker as if Empress Oak were holding Baglan to her belly. He, in turn, drew such comfort and strength in his embrace that eventually he was blessed with words.

"Cernunnos, horned god of my ancestors, I speak to you now," he paused, uncertain how to continue. "Spirits of the Ancestors whose blood runs in my veins, whose souls imparted life into my own, I ask for your assistance. Hear me." That much sounded right. But he wasn't sure what should come next. For a long moment he stared at Empress Oak, his mind blank, his lips wordless. With none of his previous confidence, he finally muttered, "Hear me. Help me . . . "

Only then did he notice how bloody his hands were from the sacrifice. To his own muddled mind, that blood was his son's blood. Baglan felt his grief give way to cold fury. Why had the gods so cursed him? What had he done to deserve such a thing? He had remained loyal to them while others turned to the new god, Iesu. He deserved better; he now demanded better.

"Cernunnos, horned god of my people, attend me," he cried in a hoarse voice. "Though I, who now kneels before you, may be only a wretched man . . . Though I, who dares to address you now, may be no warrior . . . I, Baglan the shepherd, make this vow: I will find my wife and daughter. I will avenge my son's death. This, I swear. You, who have been our god from time out of mind, you who are now made weak by the crucified one, I demand you answer my prayer and come to my aid. Cernunnos, horned god of my people, prove yourself. Assist me in my task. Should I fail . . . should I not find my family and avenge my son, then know that I will forswear you. This I vow."

Baglan still had enough sense to know that this wasn't a wise prayer, even to a god growing impotent. Yet his grief and anger had left him no other words, no other offering. He also knew well enough the folly of his choice—to set out and seek his family, to demand justice for his son. How could he, a shepherd, possibly succeed? Still, there was no other path to take, no other way to honour his duty as a father and husband. Even if it ended in sorrow, he would go. He must go.

As he started to rise, something small struck his forehead, bounced against his dry lips and rolled against his chest before landing in his cupped hands. He looked down at the object and recognized it at once as a token: small and worthless in itself, but a gift all the same. Baglan knew then that he had another guardian, one who had always remained loyal to him, and she would watch over him.

The acorn now resting in his bloodstained hand assured him of that.

—

Drichan tried unsuccessfully to concentrate on the Bishop, who was speaking to him from behind an elegant writing desk. But, as usual, he was distracted by his own agitation. His trembling betrayed him, as it always did—hands unsteady despite his firm clasp, voice tremulous when he spoke. No matter how calm he tried to appear, his body exposed him, a physical betrayal he could neither escape nor master. His helplessness gnawed at him, feeding the quiet shame he felt about his own inadequacies.

"Are you listening to me?" The Bishop's words cut through his thoughts, causing him immediately to sit up straight as though he'd been scolded by his old grammarian.

"Sorry, sorry," he replied pitifully. "I've been distracted of late."

The Bishop snorted. "I don't doubt it," he said before carefully studying the young priest. Then the episcopal expression unexpectedly softened. "Tell me again what has led to this request."

Drichan sighed inwardly. He'd already been through this with the Bishop both in writing and in person. What point was there in repeating it? But that was not a question to put to the Bishop of Isca Augusta, an imposing prelate of a city that had now been abandoned by its legion. Drichan gulped air like a suffocating fish. "I wish to become a monk."

The Bishop clicked his tongue. "I know your request, boy. I want to hear your reasons for it again. Why turn your back on a promising career?"

A promising career. His father, a prominent freeman of the city, had put the same question to him only a month before his sudden death. He had insisted on Drichan becoming a deacon like himself, not for any religious reason but to continue his family's clerical exemption from imperial taxation. When the Bishop had laid hands on him, however, Drichan had felt a warming of his heart, as though God's Spirit had enkindled it. He came away a changed man, deciding then and there that he would become a preacher like St Paul or St Cyprian rather than the businessman his father wanted. He pledged himself to help build a new kingdom for Christ in pagan Britannia.

His father had been horrified. He had not compelled his son to become a deacon only for him to squander his life on the priesthood. "You're throwing away a promising career" had been among his last words to

Drichan. Unmoved by his father's warning, however, he had sailed the next day for Burdigala in Gallia where he spent the next two years preparing for the priesthood. He never saw his father again.

Drichan brought his thoughts back to the present. "I really believed God was calling me to preach the gospel and lead people away from false gods. You know that I was even willing to defy my dying father to do so. I studied at the feet of the holy and learned Delphinus and I was eager to go obediently wherever you sent me. But a friend gave me a copy of the *Life* of St Anthony of Egypt, a man venerated among God's servants. His life opened my heart to the words spoken by our Lord: *If you would be perfect, go and sell all that you have and give to the poor; and come follow me and you shall have treasure in heaven.* That kindled a holy desire in me to renounce all my worldly goods and commit myself to God alone. I would like your permission to withdraw into my own desert, the wilderness here in Britannia. My lord Bishop, I would be made perfect."

Drichan's zeal was wasted on the Bishop, who merely rolled his eyes. "That unbearable Egyptian has caused me more headaches than I can number. I don't need another monk. I need men who can celebrate the Eucharist, preach the gospel, visit the sick, and shrive sinners. You can see for yourself that everything around us is going to rack and ruin. Isca Augusta is finished. Our poor basilica of blessed Junius and Aaron will never be built, and even now my people are preparing my household to move to Venta Silurum. The world is winding down, Drichan."

"*Those who feasted on dainties perish in the streets; those who were brought up in purple lie on ash heaps,*" muttered Drichan half to himself.

"What?" snapped the Bishop. "Oh. Yes, Jeremiah. That is indeed the age in which we find ourselves. First, our rulers geld themselves by retiring into splendid seclusion on their estates. My God, I wish they'd listen to Cicero by making themselves useful to society! Now, we have clergy retiring as hermits in God-forsaken places instead of feeding Christ's sheep. How are we supposed to preserve virtue and good order if our best and brightest are all buggering off?"

Drichan was astonished by the Bishop's rudeness. "*But the prayers of the righteous avail much,*" he protested weakly.

"Not if they know nothing about those for whom they pray because they're behaving more like troglodytes than priests. Christ did command us to love our neighbours as ourselves, not avoid them by living in some bloody cave. A fat lot of good it would have done if our Saviour had chosen to wander in the wilderness bickering with Satan rather than dying for our sins."

Drichan didn't know how to respond to the Bishop's blasphemy. By common agreement, the contemplative life was deemed superior to the active. Had not Jesus commended Mary of Bethany for sitting at his feet while scolding her over-busy sister Martha? Drichan wrung his hands anxiously. He could feel his holy ambitions evaporating like ungathered manna in the wilderness, but he lacked the nerve even to meet the Bishop's piercing gaze.

The Bishop growled. "Fortunately for you, Drichan, I can see now that you don't have it in you to be a good shepherd. Given time, perhaps you could have become one. I don't know. Frankly, I haven't the time or resources to waste on anyone who's not committed to his priestly vocation entirely. Please look at your bishop when he's speaking to you!"

Drichan sat up straight again to find that the Bishop was trying to hand him a sealed wax tablet. "Here is a letter of introduction from me to a man named Gaius Rusticelius Armoricus. He's an honourable Roman who owns a villa a few days' journey up the Isca. It's in the middle of nowhere. Just your thing. Show this to Armoricus and he'll provide you with a place where you can wrestle to your heart's content with whatever demons deign to waste their time on you. I shouldn't think they'll be overly intimidated."

Drichan could hardly believe his ears. He was about to thank the Bishop, perhaps even rise to shake his hand, but he was cut short by another episcopal growl. "Sit still, man. Before you go, may I ask whether you have made any practical arrangements?"

The question, plain and simple, caught Drichan completely off guard. He had thought long about what he would leave behind, but not at all about what his new life might demand. The consequences of renouncing possessions now began to present themselves—it wasn't just comfort and wealth he was forsaking but the ease of depending on others. He would have to learn how to fend for himself, to be as productive in practical things as he hoped to be in prayer. Nothing had prepared him for such a life.

"I thought not," sniffed the Bishop. "I give you a week. A week before you come crawling back to Armoricus begging for a hot bath and a decent meal. Perhaps then you'll have enough sense to return meekly to your benevolent bishop. When you do, please be suitably penitent. I want to see callouses on those scrawny knees of yours. You're dismissed. Go in peace."

Drichan rose from his chair without a word and began to back reverently towards the door. Just as he was about to exit, a question occurred to him. "Pardon me, my lord. But how, how do I find this Armoricus?"

The Bishop didn't bother to look up from the papyrus he'd begun to read. "Ask my porter to take you to Aurelius Rusticelius. He is Armoricus's son on his way home from Corinium. He knows to expect you. Go with my prayers, Drichan. I suspect you'll need them."

III

Corotica was uneasy. This was not a typical state of affairs for the Domina, an entirely level-headed and practical woman. Her husband, Gaius Rusticelius Armoricus, might understand how the villa worked inside and out, but no one knew its people like she did. For seventeen years, she'd dedicated herself entirely to her *familia*, which included not only her own family but also the servants, farmhands, tenants and their kin. She even knew their pets' names. Rain or shine, every day of the week, she'd do her rounds, checking up on as many of her people as she could, acting for them as a mother, governor, teacher, helpmate and nurse as situations demanded. A handsome woman with striking emerald eyes and dark coppery hair, she even wasn't above mild flirtation if it encouraged the men to do as she thought they ought. She wore her authority with grace and was therefore obeyed by almost everyone without their ever suspecting that they were being obedient.

Such was the security of her benign rule that the very fact that she was feeling uneasy made her all the more apprehensive. She had become preoccupied by her own preoccupation, and that just would not do. Setting down her distaff, she stood up, smoothed the folds of her dress and started to pace the room, stopping only for a moment to look distractedly out of the window at the rows of trees burdened with apples and pears. *What are you fretting about, you silly woman?* she asked herself as she rubbed the tightness in her chest. *What are you fretting about?* But still no satisfactory answer came.

"Ancarat!" she called towards the doorway that led to the kitchen. A moment later, her stewardess appeared, drying her hands with a cloth. "Have you seen Ria? She should be tidying the guestroom for the new priest. He may arrive any day now."

Ancarat shook her head. "I've not seen her since this morning. I sent her to gather some kindling, but that was ages ago."

Corotica sighed. "That girl of yours has been acting strangely of late. She seems distracted."

"I'll have a word with her," promised Ria's mother.

"Everything else in hand? I feel as if I've forgotten something."

"Nothing I can recall."

Corotica made a noise of exasperation. "Why do I feel so ill at ease?"

"On a lovely day like today? Let me make you a drink."

"No, thank you," replied the Domina. "Maybe I just slept badly. I'll be fine."

After Ancarat had returned to the kitchen, Corotica resumed her seat and picked up the distaff. She tried humming some of her favourite tunes as she spun, but it did little to ease the discomfort in her chest. Something was nagging her, and she knew she wouldn't settle until she'd worked out what it was. The only thing for it was to make an inventory and work through it methodically.

She began, as she often did, with thoughts of her family. Her eldest, Aurelius, studying rhetoric and philosophy in Corinium, came first to mind. His letters had been scarce of late—typical for a young man his age. When they did come, full of florid phrases, they always boiled down to the same request: *Dearest mother, please send money.* Corotica smiled faintly at the thought. He was becoming too Roman, she feared, too enamoured of city life ever to call this place home again. Had he ever really? Corotica tutted at herself impatiently. These were customary worries that time had worn weak, and, therefore, were no cause for her current restlessness.

Might she be uneasy about her other two children, Publius and Rusticella? No, she'd seen them both in the charge of her father-in-law Quercus, walking in the direction of his perch by the woods. They'd be as happy as larks in his company.

Then what about Quercus? She snorted derisively at herself. He might be old, but he was sprier than anyone his age had a right to expect. She could still remember the first time she'd seen him. She'd been only a small girl, peeking around a doorway as he strode into her father's hall. It was the early days of his visits, back when he'd come to drink fine Gallic wine and set the world to rights with her father, a German auxiliary turned farmer who'd taken a British wife. Back in the peaceful days before the Irish came, Quercus simply went by his family name, Rusticelius. He was the object of the kind of automatic deference provincials learnt to give to Roman patricians from the cradle, only laced with affectionate mockery.

The cause of the latter was Rusticelius's demeanour. People heard him long before they saw him, and the sound of him perfectly presaged the sight. He would arrive at the village dressed in his mud-stained tunic, and his black, tussocky hair making him look as if he'd been dragged through the scrub. Many a dull day in the fields was made brighter by someone dropping tools to mimic his booming laugh or his lively gesturing. He was their sprite. He took their ribbing in his stride, even shared it, recognizing that there wasn't a drop of malice in their sport.

But their Roman sprite also had mettle, which he proved when the Irish descended like vultures into their secluded valley. When almost everyone else fled, Rusticelius dug his feet on the ground and never budged an inch, even after those same evil men murdered his wife in the old bathhouse. Since then, he'd been known by everyone as just Quercus—the oak, rooted and unyielding.

No, the days were coming (given his age) when Corotica would need to fret about old Quercus, but they weren't here yet.

The only person left was her husband, now out in the fields with Cadfan and some of the villa's labourers. She snorted again. If her father-in-law was an oak, then her husband was an immoveable rock that anchored them all. He was the one who made sure the villa prospered, that they all continued to have a place to call home.

This was not to say that Armoricus was always the easiest man to live with. Corotica knew that once her husband set his mind on or against something, he was about as likely to budge as a rock. When he fixed himself steadfastly on something, there would be a hardening in his grey eyes, a barely discernible tensing of his brow, and she'd know at once that there would be no dissuading him. For an eminently reasonable woman such as herself, he could be infuriating. She recalled the early days of their marriage, when she'd try not just to move the rock that was her husband but to pulverize him. She'd rage against him in order to elicit some emotion, some impassioned response that would give her an opening for persuasion. But he'd weather her ire like granite and think not a jot less of her for the sharp words she wielded like a chisel.

Thankfully, those days were long gone. It occurred to her how rarely now the two of them quarrelled. It wasn't that they always agreed. But she had come to accept that she couldn't honestly expect to love and rely on Armoricus for his virtues while resenting him when they seemed more like vices. The stubbornness that made him unyielding in argument was precisely the same determination that made him dependable in everything he did. She could demand that he try to be a good husband, farmer and patron, but she acknowledged she had no right to expect him to be a saint.

Besides, both she and her husband had been blessed with sense that was not only good but also aligned.

"You're both sensible in the same direction," is how Cadfan often put it. She knew what he meant. Where Armorica could reliably be trusted to do what was best for the villa, she knew what was best for its folk. He had good sense about the place, she about its people. What Armoricus didn't realize, though, is that her wisdom encompassed him within its wide scope and was therefore superior. She aimed to keep it that way.

Corotica resumed her pacing. Although Armoricus wasn't the cause of her unease, her instincts suggested the solution to her anxiety lay in his direction. *What could it be?*

"Think, Corotica, think," she muttered as she rapped the knuckle on her index finger impatiently against her right temple.

As she did so, her shoe caught something on the floor, sending it rattling across the room. She looked down at the mosaic to see a gaping, grey hole surrounded by cracked and crumbling tesserae. Her eyes lit on a broken piece of tile; her shoe must have caught the edge and wrenched it from its mortar.

With a gasp, she stepped suddenly back before her foot did further damage. The blue and green mosaic floor had been laid by Armoricus's great grandfather almost a hundred years earlier. Since then, its colour had faded with use, and it had been poorly patched over the years. Artisans who could restore its beauty were rare and costly, and so the decaying floor had become a stubborn relic of a glory long past, too cherished to discard yet too broken to admire.

Corotica's gaze swept the room. Though the furnishings were intact, there were cracks in the plaster and the limewash was faded and blotched by the sun. She knew the same wear could be found in every room. Their struggle to buy what was needed grew harder by the day. And most telling of all was the old bathhouse, long since turned to a workshop and storehouse—a silent testament to how far they had drifted from their former prosperity.

"It's all falling to pieces," she breathed. "Not just here but everywhere."

She remembered how stately the villa had seemed when she and Armoricus had crossed its threshold on their wedding day. Time and devotion had not been enough to preserve that grandeur. It wasn't that the estate had failed or that they'd grown poorer—rather, the glory of Rome itself was receding, the foundation of their world was falling away. She felt it in her bones: they were living on the edge of ruin, a slow unravelling so long underway that most had grown accustomed to it.

Not Armoricus. For all his quiet endurance, he had understood their precarious place. His tireless care for the land was not just stewardship but resistance—a herculean battle against the tilt of the world. That morning, when news came of a distant villa raided, she had glimpsed it in his eyes, though only now did she begin to reflect on it. He'd been carrying the load of that struggle quietly. Perhaps he didn't want to add to the care and concerns of his household. Or perhaps (and she could well believe this of him) he bore it alone because he believed it was his alone to bear. Wise as she was in the ways of her people, she had not fully appreciated that until now.

Corotica returned to her chair and took up her distaff as the unease in her heart gave way to resolve. Armoricus must not be allowed to bear the weight alone any longer. Their good sense must be aligned again. They would hold fast to the land, their people and the graves of their ancestors. Through whatever ruin God was bringing to their land, they would remain as rooted and steadfast as Quercus had once stood. Corotica would see to it. They would endure.

The party struggled up the steep hill not far from where the remains of a long abandoned auxiliary fort lay in a wide, wooded valley deep in the territory of the Silures. Its members had trundled towards the mountains from Isca Augusta, stopping for a couple of days to resupply in Gobannium, a squalid Roman mining settlement sheltered behind crumbling wattle-and-daub walls. With each passing day of travel, the travellers sensed themselves shedding civilization. Once beyond Gobannium, they encountered only a scattering of Roman-fashioned dwellings. The other small settlements consisted of the traditional roundhouses of the Silures and looked much as they must have done before the first Roman hobnailed boots had imprinted themselves on their rich soil. They were entering a land in which Rome had, in all her days of occupation, meant little more than the to-ing and fro-ing of soldiers, the import of durable pottery and endless taxes.

Aurelius Rusticelius was travelling alongside the first cart laden with goods under a waxed canvas. Thirty yards ahead of him rode the villa's twin guards, Cunicatus and Meurig, who were his mother's half-German cousins. They were a good foot taller than Aurelius and wore their hair and beards proudly in Gothic-style. Lumbering behind them were two more similarly burdened carts with a couple of new milk cows in tow. In the middle cart rode the priest the Bishop had sent along with them.

To their left, the Isca flowed darkly through the valley, cutting its way eastward along the feet of the mountains until it snaked into the fertile fields that lay beyond Gobannium to the north of Isca Augusta. Relics of the ancients were also scattered around them. High atop one mountain stood the grassy ramparts of a hillfort that had once guarded the approach into the valley. Earlier that day, they'd passed a broken-down chambered tomb, and soon they would pass by a lonely standing stone that the locals still venerated even if they had no memory of its origin. On a late summer's day when the light breeze kissed your cheek and the smell of peat and forest tickled your nose, you could well imagine yourself in paradise.

"I never knew how beautiful these lands are," called the young priest.

"I suppose," replied Aurelius without conviction. "I'd prefer to be back in Corinium myself."

"Really?" replied the priest.

Aurelius slowed his horse until he was next to the wagon. "Nothing much ever happens here unless you like farming."

Aurelius had wanted to like Drichan. He was well educated, if perhaps more in the Christian scriptures than the great profane authors who fertilized Aurelius's own imagination. But he had found Drichan strangely uncommunicative, with the bearing of one going into exile. Aurelius concluded that he had committed some crime for which he had been banished. He wondered what the man's true story was.

"I'm not talking about derelicts," he continued, "like Isca Augusta or even a provincial town like Corinium. I want to see a proper Roman city with a busy forum, grand basilicas, theatres and baths."

"I lived for a couple of years in Burdigala," replied Drichan. "You won't find a more 'proper Roman city' on this side of the Alps."

Aurelius' eyes brightened as he imagined the Gallic metropolis. "What I wouldn't give to live somewhere like that. Instead, I'm stuck here in the backend of the Empire."

"How did your family come to be here?" asked Drichan.

"The first of them made his fortune collecting taxes from the Silures. The money he skimmed from his office could have provided my family with a respectable home in Gallia. Instead, he built a villa in this cold, sodden place with only ignorant Silures and coarse auxiliaries for companions. It's perverse. Thank the gods, I live now in Corinium."

"So, this is no longer home for you?"

"Home?" exclaimed Aurelius. "No, it was never that. Caesar, Livy, Cicero, Tacitus and Seneca taught me to think of elsewhere as my home."

"Even if only in your imagination," concluded Drichan. "I was like you before I went to live in Burdigala."

"Exactly," agreed Aurelius, not really listening to the priest. "I want to be surrounded by people who know in their bones that the gods have created Romans to rule. At least there are people like that in Corinium. My family seems content with mediocrity."

"The Bishop seems to think highly of your father," countered Drichan.

Aurelius shrugged. "I've never understood him myself. Free of all bonds, yet he ties himself to this stubborn land. Works it with his own hands, no better than a servant. What's the point of reading Virgil and Cicero, if you're going to live like a common labourer?"

"So you really hate this place?" asked the priest. "It must be hard not to belong where you ought most to belong."

Aurelius found that a strange way to describe his predicament. Where did he belong? The answer seemed obvious to him. "Perhaps not everyone really belongs where he was born and raised."

Drichan opened his mouth to respond, but then seemed to think better of it. Aurelius regretted expressing his own bitterness so openly to a stranger. Each mile closer to his parents' estate soured his mood further. Was it the homecoming or the reason for it? He intended to have it out with his father, though the thought of it made him tremble. He needed to make his position clear: he would move to Armorica, where his cousins thrived. It was the only sensible choice. Like all reasonable people in Britannia, he'd make sure that the receding tide of *Romanitas* did not leave him behind like flotsam in a rising sea of disorder.

Towards the end of the afternoon, the party forded the Isca and completed the final mile or so to the villa. They were met with great excitement as they passed through the adjoining village, where most of his father's farmhands lived. A group of boys and girls ran alongside them, calling after Cunicatus and Meurig to play with them. But they soon turned back, leaving the party alone as they approached the hubbub of the villa.

Aurelius felt his chest constrict at the sight of his father's estate. He was like an escaped convict returning to prison. He always felt this way when he came back, which is why he hadn't been home for well over three years. He imagined his friends in Corinium scoffing at the villa, mocking its bathhouse that no longer worked and its fountain that no longer ran with water. "You're more barbarian than Roman," they would have said. Their imagined words rang loudly in his ears.

A loud "whoop!" summoned him from his thoughts. He turned to see his father, grandfather, and Cadfan jogging towards him. The three had been standing in the field, overseeing the workers gathering in the harvest. Armoricus beamed with undisguised delight and Quercus pumped his walking stick in a friendly welcome as Aurelius and Drichan dismounted and left the drivers and his cousins to continue into the courtyard. Before Aurelius could deliver an appropriately dignified greeting, his father wrapped him in a strong embrace while Quercus slapped his back. "Well met, my son, well met," his father declared happily. "Your mother will be overjoyed to see you."

Their ebullience caught him entirely off guard. He momentarily dropped his adopted Roman gravitas and basked like a proud boy in their affection. But he soon recovered and attempted a formal reply. "I bring you the greetings of my patron, father. You're looking well, grandfather."

Armoricus released him and stepped back a pace to study him for a moment. "You look well yourself, my son. City life seems to agree with you."

"A bit too much," added Quercus before tapping his grandson's stomach with his stick.

Aurelius frowned at his grandfather's jesting. "I come bearing unhappy news. My tutor has closed the academy and absconded to Gallia."

"What!" exclaimed Armoricus. "But we only just paid him your fees. Did he leave any explanation?"

"No. I suspect he used the money for passage out of Britannia. Many are migrating to the continent." Aurelius didn't feel that this was the right time to mention that he planned to follow them.

"We can speak about this later," said Armoricus. "Your mother will want to see you straightaway." Then looking behind him, he continued, "First, I think you should introduce your friend."

It took a moment for Aurelius to realize that he meant Drichan. He'd forgotten about the priest, who was standing quietly a few paces back. "My apologies, Father. This is Drichan, a Christian priest that the Bishop of Isca Augusta has sent to you. I'll allow him to make his own introduction."

But before Drichan could do so, there came excited squeals as Publius and Rusticella came running towards them with arms flapping wildly like fledglings trying to take flight. If Armoricus and Quercus's delight had caught Aurelius off guard, then his siblings' unrestrained joy unmanned him. He couldn't help but laugh. It was not the polite chuckle he had learned at formal dinner parties or even the boisterous laughter of his carousing. It began as a croak before tapping into something deeper, more heartfelt, inside him.

"Aurelius! Aurelius!" his siblings exclaimed in unison. Then Rusticella continued, "We saw the most amazing stag. Up there by the woods." Publius simultaneously declared, "You must come and see my new bow!" With an apologetic look at the rest of the party, Aurelius allowed himself to be dragged towards the villa, leaving the astonished priest alone with his father and grandfather.

Though Aurelius had barely returned to his supposed prison, the sights, smells and sounds of home were already working away at his long-nurtured pretence. However much he might want to reject the villa, it remained his home. He recalled the priest's strange phrase about not belonging where he ought most to belong. Only now did he realize that really what he dreaded wasn't confronting his father. What terrified him more was summoning the courage to break free forever from the only place that had ever truly claimed him as its own.

IV

Publius looked on his grandfather with the kind of affectionate awe typically reserved for household gods. And like a devotee in the presence of his god, he was magnified in his grandfather's company. When he joined him on his rounds or lunched with him under the old plane tree or listened to him tell stories on the beech log on a warm summer's evening, he felt more man than boy. Publius wouldn't exchange his grandfather's love for anything in the world.

But his cousin Meurig came a close second in his affection. Meurig and his twin Cunicatus were sons of his great aunt, who had been killed by the Irish in the same year as his own grandmother. Tragedies from those dire years scarred both sides of Publius's family, as they did many other families in the valley. They marked Publius too, not only through the grim allusions regularly made by his elders or the stories they recounted by the fire but also through the lingering unease that those evil days might one day return.

Although, from any reasonable perspective, Cunicatus and Meurig had been born simultaneously, the few minutes that separated their births had made all the difference to their respective childhoods. Their ale-sodden, pugnacious father had pronounced Cunicatus his successor and therefore the inheritor of everything he deemed good about himself. Having declared the status of his firstborn, he could think of no other use for Meurig than as a reserve.

Thankfully, Meurig's heart could not contain enough ill-will to hate both his father and his brother. It helped that he and Cunicatus were strikingly identical. Meurig often quipped that hating his brother felt too much like trying to pick a fight with his own reflection. Yet Meurig could plainly see that to be saddled with the hopes of a father you could never love was a burden heavier than neglect. And so, as soon as they were old enough, the twins dealt with their respective predicaments by being as absent from their father as they were inseparable from each other. Thus they came to the villa, offering their swords first to Quercus and, in turn, to Armoricus.

Unlike other children, Publius didn't adore his cousins for their martial prowess. He disliked Cunicatus's soldiery bluster, preferring Meurig's skills as a huntsman, and he treasured these even more because his cousin was keen to share them. It was he who had presented Publius with the bow he had eagerly shown his own brother. It was therefore no surprise that Publius leapt out of bed early on the morning after Aurelius's return and hurried out into the damp courtyard to join Meurig for a day of hunting.

Mindful of the slumbering dogs, they slipped quietly around the main house and down to the gate that led through a hedge of hawthorns that protected the southern boundary of the villa's precincts. A low mist hung over the early dawn fields, casting a ghostly veil over the landscape as they followed a narrow path through the tall grass. When they reached the far side, both were damp from the morning's heavy dew. The dark wood welcomed them with its late summer stillness.

They knew the path towards the ford well enough to follow it blindly in the lightening gloom. By the time they had removed their shoes, crossed the river, reshod themselves and climbed the steep bank on the other side, the sun had finally risen above the distant mountains. Thousands of morning dew droplets reflected its rays, and the field shimmered as though offering a rich harvest of diamonds.

Meurig stopped by a log that lay at the edge of the wood and produced a breakfast of stale bread and hard cheese. As they dried out in the warming sun, Publius described Aurelius's return, while Meurig retold old folktales about Cadno fighting the invading Romans in the hills around them. Though a Roman himself, Publius loved Meurig's version of these stories, in which the old folk hero of the Silures outwitted blundering Romans until he was betrayed by one of his own men. Publius and his friends had spent many a happy hour in the woods pretending to be Cadno and his gang of sturdy companions. So had their elders before them, and those before them still. It was how they learnt to read the landscape, like a book repeatedly reread.

Sometime later, they began walking again, crossing through another stand of trees and into a broad meadow dotted yellow and purple with vetch, thistle and St John's Wort. When they were part the way across, Meurig stopped and reached into his pouch to produce an assortment of bleached bones. "We must make an offering before we begin to hunt," he explained.

Publius frowned. "We're not supposed to do that, are we?"

"Probably not," Meurig replied with a shrug. "But it's what I was taught to do. We must give the gods tokens of what we hope to take from the land. If we're lucky, we'll spot deer in the woods. Otherwise, we'll go beyond Baglan's hut and look for rabbits and hares higher up the valley. So I brought the bones of each animal. We'll also offer them to Iesu to be safe."

That sounded reasonable enough to Publius. Meurig snapped each bone in half and held them up to the sky. Then he bowed his head before making an awkward gesture that Publius assumed to be the sign of the cross but looked more like swatting a fly. "Help me dig a hole." After they were done, he placed each set of bones in the shape of a cross inside and sprinkled them with yew needles before replacing the soil.

The ritual complete, they crossed to the far side of the field, where the ground climbed gently into an ancient wood of oak, beech and ash. Iesu or the gods must have paid no attention to Meurig because they spent the entire morning searching and listening for potential game without luck. After an overhead buzzard seemed to mock them, they returned to where they had buried the bones and headed southward into the narrow valley that lay between two of the great northern arms of the mountains.

From time to time, breaks in the canopy gave them a view of the villa surrounded by a broad landscape of cultivated fields, pastures and woodlands. Publius could see people gathered besides the fields that would shortly be mowed. He and Meurig stopped to enjoy the view while they snacked on more stale bread and refreshed themselves with some of Meurig's bitter-tasting ale. Afterwards, Publius picked and ate some of the last raspberries of the season while Meurig dozed in the warm sun.

Refreshed, they continued up the valley, where breaks in the canopy began to afford a different view, mountainous and wild. To their west, a pair of craggy, flat-topped peaks poked above the hump of a high ridge, like fins cresting a wave. These were the lofty places from where, on a clear day, you could see all the way to the sea itself, or so Publius had been told. He often wondered what it must be like to stand atop them and glimpse the sea. Since he had travelled no farther than a few miles from the villa, the wide world existed only in his imagination. Cities like Isca Augusta and Venta Silurum were as fanciful as Rome or Athens.

Shortly later, they reached the depths of the woods, where bracken and trees clothed with moss surrounded them, and the damp musk of earthy decomposition filled the air. The song of thrush, blackbird and robin regularly broke the silence, joining the constant but fainter trickling of the stream along the bottom of the valley. They stood listening for a few seconds before they heard another sound, a quiet rustle of leaves and the cracking of twigs. A large animal was approaching.

Publius stared with ecstatic wonder when an enormous stag emerged around the side of an uprooted ash. It knew they were there and stared at them as it stepped forward a few paces. From the bold creature's markings and antlers, Publius recognized it immediately as the same stag he had seen before. It stood watching them, still apart from a wrinkling of its coal black nose and the flicking of its ears. Publius caught a movement on the periphery of his vision and turned his head slowly to find Meurig beginning to aim a deadly arrow.

"No!" he cried and desperately knocked the bow just as Meurig released the string. Publius turned in dread back towards the stag, but neither it nor the arrow was visible.

"What's wrong with you, boy?" demanded Meurig.

Publius was shaking with emotion. "Did you hit it?"

He could tell that Meurig was angry. But his cousin did no more than study Publius's face for a moment. His anger faded, and he said, "It's fine, cousin. The arrow missed him by an inch or so. Now, tell me what that was all about."

Publius explained about the stag's prior visit and the connection he had felt with it. Meurig seemed to understand at once and accepted Publius' account as though it were the most natural thing in the world. He put away his bow and began to search for his arrow.

"I don't pretend to understand the ways of the gods, cousin, especially in these strange days. That stag's visit could just be chance, or it could be the gods, Iesu, or the Ancestors trying to tell you something. I can't say.

But pay attention." He bent down and retrieved his arrow. "Come, let's see if we can follow this friend of yours. Perhaps the horned god is trying to take us somewhere."

It was easy enough to follow the stag's path. After a while, they were able to track its footprints as the ground gradually turned into spongey peat. By then, the woods had begun to open up onto the broad, open space of mountain and moor ahead of them. Publius had never been this close to the high moors, but he knew his bearings well enough to know they couldn't be far from the *hafod* of Baglan the shepherd.

Suddenly, Meurig stopped, grabbed Publius, and pulled him roughly behind an alder. Ahead of them, around a dozen scattered sheep grazed on tufts of grass amid the trees. It was only then that Publius noticed the smell of smoke.

"What's wrong?" whispered Publius.

"Those are Baglan's sheep. They should be up on the hill, not unguarded down here in the woods. He would never be so careless. His *hafod* is just over there, beyond the trees. Stay here while I go investigate."

Publius didn't want Meurig to leave him alone in the suddenly menacing woods. His cousin squeezed his shoulder reassuringly, though he looked stern. "I won't be more than a few minutes. If you hear anything strange, fly like your stag back to the villa. Do you hear me?"

Publius nodded. Meurig lay his bow on the ground and quietly removed his quiver. Then, gripping his sheathed hunting knife, he crept through the wood, careful not to startle the sheep. Publius watched him through the alder until he had disappeared behind the slope of the hill, leaving him to sit in a forest silent except for the rhythmic sounds of munching ewes.

When Meurig finally returned, Publius knew at once from his expression that he brought unwelcome news. "What is it?" he asked as he rose to meet his cousin.

Meurig frowned. "There's been an attack. Baglan and his family are gone. There are dead sheep scattered everywhere. And . . . "

"What?"

But Meurig only shook his head and said firmly, "Come. We must return to the villa at once. I need to report this to your father."

V

Drichan had slept surprisingly well. His bedchamber was comfortable, if small, containing a single wooden bed with a feathered mattress. His bags were piled against a corner near a window draped with linen curtains billowing in the morning breeze. He sat up, made the sign of the cross on his forehead and quietly recited the Lord's Prayer before reaching for his tunic.

Next, he fumbled through his bags until he found his most precious possessions: his psalter and Gospel book. Both were enclosed in undyed linen, which he unfolded reverently, edge by edge, as though unwrapping a delicate gift. The books were bound in dark leather with crosses etched into their covers. The Gospel book was held shut by two bronze clasps incised with elegant tracery, while the little psalter was bound with only a leather strap. Drichan picked up the psalter and sat back down on his bed with the volume resting open on his lap. He composed his mind for his morning devotions.

Although it had become his intention while in Gallia to pray seven times a day as stipulated by Psalm CXVIII, it turned out that his mind was less devout than his heart. No sooner had he begun his contemplation than his attention would scurry after little anxieties, memories, grumbles and wants, like a cat darting after scattering mice. He would try to corral his thoughts by concentrating on a holy phrase or image only to find that this would comprise the sum of his devotions. He constantly berated himself for his lack of concentration.

So when he closed his psalter a little later, he wasn't surprised that his time of prayer had been squandered on reflecting about his new environment. He blamed the verse from Psalm XXVI:

> *One thing I have asked of the Lord, this will I seek after; that I may dwell in the house of the Lord all the days of my life. That I may see the delight of the Lord, and may visit his temple.*

The verse had initially turned his thoughts towards his impending life as a hermit. Whatever cave or cottage that Armoricus gave him for a cell would become his "house of the Lord". His prayers and devotions would ensure that. He yearned to taste the sweetness of his Lord, to draw as close to heaven as his sinful soul would allow on this side of the grave.

But no sooner had these pious thoughts begun to inflame his heart than the image of another house rose up in his mind: the villa. It was a shabby place compared to the stately homes he knew, more farmhouse than aristocratic estate. He noticed straightaway the parched, ivy-covered fountain in the courtyard, the flaking whitewashed walls and the monstrous bathhouse. The last of these was a garish affair, a tasteless status symbol inappropriate for only a very modest villa rustica. He suspected it had been built by some *nouveau riche*—perhaps a tax-collector, land speculator or an auxiliary commander fattened by plunder.

At first, he wondered why the Bishop had formed so high an opinion of the family. But then he met the Domina. He warmed to her at once. Though the blush of her youth had faded, there were still enough hints of it easily to imagine how alluring she must have once been. She was as tall, with a figure that suggested the kind of matronly strength he associated more with plebian women. No reclusive lady she, he suspected. Her hair, streaked with grey, was bound up and partly hidden under a brightly coloured shawl that complimented her emerald eyes.

His admiration for Corotica only increased during their dinner the previous evening. Both Armoricus and she had made him feel at ease. While he didn't detect any deep piety, they spoke openly about their Christian faith and assured him of how much they and others missed receiving the holy mysteries. As the meal had progressed, however, he had become increasingly worried that Armoricus and Corotica supposed him to be their new priest. He kept intending to bring up the subject of his hermitage, but the opportunity never presented itself. They were far more focused on their son and his news about his tutor's unannounced departure.

By lunchtime, Drichan had managed to explore his surroundings and meet a few of its residents. While his opinion of the villa itself hadn't improved, he had been entirely seduced by its setting. The quality of the light that morning was such that the woods, fields and mountains were remarkably vivid. The leaves were blushed with autumnal colours and broad patches of purple heather were beginning to darken the green slopes of the mountains. It was too beautiful for the austere life he had planned, yet he understood now why someone might choose to live here, away from the crowded, noisy world.

Drichan was somewhat astonished to find Armoricus and Corotica dressed casually in tunics when he arrived for lunch. While the matron looked fresh and relaxed, her husband wore a stained and soiled tunic, and picked at his grubby fingernails. A dilapidated *petasus*, a broad-brimmed straw hat favoured by farmers, lay on the couch at his side. He welcomed Drichan with a smile and beckoned him towards one of the couches that surrounded a low table laden with dried meats, cheese, bread and fruit. As he reclined, a young woman poured him watered wine.

"Apologies for our appearance," greeted Armoricus, looking at his hands. "I've been harvesting onions and leeks, and we both must go straightaway after lunch to help with the mowing. I'm afraid our meal will be hasty."

"You must forgive our familiar ways," explained Corotica. "I fear we've been too little improved by the kind of society you must be used to. My son says we live too modestly, by which, I dare say, he means we're too common."

Drichan swallowed his cheese before replying. "Your modesty is becoming, Domina. Like that of St Anthony who, as a child, was said to have been *content with what he had nor sought to have anything more*. I myself am seeking to escape the trappings of civilization."

"The Bishop says in his letter that you trained in Burdigala," said Armoricus. "Although I was born here, much of my childhood was spent with my cousins in Armorica to keep me safe from the Irish. I never made it as far south as Burdigala, but I often heard about it. Is it as magnificent as they say?"

"I found it so," replied Drichan. "It's justly famous for its learned teachers and eloquent orators. I was blessed to undertake my studies there. It seems as if the sun always shines there."

"What a change to find yourself here now," laughed Corotica with just a hint of defensiveness.

Drichan shook his head. "Yes, but for the better." He briefly recalled when he had first arrived in Burdigala and felt so overwhelmed by the city that he'd hidden away for a week in his cell. "I eventually tired of all the sophistry. And I could never get used to the crowds and the noise."

"So you returned to Britannia," concluded Armoricus.

Drichan nodded. "Ironically, it was among all that opulence that I encountered the life of St Anthony. He was such a holy man and his life is so inspiring. Reading his *Vita* changed me." Drichan realized he was speaking too excitedly among strangers. He reached for his cup and took a large swallow.

But his hosts seemed not to notice. "Tell us more," encouraged Corotica as she tore herself a chunk of bread. "Was he a priest like you?"

"I pray to be even half as holy as he," replied Drichan earnestly. "Blessed Anthony was born into wealth, yet when he heard the gospel calling the rich to sell all and follow Christ, he did just that. He gave away everything to the poor and retreated to the desert, living in solitude and prayer. It is said that he fought legions of demons."

"That seems rather a lot," commented Armoricus through a mouth full of food. "Do demons congregate in the Egyptian desert?"

"What do you mean?" asked Drichan, confused by Armoricus's train of thought.

"Only that I've never seen a single demon here. Spirits, I could understand. They're all around us. But I've never heard talk or tale about demons. So there must be something about the desert that attracts them. Like flies to a midden. Perhaps it's the heat."

"No, no. Demons are evil spirits—*daimones*, the Greeks call them—but not of the dead. They're all around us, invisible. They tempt us, putting evil thoughts into our minds, stoking wicked desires. Because Anthony was so good and holy, he drew them to himself like light attracting moths. But he vanquished them, which meant they couldn't prey on others. He even overcame the devil himself."

"Like Iesu casting out demons in the Gospel stories," added Corotica helpfully. "You must tell us more about Anthony sometime. He reminds me of a holy man who visited our home when I was a girl. A strange, wild creature, but with a kind heart, I think. We thought him a druid of old returned to life. He said he fought demons too. I remember his forearms were often covered in lacerations."

"What became of him?" asked Drichan.

Corotica frowned. "Tragically, the Irish murdered him. Afterwards, they left with his head, as my people did in days of old."

Drichan blanched. "Surely, the Irish don't still come this far inland?"

Armoricus snorted. "We've not seen them around here in many years, but they frequently attacked us when I was young. They killed my mother too, which is why my father sent me away to Armorica. We'll see them again, sooner than we'd like, I imagine."

"So we may need your prayers even more," offered Corotica diplomatically.

Armoricus picked up and glanced over the wax tablet that sat on the table by his plate. "Which brings us to your arrival. Your Bishop speaks well of you, so we look forward to your services here. As we said earlier, we've not partaken of the holy mysteries for a long time. We also lost a few people in the village over the winter, who we've had to bury without benefit of priestly prayers . . . "

As Armoricus continued to describe the villa's spiritual and pastoral needs, Drichan could feel his temperature rise. He began to reach for his cup again but realized that his hand was trembling. He felt Corotica's eyes fixed on him.

"I think our guest wishes to say something," she said.

Drichan met her gaze briefly but couldn't bring himself to look directly at Armoricus. "I-I-I don't know how to begin," he stammered. "I think there's been a misunderstanding. I'm not here to be your priest."

"You're not?" barked Armoricus in astonishment. "But we've been expecting you for some time! Why are you here then?"

Drichan wanted to ask the Dominus if he had actually read the Bishop's letter but decided that would be undiplomatic. "That's why I was trying to tell you about St Anthony," he explained, instead. "I've vowed to God that I will follow his example. I've sold all my possessions and have given them to the poor. I wish now to become a monk and aid people with my prayers."

Armoricus stared at him for a long moment before breaking into a long, full-throated laugh. "You're having us on! You've come to the mountains of western Britannia to live like an Egyptian monk? You'll have to search long and hard to find a desert here in the land of the Silures! This has got to be about the most sodden place in the entire Empire."

Drichan shook his head vigorously. "Perhaps we can't be in a desert like the Hebrews when they followed Moses, or Iesu when he was tempted by Satan, or Anthony wrestling with his demons. But many like me are searching for lonely places in Gallia and here in Britannia where they can be monks like Anthony. The Bishop sent me here because he thinks you can offer me just such a place."

Armoricus was quiet for a long time, mulling over Drichan's words. Then he said, "I'm sorry, Drichan, but given the situation, that's impossible. I need a priest here in the villa looking after my people, ensuring that we remain right with Iesu, and we're fed by his body and blood. I gathered that much from your predecessor. A priest praying alone out in the woods or up in the hills does us little good."

"But, but . . . " stammered Drichan. "My prayers would greatly benefit your people. God would smile on your benefaction."

"Perhaps," countered Armoricus in a suddenly sterner voice. "Or he might punish us for abandoning you to wild beasts and the elements. No, what you ask is utterly impractical."

Drichan was growing desperate. "But has not the Bishop directed you to provide for my needs?"

"No," replied Armoricus sharply. "No, he has not." He offered the wax tablet to Drichan. "If you don't believe me, you can read the letter yourself. All it contains is a letter of introduction and the Bishop's desire that I use you however I wish. There's nothing about your being a monk."

Drichan made to receive the tablet but then checked himself. Custom bound him to accept Armoricus's word—he was the master of this household and of higher rank. Drichan's hand fell harder than he intended on the table, rattling his plate. "Then I must return to Isca Augusta," he said, his voice cracking with frustration, "and speak with my Bishop."

"Of course, you're free to do so," replied Armoricus. "My own advice is that you consider your options carefully. Your Bishop might not be best pleased if you return to complain about the inadequacy of his letter of introduction. Perhaps he doesn't approve of your ambition to be a monk."

"What if," Corotica began in a gentle voice, breaking the awkward silence that followed her husband's words, "what if you remain with us for the winter? In return for your ministering to our *familia* and to the village, I'll ask our shepherd Baglan to teach you skills you'll need to live as a hermit. And you would have the liberty of our lands to go wherever you like to pray and wrestle with your demons. If it's still your wish in the spring to follow in the footsteps of St Anthony, then I'm sure my husband will gladly offer you a place on our estate where you may find your solitude."

Corotica's offer was so reasonable and so graciously stated that Drichan could only acknowledge it as a firm and final decision. He couldn't see what other choice he had. If the Bishop intended that he serve here as a priest, then he must obey. He would have to rein in his ambitions until the spring,

Lunch came to a quiet end, the easy rhythm of its beginning lost somewhere between the first few bites and the last few words. Afterwards, Drichan returned to his quarters to ponder the unexpected change to his plans. He found an unexpected relief in himself now—a strangely welcome reprieve from the ambition that had driven him so far and so fast, without thought for the season or for what was required. He now saw that his intention to follow St Anthony's example had been naïve. But now, thanks to Corotica, there was time to make his way in a manner both practical and spiritual. Perhaps this delay—this unplanned turn—was not a hindrance, but a grace. If it allowed him to ground himself more firmly in both body and soul, then he could have no cause to complain. This wisdom was undeniable, in truth, even if he had been misled, which he now felt he had been. What he couldn't answer, without reading the letter himself, was whether the deceiver was the Bishop or the Dominus.

VI

Whenever they were waiting to start a big job, the workers of the villa milled around in groups segregated by sex. On this occasion, some men were joking with Armoricus and Quercus while others sharpened scythes to a fine edge. They laughed, whooped and carried on like boys at a dance while Cadfan organized the workers into two teams, each to a field. All wore light, sleeveless tunics and the wide-brimmed *petasus* hats long favoured by Roman fieldworkers.

Ria stood with the women outside the open doors of the barn. They were dressed in ankle-length tunics gathered with cords beneath the breast. As Corotica and Ancarat handed out hay rakes and pitchforks, the older women set out a long table with water, sweet wine, dried meats, bread, fruit and cheeses. The ever-hopeful Lupus and Flox sat as still as statues among them, drooling as they waited patiently for a sympathetic soul to take pity on them.

The women gossiped about the villa, about domestic affairs, the latest courtships, and the health of newborns who were keeping their mothers at home. With Corotica and Ancarat within earshot, their conversations remained congenial, though a little spice was added by the occasional ungenerous but veiled comment about anyone absent or out of earshot. The older women talked about the new priest, anticipating (as only elderly ladies can) his devotion to their spiritual and moral requirements.

By the time the women ambled out to the edge of the field, they had mostly set the place and her people to rights—or at least, knew what needed to be done to ensure peace and good order. Though none of them had considered it, this permanently convened informal council of women functioned in a remarkably egalitarian fashion, its concerns, judgements and decisions encompassing everyone from Armoricus down to the lowliest among them. Though the men casually dismissed it as idle gossip, within the narrow scope of their settlement, it played the part of senate alongside Armoricus's emperor.

With the preparations complete, everyone gathered around Armoricus.

"Now, let an old hand show you how it's done," he declared as he stepped towards the thigh-length grass with his scythe. He spread his legs slightly, dropped the blade towards the ground, and then stepped forward with a long, graceful movement that swept away the grass with each swing. After he'd repeated this for a few feet, he turned around with a broad grin.

"If I were a few years younger," said Quercus, swinging his walking stick like a scythe, "I'd show you how it's done." But everyone knew that his joints wouldn't back up his boast. His body, having long retired from such back-breaking work, consigned him to the role of bystander, though he conducted himself more like a field marshal.

"Boys," announced Armoricus, leaning on his upturned scythe, "we're going to mow this field as well as that one over there by the stream. The first team to finish gets an amphora of my own wine. You must cut well, mind. I want that grass low and clean." The announcement, part of the usual ritual, still brought cheers, the men lifting their scythes high.

"And," he added, a mischievous grin spreading across his face. "The losers get to turn the midden when they're done. Tonight, some of you will be in your cups, and some in the shit!" This pronouncement was met with cheers and groans. Those working alongside Armoricus faced a much larger field, meaning they'd have to work twice as hard to avoid an inglorious end to the day. But that was all part of the game.

As the men moved forward with their cutting, Ria and the other women fell in behind with rakes and pitchforks. Their job was to turn and spread the cuttings to dry in the sunshine. If the weather held, they'd return the next day to turn it all again to dry further before gathering it into haycocks for curing. Then the men would bale the hay and haul it into the barn, where it would be added to the earlier summer's crop for winter feeding. Thanks to a summer of balanced sunshine and rain, the barn would be well-stocked with nutritious fodder.

Ria fell in alongside her old friend Gwen, the carpenter Riderch's eldest daughter. She was a short but sturdily built girl with a friendly face and curly black hair, who wielded her pitchfork as though she were in the front ranks of a phalanx. Ria had to be on her guard constantly when working across from her.

"Look at Rhodri swing that thing," she declared as she stabbed the ground with her pitchfork. Ria glanced over to where the men were working, their scythes flashing against the pale green. Rhodri, tall and broad-shouldered, was cutting with such skill and speed that he was steadily gaining on Armoricus. Ria nodded but said nothing. Though Gwen was her closest confidant, she had kept her entirely ignorant of her relationship with Brochfael.

"He's a handsome hunk of meat, that one," exclaimed Gwen. "I bet you'd like to see what else he swings."

"Girl," Ria replied with a roll of the eyes, "you can be so vulgar! Now watch where you put that fork. You'll stab my foot if you don't watch what you're doing."

Gwen's conversation continued in this vein until sweat and labour reduced her to purposeful silence. By then, almost everyone else was working quietly too; like Armoricus's initial banter, this was part of the field liturgy. Idle chatter would disappear as people settled into the rhythm of their work under the bright sun.

"They're doing fine work over there," declared one of the hands whom Armoricus had sent to check the progress in the other field. "They'll surely be done before us."

"Then we'll have to pick up our pace," replied Armoricus as he removed his hat and wiped sweat from his brow. "No wonder. How can you be such a sluggard, Rhodri? Why, when I was your age, I'd have reached the hedge by now!"

Although the jest was clearly absurd, Rhodri's face darkened, and he began to attack the grass with such ferocity that Ria found herself feeling sorry for it. Armoricus laughed as he straightened his back and stretched. "That's the spirit. Now, who's going to get us singing?"

One of the hands cleared his throat and began to sing in a fine baritone:

> *Oh, lucky the farmer, if only he knew,*
> *How grand is the life that he lives, pure and true!*
> *Far from the battle and far from the blade,*
> *With earth's gentle bounty, his fortune is made.*

To this, all the workers replied haltingly with the refrain,

> *Oh, the fields are your kingdom, the sky is your crown,*
> *You live with the seasons, no need to bow down.*
> *No honour, no purple, no troubles to bear,*
> *The simple life's fortune is there to be shared.*

With each stanza, the singing grew stronger, until their voices filled the field. The rhythm of their labour matched the song's cadence, scythes swinging in arcs and pitchforks spreading the hay into broad, even carpets. Workers from both fields checked each other's progress. Though Armoricus's team faced the larger field, the grass in Cadfan's plot by the stream was thick and damp, slowing their pace. The competition tightened as the sun climbed higher.

Ria paused beneath the shade of the plane tree that overhung the barn as Corotica approached, her face glowing from work and her dress flecked with green stains. Like her husband, she had been taking her turn at the work and encouraging the others. She also enforced a fair division of labour, gently but firmly ensuring that no one shirked their part or bore too much alone.

"You're doing fine work today," Corotica said with a smile, brushing a stray wisp of hair back under her hat. "How's Gwen holding up? Still swinging that pitchfork like she's at war?"

Ria laughed, glancing towards her friend, who was working with her usual vigour. "She'll outlast us all."

"And how was the other day?" asked Corotica quietly, though no one else was within earshot.

Ria made to rise, but Corotica gestured in a friendly way for her to stay put. Ria replied evasively, "What do you mean, Domina?"

"Oh, come now," replied Corotica with a sparkle in her eye. "Do you think me blind? I know you and that shepherd boy have taken a shine to each other. Ever since Midsummer's Day, you've been mooning about the place like Psyche pining after Cupid. And don't think I didn't see you slipping off towards Baglan's *hafod* when you ought to have been churning milk."

"I was only going to the woods for a think, Domina!" protested Ria. "And I did finish my chores."

Corotica sat down next to her and started munching on an apple. "I'm not angry with you, child. I was a young woman once. Do your parents know?"

Ria could see there was no point in trying to deceive an all-knowing *materfamilias*, so she dropped her pretence of innocence. "Oh, Domina," she confessed, "I don't know what to do. I don't know what to say to them. I don't even know how to feel. My parents have their hearts set on Rhodri."

"With good reason, too," replied Corotica thoughtfully. "He's a fine boy and will make a strong match. But you're young yet, and a girl should enjoy the attentions of boys. Still, this place is too small to keep a secret like this hidden for long. Either you need to end your fling with Brochfael now or else speak with your parents."

"But I don't want to disappoint them!"

"I'm afraid that's part of being young, especially for us girls who aren't supposed to have wills of our own. But you will come into your own soon enough. Enjoy yourself while you can. It might even do Rhodri good to have some competition."

"Competition?" Ria frowned.

"Girl, you've so much to learn about men." Corotica leaned back, her green eyes full of mischief. "They're not sensible like you or me. They're creatures of battle. They appreciate most what they must fight hardest for."

Ria flushed. "But I'm not a prize to be fought over!"

"Of course you are. All beautiful women are," replied Corotica. "If you're fond of Brochfael, admit it. If Rhodri genuinely loves you, he'll rise to the challenge. If not, Cadfan will see reason. You're his jewel—he won't give you away lightly."

Corotica tossed her apple over the fence to the pigs and wiped her hands on her dress. Rising to her feet, she held out her hand to Ria. "You've a good head on your shoulders, Ria. Trust it, and all will be well. Now, back to work, young woman."

Not even the baritone's lusty lungs could sustain the workers against the rising humidity of the afternoon sun. The scythes kept swinging, the sharpening stones kept screeching, and the rakes kept gnawing at the cuttings, but the people wielding them were growing weary and quiet. Even Armoricus surrendered his scythe, undone by a lower back unequal to the full measure of his task. He sat in the shade with Quercus, shouting cheerful taunts and encouragements to those still at work.

But Rhodri kept going, refusing, except under duress, to take his allotted breaks. It was a pleasure just to watch him. The scythe had become an extension of his body: legs, back, hips, arms, snath and blade flowed in one fluid, sweeping movement. The lad was entirely focused on the ground in front of him, unmindful of the sun that was turning the nape of his neck bright red. Many on their breaks gathered near to enjoy the sight of work that had become an art.

By the time Rhodri and the other scythers reached the final stretch of their field, a strong south-westerly wind had risen and the sky over the mountains had darkened to an ominous blue-purple. The cheerful rivalry between the two fields shifted into a grimmer contest: workers against the deteriorating weather. Arms ached and backs groaned as the men quickened their pace to match the wind's growing urgency. Others scrambled to gather tools and secure anything that might be tossed or drenched by the rain.

Ancarat sent Ria and a couple of the younger women to shutter the villa's windows against the coming storm. As Ria bolted the last shutter, a chorus of triumphant huzzahs erupted from the fields. Her heart lightened; their team had won and so would not be dealing with the midden. She emerged smiling onto the veranda, just in time to see Armoricus toss a skin of wine to Rhodri, who caught it with an air of victory.

"Well done, my boy, well done, indeed!" he called over the din of the crowd. The gang cheered again as Rhodri unstoppered it and took a long drink. Armoricus warned, "Go easy! Judging by the colour of your neck and arms, tomorrow's going to punish you enough already!"

Rhodri lifted the skin high, prompting another cheer from the crowd. Like a child who'd won his first prize, his eyes sought Ria's and he beamed proudly at her. It was then that she realized that he'd been trying to impress her all along. She forced herself to return his smile, but it wavered, and before she could stop them, tears welled in her eyes. A sob escaped her lips. Covering her face with her hands, she fled back into the villa, her tears spilling faster as the first drops of rain splashed against the roof tiles.

The courtyard was deserted by the time Ria had wiped her face and ventured out again. The rain washed across the courtyard in sheets carried by the howling wind. The trees bowed against its force in the afternoon's preternatural darkness. Across the courtyard, the barn glowed warmly, alive with music, laughter and voices raised in good spirits. Just as Ria was covering her head with her shawl and preparing to dash over to the barn, she saw two figures stagger into the courtyard, silhouetted in the dim light. It took her a moment to recognize them: Meurig, drenched and grim, half-carrying Publius, who stumbled alongside him, looking scared and exhausted.

"Where is Armoricus?" Meurig demanded, his voice sharp and urgent.

"I—I don't know," stammered Ria.

"Find him. Find him now."

Before she could move, Armoricus appeared from his office, rubbing his back with one hand and smiling faintly. The smile faded as soon as he saw their faces. "What is it?"

"Something's happened at Baglan's farm. It's bad. But we should speak in private."

Armoricus nodded. "Ria," he ordered, "find Quercus and Cadfan. Tell them to come to my office. And let your mistress know Publius needs her care."

Ria held her hands to her mouth and stared uncomprehendingly at all three of them until Armoricus dismissed her with a wave of his hand. Hurrying out into the rain to find the others, her heart thumping, she recalled the eerie wail she'd heard in the woods earlier that day. She had dismissed it then. But now her heart knew what her mind refused to believe: death had come. And Meurig had found it.

—

Rain lashed Baglan's face as he huddled miserably in a low cleft among the rocks, partly sheltered by a stand of hawthorn that clung stubbornly to the earth. The downpour that battered him relentlessly through the grey emptiness around him bore the first chill of winter: a cold rain carried on a bitter wind. He yearned to be somewhere warm and dry but could do no more than cling tightly to his sodden cloak and sink as far into the gap as he could manage.

Only a short while earlier, Baglan had stood on the edge of the world looking at a vista that extended miles and miles over the countryside. At any other time, he might have lingered, luxuriating in the view that was as clear as only an early autumn's day can be. But it had given him no pleasure. There was no joy in him, and the taste of the wind had warned him of approaching rain. Sure enough, an impermeable fog had suddenly descended, wrapping his world in a veil so close it might have been spun from his own breath. A few minutes later, the wind and the rain had hit him with a fury that made him stagger.

Since parting ways with Empress Oak, he had made excellent time. Grief and fury propelled him forward on his journey. His son's killers had come from the south and had returned that way afterwards, probably circumventing the valley. That meant they had come over the high country, more likely along its edge, as he could not imagine them crossing over the top from the more settled lands on the south side of the mountains. He was convinced they were Irish, and the Irish had always come from the west.

After laying his son to rest, Baglan had wasted no time. He took what he could carry, leaving the scattered flock to fend for itself, though it broke his heart to do so. Although the raiders had a day's advantage over him, Baglan could travel swiftly. Judging from the tracks, the band consisted of at least a dozen men. He had not stopped to ask himself what he might do when he caught them. The question seemed irrelevant; his course had been set by his vow to the horned god.

Baglan had descended into the narrow valley below his *hafod*, crossed the stream above a waterfall overhung by a rowan tree red with berries, and scrambled up the steep slope on the far side. A trail of scarred earth showed where people had ascended, but it was too widely churned to be those of only the raiders. He was now on the drovers' path that traced the edge of the mountains from the west all the way to Gobannium in the east. It led him across open moors browned with bracken's dying fronds, expanses of marshy peat and fields of scattered rock. To his left, the slope stretched steeply upwards, while an almost unbroken border of oak, birch, ash and alder covered the lower slopes. It was under their canopy that he had spent his first night.

The following day, after crossing a broad valley beyond the highest peaks of the mountains, he risked leaving the drovers' path to ascend through sparse aspen and gorse onto the moor and up to a high vantage point. From there he could see a broad expanse of the mountains to the west as well as a long stretch of the great Roman road that crossed from Nidum in the south to forts and settlements in the north. This had fallen into some disuse after the forts had been abandoned many years earlier.

But Baglan could see that at least one band of travellers was using it now, only a mile or so away. He hoped it was the Irish. If only he had the eyes of an eagle, he might see his wife and daughter, his precious Awen and Ceridwen. But the hope that had risen so swiftly faltered just as quickly when he noticed the sky beyond them—low and heavy, carrying the threat of storm. Shelter, he realized, would have to come before everything, even though it meant losing sight of his quarry.

An hour or more later, he now huddled miserably amidst the rocks, lamenting the capricious gods who seemed intent on cursing him. The elements would have been hard enough to endure on their own, but to be so close to his family and yet unable to catch up with them was intolerable. Indeed, it was more than he could bear. When a rivulet snaking down between the rocks started filling his left boot, he decided he'd had enough.

"To hell with it," he growled as he stepped back into the teeth of the wind. If he must be wet, let him be moving. He stumbled and slid down the hill, moving faster than he ought across the thick turf and uneven ground. Just as he was about to reach the road, his foot caught on a low tussock, and he pitched forward, striking his head against a half-buried rock.

Dazed and bleeding, he rose immediately back to his feet and stumbled onto the Roman road.

Here, the road led him southward, its hard surface a kind of grim mercy that directed him through fog and rain. The landscape around him was among the most desolate he'd ever seen: his lasting impression was of pale grass, dark earth and grey rock washed out by the enveloping fog. He leaned into the wind, his body failing but his stubborn will carrying him forward step by step. The night thickened. The rain stung. At last, when his strength was wholly spent, he came upon a small stand of trees beside a cairn. There, in that fragile refuge, he collapsed. The rain tapped softly on his weary body as the night gathered him into its lonely embrace amid the eerie silence of the earth.

VII

Meurig's news fell on Aurelius's family like a hammer. Aurelius sat in the office with his father, Quercus, Cadfan and Meurig, the air between them heavy and tense. Corotica and Ancarat offered to look after the hands in the barn to avoid suspicion. When all had gathered in the office, Meurig explained, "There has been a raid on the *hafod*. The sheep scattered or slaughtered, their bodies left to the crows. The cottage—ransacked. There's a fresh grave but no sign of Baglan or his family."

This was greeted with murmurs of dismay. There had been no attacks on any of the local settlements in over ten years and on the villa in almost thirty. But now, with one cruel act, that long calm was broken. Aurelius felt far from the security of Corinium.

"Tell us what happened," said Armoricus.

"Publius and I were up in the hills yesterday, hunting. As we neared Baglan's place, I noticed stray sheep, which didn't seem right. Baglan's a good shepherd. Too good to let them roam. I had your boy stay hidden while I went on. Just beyond the trees, I found the carcasses—a dozen, maybe more, all butchered, some bludgeoned, some impaled. A bonfire still smouldered in the yard. The cottage had been ransacked."

Cadfan interrupted. "Now that I think of it, I recall seeing smoke up that way the other day. But I didn't think twice about it. I just figured it was Baglan burning brush."

Meurig nodded. "I can't imagine what the raiders thought they'd find in a shepherd's hut. As I said, there was no sign of Baglan or his family. But I stumbled across a fresh mound nearby, which looked to me like a grave. Since I had Publius with me, I thought it better to get him to safety rather than to spend too much time investigating."

"This damned rain will now make that difficult," grumbled Cadfan. Everyone muttered in agreement.

Aurelius observed that everyone was looking at his grandfather. All of them had been nursed on stories about his defiance of the Irish, and they instinctively looked to him as their leader. His grandfather's eyes, however, were fixed steadily on Armoricus. It was his place, as the Dominus, to speak first.

"Let's see if we can find out what's become of Baglan and his family. I also want to know who's buried there. We'll go in the morning to investigate."

"The grave, if it is one, is very strange," observed Aurelius, more to ensure he was the first to speak after his father than to be of help. "Might it be for one of the raiders?"

Quercus shook his head. "I've never known raiders to take the time to bury their fallen. It's more likely to be one of Baglan's family. Did it look large enough for more than one body?"

Meurig shook his head. "No. Nor did it look deep. But if it was dug by one or more of Baglan's family, where are they now?"

"Whatever the answer may be," said Quercus grimly, "we're missing all or most of the family. I'm guessing they've been kidnapped or are hiding. Finding them must be our priority."

"But surely they won't be hiding," suggested Aurelius. "If they were, wouldn't they have sought help by now?"

Quercus replied, "Back when the Irish were attacking us, fear caused a lot of people to behave strangely. They may be too terrified to come out from hiding, especially if it's Baglan in that grave."

"Why kill the sheep?" Armoricus asked. "I can understand stealing them. But killing so many would have taken time. It seems a strange thing to do."

"If they came from a distance," explained Meurig, "it might have been impractical for them to steal them."

Armoricus nodded. "But why kill them? And why raid a *hafod* for that matter? Where's the gain unless you're going to steal the sheep?" Armoricus thought for a moment. "Cadfan, gather some men in the morning. Arm them, but let me tell them what has happened. Meurig, you and I will lead them up there. We'll see what else we can find and exhume the body. Maybe we can get some answers."

"We'll need donkeys," added Cadfan, "both to carry tools there and, if necessary, for bringing the body back. I assume you'll want to round up and bring back the remaining flock. We'll take the dogs."

"I'll go too," said Aurelius, as much to his own surprise as everybody else's.

"You will?" Armoricus' tone revealed more than his words. The sting of it confirmed Aurelius's decision.

"Yes, Father," he replied without further explanation. He had none to offer. Honour compelled him to do other than his heart desired.

Armoricus looked pleased. "Then you will come," he confirmed before turning back to Meurig. "Find your brother. Explain to him what's happening. He should remain here to keep a sharp eye out for strangers. Now, everyone, try to get some sleep."

It was a weary crew that splattered out of the villa's courtyard and across the sodden fields on the following morning. Initially, the hands who joined them were quiet as they digested the news they'd only just received. But as they made their way up the valley and the rain eased, their disquiet formed itself into anxious chatter. Aurelius thought that his father ought to silence them, but neither he nor Meurig seemed to mind the noise. Only Lupus and Flox seemed untouched by the sombre mood, darting through the undergrowth and scattering birds with gleeful abandon.

"Why Flox?" Aurelius asked suddenly.

"Hmm?" replied his father, obviously lost in his own thoughts.

"Why did you name her Flox?" Aurelius pressed, his eyes on the wiry dog.

"When your sister was little," his father began with an affectionate smile, "she couldn't manage 'Ferox'. It came out as 'Flox'. The name stuck."

They walked on in awkward silence, trudging side by side yet apart, their thoughts winding in separate channels. Aurelius felt it keenly—the distance between them, the way their words faltered and fell. Their personalities were like two different dialects. Even before Aurelius left for Corinium, they'd both largely given up trying to talk much to each other. They might be of the same blood, but their minds were like strangers.

They found the *hafod* as Meurig had described it: a dismal scene of death and wanton destruction. Bludgeoned and bloated carcasses lay all around, some of them now partially eaten, their entrails putrefying. Buzzards wheeled above, their cries sharp and greedy, and carrion crows picked at the wreckage.

"Wolves," one of the hands murmured, crouching to examine deep prints in the churned earth. "Glad we brought the dogs."

"They must have fled at the sound of our approach," said Meurig. "Those were made after the heavy rains. Lucky for the surviving sheep that they had plenty to scavenge here."

Aurelius hung back, unwilling to draw any closer. The sight of such brutality churned his stomach, the bile rising sharp and bitter. He pressed a trembling hand to his mouth, swallowing hard against his shame. Why had he come? What good could he do here, where books and civilized manners were of little use? He stood frozen, helpless, a witness to a horror that left his heart as sick as his stomach.

After they were satisfied that the place was secure, Cadfan sent a few men with the dogs to watch out for the wolves and begin herding the sheep into the nearby fold. Meurig went to investigate the surrounding area, stopping from time to time to study the ground. Armoricus gestured for his son to join him as he and the other men searched the hut.

The *hafod* consisted of poorly made stone walls with a thatched roof, spanning an area that Aurelius thought too small for a family to live in. Light filtered through the broken shutters of the one small window. The roof had been largely ripped apart by the raiders, so that the interior was soaked and its contents ruined. A lean-to behind the *hafod* now lay empty except for a scattering of crumbs and crushed vegetables covered in a congealing morass of flour, millet and oats.

"I don't think we'll find much useful here," said Armoricus. "What do you make of it?"

"It all seems senseless," replied Aurelius. "Meurig was right. Who would ransack such a place?"

But Armoricus nodded. "This is brutal, feral. They didn't want to steal but destroy." Then he sighed deeply. "Go and gather up a few men with the shovels. I think it's time we faced uncovering the body."

The grave lay a few yards away, where the ground flattened out, free of the lichen-covered rocks that dotted the ground closer to the hut. As Meurig had indicated, it was a shallow grave, hastily dug; the shovel used to make it still lay by its side. The rain had pressed the loose earth into a damp crust, partly concealing a handful of wildflowers left wilting atop it. For all its haste, there was care in the burial, an offering of love that contrasted sharply with the surrounding horror.

Aurelius hung back as the men carefully removed the black earth. But he knew the moment when they uncovered the body because they collectively recoiled, groaning and gasping as they turned away from the grave. One young man retched. Only his father remained impervious. When he glanced at Aurelius a minute later, he looked ashen, his eyes shadowed with grief.

"I believe it's Brochfael," he announced hoarsely. "Though his face has been so savagely beaten in, it's hard to tell. Poor, poor lad."

The men steadied themselves, then reverently cleared away the remaining soil. Brochfael's body was wrapped in canvas, the fabric stained and heavy with damp. One glance at Brochfael's face caused Aurelius's throat to constrict. No amount of self-respect could hold his rising nausea in check. He staggered back and vomited, the acid sharp and bitter. He had known Brochfael only in passing, a quiet lad who had worked alongside him on occasion. Yet to see him now, so brutally disfigured, brought the horror of their circumstances into terrible clarity. If the Irish had returned, if they had done this—he shuddered at the thought of his own family meeting such an end.

The horizon had begun to darken again by the time they lifted the body from its resting place. They decided to return to the villa, the sheep in tow and Brochfael's corpse bound for a proper burial. Only Meurig would stay behind, determined to search for clues about the missing Baglan, Awen and Ceridwen. Most assumed now that Baglan had buried his son. But where had he gone since? And why?

As they gently placed Brochfael's corpse on the mule, Aurelius noticed something fall from its limp hand. He bent to retrieve it, holding it up between his fingers.

"What is it?" asked Armoricus, stepping forward.

"An acorn, Father," Aurelius said, his voice hardly more than a whisper. "Just an acorn. It must have got caught in his shroud."

The flock, led by Lupus and Flox, moved reluctantly ahead as the party formed into a slow procession back to the villa. They had come to the *hafod* as a crew of farmhands and fighters; they returned a funeral cortege, silent in sorrow. No sooner had they started their sad journey than the heavens opened, and the rain once again fell heavily.

VIII

A sharp pain in his side roused Baglan rudely from his sleep. Instinctively, he reached for his ribs, only to feel his arm jerked back violently as he was dragged roughly across the ground. Before he could grasp what was happening, he was bound to a tree with only his head and shoulders upright against the rough bark that dug painfully into the nape of his neck.

A circle of men loomed over him, their faces grim and wet, streaked with mud. Their clothing hung heavy with rain and filth, their boots caked in black earth. One stood apart, older than the rest, with a full red beard that glistened in the dim light. Another, barely more than a boy, rifled through Baglan's belongings with quick, careless hands. He was about to protest but his words were cut off by a brutal blow across his cheek. A gag was forced into his mouth, the rope tightening around his head. Another man stepped forward, his fist descending hard onto the crown of Baglan's head. The world tipped, blurred and faded. When the next blow came, Baglan barely felt it.

The world returned in fragments: the cold press of wet ground, the bite of the ropes at his wrists, the ache of his battered body. When he opened his eyes, the woods stood empty. The men had gone. His bag lay discarded atop the cairn, while his few remaining worthless possessions were strewn across the woodland floor, half submerged in black puddles. Baglan's head throbbed, his shoulders and neck were painfully stiff, and his body felt leaden with cold and damp. He felt mildly feverish as he struggled half-heartedly against the rope binding him, but it held firm. Only gradually did he recognize it as his own—a cruel irony adding insult to injury.

He slumped against the tree, defeated. Death seemed inevitable, and he now welcomed it as self-pity robbed him of any determination. He couldn't tell how long he slipped in and out of sleep. His dreams and waking thoughts merged into a parade of haunting visions of Awen and Ceridwen, of what their capturers would do—may have already done—to them both. He didn't have the strength to be angry any longer. That would have required a degree of hope. He could feel only an all-encompassing desperation. He would have given up in that moment and died. Instead, death would come slowly like a cat upon its prey, teasing him first with dark thoughts and biting shame.

Why had he bickered with his wife? Why had he been absent when his family was attacked? He shouldn't have been away. He had gone into the high country only to be alone with the stars and the gods. If he had been at home—if he had been there to protect them as he ought—he would have known by the sound of his sheep that people were approaching. They would have had time to escape. Everything was his fault.

He flailed himself with a litany of *if*s. *If* he had stayed with his family, they would now be warm and sheltered in the villa. *If* he had gone to the Dominus for help, Cunicatus and Meurig might even now be searching for Awen and Ceridwen. *If* he had fallen asleep a few more yards into the woods, his attackers would never have seen him. The gods really had set themselves against him. Knowing this, Baglan could not even pray for himself. No god would give ear to his pleas. Forlorn, he fell gradually into a fitful sleep.

He awoke to find himself stretched on the ground, wrapped in a wool blanket that stank of sweat and damp. A sun had warmed the woods, and the crisp autumn air was filled with the scent of cooking that tickled his nose and made him realize how hungry he was. His stomach growled fiercely as he sat up gingerly and looked in the direction of the aroma. His head swam.

By the cairn squatted a strange figure—a man who seemed little more than skin and bones wrapped in rags and shreds of leather. His beard, long and unkempt, was thrown over one shoulder, and his hair fell about his face as he stirred a pot hanging over a low fire. Disconcertingly, he was wearing a small set of antlers, which would have been impressive had they not slipped precariously to one side. He seemed like some strange parody of Cernunnos, as though he were mocking the horned god's impotence. Baglan could only stare.

He coughed to get the stranger's attention. "Who are you?" he asked.

The man swept aside his hair as he turned to welcome Baglan with a smile. Although the wan features of his face made him look advanced in years, Baglan was struck by the vitality of his green eyes. Without saying a word, he walked over to a pile of bags and began to ferret through them. He was even shorter and slighter than Baglan imagined. He couldn't help but wonder if he was a faerie.

"Bread, bread, bread, bread," said the stranger in a strangely syncopated manner. He had a surprisingly sonorous voice for one so small. "Where is that . . . oh, here it is. Yes, bread. Good, tasty bread." He walked back over to the fire, dipped a chunk into the cauldron and began to eat with loud slurping noises. He was in the process of repeating this when he stopped and turned to Baglan. "Come, come. You must eat."

Whatever his doubts or suspicions, Baglan was incapable of disobeying. He pulled off the blanket and crawled weakly over to the fire. After accepting a large chunk of bread, he dunked it into steaming broth that tasted deliciously of wild mushrooms and herbs. He gobbled it down at an obscene pace and accepted another portion from the stranger.

"This is very tasty," he said through a mouthful of food. "Thank you."

The stranger clapped his hands and hopped side to side in his crouching position. Then he sprang over to his bags, returning with a wineskin that he offered to Baglan. "Drink. Drink quickly."

Baglan warily sniffed the contents of the skin and was greeted by a wonderful but strange combination of honey and humus. He began cautiously to taste it.

"No!" exclaimed the stranger. "Drink quickly. We must go now."

Baglan obeyed, tilting the skin back and swallowing in quick gulps. The liquid burned as it coursed down his throat, then spread a warm and welcome heat through his chest and limbs. He gasped, coughed and then, without hesitation, drank again. When he handed the skin back, the stranger seized it with an eager grin and drank so violently that the liquid poured down his beard and ragged tunic. Back and forth they passed it, until it was drained.

"Good, good," the man chirped. "Now, we must go. The Stone won't wait. No, no, it won't. The Stone won't wait!"

Before Baglan could ask what he meant, the man grabbed his hand and began pulling him forward with startling strength. Baglan stumbled after him, his legs unsteady and his head swimming.

"What stone?" asked Baglan. "Where are we going?" He felt as though he might be sick.

"The Great Stone. It will drink. The Stone will drink. We must go!" The stranger's voice carried a wild urgency that stirred something inside Baglan, part fear and part elation.

They quickly emerged from the far end of the small wood and tumbled down a treacherously slick embankment into a small stream. Baglan lost his footing and fell heavily to his knees into the rushing water. The world was spinning quickly now. His body felt light, his mind hazy, yet strangely alive. A small hand gripped his arm and pulled him to his feet.

When Baglan looked up, he found himself staring into the face of Cernunnos, the horned god of the wild. His breath caught, and he trembled as the god spoke, his voice like the music of rustling leaves and flowing rivers: "Come, come."

Baglan followed. The horned god led him up the embankment and onto a broad, boggy plain. A few hundred feet ahead of them stood the most magnificent stone Baglan had ever seen. Even if Cernunnos had not been leading him, the Stone itself would have drawn him forward. It stood as a solitary sentinel in that desolate valley. Baglan had to touch it, had to feel the rough contours of its hard surface and come into the presence of the Ancestors who had erected it, to feel with his own skin the presence of the gods.

In its shadow, Baglan stopped, overwhelmed. Around him, Cernunnos danced, leaping and swirling and singing with a sprightly vitality that reminded Baglan of the springtime. The dark Stone was the height of more than two men and almost as broad, covered all over in pale green lichen and by thick moss along its top. He could feel the Ancestors congregating around him. He reached out a trembling hand to the Stone and felt it—a deep, timeless power. A shiver of ecstasy rippled through him, and he dropped to his knees.

He burned. Heat coursed through him as though the Stone had filled his body with fire. His faintness felt now more like a fog that made it impossible for him to think straight. But the horned god took him by his hand and led him in a dance around the Stone. Thoughts now became a whirlwind of dreams and sensations. The wild horned god and he became stationary while everything else spun around them. They had become the earth's pole, the axis upon which it turned. But, no, that was the Stone: *it* was the axis, the fulcrum, the centre of the world. Baglan could sense its ageless endurance in the face of wind and rain and ice and storm.

He was suddenly thirsty.

"Look!" cried the horned god, pointing to the shadow cast by the Stone. Baglan turned and saw it: the shadow stretched across the tussocky moor, touching the stream they had crossed earlier.

"It drinks!" exclaimed the horned god in triumph. "The Stone drinks!"

The Stone was drinking. It was being refreshed, fortifying itself against the cruel claws of winter. It would stand. Baglan raised his arms, his voice joining the wild cry. It was the last thing he remembered.

IX

Corotica sat on the stone bench at the outer end of the orchard, admiring the heavy clouds that dappled and shadowed the green mountains. A windfall of pears and apples from the storm lay around her, and the steady buzz of feasting wasps filled the air. Rusticella was happily playing with muddy Lupus and Flox, watched by Ria, who was still blissfully unaware of her approaching calamity.

She had chosen the orchard carefully. The diffused light filtering through the autumn leaves, the hum of bees and the soft laughter of Rusticella playing with the dogs all conspired to weave a fleeting, gentle respite. Here, surrounded by ripe fruit and the earthy smells of late harvest, Ria might have one last breath of peace before sorrow claimed her. Corotica watched as the younger woman reached down to toss a bruised apple for one of the dogs, her face unguarded in a moment of distraction. It was a face Corotica knew would soon change, would harden or break, under the weight of what she must share.

The tasks ahead loomed in Corotica's mind, steadying her even as it threatened to overwhelm. Soon they would lay Brochfael's body to rest, but first they must prepare him. The women of the household would gather in that solemn, shared labour, their hands moving with practised care over his broken body. They would channel their grief into the ageless ritual of washing, anointing and dressing for burial. Only with the start of the funeral procession could they finally express their sorrow usefully—their loud lamentations would frighten off the evil spirits drawn like jackals towards death. Ria would need space for her private grief before she could join the others in the burial rituals; only in that way would Brochfael's spirit be allowed to rest and Ria find healing in the company of the *familia*. If she allowed it.

Corotica refused to yield to the evil spirits that threatened her. Brochfael's death and the disappearance of Baglan, Awen and Ceridwen had shaken her badly. The day's auguries rattled her composure. The tightness in her chest had returned, along with the sense that they now stood on a precipice. The attack on the *hafod* had, in a moment, dispelled the serenity that they'd been struggling so long to maintain. She, who had devoted her life to sustaining her people, now felt powerless to protect them.

"Come, child," she called to Ria as Rusticella occupied herself with throwing sticks for the dogs.

Ria walked over and sat down next to her on the bench. "Are you well, Domina?" she asked. "You look tired."

Corotica sighed deeply and took the girl's hand in her own. It was a shapely hand, still youthful and even elegant despite the hard tasks to which it had been put over the years. "I have sad news, Ria, that you need to hear away from the others."

Ria frowned. "News?"

Corotica suppressed the tears that now welled up. "Oh, my poor, poor girl! My dearest Ria. They have found your sweet Brochfael dead."

Ria's eyes opened wide, her mouth fell open and she gasped. "What do you mean? Dead? Dead! But how?"

"Killed. I know no more than that now, except that his father and family are missing and the *hafod* has been ransacked. I fear it may be the Irish."

Ria shook her head violently. "No, no!" she exclaimed as her eyes filled with tears. "That can't be! Brochfael, dead? No!"

With no comforting words to offer, Corotica instead took Ria into her arms and clasped her tightly. At first, she resisted the embrace. But then, with a heaving gasp, she yielded and sobbed freely. Corotica, unable to hold back her own grief, wept with her. There they remained until Lupus and Flox nosed into their silence. Lupus pawed at Corotica's lap, his muddy print a gentle interruption, while Flox nudged Ria's hand until it rested on her soft, grey head.

Rusticella, ever curious and unbidden, squeezed between the dogs and climbed onto their laps. "Why are you crying, Mummy?" she asked, her wide eyes earnest.

Corotica smiled through her tears, brushing a stray curl from her daughter's face. "Hush, child," she murmured, her voice soft as the breeze stirring the orchard's branches. "Shh."

But Ria pulled Rusticella close, holding her as though she might borrow the child's innocence for a moment. "Your mummy is crying for me, sweet one. I've had sad news, but there's no need for you to be sad. It's much too nice a day for that."

Rusticella wriggled free and darted across the orchard towards the villa without a word. Ria stirred to follow, but Corotica placed a steadying hand on her arm. "Let her go. She'll be fine. But you, my dear, must gather your strength. There's much ahead that will demand it."

"What do you mean?" replied Ria.

Corotica's voice was quiet but firm. "The moment you leave this orchard, Brochfael's death will be waiting for you in every look, every word. His body will return, and the grief of this household will be overwhelming. Everyone will speak of the manner of his death, yet no one will understand the depths of your own sorrow, because they don't know of your love. Unless you tell them."

Ria wiped her nose on her sleeve. "What must I do?"

"Our first duty is to commend Brochfael to his Redeemer with honour. Evil spirits are drawn to souls by the violence of their deaths, but love— true love—can protect them. Until his family can take him to rest, you are the keeper of that love. You must help prepare his body, shielding him with your tenderness. But before that, you must decide: will you reveal your love or keep it hidden?"

"What do you mean?" asked Ria. Her face now expressed bewilderment as much as sadness.

"Are you going to tell your parents and Rhodri about your love affair or keep it secret? I think you should tell them. But I suspect you'll want to keep the secret that bound you together in life to do so after his death."

Ria covered her face with her hands and began to weep again. "Oh, Brochfael!" she sobbed repeatedly. Corotica sat quietly and allowed her the space to cry. She stroked Ria's arm gently with the back of her fingers. Finally, Ria looked up and wiped her eyes with the hem of her sleeve. "Why must I decide now?"

"Because there is a duty to be done," she replied matter-of-factly. "We must prepare Brochfael. That's all that matters now. You can do that with the support of your parents. But you must tell them. And you must tell Rhodri. On the other hand, if you keep your love secret, then you must find the courage to bear yourself appropriately in the days to come. Does your heart have strength for that, I wonder?"

"I hardly know," admitted Ria. "How can I know? I can't think straight right now."

"That's how life is, I fear," replied Corotica. "We must decide and pray God that our judgement is right. And those choices so shape our memories that we can hardly tell what happened from what we tell ourselves happened. The way I remember Armoricus and even Quercus from the days of my maidenhood is filtered, like light through coloured glass, by my decision to accept his hand in marriage. And I am who I am now because of that choice. That is the way of love."

"So, if I tell others about our love, that will affect how I remember Brochfael?"

Corotica nodded. "Or if you keep it a secret, the same. The first and more sensible choice will draw away the sting. We aren't made to bear grief alone. Keeping it a secret will bind your heart to Brochfael powerfully, but it may also twist it in the remembering."

"But why must I choose now?" protested Ria.

Corotica's heart went out to her, but she did not waver. "Because duty does not wait. We women bear this burden—to care for the dead as we do for the living. Your choice will shape how you fulfil that duty, and the way you remember your love."

Ria looked down at her lap as she wept more. Corotica watched her tears drop into the folds of her dress and thought of how she would respond had it been Armoricus who was found dead. But their love was different from Ria and Brochfael's: open, generous, inclusive of others. It was the secret of the thing that made Ria's predicament so agonizing. A grief that cannot be shared is the sharpest grief of all.

"What would you have me do, Domina?" asked Ria in a voice so soft it could hardly be heard.

"Only you can decide," she replied before pausing to consider her next word. "I will say only this: memories are meant to be shared so that they may heal us in the telling."

Before Ria could respond, Rusticella dashed back into the orchard, closely followed by the dogs. She bore a bouquet of aster, cosmos and dahlias she had picked from the garden. "These are for you, Ria," she said bashfully as she held them out at arm's length. "They will make you happy again."

Ria accepted the flowers and tightly hugged Rusticella. "You are a precious girl."

A loud cry and a chorus of murmurs announced the arrival of Armoricus and the hands. Ria looked up at once with such trepidation in her red, swollen eyes that Corotica couldn't resist leaning over and embracing her tightly. Rusticella spread her little arms wide and tried her best to hug them both. They remained that way until Flox began to whine impatiently at them. Corotica felt Ria stiffen before pulling herself gently away from the embrace.

"I can't make that decision, so, I won't," she declared firmly. "Telling my parents, and even Rhodri, now would be self-indulgent and distract me from mourning Brochfael wholly. So, I'll keep my secret for his sake. At least for now."

She rose to her feet with a look of determination in her eyes, straightened her dress and tidied her hair. Then, quickly bowing to her Domina, she turned and walked with her chin held high in a sign of resolution. Corotica watched her go with a profound sense of sadness. She would spare Ria the pain of the next few days if she could. But some things remained beyond the power of even a Domina.

X

Drichan's hands were trembling again, but this time he didn't castigate himself unreasonably. The heavy burden of expectation placed on him without warning would have disturbed even a more seasoned priest. How had he gone so quickly from the prospect of holy solitude to shouldering the pastoral needs of a frightened and grieving household? He had no experience to draw upon and no practical wisdom to help him cope with what he knew was expected of him. Where would he find the words?

It was the lack of words that most alarmed him as he knelt with his psalter and Gospel book in front of him. He implored God to show him where to turn to find the comforting words the people needed and the wisdom to intercede profitably on their behalf. But in his panic, he couldn't even decide which book to open first. He didn't know these people or the deceased. How could he know what words would speak to their hearts? A jumble of remembered verses ran through his mind, but he could take hold of none of them. It was like trying to catch sparks to light a fire. And yet he had a duty to perform. However inadequate, he was now the villa's priest.

He had been inspecting the small chapel when they came to find him. "Come quickly," the woman had said, "you're needed."

The people parted at his approach. Some even bowed reverently to him. A woman bent over with age grasped his tunic, pleading with her tears for him to do something. The keening chorus clouded his thoughts; he couldn't comprehend what was happening. It was like a scene from the Gospels, like the raising of Lazarus, except that Drichan could perform no miracles. Unlike Jesus, when he saw the body wrapped in a shroud, he didn't restore it to summoned life but recoiled in disgust. Only shame armed him against the temptation to run away. He jerked violently when Armoricus placed his hand on his shoulder and squeezed it tightly.

"How glad I am you are here," he said in a reassuring tone. Their eyes met, and Drichan knew that the Dominus saw his apprehension. "We need only your prayers now. The rest can wait."

Drichan nodded passively, accepting in that moment that he was no more than the Dominus's instrument, the surest means for calming the disturbed *familia*. "Wh-what happened to him?" he asked weakly.

"We found him dead, beaten to death. He was our shepherd's son, only a boy."

Drichan winced at the violence indicated by Armoricus's reply. He momentarily recalled Armoricus's concern in their earlier conversation that the Irish might soon return. He was not unused to bloodshed, but he had never seen it so close and had never personally experienced the threat of it. He felt exposed and unequal to the task of even offering a prayer. His tongue clung to the dry roof of his mouth.

Despite this, he stepped towards the corpse and gently laid his hand on its head. The moment his fingers met the broken skull beneath the linen, he knew the mistake he had made. It was all he could do to keep from jerking his hand away in horror. Instead, he willed it to remain motionless while he bent his head in silent prayer. The crowd grew hushed around him, waiting. He felt their gaze pressing, could sense that more than prayers for the tragic death of a boy, they needed a deep wound salving. They were looking to him for the balm of Gilead.

While it probably appeared to the onlookers as though he were praying earnestly, his mind scrambled for words. For all his learning, for all the times he had decorously declaimed Cato and Cicero in the forum, all eloquence escaped him now. He opened his mouth, then closed it, panic choking off his words. Finally, he prayed the only prayer that came to his mind: that God would give him the words. He turned to face the people.

"O Lord God of spirits and of all flesh, remember this poor soul . . . " His voice faltered as he realized that he didn't know the boy's name. "Er, accept a sinner of Christ's own redeeming and grant unto him eternal rest. Receive him into your heavenly kingdom, into the bosom of Abraham, Isaac and Jacob, where there is neither pain nor sorrow and where sighing has fled away. May the light of God shine upon him. Amen."

The "Amen" repeated by the *familia* was as much a signal for their wailing to resume as it was a conclusion to Drichan's prayer.

He thanked God for giving him words. He knew he had heard or read the prayer elsewhere, though he couldn't remember where or if he had quoted it verbatim. Whatever its source, it had done what was needed. Armoricus nodded to him approvingly.

Drichan turned back to the corpse to sign it with the cross. Only then did he notice that blood had soaked through the shroud where he had laid his hand. He looked on it in horror and disgust. Now his heart failed him, and he stumbled away, barely escaping the crowd's gaze before violently vomiting.

—

Drichan had only just managed to clean himself up, change his clothes and return to the chapel to say prayers when Corotica entered and sat quietly on a bench against the wall by the door. She gave him time to continue his prayers before disturbing him, though her presence alone was enough to achieve that. Finally, she said, "I must confide in you."

Drichan rose from his knees and walked over to her. "Yes, Domina?"

Corotica studied his face for a long moment before answering. "I relied on your predecessor's discretion. May I trust yours as well?"

Drichan nodded. "You may."

"Good," she said, her voice softening. "What I must tell you now is not mine to share, but you must know. As you prepare to offer us the Lord's consolation, you need to understand how things stand."

"I understand, Domina," though he, in fact, did not. He wondered what further burden was about to be committed to him.

"There is a young woman," Corotica continued, her eyes lowering briefly. "She was Brochfael's secret lover. A first love for both of them, I believe. Only I know of it. For a young maiden, to have such a love end in this way—" She stopped, as though she could not bring herself to finish the thought. "It's too cruel. She's afraid, Drichan. I tell you this because this funeral will be a trial for her, and I fear her silence will only harm her. She's too sweet to bear this pain alone. I will try to be a mother to her, but I think she will need your care as a priest."

"But how can I offer that care if I am not to betray your confidence?" Drichan did not add that he hardly knew how to offer a young woman such care.

Corotica's gaze met his. "I'll encourage her to seek you out. If she knows she can confide in you, her grief may open the door. If not, I only ask that you watch over her. Perhaps you can ease her pain while pretending not to know its full extent. Surely, priests must often do so without knowing every detail."

"I suspect so," replied Drichan, inadvertently revealing his own inexperience. "Domina, I am new to this way of life and have ministered to few. But I will do as you say."

Corotica nodded. "Her name is Ria. She is my handmaid. I will point her out to you when I have the chance."

—

Before Drichan could return to his room to begin preparing for the funeral, he was given yet another weight to carry. A grim-faced and worn-looking Armoricus met him on the veranda and beckoned him in a perfunctory manner into his study. The Dominus sat down heavily in his seat, placed his elbows on the table, and rubbed his face and eyes. He then sat with his head in his hands, looking absently down at the table as though he'd forgotten about Drichan's presence. Finally, he sat back, invited him to sit, and said, "I fear, Drichan, that God seems to have different plans for you from those you wanted."

Drichan frowned. "How do you mean?"

Armoricus sighed. "What do you know about the state of things?"

"Here at the villa? Or do you mean more generally?"

"The latter," replied Armoricus. "I mean Britannia. Hell, I even mean the Empire."

Drichan shrugged. "I suppose I know no more than anyone else. We're living in dark times. The glory of Rome fades, but I believe that by the light of Christ it will return."

Armoricus snorted. "That's more than I know. Some say that your so-called Christ has made Rome weak. But I've not asked you this for a sermon, though I dare say you may want to give me one. So, you think the evils that are upon us are only temporary?"

"Yes, in the grand scheme of things I do, though I know some who think we're in the End of Days. Yet I begin to wonder if these evils may last beyond our lifetimes."

"Then whatever good may come will be of little use to me," replied Armoricus derisively.

Drichan felt that something more was weighing on Armoricus's mind and so refrained from responding.

The Dominus continued, "People talk of evils, bad omens and hard times as if they were clouds in the sky, distant and formless. But such things are made of flesh and blood. Evils are a boy, scarcely grown, beaten to death by cruel men. Hard times are a household trembling with fear when courage is needed for the fields. Bad omens appear when a failing Empire emboldens the wicked. No master can run his villa, support his *familia* and protect his people in such a world. There is no harbour from such a storm."

"Except faith," offered Drichan.

"Spoken like a true Christian priest," scoffed Armoricus. "But faith does not raise the dead or feed people, whatever your Gospel book may tell you."

"Perhaps not as often as we may want," countered Drichan. "But it gives us the strength to endure. Some may say that Christianity has weakened the Empire, and perhaps that's true. If so, we may deserve such weakness. What is it that Tacitus put into the mouth of the British king of old?"

"*To robbery, slaughter, plunder, they give the lying name of empire; they make a desert and call it peace,*" quoted Armoricus. "The king's name was Calgacus."

"Yes," replied Drichan. "Perhaps we are being punished for the sins of our forefathers. If so, perhaps God, in his mercy, has given us the hope of Christ because he knows we need it for these dark days. That's why so many are becoming monks and why many of your fellow patricians are turning their villas into monasteries."

"For all the good it will do them when barbarians appear at their gates. Still, I respect them more than those who are selling their homes, abandoning their people and fleeing like cowards to safety. I will not abandon this place so cheaply."

Drichan admired Armoricus's resolve. "What do you need from me?"

Armoricus rubbed his eyes again. "I don't think you were far wrong when you said that faith can provide some people protection from the storm. If Brochfael's death is an omen of dark days ahead, I need you to provide that faith. The old gods are passing. They provide neither the strength nor what you call faith to help my people. I think Christ can. If we're to survive, I need my people to feel as secure as they can. They must have hope that God will guard their souls, at least, if not their lives. And if they fall, they must believe he will welcome them into heaven."

"I think your words wise," replied Drichan, little considering what it might actually mean if the omens were true.

Armoricus looked at him intently. "But are you up for it?"

"What do you mean?" Drichan's voice wavered as he felt a warmth creep into his cheeks.

"I've seen you tremble," Armoricus said, his tone blunt but not unkind. "I saw you flee from Brochfael's body. My wife told me you were sick in her flowerbed, though I commend you for choosing a place out of sight. You are young, I know that. And I understand that your duties are not light ones. But I need to know that you won't falter or shame yourself should things grow hard here. Can you be the priest my people need?"

In that moment, Armoricus reminded him of the Bishop, speaking with the same authority and piercing clarity that left no room for evasion. He felt his heart quail at such candour, and he dropped his gaze submissively to the tabletop. He knew what the Dominus wanted—a proud and swift assurance, a declaration of strength and purpose. But the confidence to give such a reply eluded him. Instead, he said, meekly, "I hope so."

Armoricus sighed, the sound laden with disappointment. "That is hardly the reassurance I am seeking. Convince me of your worth, or I'll send you back to your bishop. I need a priest, not another mouth to feed."

Drichan imagined the shame of being returned in such a manner. It would be an end to his ambitions, a failure that would follow him. Whether he liked it or not, this was his place now. If God had sent him here, then God must have reason for it. He thought of Moses at the burning bush, trembling at the magnitude of his task, yet summoned to it all the same.

Drichan's reflection was brief, more flicker than flame, but it gave him just enough confidence to look Armoricus in the eye.

"With God's help," he said, his voice steadying as he spoke, "I will do my best for your people."

Armoricus studied him for a moment and then nodded, his expression softening. "Excellent. That's all I need for now. Go and prepare for the burial. Your first test comes soon."

Drichan rose, but hesitated, a question forming. "May I ask you something, Dominus?"

"Go on."

"You speak of your people's need for faith. But what of your own? Are you not a Christian?"

Armoricus leaned back in his chair, his eyes drifting to the window and the land beyond. "I think I am neither fully Christian nor truly pagan," he said after a pause. "I admire your God, and I think Iesu would have made a fine farmer if he hadn't found himself nailed to a tree. But I don't have my wife's faith, though I am baptized."

"Then who do you worship? Or are you an Epicurean, believing in no gods at all?"

Armoricus smiled faintly at the question, the lines of his face softening. "No, I am no Epicurean nor a follower of Lucretius. I accept what I've been taught—that Iesu died for our sins. But my sins concern me less than the duty I owe to my people. What do I worship, you ask? The soil, I suppose. It is the soil that sustains us. If I care for it, it blesses me and my family. If I neglect it, it curses us. Yet even when I care for it well, I can't be sure of its favour. In that, it's not so different from your God."

Drichan listened intently as Armoricus continued, his voice growing quieter as if speaking to himself. "When I look to the sky, it's not towards heaven. It's to gauge the rain or sun, to see what's coming for my crops. My devotion is to the earth beneath my feet, and my offering is the sweat of my brow. It asks for nothing more than that." Armoricus paused and then chuckled. "Well, except for shit. What humbler offering could any god ask for than that?"

XI

Providing consolation, faith, strength and a safe passage for a soul to heaven were now Drichan's burdens. They had been laid on him, though he was a stranger to this place and its people. These folk, who knew each other so intimately, who worked, played, loved and lived alongside each other, were as tight knit a *familia* as he'd ever encountered. And yet, they turned to him—an outsider, a young man they scarcely knew—for consolation. They scarcely knew him, could not know if he were wise or foolish, serious or frivolous, compassionate or hard-hearted. Yet without hesitation, they placed their burdens on him to bear to the God they had hardly begun to worship. Why? Because he was their priest.

A broken and contrite heart you will not despise. The verse from the psalms drifted into his muddled mind, followed by another: *Judge my cause against the ungodly people; deliver me from those who are deceitful and unjust.* Had God sent him to this place because he knew their hearts would be broken? Was he there to defend their cause against the wicked and the ungodly? The weight of his responsibility pressed upon him, yet it was all the same burden: to stand with these people before God. They may hardly know Christ or believe in him. But he knew Christ, he believed in him, loved him with his whole heart. Despite his own failings, perhaps God had sent him to be a consolation to these people.

The story of Moses before the burning bush rose unbidden in his mind again. When God called him, Moses had protested. *They might not believe me!* Drichan now understood that protest fully. He might speak truth, but why would the people believe him? He had been trained in rhetoric, yes. He had stood before the forum and before altars with words of elegance and formality. Yet now, when he most needed them, the words eluded him. It was as though God's Spirit had abandoned him once more, just as it seemed to abandon him whenever he truly needed strength. *Where are the words?*

What had Moses said next? *O my Lord, I have never been eloquent.* That, too, seemed a painful truth. He had never been eloquent, not in his own eyes. Even now, he struggled to find the words to offer solace to these grieving souls. How could he possibly be the one to bring them comfort? He'd been sitting there for close to an hour trying to compose an oration for the burial, yet still there were no words. Now, he compared himself not with Moses but with Zacharias after the angel had struck him dumb. He had no words.

He reached out and touched the cover of the Gospel book. Laying his hand flat on top of it, he recalled his bloody handprint on Brochfael's corpse and the revulsion he had felt. Gently picking up the book, he unclasped and opened it to a page in Luke's Gospel. He read:

> *And when they bring you into the synagogues, and to magistrates and powers, be not anxious about how or what you will answer, or what you shall say; For the Holy Spirit will teach you in the same hour what you must say.*

He ruminated on the passage, recalling how the words had come to him when he had prayed beside Brochfael's body. His mind had been blank until the very moment he'd begun to pray. Had the Spirit given him those words? In a way, no. He had heard them elsewhere, and they had come back to him suddenly and surprisingly in his panic. But perhaps that *was* the Spirit. He was a learned cleric, and his mind was a deep well of memorized words. Where were the words? The answer was obvious: they lay within him. He had to learn to trust that the Spirit would draw them out. He had done so earlier; he would do so again.

As he closed the book, the final verse of the psalm came to mind. *Why are you sad, O my soul? and why do you disquiet me? Hope in God, for I will yet give him praise: the salvation of my countenance, and my God.* Reassured by those words, he replaced both books in his satchel, changed again into his robe and left the room.

—

The din was astonishing. It swept from the villa's courtyard out into the fields, startling the flock of sheep grazing in their winter pastures and causing the cattle to low and horses to neigh their displeasure. Horns tooted, bells jangled, drums reverberated, and an assortment of pots and pans clanged amidst the ebb and flow of the piercing wails of women and the drone of groaning men. The entire village seemed to grieve as one. Amid this explosion of sound, six farmhands bore a litter carrying Brochfael's body. They were led by Drichan, followed by Armoricus, Corotica, Quercus, Aurelius and the two children. The Dominus, Domina and Quercus wore matching togas as dark as blood and trimmed in gold; like all the women present, Corotica's head was covered by a shawl.

It was an old Roman custom, this tumultuous procession. The sounds were meant to ward off evil spirits that might seek to snatch the soul of the departed before it was safely in the hands of the gods—or now, Drichan hoped, in the care of God. The tumult was the *familia*'s final act of service to Brochfael before he was laid to rest, though it was a service some performed as much for themselves as for him. They feared the likelihood that one killed so young and unjustly would return to haunt the living. Brochfael's peace, they believed, depended in part on the volume of their grief.

Drichan turned to face the bier and splashed it with water he had blessed earlier. Although he found it hard to focus amidst the loud lamentations, he was uncharacteristically calm. His heart nearly quailed beneath the tide of woe that washed over him, but the solemn ritual stirred a resolve that let him fulfil his priestly duty with quiet dignity. With a nod from Armoricus, the procession began its slow march towards the village cemetery.

In early evening light, the mourners slowly processed past the empty bathhouse and down the lane that led to the village. People from the village had positioned themselves at stations along the way, greeting Brochfael's body with their own cries of anguish before falling into the procession. Drichan followed a young lad leading one of the sheep that had been brought back from the *hafod*. It occurred to him in a strange and fleeting moment of reflection that the sheep may well have witnessed the boy's death. Had it the wit to think and the tongue to speak, it could tell them what had happened to Brochfael and his family. He shook away the silly notion; such thoughts did not befit the occasion.

At first, the village itself was strangely quiet with only a few elderly watching from windows and doorways. But as the loud dissonance of the mourners entered the village, they were joined by the howl of dogs, which rose even above the keening of their owners. Drichan thought of the Psalmist's words, *Deep calls to deep*.

The cemetery lay in a secluded field to the north of the village. On one side stood a few modest tombstones, each engraved with what Drichan assumed to be the epitaphs of the Rusticelii. He wondered if Armoricus's mother was among them. He had expected to find something like an open pit for Brochfael's body. In the city and towns, people of low estate were mostly given a common burial in pits dug to accommodate their decomposing bodies, along with those of animals. But he could see that the field was dotted with individual graves, perhaps not equal to the number of all who had died in the village but a great many, nonetheless. The people here may not have been able to enjoy in life the benefits of Roman city-dwellers, but at least in death they had been treated with greater honour.

The lad leading the sheep came to a halt on the far side of an open grave. Drichan assumed his position on the other end while the pallbearers drew to a halt alongside the pit. The hole was already occupied by a couple of urns and a pile of bones that had been reverently piled to one side. Drichan then understood that the graves around him were not all of individuals but rather the earthen beds of families, buried so that they might be together in death as in life.

Armoricus, Corotica and their family assembled next to the boy with the sheep as the crowd gathered around the grave. Having warded off the evil spirits, the clamour gradually turned into a sombre dirge, which Drichan recognized as the traditional song of the Silures that commended their dead to their Ancestors. It was a pagan elegy replete with pagan imagery and therefore inappropriate for a Christian burial. But there was no stopping it; indeed, so moving were its words that Drichan had to restrain himself from adding his voice to theirs.

They sang the dirge over and over while men strung ropes beneath Brochfael's body and lowered it reverently into the grave. Drichan patiently waited for the sweeping chords of the funeral song to end so that he could begin his eulogy. He understood that they sang not just for Brochfael but for themselves. They were crying for peace and security; perhaps in its own way it was also a lament for Rome. If Armoricus's fears turned out to be prophetic, he wondered how many more such scenes he would witness. Who would scare off the evil spirits when there were none left to sing?

However hard things became, he knew now that these people would not willingly leave their home. No matter how many of them joined their company, they would never abandon their dead. This place was the span of their world, the land to which their ancestors, customs and even the law bound them. To leave would be to experience a kind of death in life, but more so, because they would be exiled from their Ancestors. How different this was from what Drichan knew from his life in cities. These people enjoyed the same rootedness, the *stabilitas*, which monks sought within their monasteries. They lacked only the prayers of the righteous to be holy.

The elegy finally began to trail away raggedly as the mourners tired. As eyes began to turn towards him, Drichan sensed that the moment for his Christian prayers and eulogy had arrived. The priest who now spoke was not the timid man who had earlier fretted over his Gospel book. Whether God, the people or the occasion gave him words of consolation, all that mattered to him was that the words now flowed.

After sprinkling water into the grave, he made the sign of the cross, and prayed in a clear voice over Brochfael's body, commending his soul to the angels who would carry him to God and away from the evil spirits that looked to claim him. Then, with his voice steady and clear, Drichan began his eulogy.

"*The days of men are like grass; like the flower of the field so does he flourish. For his spirit shall pass away from him, and he shall not be: he shall know his place no more.* So sang the Psalmist. Our lives are fleeting; this world is fleeting. We, who would prefer never to let go, must endure the passing of all things. For as long as we live, we must be prepared to grieve. This is what it is to be mortal."

Drichan noticed Armoricus watching him closely and thought about their earlier conversation about strengthening his household with faith. He turned his oration towards answering that plea.

"Thus, we are gathered here to mourn. Our sorrow is not just for a death nor even for one who died before his time, as sharp as that anguish may be. We grieve also for what the wicked murder of Brochfael portends: our loss of security. We have been made fearful—we know dark days may lie ahead. While we grieve, we therefore tremble."

His voice grew stronger as he continued. "Yes, we should be sorrowful when our loved ones are parted from us by death. That is the way of things. Even if we have the faith to know that, in God's mercy, we have not lost Brochfael for ever, yet our hearts are saddened by death itself. But in our grief, we are not without hope. In our sorrow, we are not alone. Hear the comforting words of the Apostle Paul: *We would not have you be ignorant concerning them that are asleep, that you do not grieve like those who are without hope.*"

It was then that he saw her—the woman standing beside the steward and his wife, the woman with tears that washed her face, marking it with angelic beauty. The sadness in her eyes pierced his heart. He knew at once that she must be Brochfael's lover, the woman whom he had loved in secret, who was now bearing the grief of it in secret. Without even considering it, Drichan now turned his words towards comforting her alone.

"Grieve," he urged softly. "Grieve. Weep for Brochfael's death; mourn even our own mortality in this wicked world. But don't grieve like those without hope. Know that in this darkening world, God does offer us his hope. If we are afflicted, he will give us consolation. If we are weak, his faith will keep us upright. If we lament our mortal condition, we can find healing in his promise of eternal life. By God's love and through faith, our tears will turn to joy and our sorrow into gladness. If only we have hope, we need never fear the evil spirits that seek to snatch our souls away."

All Drichan's schooling in rhetoric came to his aid now. The gathered mourners listened keenly, their faces a testament to the grief they carried and the solace they sought. His voice, steady despite his trembling heart, drew out their tears and left them with a flicker of hope—a balm for wounded souls. He had no idea if he could do it again, but in the quiet gratitude that met him afterward, he glimpsed something new: their trust. No longer was he the stranger who had come to make them right with the God they hardly knew. Now, he was their priest.

A soothing stillness had settled over the land as they made their way by moonlight back to the villa. Drichan walked apart, drained by the day's exertions. The first owl calls of the autumn greeted them from the woodlands while bats flitted in the dim light. It was the sort of silence that seemed to stretch to the stars; the silence of the earth sliding towards the slumber of winter. But what made the stillness so comforting was what it suggested: the evil spirits had fled, driven off as much by the people's lament as by Drichan's prayers. None could now doubt that Brochfael had received the burial he was owed and that his soul now rested in peace.

XII

The dispute raged so loudly that it could be heard out in the fields by the men binding and gathering in the hay. Even though it came from the sanctuary of Armoricus's office, such was its volume and passion that it was impossible for anyone to ignore. People flinched at the sting of their words, exchanged regretful looks when one of the quarrellers spoke inadvisably, and dreaded the consequences. Even young Publius knew that some of the things they were yelling at each other were not meant for the ears of others.

Publius wanted to run to his mother but told himself that he was too grown up to borrow her courage. Instead, he closed his eyes and summoned the image of the stag, standing bold and unmoved, as a talisman to calm his anxieties. With the thought firm in his mind, he walked purposefully calmly towards his room to gather his bow and arrows. He would practise his archery somewhere in peace. Moving towards the fight felt enough like walking into a hailstorm that he was tempted to lean into it. Tears began to well in his eyes.

As he reached the dry fountain in the courtyard, he heard gentle sobbing. Looking around to the far side, he found his sister Rusticella sitting against the fountain's edge, hugging her knees. Her tear-streaked face looked up at him, and without a word, she reached out her hand. Publius took it at once, pulling her gently to her feet.

"Come on," he urged softly, though his voice trembled. "Let's go to the old bathhouse. It'll be better there."

She nodded, sniffling, and clung to his hand as he led her away. The acrid tang of the smithy and workshops caused them to wrinkle their noses as they slipped into the shadowed building. As soon as they closed the door, the sound of the quarrel dropped to a muffle, overtaken by the clamour of the smithy, the carpentry shop, and the loud conversations of the men working in them. Soon, they forgot why they had come.

"Don't let go of my hand," warned Publius, perhaps a little too sternly. Strictly speaking, Rusticella should not have been there unaccompanied by an adult. Too many hazards lurked in the dark rooms of the large building, nor was the workmen's chatter fit for the ears of a young girl. Still, it was preferable to listening to their father and brother quarrel. The thrill of watching the craftsmen at work would also be distracting.

They walked down a long, broad hallway lit dimly by a few small, glazed windows in the western wall and lined with piles of firewood and kindling. The corridor—once grand with plastered walls and ornate rugs—was now a neglected space piled with firewood, its former elegance stripped bare. The sound of their footsteps echoed faintly, blending with the distant clang of tools.

"I'm going to show you something you'll like," said Publius as they entered a square room with a much-damaged geometric mosaic floor. Stacks of dressed timber lay piled around them.

"What is it?" asked Rusticella with eager eyes.

"You'll have to wait and see," replied Publius.

He tightened his grip and quickened his pace, determined to show her the wonder he had discovered. They entered a massive room filled with the din of carpentry and loud-voiced men. Once a lavish receiving room for the baths, it now served as the villa's woodshop. Light spilled through a wide gap in the northern wall that had been knocked through and shored up with oak supports to create an opening onto a small, paved area with the fields and village lane beyond. The air was choked with sawdust that covered the furniture, floors and the carpenters' clothing. Riderch, the master carpenter, glanced up from his work with a frown.

"What are you two doing here?" he asked, wiping his hands on his leather apron. "You know your sister shouldn't be here. It's no fit place for a young child."

"Just exploring," replied Publius. He knew that Riderch's words held no real threat; they understood each other well enough. If Publius didn't get in the way of the workers, he was free to come and go as he pleased. When he was only a little older than Rusticella, a couple of older carpenters had even begun to teach him their craft, letting him take a turn with a hammer and saw or at the lathe.

"Your brother's making a hell of a ruckus mouthing off to your father," continued Riderch as he placed a plank onto a sawhorse. "Hell of a row."

"I suppose," replied Publius in a non-committal tone. Rusticella squeezed his hand more tightly as she hid bashfully behind him.

"Disrespectful. I'd belt my son if he talked to me that way. I expect he thinks it's crazy for us to stay here unprotected if the Irish have returned. He's not wrong, mind. But what can you do?"

Publius had nothing to say to this. Despite the danger, the idea of leaving the villa was too far beyond his imagination for him to consider it seriously. He knew nothing other than this place and the land lying between it and the farmstead where his mother's family lived. He presumed the world to be just like his home—wider and stranger perhaps but filled with the same kind of people and the same kind of dangers. No threat could ever be more real than the home where he'd always lived. People just had to weather the danger as they did the winter.

"You two run along now," said Riderch as he began searching for his mislaid saw. "Keep your sister out of trouble. If anything happens to her, I'll be the one to answer for it."

While the carpenter's back was turned, they scurried through an archway in the south wall that led into Publius's favourite room. At the entrance was an enormous mosaic, partly obscured near the entrance by sawdust. Although it had been strangely cut in half by one of two bathing pools, they could still see a depiction of a long sapphire-blue fish entwined with an aquamarine sea serpent. The flicker from the few lanterns in the room made the fish seem to swim. Beyond it lay the two empty baths, each about fifteen feet wide and four feet deep.

"What do you think?" he asked, trying to spark a flicker of wonder in his sister's fretful eyes.

Rusticella barely glanced at it. "It's nice," she murmured, her voice small and flat.

Publius sighed but pressed on. "Come on. There's something better."

The clatter of the carpentry shop behind them met the banging of the smithy on the other side of a doorway in the eastern wall. The din of the two workshops meant that this room was hardly used for more than storage, a place to gather much of the villa's refuse.

"Come with me," replied Publius gently. "We're almost there."

They walked across the mosaic and entered the first bath down a few tiled steps. Publius released his sister's hand and pushed aside an empty crate to reveal a large gap in the side of the bath. He fetched an oil lamp he had hidden on earlier visits, which he lit from one of the lanterns on the wall.

"Don't be scared, Rusticella," he said as he entered the hole. "I want to show you where this goes."

Rusticella hesitated, eyeing the dark gap warily. "I don't want to. There might be spiders."

"Don't be silly," replied Publius. "You'll see. It'll be fun. Like an adventure."

"Don't want to." Rusticella folded her arms defiantly.

"Tell you what. If you follow me, afterwards we can go to the kitchens and have some honeyed nutcake. I saw Ancarat making some earlier."

"And some pears, too?" suggested Rusticella, already taking a step towards the hole. There was no fear so great as to keep her from sweets.

They crawled into a narrow tunnel that soon opened out into a dark expanse that reverberated with the clang of the smithy only four feet above them. Thanks to a shaft of bright sunlight in the far eastern wall, they could just discern a forest of stout stone columns supporting the floor above them. Publius's lamp lit the nearest of them, creating nightmarish shadows through layers of cobwebs so thick they seemed like drapes. The air was damp and cool, carrying the faint sounds of scurrying rodents.

"I don't like this, Publius," whimpered Rusticella. "I don't like it at all!"

"Nothing here will hurt you," he replied. "I come here often to explore. Isn't it amazing? It's the old hypocaust that once heated the baths."

"No," said Rusticella firmly. "It's scary."

"Just think, though," he continued, ignoring her indignation, "once upon a time, this would have been filled with hot air that made the rooms and baths above us warm during the cold winters. Imagine taking a hot bath or sitting in a hot room when it's wet and cold outside. It must have been amazing."

"What happened to it?"

"It stopped working a long time ago. When I grow up, I want to repair it. Wouldn't it be grand to have it working again?"

"I still think it's scary," replied Rusticella. "Can we go now?"

Publius sighed again, reluctant to leave his secret hideaway. "All right," he said at last. "But I'll come back later and clean it up. I'll clear out all the cobwebs and make it nice. Then it can be our secret place. What do you think?"

Rusticella shook her head emphatically. "I think it's dark and smells bad. Let's go."

Relenting, Publius led Rusticella across the short, shadowed stretch to the furnace and through its narrow mouth into the sunlight. They brushed off the dust and cobwebs as best they could and made their way back towards the villa cautiously until they were satisfied the quarrel had ended. Then, like young birds freed from a cage, they raced to the kitchen, where the sweet promise of honeyed nutcake awaited. As they reached for the treats with their grubby hands, their laughter was met by the cooks' startled cries, which made the taste of the sweets even more delicious.

—

Aurelius was fuming. How could his father be so stubborn, so wilfully blind? He was an obstinate fool whose inexplicable love for the villa was going to end in tragedy for them all. With the markets in chaos and the Irish raids creeping closer, surely the prudent thing would be to try to sell up and flee to somewhere safer. Even a ramshackle villa in Glevum or Venta Silurum would be preferable to clinging to this precarious patch of earth.

Quercus had pulled him away after the shouting match, dragging him to the orchard bench beneath a gnarled apple tree. Now, the old man leaned heavily on his walking stick, his weathered face sharp with disapproval.

"You need to cool down," said his grandfather, rather more harshly than Aurelius thought necessary.

"I need to cool down! I need to cool down?" Aurelius snapped. "You heard him! He's as stubborn as a mule. What I ought to do is march back there and—"

"What you ought to do," Quercus interrupted, "is stop carrying on like a fishwife at market. You call yourself a patrician? Then act like one!"

The rebuke landed squarely, and Aurelius faltered. "What do you mean?"

"I mean that you've forgotten yourself," replied Quercus. "You and your father both. To yell and bicker like children—do you think that helps anyone? The whole household has been on edge for the past week, and now you've stirred it up even more with your outburst. Your business has become everybody's business."

"That's not my fault." Even as he said it, Aurelius knew that to be untrue. He'd been the one to press the matter, despite his father warning him repeatedly to stop. He should have been more patient, waiting for the moment when he could approach the subject like a diplomat rather than a soldier. But he had never known how to do that with his father.

"And tell me," Quercus went on, "what did you hope to achieve by confronting your father?"

Aurelius shrugged. "I didn't stop to think about it. I just thought the subject needed addressing. No one else has."

"Why might that be?"

"I've no idea," exclaimed Aurelius. "Everyone's pretending life can go on as usual. Even after Brochfael was killed. Even after Meurig brought word of the raids."

Quercus nodded. "Good for them, too. What would you have them do? Run around like startled hens?"

"Don't be ridiculous," Aurelius snapped, his frustration bubbling again. "But we ought to prepare. Brochfael's death should be warning enough. We can't defend this place. We need to leave while we still can."

Quercus tilted his head thoughtfully, and the light filtering through the branches cast shadows across his face. "And what of the villa?"

"What of it? Look around you. The place is falling apart."

"I don't mean the buildings," replied Quercus with a frown. "I mean the people. The *familia*. What do you propose? Dragging them to the city? They're farmers, boy. The land is their life. Take that from them, and you might as well cut their throats yourself."

"That's absurd," protested Aurelius. "We wouldn't need more than a few of the household servants. The rest can stay."

"Stay and die at the hands of the Irish you're so afraid of?" Quercus's voice sharpened. "Is that your honourable plan?"

Aurelius threw up his hands in exasperation. "You're just like Father! It's not a matter of honour. We don't have the means either to defend these people, or to take them with us. And why should we? This is their land, their home. They're Silures, not Romans."

His words hung in the air, brittle as frost. Quercus said nothing, letting the silence stretch long enough for Aurelius to reflect on his own words. Brochfael's murder had been gnawing at him, and the image of his own family being dragged away in chains haunted his sleep. He could not shake the vision of Hibernian ships slipping through the waves, their holds filled with captives. Status would mean nothing if the pirates came. Nothing would.

Finally, his grandfather spoke, his voice low and calm. "Do you remember Cadfan's father?"

Aurelius blinked, caught off guard. "Yes, he was your steward, wasn't he?"

"One of the best men I ever knew. Smart as a whip. He understood the soil as if it spoke to him, and he knew livestock the way a mother knows her child. When the Irish came raiding, he stood by me. He buried your grandmother that same year—just after he buried his brother. That man carried more grief in those months than I hope you ever know, but he never faltered. His father, now—he was steward before him, though not so skilful. Then, there was Cadfan's uncle—he could raise a horse like no one else. Tough as leather, foul-mouthed as a stable hand, but he had a way with those beasts. Talked to them like they were sweethearts. Folks used to joke he didn't train horses; he made love to them."

"What does this have to do with anything?" Aurelius interrupted, his impatience rising.

Quercus ignored the outburst. "And Ancarat's aunt—do you remember her? I recall she was like a grandmother to you. Always slipping you nutcake when your mother wasn't looking."

Aurelius frowned, the memory rising unbidden. Ancarat's aunt had indeed been a kind and constant presence when he was young, though he hadn't thought of her in years. She'd died when he was still a boy, and her absence had faded into the fabric of his childhood.

Quercus pressed on. "There's not a soul in this villa whose life isn't entwined with ours. People whose names you don't even know but whose bloodlines have served alongside ours for generations. You say they're Silures and we're Romans. But what the hell does that really mean? I've never been to Rome, nor have you. You say that this is their land, their home. Well, Aurelius, you're right. In fact, that may be the rightest thing you've ever said. But it's true for us as much as them. This is our home, for good or ill, and you damn well better believe it's our land. No one with a shred of courage or honour abandons his home and his land cheaply."

"But we may have it taken from us," replied Aurelius, his resolve slipping.

"Not without a fight, we won't," responded Quercus firmly. "And even if we die, our bones will lay claim to this place long after we're gone. We've held this ground for two centuries, boy. We won't be shifted easily."

"Then all is lost," sighed Aurelius, his voice hollow. "Even if we survive these raids, how long before we're nothing more than poor smallholders? How long before we forget what it means to be Roman?"

"Honestly, Aurelius, questions like that don't keep me awake at night. Deep down, I'm a gloomy bastard. I've always thought Virgil had the right of it—*All things are ready to grow worse, to slip backwards, to fall away from what they were.* The world's always been like this, boy. All we can do is care for what's ours as best we can while we have it."

Aurelius accepted defeat. He stood and reached a hand towards Quercus, but the old man waved him off. "No, you go on. Find your father. Make amends. It's no good for the two of you to be at odds."

"And you?" Aurelius asked.

"I'll sit here a while longer," Quercus said, leaning back against the bench. "There's peace in this place, even in troubled times. But I'll speak with your father later."

"About what?"

Quercus scratched the stubble on his cheeks. "You'll have to accept that we're not budging. There's no changing that. But your father will have to understand something too: this land doesn't hold you the way it holds him—or me. It's not your home; I suspect it never has been. Not really. If you feel you need to go, then we must let you. Clipping your wings will only cause misery for everyone."

XIII

A shaft of sunlight glared into Baglan's face, rousing him from a deep sleep. He blinked, the brightness sharp and unkind, and turned his head instinctively towards the shadows that framed the crude shelter. He was lying in a low enclosure, hardly bigger than his bed, which was made of cut branches and thatch so poorly put together that he could see the blue sky above. He touched his dry, cracked lips, trying to orient himself, but his memory was disjointed. But only odd, distorted images of the dancing horned god and a looming stone came to mind.

"Awake! Awake!" chirruped a familiar voice. "The stranger is awake! Must fetch him food and water. He's awake!"

A scrawny hand reached through a small opening with a wooden bowl and a large cup. Baglan grabbed the cup and drank greedily, enjoying the cool of the liquid as much as the unexpected sweetness of rosehip. He glanced into the bowl, which held a pale, cold gruel with the faint scent of nuts. But its taste was less offensive than he expected, and he ate it quickly, licking his fingers clean.

He felt the eyes of the strange man peering at him from behind his curtain of hair. He cooed like a contented dove before suddenly springing out of view. Baglan crept out of the shelter into the warm sunshine. He was once again in the small wood near to the cairn where he'd been roughly handled by the bandits. He could see the Stone in the distance, standing now without its former potency, a charcoal smudge against a pale-brown background.

The stranger popped out from behind the cairn with another cup of rose water and a morsel of bread. "I must find more food," he said as he handed these to Baglan. "Didn't plan to feed two mouths, did I? But Nodens healed you, and Nodens will provide."

"How long was I asleep?" asked Baglan after he'd drained half his cup.

The man frowned. "Many days. Many, many days. You were not prepared for the Stone. No, not strong enough for it. Its power overcame you and made you prey to wicked spirits. Wicked, wicked spirits roam these lands. Driven here. Driven here, yes, but by whom? No one knows. But they are here all the same, and they tried to drag you down with them. Down to Annwn, Hades, Hell. But with Nodens' help, I saved you." He thumped his narrow chest. "Though you were at death's door, I dragged you away from those wicked spirits. Nodens fought them off through me."

"Many days!" exclaimed Baglan with despair. "That can't be! I must go. I must find my wife and daughter."

The man looked at him as though he'd lost his mind. "Where? Go where? There is nowhere to go."

Baglan was shaking now. "My wife and daughter. They have been kidnapped by men who killed my son. I must find them." He staggered to his feet, looking around frantically for his belongings. As he did, the world suddenly upended itself, and the ground crashed painfully against his head and side. Only gradually did he realize that he'd collapsed.

The man crouched beside him, his odour a pungent mix of sweat and unwashed skin. "Now Gwas knows. Now Gwas understands. The evil within you drew the evil without. Darkness attracts darkness. That is the way of things. Nodens must heal your mind even more than your body."

"Never mind that!" replied Baglan impatiently. How would he even begin to look for Awen and Ceridwen now? "I must go. I must find my family." He picked himself up and sat wearily against a tree. He felt weak again.

"The stranger is going nowhere today," continued Gwas. "The wicked spirits are still clutching at you with their claws. Wicked claws. Evil claws. Claws of death." He then leapt like a grasshopper and dashed back behind the cairn, leaving Baglan perplexed.

He was just starting to climb gingerly back to his feet, when Gwas returned with a clump of soggy mistletoe. Much to his astonishment, he started to beat him over the head with it as he declared, "Begone, spirits! Begone, wicked ones! Go away! Go away! Shoo!"

Baglan raised his arm to deflect the blows. "Stop it! Stop it now!"

But Gwas kept striking him with the mistletoe. Summoning what little strength he had, Baglan snatched it from him and threw it as far away as he could. Gwas looked at him with such outrage that he feared he might attack him. Instead, he suddenly wailed with a sadness that instantly extinguished Baglan's anger.

"I'm sorry," he said, though he could think of nothing he'd done wrong.

Gwas gave him an evil look, turned and ran off in the direction of the Stone. Baglan tried to follow but managed only a few steps before his legs gave way. Leaning against another tree, he called after the strange man, but his cries went unanswered. He didn't even stop at the Stone but continued across the moorland until he finally vanished in a far wood. As he disappeared from view, Baglan felt very alone.

Using a sturdy branch for support, he searched the camp for more food and drink. Gwas had left supplies behind as well as the remnants of Baglan's own possessions—at least, whatever the bandits hadn't stolen. From these, he managed to start a fire and prepare a large bowl of porridge. Although he made enough for two, by nightfall his mad friend still hadn't returned.

But he could hear him. Somewhere out in the darkness in the direction of the Stone, Gwas was singing. He sang and sang. The words were indistinct, but the songs flowed seamlessly into one another, their tone unmistakably elegiac, endlessly repeating until Baglan thought he could bear it no longer. As Gwas's beautiful baritone echoed hauntingly in the darkness, Baglan found it impossible not to think of the Stone and its solitude in that ancient landscape, the years flitting by undetected in the shadow of the long ages it had seen and would see.

Baglan lay by the fire, listening long into the night. His eyes closed, but the singing lingered in his mind, merging with dreams of his family. He saw his wife, Awen, her face shadowed with fear, and his daughter, Ceridwen, clinging to her. They were out there somewhere, beyond the moors and woods. The thought was unbearable. He ached for them, for his home, for the life that now seemed impossibly far away until, at long last, he fell into a fitful sleep.

There was no sign of Gwas the next morning when Baglan staggered back onto the Roman road and turned south. Though he now had enough strength to walk slowly with the aid of his stick, he was weighed down by the impossibility of his task. He could travel only at a snail's pace, stopping regularly to allow his heart to slow and his vision to settle. He carried his pack with a few of Gwas's supplies. It was only fair to leave most of the food and drink behind in the assumption that Gwas would return. Baglan would have to forage.

The road took him across a shallow river and into a large, wooded valley that seemed as old as the world. Banks of bracken, tipped yellow in the late season, lined the road that wove its way through the encroaching shade of immense oaks, beech and ash. A thick carpet of moss muffled the woodland sounds around him, except for the music of birds chirping their early autumn songs. Baglan continued slowly through the unbroken canopy for much of the day, never knowing whether his footsteps were taking him any nearer to Awen and Ceridwen.

Late during the following day, the quiet of the woods was suddenly broken by the sound of voices and human activity. Baglan's ears sharpened to the sound, but it did not grow louder. Curiosity and desperation pushed him to follow. Moving cautiously, he crept along the road until the forest opened onto a boggy field that sloped down to a brown stream. Beyond it stood a Roman fort behind imposing walls of turf and timber.

Baglan's immediate reaction was despair. Surely no band of Irish raiders would have taken a path that brought them so near to Roman authority. The thought was almost too much for him, but he clung to a slender hope. Perhaps the raiders hadn't known about the fort. Perhaps they had stumbled upon it or been caught by a patrol. His family could be inside those walls. He had to find out.

As he approached, two horsemen rode out of the fort towards him, followed shortly afterwards by three men on foot. None wore Roman uniforms, though they were armed with swords and spears. Baglan stopped, knowing he could neither outrun nor outfight them.

"Who are you?" the first rider called out sharply.

"I am Baglan," he replied, steadying his voice. "I'm searching for my wife and daughter."

"Where have you come from?" barked the other horseman.

"From the east," Baglan said, gesturing vaguely. "A few miles beyond the old Roman fort at the far end of the road. Have you seen a band of Irish raiders?"

The horsemen ignored the question. Pulling up on either side of him, the first man asked, "Are you alone? Do you have permission to travel?"

Baglan hesitated. "Yes, I'm alone. I'm trying to find my family. They were taken from my home over a week ago."

"I asked if you have permission to travel."

"I—" Baglan faltered, the implications dawning on him. A *colonus* like him, bound to the land of his Dominus, had no right to wander freely. "I had to leave immediately. I couldn't wait for permission."

"A fugitive," the first horseman muttered. "Thought you'd escape west. Who is your Dominus?"

"No, no!" Baglan protested, his voice rising in panic. "I'm no fugitive. I'm searching for my family. Please, let me go on."

"Not likely," the second rider said with a sneer. At his nod, the men on foot moved in. Two grabbed Baglan's arms, their grip rough and unyielding.

"Please!" exclaimed Baglan. "I've done nothing wrong. I just want to find my wife and daughter."

The first horseman leaned down, his face full of scorn. "You can forget about them, fugitive. You're coming with us. And unless you can prove otherwise, you'll be staying with us."

The man holding his left arm added sarcastically, "Welcome to your new family."

—

Years of daily chores had trained Ria's body to go through the necessary motions without needing to think. She might be sweeping or dusting, milking cows or feeding the pigs, washing laundry or baking bread: whatever the task, she would mindlessly trudge her way through to the end like an ox ploughing furrows.

The people around her did not fault her work. Yet they noticed her—how her cheer seemed worn at the edges, her laughter hollow, her eyes burdened with shadows that didn't lift. To those who cared for her, this dissonance unsettled, even pained them. Yet, they did not press. In the peculiar, unspoken way of the *familia*, they embraced her sorrow as a reflection of their own, an acknowledgement of grief they all shared in some measure. And so, Ria, with her hushed melancholy, became a kind of household spirit—a presence both comforting and sombre.

She could abide that. What troubled her most were the attentions of those few who sought to cheer her, as if grief were something to be mended and set aside. Their efforts only stirred up her pain and made the heaviness harder to bear. She didn't believe herself destined to remain untouched by love or kindness—she was too practical for such sentimentality—but she was tangled in two fears she couldn't quite face. The first was rooted in her silence about Brochfael. To tell her parents, to speak openly to Rhodri, seemed impossible. The longer she held her tongue, the more the truth seemed to knot itself in her chest. She created for herself a burden she need never have carried but now could not put down. This, in turn, bred in her an unacknowledged resentment towards them all. Her ill-will wasn't so consuming as to make her love her parents less, but it erected a wall where before there was none. It made her home feel less like a home.

Rhodri was another matter altogether. He had sensed her pain, though he knew not the cause, and had responded by giving her his devotion, which she did not want. His ineptitude made it worse. He would suddenly sidle up next to her, put his arm around her, and say something stupid like "We miss your smile" or "You've got to try to cheer yourself up." His presence felt oppressive and his words fatuous. She hated herself for snapping at him, for pulling away from his touch, for the sharp words that would sometimes escape her lips before she could call them back. She hated him more for giving her cause.

Yet, strangely, the worst of them all was the new priest, whose attention was more constant than almost anyone else's. She couldn't decide whether he was just an inept pastor or he had become infatuated with her. In either case, his presence robbed her of the one refuge where she had found peace: the small chapel. Before Brochfael's death, she'd thought little of the place. It was simply where services were held and their offerings made. But when she went there in the days following his burial, she found there a presence that healed, that invited her to weep. It put her in mind of when the farmers bled the bad humours out of ailing livestock. *Wash me, and I shall be whiter than snow.* The words, recalled from somewhere distant, seemed to name the work of her tears.

After a couple of days of slipping into the chapel unobserved, she had arrived to find the priest at his prayers. She had found the look he had given her unsettling. No one had ever looked at her in that way. It contained something of the quality of the leer of men but also the tenderness of her parents. It was as though he longed for her but not necessarily in a carnal fashion. Or did she just tell herself that because he was a priest? She didn't know. But once she saw his look, she couldn't unsee it.

Worse still, he insisted on peppering her with platitudes. "The Lord knows your pain," he'd say in a familiar tone, as though he really meant "*I* know your pain." Or he'd mistake her silence for prayer and quietly say something like, "*Come to me, all you who suffer, and I will refresh you.*" Worst of all was when he referred to her as "my child", his voice carrying a mix of authority and something else she could not name. For a man of God, he had a knack of getting in God's way.

So she was trapped. The priest wouldn't leave her alone with God in his chapel, and it was too dangerous now for her to go alone into the woods, as was her custom. Often, she was tempted to pour out her exasperated sorrow to the Domina, but even here, something in her held her back. And this, she knew, was the deepest wound of all: a solitude born not of others' neglect but of her own making.

It might have gone on this way, her grief spiralling inward, had it not been for one unexpected arrival. Late one afternoon, when the light slanted low across the courtyard, Meurig rode in bearing a gift that seemed as miraculous as spring after a long winter: Brochfael's little sister, Ceridwen.

Familia supra omnia

XIV

Corotica rode her grey-white mare alongside Armoricus, Cunicatus and Drichan on the old track that led towards the river Isca. In her younger days, the land around them had been cultivated for the legions in Britannia and along the Rhine, the fields sown with grain and blanketed in winter by green forage and manure. Now, the thorns had returned, brambles stretched over the furrows, and the wild things—rabbit, fox, badger and deer—reclaimed what had been taken from them. The workers were gone and fewer farms remained.

They passed a half-collapsed roundhouse that Corotica remembered from her younger days. It had belonged to cousins of Owain the blacksmith. She noted three or four other smallholdings in similar ruin, the once-busy farmyards now silent. But her mind refused the silence. Recollections rose like spring shoots: a farmer joking with his wife, children chasing hens, the comfort of a warm drink on a chilly day. These were sharp, vivid memories, recalled as if from yesterday. How strange, she thought, that none of them had foreseen how easily their lives could fall into tragedy, their homes to ruin. Unless their world revolved back from darkness into light, one day not a trace of the farms would remain. *Who will remember their stories?* thought Corotica. *No one, I suppose.*

A heavy frost gripped the landscape, and a dusting of snow covered the crowns of the northern hills. The mountains to the south were hidden in cloud, though she knew their peaks were wrapped in the season's first snowfall. Everything seemed drained of colour, which made the cold seem somehow colder. Corotica pulled her cloak close, knotting the cord tighter at her throat. She felt the chill now more than in her youth.

A month had passed since Meurig had returned with Ceridwen but also with grim news of Awen's death. Baglan's whereabouts remained a mystery. The poor girl had been in a state of shock, too traumatized to do more than clutch a small figurine that Meurig had made her from straw. Without asking, Ria had taken Ceridwen into her home. Corotica allowed and approved of it, knowing that each might find healing in the other's companionship, sheltered in the blanketing care of Cadfan and Ancarat, like seeds tucked into soil, waiting for the warmth to return.

Meurig had also brought back further terrible reports of ransacked villas and roads menaced by roving bandits. All this time, they had been dreading the Irish when it looked as though it was their own people they needed to fear. Many of the bandits were workers from the mines to the west or the huge estates to the south and east. They were another sign of the breakdown of Roman order, but one with grave consequences for them all. Even if bandits never attacked their villa, the obstruction of trade would make their survival difficult. The intended shipment of their goods to Glevum had never departed—the danger was too great in the wake of the attack on Baglan's *hafod*.

Corotica had convinced Armoricus that security lay in numbers. Every estate or farmstead in western Britannia was in the same predicament as their own villa. Theirs might be the only villa rustica for miles around, but there were numerous Silurian farmsteads tilled and kept by honest folk. They would be worried about their livelihoods as well.

After crossing the stream and the boggy ground beyond it, they followed the byway along a ridge through a hardwood forest. They could now see the banks of the Isca on their right through the naked trees, though its dark, fast-moving waters lay hidden behind the lie of the land. The woods deepened and the path climbed briefly before dropping into a broad meadow dotted with groves of oak and ash that Corotica knew well from her childhood when she and the other children often forded the river to pick wildflowers. Although she had not lived there in more than twenty years, she felt a familiar pang of homesickness.

"Your family appears to be doing well," commented Armoricus as they carefully crossed the ford through the swollen Isca and entered newly cultivated lands. A fox in the middle of a field scurried away with its half-eaten quarry, stopped once to look back at them sullenly, and then vanished into a stand of trees next to the river.

"Indeed," replied Corotica with pride. "I do spring from an industrious family."

Armoricus grunted. Unlike Quercus, he had never formed a particularly close friendship with either her father or brother. She could never work out why. They had much in common as prominent local farmers facing many of the same challenges. Though they certainly respected each other, she had long ago accepted that they were too proud and independent ever to be close. Being men, they were unaware of how much it grieved Corotica and her sister-in-law Gwladys that theirs would never be the large family they both wanted for their children.

"Look over there," said Cunicatus as he pointed to smoke rising from a high hill to their west. "The old fort has been reoccupied."

"Goodness!" exclaimed Corotica. "It hasn't been used since before the Romans arrived. Do you think my father has reclaimed the fort, or is it someone else? A possible rival?"

"I doubt it's your father. Better to occupy the fort over there," he replied, pointing towards a higher hill to the north-west. Though its ancient ramparts were visible even from their distance, it appeared unoccupied. "Or even the old cavalry fort. But he'll be reluctant to move away from this rich land," he added.

They could now see a large timbered hall surrounded by a dozen or so roundhouses, partly obscured by a dense hedge of thorn. It lay on the edge of a high bank above the Isca amidst a broad plain of pastureland where sheep and cattle grazed. It was an enviable position, benefitting from rich farmland, woods and the proximity of the river stocked with trout and salmon. It also lay close to the main Roman road that led eastward along the valley towards Isca Augusta. No wonder her family had prospered.

"It's a lovely view," commented Drichan, who had remained largely quiet during their journey. "Did my predecessor ever visit?"

"Do you mean are they Christians?" replied Corotica with a wry smile. "No need to fear. Remember I once told you about the holy man that lived with us? He did his job well before the Irish murdered him. I'll show you where he lived while we're here."

Waiting for them at the gate through the hedge were three men, two of whom Corotica knew well. The first was Corotica's father, Theodwald, roughly the same age as Quercus, though visibly without his robust health. Once a Roman cavalry officer who had seen action thirty years earlier when the great Count Theodosius restored order to Britannia, he was now only a shadow of his former self. Just one look was enough to confirm Corotica's worst fears about his condition.

With a staff in one hand, he leaned heavily on his son with the other. Although Corotica's brother's given name was Theodoric, everyone called him Tewdrig—his British name, chosen by their late mother, who had insisted on it from the day he was born. Two years Corotica's junior, he had been her constant childhood companion. He looked every inch a warrior, though he had never raised a sword against any man, devoting himself instead to running his father's estate. He might not be the farmer that her husband was, but his knack for navigating local politics had made him indispensable to government officials.

The third man was a stranger. Roughly the same height as Cunicatus, he was clad in brightly coloured trews beneath a bearskin cloak that made him seem like a giant. He stood slightly apart from the other two with an air of self-confidence. He wore his black hair long, though his cheeks were clean shaven. Corotica noted how carefully he was assessing Cunicatus. She instinctively didn't trust him.

"Well met, Gaius Rusticelius Armoricus," called her father rather too formally as the four of them dismounted. "It has been too long. How is your father?"

"In fine health, you'll not be surprised to hear," replied Armoricus amiably. "He's as immovable as an old oak and likely to live as long, too. And you?"

Theodwald shrugged. "Much as you see me, alas. And how is my daughter? You look very well."

Although she knew some message was contained in the overly formal salutations, she chose to ignore it and instead marched up to her father and brother and hugged them both hard. "It's so good to see you both! I'm sorry it's been so long."

They returned her embrace awkwardly, and their unease told her all she needed to know: they were anxious about this visit. She chose to cut through the tension with further pleasantries. "Allow me to introduce our new priest, Drichan. We've invited him along so he can meet the household and offer them the holy mysteries. Perhaps for you as well," she added, glancing at her father.

He nodded gravely. "I would be grateful for that. Welcome, Drichan. My household is yours."

Drichan bowed respectfully. "May God bless you and your family."

Now all eyes turned to the stranger. He stepped towards Armoricus, bowing respectfully before greeting him in Irish. "Slántu."

Tewdrig cleared his throat. "May I introduce our new protector, Cormac mac Urb of the Irish."

—

"She still hasn't made a peep?" asked Ancarat as she walked into the room, where Ria was spinning wool. Ceridwen lay beneath a heavy blanket, asleep at her side.

"Not a word, the poor chick," she replied quietly, "though at least she's eating more now."

"That's good. Her colour is much better," continued Ancarat as she sat down opposite Ria and picked up her own spindle.

"She's also begun to follow Rusticella around. She doesn't do anything but watch. But it's a start."

"Time heals all," offered Ancarat, "or so they say."

They spun wool silently. An iron brazier struggled to warm the room against the damp cold outside; wisps of smoke eddied and swirled along the high ceiling. Cadfan could be heard snoring in the adjoining room, where he had retired earlier for a short nap after a night of broken sleep.

Ria stopped her spinning to stroke Ceridwen's hair. A month had passed since the girl's return. She would not soon forget the image of the poor child, pale as death, being handed down by Meurig from his horse. Although he had bundled her against the rain, her umber hair had been soaked and her face streaked with water. Ria had at once rushed over and wrapped her own woollen shawl around her. As she crouched down and tried to rub heat into the girl, she had been dismayed by Ceridwen's expressionless face. She had seemed not to understand what was happening around her.

Ria immediately took responsibility for Ceridwen and no one questioned her right to do so. Thankfully, Corotica excused her from her duties that week so she could devote her entire attention to the girl. She needed it. At night, Ceridwen slept fitfully by Ria's side, occasionally waking and crying or suddenly screaming. During the day, she was like a lifeless doll, refusing to do more than stand or sit as directed and never responding to the people around her, not even with her eyes. Ria found herself chattering away or singing lullabies to Ceridwen just to lift the weight of her sorrowful silence. But nothing seemed to get through to her. It was as though her spirit had fled her delicate body.

Yet, however physically exhausted Ria became, Ceridwen's need awoke within her something far more powerful than a young woman's grief. Her own sorrow drew and bound her to Ceridwen like a mother to a newborn child after the ordeal of childbirth. Her ache blossomed into a tender and nurturing love that restored her broken spirit and made her want to be happy again.

Following the discovery of the attack on the *hafod*, Meurig had scoured the hills and byways, relentless in his search for Baglan and his family. Unlike his brother, who had only raged about the cowardly bastards, Meurig had taken Brochfael's death and his family's disappearance as a personal disgrace. He had one purpose, to protect the villa, and he had failed. He never had to articulate this shame—everyone knew how he felt, just as they knew that he would not rest until he had redeemed himself.

It was during this time that Meurig first brought back news of lawlessness spreading through the region. Travellers were set upon, robbed and murdered. Villas like their own were looted, some burned to the ground. A village over the mountains had lost its winter stores to raiders. Meurig himself had barely escaped an ambush not ten miles from home.

News of the banditry caused even more dismay than the prospect of the return of the Irish. The Irish were foreign, their threat distant and recognizable. But bandits—they were kin, neighbours, the faces of their own people turned against them. Ria had heard, of course, about places where conditions were much worse than where she lived—the mines to the west, for example, or the massive villas where the farmhands, though technically free, were treated like slaves. But surely even such a life was better than violence and disorder. Surely, they must see that their way would lead only to the ruin of all.

Everyone had given up hope of ever finding Baglan's family alive when unexpectedly Meurig rode into the villa's courtyard on that wet night with Ceridwen snuggled in front of him. While Ria and Ancarat had taken her away to be dried, warmed and fed, Meurig had made his report to the others. From what Ria could gather later, his discovery of Ceridwen was entirely by chance. He had stumbled upon the half-starved girl asleep next to Awen's dead body. Ceridwen bore only a bruise, but her mother had clearly been ill-used before she was killed. Meurig brought Awen's body back a few days later for proper burial. People feared that no amount of funereal noise and wailing would keep away the evil spirits from her restless soul. Only the priest had expressed confidence that she would find everlasting peace in heaven. Few believed him.

Not once did people fault Meurig for failing to protect Baglan and his family. But when he brought back Awen's body, they cursed him under their breath. If Brochfael's death had shaken their spirit, the discovery and manner of Awen's death broke it altogether. While no one dared openly to blame Meurig for bringing back bad luck, many began to associate every misfortune, small or great, with his refusal to leave well enough alone.

"Better if he'd left Awen where she died," said some. "Let the evil spirits haunt there rather than here. In times like this, honest folk don't need bad luck."

A knock at the door stirred Ria from her ruminations and woke Ceridwen from her sleep. The girl sat up, clutching the blanket close to her chin as Ancarat set down her spindle and rose to open the door. A moment later, Flox and Lupus padded eagerly into the room, spraying the room with their wet tails as Rusticella followed them with a doll cradled in her arms.

"Well, hello, my dear," greeted Ancarat. "What brings you here on such a foul day?"

Before she could answer, they were all surprised by a giggle. As soon as he had entered the room, Lupus, ever the mischief-maker, had taken a corner of Ceridwen's blanket in his teeth and tugged with such force that he now stood with it draped over his head like a shawl. That one silly canine antic worked more balm into Ceridwen's spirits than all the love and care she had received thus far. She reached to pull the blanket back, but Lupus, emboldened, gripped tighter, and Flox joined the game. Together, the dogs tugged with such enthusiasm that Ceridwen tumbled from the couch. As Ceridwen landed on the floor, the dogs staggered backward, bumping into the brazier. Just then, Cadfan strode into the room and, with practised ease, steadied it before any coals could escape. It had all happened in an instant, but it was a moment that no evil spirit could endure.

Ceridwen lay on the floor, giggling uncontrollably as the dogs eagerly licked her face. Rusticella, wide-eyed with guilt, stammered, "I'm sorry! I didn't mean—"

Ria shooed the dogs away and swept Ceridwen into her arms, holding her close. Tears shimmered in Ancarat's eyes as she watched, her expression soft with relief. Overcome, Rusticella climbed onto the couch and burrowed into the embrace, her own tears spilling freely. Even the dogs whined.

Cadfan scowled, crossing his arms. "By Jove! First, I'm woken from my nap, and now I'm surrounded by a pack of weeping girls. Why, oh why, couldn't I have had a son?"

XV

Drichan's backside ached from hours of sitting on a wooden stool that age had split down its middle. Despite his woollen cloak, the cleft had begun to bite into his tender flesh by the end of the first hour of formalities and discussion. After the second hour, he was wondering if he had blisters on parts of his anatomy where they didn't belong. No matter how he shifted and squirmed or however often, he could find no relief. His only comfort came through offering up his pain to the Lord as mortification of the flesh.

He was sitting across a roaring fire from Tewdrig and next to Cunicatus and Corotica in the midst of a great hall. It reminded him somewhat of a Roman basilica, only on a smaller scale and constructed entirely of timber rather than dressed stone. Massive oak beams, supported by parallel rows of six oak columns, spanned the hall's width, and from these hung ornate bronze lanterns, hooded so that their light fell downwards. Smoke gathered in the gloom of the arching thatch of the roof. Pigeons nestled together on the beams for warmth, their gentle coos a background hymn to the weighty conversations below.

"I still can't see how this is acceptable," said Armoricus, his sharp tone dulled by repetition. This was translated into the Irish tongue by a man dressed in a striking green robe who was sitting between Cormac mac Urb and Theodwald.

Cormac shook his head and exclaimed something that his companion saw no need to translate. Drichan felt some sympathy for the Irish prince, though he was as appalled as anyone by his presence and his news. He might be a great warrior and leader of his people, but he could never have encountered anyone as immoveable as an obdurate Armoricus.

Their discussions came to one of those lulls that fall heavy in long debates. Although Cormac's case was a hard one for any of them to digest, it could be simply put: the Romans had authorized Cormac's father to keep the peace in the lands to the west, and he now wished to extend that authority to include the territory along the Isca, known of old as Garthmadrun. This decision had been hastened by continued attacks from

Irish raiders and the rise of banditry. It wasn't conquest, he had assured them—only peace and security so that all in Garthmadrun could prosper.

No one believed him.

Their host certainly couldn't be blamed for their scepticism. Theodwald had done all in his power to set his guests at ease. Upon their arrival, he had welcomed them with a feast. Spiced wine had warmed their blood, and Gwladys, Tewdrig's wife, had sung songs of the old days—tales of warriors and love, of Silurian defiance against Roman iron. But even her voice, sweet as spring rain, could not rival that of Cormac's companion, who played his harp and sang at length in a tongue no one understood. Even so, he stirred the hearts of all who listened, ending with an elegiac melody that left even grim Cunicatus with moist eyes.

Yet the spell of the music had not lasted. As the fire had burned lower and the wine cooled, hard truths began to press upon them like winter's frost. Drichan, for his part, felt a strange stillness, a clarity amid the tension. He could see the turning of the world. Life as they had known it had reached a moment of irreversible change, the same as when the highest tide starts to fall. But he could also see that Armoricus hadn't grasped this yet—that he still thought of himself as a Roman, secure in the privileges of a civilized world. Drichan's eyes lingered on the Irish prince, studying his face, his bearing. A verse came to mind: *Let them become as chaff before the wind, with the angel of the Lord hemming them in.* Was Cormac, he wondered, the instrument of God's judgement?

Theodwald rose creakily from his chair, beckoning Gwladys to her feet to help him. "Brother," he said with a weary voice as he looked at Armoricus. "I know how hard this is for you. Your family has borne the scars of Cormac's people as deeply as mine. I can't forget, nor forgive, their murder of my own beloved sister. Were it within my power, I would not for a moment have treated this man as a guest. I would have met him with sword and shield rather than the handclasp of friendship.

"But you and I are no heroes of old. I stood alongside Magnus Maximus himself, yet I am no Birinius, who drove back the proud legions come to conquer our fatherland. And you"—here he managed a faint smile—"you are no Cincinnatus, laying down your plough only long enough to vanquish Rome's foes. Neither of us can make this world be as we want. We're just farmers. Yet what more venerable and noble people are there than we? Leave us alone, and we'll dedicate ourselves entirely to the scrap of land under our care; attack us—well, attack us, and we'll simply endure until we are finally left alone again to return to our ploughs. My brother, we have entered a season of endurance."

Tewdrig took up his father's thought. "This is why we must accept what we cannot change. Rome has decided it needs Cormac and his people to keep order from here to the western sea. Our approval was neither asked nor required. It is what it is, and we must take the world as it comes, not as we would wish it."

Through the interpreter, Cormac finally spoke, his tone firm but reflective. "My people were once as you are now—peaceful folk who tilled their fields in northern Britannia for many generations before you Romans arrived. My ancestors fled to Ireland rather than bow to the Roman yoke, only to be made subject to an Irish one. My people are called the Déiri, which in your tongue means 'vassal'. That is what we became.

"Still, we settled. Like you, we farmed. Also like you, Roman, we tilled fields that were not ours—but not, like you, as masters. That was until my people were unjustly expelled. For almost a hundred years, we've been a wandering people, an exiled people, a people without a home. Can you blame us if some turned to piracy? Can you condemn us for seeking to survive?"

At this point, Cunicatus rose angrily to his feet. "That is a weak man's excuse! It is no fault of the Silures that your people have suffered."

Though a lesser man would have either quailed in the face of Cunicatus's anger or else risen belligerently to the challenge, Cormac remained impassive. He hardly even looked at the Silurian warrior. *Again*, Drichan thought, *he displays his position. He knows he holds the power.*

Corotica, who had been so far silent, spoke with measured calm. "My cousin is right. Misfortune doesn't excuse evil. You should have turned your swords against those in Ireland who wronged you, not us. My mother-in-law and my aunt were both brutally murdered by your people."

She paused, her voice softening as she sighed. "It takes more than fine words to heal such wounds."

Cormac inclined his head, his tone respectful but firm as he replied to Armoricus. "Your wife is wise. Yet I have not come seeking your forgiveness. To speak plainly, I do not need it. In my grandfather's time, my people settled in the lands of the Demetae by the western sea, with Rome's consent, on the condition that we defend those lands against others of our own kind. After all we had endured, we took that hard bargain. We traded the Irish yoke for the Roman one, which our ancestors had fled. It was bitter, but we accepted it for what it gave us: land to call home. Your emperor Magnus Maximus understood this need. That is why he entrusted Demetia to us when he marched away with his Roman legions."

"And yet your people still raid," replied Armoricus. "Have you failed in your charge, or are you exploiting our weakness?"

Cormac shrugged. "Perhaps both. Brave men will seek plunder where it can be found. The world has been ever thus. Your own people conquered these lands where hardly any plunder could be gained. Can you blame ours for doing the same after you enriched it? Theodwald was right to praise the nobility of farmers. But no man farms land that was not first claimed by conquest. Peace must be won and kept. The plough depends upon the sword."

"And you would have us submit our ploughs to the Irish sword?" spat Cunicatus.

"No!" declared Cormac in a loud voice that silenced everyone. "I have not come to be your overlord. If that were my aim, I would have come with sword and spear. I have come on my father's behalf to be your friend, your protector. The legions are gone. If you believe they will return, then tell me to go, and I will. Otherwise allow the authority your late governor gave to my father to encompass Garthmadrun. Theodwald will continue to govern these lands, as before, and his son after him. But he will do this in league with my people. You will look west to Moridunum rather than east to Venta Silurum or Glevum. Together, we will protect Garthmadrun, and together we will make these lands prosper."

A long silence followed Cormac's speech, broken only by the cooing of pigeons and the crackling of burning wood. Drichan saw in the Irish prince some of the same barbaric nobility that Tacitus described in his annals. Only Cormac was not Caratacus in chains or Calgacus on the verge of defeat; he sensed a man who knew that his people would one day rule where Rome now governed.

He wondered if Armoricus believed he really had a choice. Earlier in the conversation, the bard had presented them with a wax tablet bearing the late Emperor's seal, authorizing Cormac's father to work with the Roman administration in governing Demetia. It carried exactly the same legal weight as Theodwald's own commission; indeed, it had been given at almost the same time. The villa was caught between the waning power of Rome to the east and the ascendant power of the Irish to the west. Armoricus's decision was obvious. Yet the Dominus could not bring himself to make it. "Tell me, Cormac, do you know Virgil?"

Cormac furrowed his brow and shook his head. "No. Is he a Roman official? A general perhaps?"

Armoricus smiled. "Neither. He was a poet. My father's favourite, in fact. Were my father here, I think he would respond now with a quote from his *Georgics*. Let's see if I can recall it:

> *Too fortunate farmers, if only they knew how happy they are!*
> *Far from the clash of arms, the generous earth*
> *lavishes on them from the soil a life of abundance . . .*
> *He is unmoved by popular applause, or by*
> *kingly purple, or by the maddening*
> *discord among treacherous brothers, or by*
> *conspiring barbarians swarming from the . . . west,*
> *Nor Roman power nor kingdoms destined to perish.*
> *He neither pities the poor nor envies the rich.*
> *He gathers from his fruitful boughs and from his fields*
> *What they give of their own free will.*

Cormac continued frowning, though Drichan could not tell whether it was because his companion had failed to translate the poem or because the Irish prince could not fathom its meaning. In Drichan's recollection, Virgil referred to barbarians invading from the Danube in faraway Dacia, not from the west. But the reason for the amendment was obvious enough.

Armoricus continued, "I cannot deny the authority claimed by you or your father. Nor do I wish to comment on how you exercise it in your lands. If Magnus Maximus made your father sub-king of Demetia, that was his choice. But let us not forget: Maximus was declared a usurper. His commissions were nullified. And you've shown no proof that the Governor has renewed this authority."

He held up his hand as both Cormac and Theodwald made to object. "Hear me out. I am content to leave such high matters to others. I have no interest in the 'kingly purple'. My only concern is the welfare of my people and the prosperity of my lands. I want nothing more than what my fields and orchards freely offer."

Cormac leaned forward. "Then you accept my offer to be the protector of these lands?"

Now it was Armoricus's turn to sigh with exasperation. "No. That is not what I am saying. If I must put my words plainly, then what I am saying is that I wish for you and your people to leave me and my household in peace. If Theodwald chooses to cooperate with an authority that does not extend to these lands, that is his choice. I believe he will regret it—or his son will. You say you've not come as an overlord, else you'd have brought warriors. Yet we both know that the threat of them is sufficient. You ask us to look west rather than east. Very well. Secure the roads, and our goods will flow westward. But they will go as trade, not tribute. Should you send men to impose your will, we will oppose them. If you attack us, we will endure. And if you make endurance impossible? Then we will leave, and the wilderness will reclaim what my ancestors long ago wrested from it."

Cormac mac Urb glared at Armoricus and uttered something in Irish that the bard dared not translate. "You are a fool, Roman. In a world falling apart, those with power must gather the fragments to make things whole. Be warned, Gaius Rusticelius Armoricus: no piece can be left discarded."

Once his bard had finished, the Irish prince strode from the hall. The heavy silence left behind was broken only by the soft cooing of pigeons in the rafters. Drichan recalled the psalm once more: *Let them become as chaff before the wind, with the angel of the Lord hemming them in.* The time of the Lord's winnowing was drawing nearer.

XVI

Baglan was crouching arse deep in frigid water, engulfed by a total darkness that resounded with panicked voices and the relentless roar of inflowing water. Given the slope of the shaft, he knew that most everyone behind him had drowned by now, while those ahead were almost certainly near enough to the surface to gain safety. He couldn't figure out where he stood in this matter, but the rate that the water had risen from his feet to his waist didn't bode well. He frantically scrambled up the roughly hewn slope of the shaft. The terror of drowning gave his exhausted legs strength and speed.

The disaster had struck without warning. A crack like a thunderclap had split the air, and then came the deluge, an inescapable torrent. Baglan had been making his way towards daylight with a load of lead ore when the flood began. He was at the rear of a procession of miners, all of whom crouched paralyzed as the sound grew louder. Within a matter of seconds, icy water lapped at their ankles. Once the first shock had passed, and they had dropped their loads, water was already at their waists, numbing their bodies and rendering the tunnel floor treacherous and slick. Twice Baglan slipped, the frigid water stealing his breath, leaving him gasping and trembling, his heart pounding as though it might break free of his chest.

He began to feel sluggish, as though the water around him were turning to mud. He thought about how comforting the darkness around him was. It enveloped and enshrouded him, protecting him from the glare of the light above. Perhaps he would stop for a moment. The bright surface was where suffering lay; here in the darkness, halfway to Annwn itself, he could be left alone, free from the cruelty of hard men. Ever since he had been captured by the Roman authorities, the toing and froing between comforting darkness and the tyrannical light had been the summation of his life. Now, it appeared it would also be its ending.

But there was still enough life in him to push him onwards. His perseverance was more instinct than willpower. Although he was ready to yield to the gods' unremitting cruelty, his legs kept working hard until at last he began to feel the water level drop. By the time it had ebbed to his knees, he could see dim lights and dancing shadows ahead of him. Soon, hands—strong, calloused and rough—reached out, grabbing him, pulling him from the yawning darkness back into the horror of his imprisonment.

Christians spoke of a place called hell where the damned, like himself, would be made to suffer for their sins. There were too many signs of it around him for Baglan ever to doubt this belief. He had always accepted that the world of man is filled with unequal measures of beauty and brutality, of kindness and cruelty. Why else supplicate the gods except to try to redress the imbalance? But the hounds of Annwn ever prowled for souls—or so it now seemed to him—and the gods cared nothing for mercy. No, while he thought it foolish to worship a god who allowed himself to be crucified, he could easily believe in hell—especially now that it had become his home.

He didn't know how much time had passed since the Roman authorities had arrested him. Despite all his protestations, he had been hauled before the local magistrate and questioned hard about his movements and home. He had tried to explain his actions, appealing to them to let him resume his search for his family, but he had been met with only disapproval and suspicion. To them, he was no more than a slave or a *colonus*; in either case, bound by imperial law to the land on which he lived and worked. By that same law, he should have been returned to his Dominus for punishment, but the judge's sentence had been as predetermined as it was perfunctory: "Send him to the mines."

And so, a man long accustomed to the wide-open spaces of meadows and mountains now found himself entombed in cramped darkness. Nurtured throughout his life by the villa's gentle abundance, he was now weakened and wrecked by the barren grind of industry. His world had been bleached into the grey of rock and silt, which seemed to leech the humanity from those it claimed. A landscape as grey as old bones produced men as cold and unfeeling as death.

Yet within the mine's black depths, Baglan's mind wandered freely. The press of rock seemed to release his imagination, and in the refuge of his memories he saw again the green hills rolling into the horizon and heard the wind in the high grasses. In that space, he somehow found enough comfort to endure. He was sure his happiness would from now on exist only in the past tense.

Prickling sunlight greeted him as he was hauled out of the adit to where other survivors were sitting. They sat in stunned silence, their faces pale and drawn. Baglan turned back to the mine entrance, where a foreman was ranting in frustration. After three or four others were pulled from the earth, no one else emerged. A dozen or more remained below, all now either dead or wishing they were.

A shadow crossed over him, and he looked up to find a man holding out a towel. "You'd better dry yourself off before you catch cold." Baglan accepted the towel without comment and started to rub himself down as he watched the man walk over to a cauldron and return with a mug of hot broth, which he offered to Baglan.

"It'll put some life back into you. It's supposedly made from meat and turnips, but it tastes more like boiled boots. Still, drink up."

The man's description was entirely accurate. But the broth filled Baglan with a welcoming warmth, and so he forced himself to consume it slowly. He reflected on the fact that this was the second time since leaving the villa that he had emerged from near death to be offered sustenance from a stranger. He wondered where Gwas was now.

Handing back the half-empty mug, Baglan murmured, "Thank you. Yours is the first kindness I've known since coming here. What's your name?"

"Potitus," the man replied. "I live down in Bonaven Taberniae. How about you?"

"Baglan. I come from over beyond the mountains that way," he replied as he gestured towards the east. "But now I suppose I belong here."

"Then you're a long way from home, Baglan. How did you end up in this hell hole?"

Potitus was a late middle-aged man, short in stature with a receding hairline, but with a strikingly youthful and friendly face. There was a delicateness to his features, which suggested someone unused to demanding work or the sun. Baglan wondered what he was doing here at the mine; he seemed better suited to a shop or a library. Although there was something about his brown eyes that suggested cleverness, the soft features of his face invited trust and confidence. Although Baglan had learned to keep to himself since coming to the mines, he found himself drawn to the quiet pull of this man's presence. His story spilled out like the water from the fissure below.

"That has to be one of the saddest stories I've heard," Potitus said plainly when Baglan finished his tale. "And I've heard my share of tragic ones. I can't imagine what it must be like to lose your loved ones as you have. The ways of our world can be so cruel, so heartless. But don't give up yet. As old Cicero said, where there's life, there's hope."

Baglan scoffed. "Hope? I gave that up long ago, however much life still clings to this sack of bones. My son is gone, buried in a grave I'll never see. And the gods only know what horrors my wife and daughter endure. Tell me, what's left for a man like me to do?"

Around them was the broad scar of churned up earth, the workers' dilapidated shanties and the frenetic flow of the workmen. The air was filled with the shouts of foremen and the groans of the cold and weary. It was a place repurposed to profit an empire; an ugly place that degraded men as much as it did the land. Yet beyond the ugliness, there was something else.

"Look there," Potitus said, his voice soft.

Baglan followed his gaze to the hills. The setting sun cast its long, golden rays across the land, causing the green slopes to blush. The effect was remarkable; it was as if the gods had chosen to clothe the green hills and grey rocks in rose array. Above, the sky burned with fiery hues beneath a ceiling of deep purple clouds. Despite himself, Baglan felt a stirring. It was strange how beauty had a way of reaching even into his pit of despair, piercing through his calloused sorrow. He couldn't argue with it, couldn't push it away. It simply reached beyond his despair to caress his soul. And his soul awoke at its touch.

I lift my eyes to the mountains from where comes my help, whispered

Potitus as a murmuration of starlings ebbed and flowed and rose and fell against the blushing landscape.

"What?" Baglan asked, his voice distant, his mind still caught in the wonder.

"Perhaps there's a way to hold onto hope. You're a shepherd. The hills, the mountains—they're in your blood. Instead of looking around at all this misery or inside at the sorrow that poisons you, why not try looking up? Let the beauty of those hills hold you for now. It's not much, I know. But maybe it's enough to keep you alive. And while you're alive, hope will find you. I promise you that."

Baglan turned to Potitus, studying his face. Here, in this place of despair, among people degraded and broken, was a man offering unlooked-for kindness. Potitus owed him nothing; he had nothing to gain. It was pure grace, unmerited as it was disarming. In the kindness of a stranger and in view of ravishing beauty, he felt the faint stirrings of renewed life. And perhaps, just perhaps, the first glimmers of hope.

—

Aurelius stood with his grandfather and Cadfan beneath a plane tree, watching workers skilfully erect a pavilion. The tent was normally used for festivals, but now it provided shelter for those fleeing ruin. The refugees had arrived in small groups a couple of days earlier from the other side of the mountains. They brought little with them other than grim reports of great estates being ravaged, their lords lynched, their homes burned to ash. Aurelius vaguely knew the eldest son from one of the villas and wondered whether he had suffered the same fate.

A one-armed, middle-aged veteran with a face weathered as old leather approached them. He had introduced himself as Muconius, a foreman from the estate, who had made himself leader of the refugees. He seemed trustworthy enough, though Meurig and Cunicatus had objected to sheltering any of the refugees so near to the villa. They had only relented when assured that some of the farmhands would be posted as guards.

"We can't thank you enough for taking us in," said Muconius in strongly accented Latin.

"Do you think there will be many more?" asked Cadfan.

"From the south? Hardly. Only a handful of us chose to cross the mountains. The rest headed towards Isca Augusta."

"Why did you come this way?" asked Aurelius. "Pretty mad thing to do this time of year."

Muconius nodded. "Not my idea, I can tell you. But a few of them are from somewhere a little north of here, and the rest just want to put the mountains between them and the brigands. Plus, the Irish have begun raiding along the coast. The world is going to shit."

"That accent of yours," said Quercus. "Where's it from?"

"Far north," replied Muconius. "Up near the Wall. I was an auxiliary once—a Briganti slinger. Pretty good one, too. But ten years ago, I lost this." He raised the stump of his arm. "Army doesn't have much use for a one-armed slinger, so I found myself a pretty girl who thought she did. Followed her south to work as a foreman on an estate."

"And the girl?" Aurelius asked, though he wasn't sure he wanted the answer.

Muconius barked a laugh. "Turned out she had less need of a one-armed man than one with two arms. But it didn't end too well for her."

The gist of this comment hung heavy in the autumn air. Aurelius shivered. Their villa felt safe enough. But ruin wasn't far away. Sooner or later, it would find them, unless the legions came back. And there was no sign of that happening. How could they ever hope to avoid the destruction that seemed to be engulfing everything around them? *We should just pack up and leave*, thought Aurelius.

Cadfan spat on the ground and rubbed his spittle into the dirt with the tip of his boot. "Well," he said, "you and your folks can stay in the tent till the Dominus gets back. Can't live out there all winter, though. You'd freeze. Got any plans?"

Muconius laughed uncomfortably while shaking his head. "You don't have need of a one-armed man, do you?" When no one answered, he scowled and turned towards the tent. "Some of them will move on once they've rested and eaten. The others don't know what to do. That estate was their entire world. What's a man to do when his home is gone?"

"Make another one," replied Quercus simply. "I'm sure there are jobs around here or on some of our tenant farms that Cadfan can find for you to do. My son should be back any time. We can decide then what's practical."

After Muconius left to rejoin the others, Quercus, Cadfan and Aurelius returned to the villa. It had begun to drizzle, and the air was cooling quickly. "Might see snow by morning," commented Cadfan as they stepped onto the veranda. "I'll see that our guests get some extra blankets."

"Do we have the supplies to feed them over the winter, if they stay?" asked Aurelius.

"We're fine with that lot. I'm just afraid they might be the first of many more. I suppose it may work out all right that we couldn't sell as much of our produce as we'd hoped. Grain supplies are pretty good. We may have to slaughter a few more of our livestock than I would like. But we'll manage. Winter should keep others from trying to follow them across the mountains."

"Brigands, too," added Aurelius. "I can't imagine they'd try to come this far north when there's easier pickings down south."

"For the time being," countered Quercus. "But if word gets out that we're well-stocked, we'll have trouble soon enough."

Cadfan's jaw tightened. "Been thinking about that. Might be time to do more than just wait for it."

"I thought we were," replied Aurelius. "Isn't that why Meurig has been training the men to fight?"

Cadfan shrugged. "Yep. But that's not what I mean."

"What are you getting at?" asked Quercus.

"Two things," said Cadfan. "The first is for you, Armoricus and Corotica. Find somewhere secret and secure to stash some of your valuables. If the worst happens and we've got to run, you'll need something to start over. Second, we stash supplies. Not all of them, but enough to get by if it comes to that."

"Where would you store them?" Aurelius asked.

"Old hypocaust under the bathhouse," Cadfan explained. "No one's touched it in years. Thieves won't think to look there."

"Hard to think of a better use for the old place," agreed Quercus. "Start on it in the morning?"

"But that only works if we don't get many more refugees," suggested Aurelius. "We don't have enough to feed them and keep anything back. It's one or the other."

Cadfan shrugged. "Nothing we can do about that. Just hope no one else gets the idea we're taking all comers."

Later that night, Aurelius lay awake beneath layers of wool blankets. Outside, rain mixed with sleet lashed against the shutters, and the wind made a mournful sound in the eaves. Although he was tired, he couldn't sleep. He kept replaying the earlier conversations in his head, ruminating on what they might mean.

The world, it seemed to him, had come unmoored since he left Corinium. Back in August, news from this part of Britannia had been troubling but not dire. Reports then were about the Saxons to the east. It was as though the chaotic forces in the world had been waiting for a signal to be unleashed, like Nodens' horn summoning the hounds of Annwn to the wild hunt. Was anywhere west of the Severn truly safe anymore?

He began to feel angry. What infuriated him most wasn't just that barbarians and brigands were defying Roman authority—it was that they were succeeding. Home was supposed to mean order, prosperity, civilization itself. To defy Rome was to invite anarchy and terror. And as Euripides had said, anarchy is stronger than fire. Unless checked, such a fire would turn into a conflagration that would consume everyone. The thieves and brigands needed to be crushed. But what had become of Rome's strength to do that?

Then he realized what truly grated on him: this was his home. It was his to hold, his to reject if he wished—but not for others to destroy. Contradictory moods afflicted him: one moment he was determined to convince his family to leave, the next he was thinking of ways to guard against the approaching disaster. He'd no sooner outline his case for decamping to Corinium than he'd imagine himself standing with Meurig, spear in hand, ready to fight. All the news encouraged him ever more urgently to forsake his home. But the more he was convinced to do so, the more openly and fiercely his heart clung to the place that had given him life.

Familia ante omnia? he thought to himself wryly. Hadn't he always told himself his ambitions were for the sake of his family? That seeking a better life, one with prospects for advancement, was about securing their future? Wasn't that what the great men of Rome—Octavian, Severus, Constantine—had done? They achieved greatness for their families and not just for themselves. *Familia ante omnia*. His sharpest criticism of his father, grandfather and forefathers had always been their lack of ambition for the *familia*. Each had allowed personal contentment to come before the good of the family. Their selfish decisions had doomed their heirs to mediocrity and perhaps now to ruin.

And yet now he was not so sure. *Familia ante omnia*? The slogan took on new meaning when others were threatening his home. Now, it was the family *in the face of* all others. Could he refashion his ambitions into defiance? Perhaps greatness wasn't found in leaving but in standing firm. He was not yet ready to concede that point. But the fate of Muconius's former masters loomed in his thoughts. He resolved, then and there, that he would do whatever it took to ensure his own family didn't share their ruin. An old proverb came to mind—Seneca the Younger if he remembered rightly: *Sometimes simply to live is an act of courage*. Perhaps in times such as this, it was also an act of defiance. And if so, maybe it was a kind of greatness. With that comforting conclusion, Aurelius finally settled down to sleep.

XVII

"She's a cheerful little doll, isn't she?" commented Corotica as her niece Marcella played with a jumble of yarn on her lap. Gwladys was sitting next to her on a roughhewn bench outside Theodwald's hall. Sleet had fallen during the night, and the morning had brought with it a confining and depressing fog. But by midmorning it had lifted just enough for Armoricus and Tewdrig to go out and survey Theodwald's domain and to visit the neighbour who was refortifying the nearby hill. Cormac had stayed behind, stricken by a vicious cold that was sweeping through the estate.

Marcella wiggled off her mother's lap and scampered off to play hide and seek with a group of girls. As she watched her go, Corotica recalled her own childhood, imagining herself in her niece's place and the children as her old playmates. Despite all the changes, some things remained perennially the same. She wondered if her niece would grow up to marry a fine man as she had done, to mother her own children, and perhaps even one day sit on the same bench and imagine herself a child again. "The roles never change, only the players."

"What's that?" asked Gwladys, turning towards her.

Corotica hadn't realized that she had spoken her final thought. "Oh, just thinking about the times we're in." She shifted, drawing her cloak closer. "How is your family?" Gwladys's father was the chief of a settlement near a lake on the other side of the hills to the east.

"They're well, as far as I know," Gwladys replied. "But I haven't had word since summer. We plan to visit them near the solstice, though. The Irishman will accompany us."

"He's staying as long as that?"

"No, no," replied Gwladys. "We'd hoped he'd be gone by now. His presence here unsettles the people. Many agree with your husband, but I think Theodwald is probably right. The Romans are growing weak."

Corotica nodded. "What will become of us, I wonder?"

Gwladys looked towards Marcella with concern written on her face.

"When I was a girl, I thought we were strong. We were once, I think, or at least that's what the old tales want us to believe. But we're not the heirs of Caratacus any longer. The last time the legions left, we proved ourselves no match for our enemies. I tremble to see such days returning."

Corotica had long ago dealt with the memories of the terror and loss she'd known as a girl. But she could feel them returning, especially as she saw that same fear now on the faces of the people around her—a different cast, but the script felt the same. No wonder they looked for strength wherever it could be found, even in the guise of a supposedly friendly Irish prince. Or in the presence of a priest.

The last thought occurred to her as she saw Drichan emerge from one of the roundhouses. His book satchel was slung over his shoulder, and he was carrying a large goblet and a small plate towards a table that had been set out in the courtyard in front of the hall. He was preparing to celebrate the holy mysteries for the estate as he had done on the previous day in the hall for Corotica and Gwladys's families. Corotica watched Cormac's interpreter trailing after him, the man's curiosity unmistakable as he lingered close to the priest.

"I'm glad you brought him," Gwladys said softly. "I think we'll need his prayers before long."

Corotica nodded. "I thought I would show him where the holy man used to live. Drichan wants to become a hermit like he was. At first, I thought him mad. But now I wonder. Iesu has shown himself to be a powerful God throughout the world, and I begin to see that we need more than the strength of men if we're going to survive."

Gwladys gave a quiet laugh, more rueful than amused. "We always need more than the strength of men, though they'll never admit it. Perhaps our new God will protect us better than the old ones."

Corotica rose from the bench, reaching out a hand to Gwladys. "Come. Let's join in the mysteries. The fog sits heavy on our spirits, and we have need of grace."

After the service and a light meal, Corotica enlisted a couple of strong men and went in search of Drichan. She found him once again in the company of Cormac's interpreter. He greeted her with a polite bow. "How is the Domina? I'm pleased that you and Gwladys could join us for the mysteries."

"I am fine, Drichan," she replied. "You seem to be getting on well here."

Drichan smiled. "Yes, I'm going to baptize eight adults and fourteen children. Your brother is also arranging for me to come regularly to celebrate the holy mysteries and tutor your niece."

Corotica laughed, her eyes glinting with humour. "Why, you almost sound like you're enjoying being a priest."

"Almost," replied Drichan a little too seriously. "But I've not changed my mind. In the summer, I'd still like to go through with my original plans. But perhaps it could be combined in some fashion with continuing to be of service to you."

"That's why I've come to find you. Would you care to see where our old holy man lived his solitary life? Bring your Irish friend along if you like."

Drichan turned to his companion. "Would you care to join us, Aongus?"

"Thank you, I would," he replied, his voice a gentle lilt. "Kind of you to include me."

"It's about two miles up the road. Close to the old Roman fort. I've asked these two to come with us for protection." She gestured towards the armed retainers who followed at a short distance. "You can't be too safe."

The road that edged along the northern slope of the hill behind Theodwald's estate showed them grand views across the broad valley, itself dominated by the long-derelict fort atop a high hill to their north and east. Locals still vaguely recalled that it had once been the capital of their kings, but it had been destroyed by the Romans who demolished its walls and turned its roundhouses into ash heaps. Though generations had looked to it as the centre of their world, no memory of its people had been handed down the intervening three centuries. They were now simply among the faceless company of Ancestors, who even good Christians knew watched over them from the afterlife with care and affection.

Not long afterwards, the road dropped gradually towards a narrow river that flowed from the north into the Isca. To their south, not far from the confluence, stood another abandoned fortress: Bannium, which the Romans had built after destroying the hillfort. Its high walls of dressed stone overlooked the road where it crossed the Isca. It had once been a base for a detachment of Roman levies tasked with protecting the roads and industrial sites. But it had largely fallen into disuse long before it was completely abandoned, ending its life as a base for a small detachment tasked with tax collection. They had scarpered back east at the first sign of the Irish, and only shrubs and small trees now stood sentry.

"How incredible that it should be left derelict," remarked Drichan as they approached the fort. "I imagine thieves or the Irish could make good use of the place."

But Aongus shook his head. "Not unless there are many in number and they have brought masons with them. The fort is enormous, and it looks as if all the gates have been broken down. Look, there are gaps in the walls."

Corotica nodded. "Engineers came after the troubles and destroyed much of it. You're now more likely to find wayward sheep than brigands. One day, it will be like the old hillfort we saw earlier—crumbled and forgotten. No one will remember who lived there. Perhaps it's the Romans' turn to fade into history, just as others before them. Perhaps eventually your stories will also be forgotten. No more Virgil, no more Cicero."

They walked their horses into the fort's deserted precincts. The walls surrounded an astonishingly wide area, marked now only by the skeletal remains of the principia, praesidium, granaries and bathhouse, amidst lines of mounds where timber structures once stood. Corotica vaguely recalled visiting the soldiers here with her father when she was a tiny girl and how ugly she had found both the place and its men. By then, the place was already dilapidated, and the sorry souls stationed there were more thugs than soldiers. It occurred to her that except for a couple of brief visits to Venta Silurum, she had never been to a Roman-built place that wasn't decaying. The only glory of Rome she'd ever seen was a fading one.

"What astonishes me," Aongus said after a moment of quiet, "is the stonework. If we Irish built a fort like this, it would be heralded throughout the ages as a mighty feat of kingly strength. But you Romans build such a place and then abandon it as though it were nothing. Someone once described legionnaires to me as deranged masons: as ready to build a wall or a bridge as run you through with their sword."

They remounted their horses and ambled down towards the little river just a little north of where it met the Isca. After splashing across onto the far bank, they entered a dense wood that seemed cold and lifeless in the wintry damp. Corotica recalled its summer lushness when she and her mother used to visit the strange holy man. She remembered him as a good man, in his way. Affectionate, even. But there had been a wildness in him too, an unbroken spirit that seemed, to many, a sign of God's hand upon him. He had proven them right in the manner of his death. She shuddered as she recalled it and his final prayer for God to deliver him. God had not listened.

After a short but steep climb from the river, the path opened onto a gloomy glade, in the middle of which stood a small stone hut next to a venerable yew tree. Its evergreen foliage transformed the glade into a fragrant sanctuary hemmed about by oak and birch and carpeted with fine needles. Boughs undergirded an evergreen canopy that kept the ground largely dry against even the winter's damp. It was like entering a humbler version of the Temple of Solomon. The hut formed a kind of inner sanctum, a Holy of Holies sheltered amid gnarled branches that stretched out on either side like the wings of the seraphim atop the Ark of the Covenant. The cottage was positioned as though it were an entryway into the yew itself. The overall effect was more pagan than Christian, as though the holy man had imposed himself on a shrine built for druids. Yet for all that, Corotica remembered him being utterly of this place, guarding it with his presence and prayers as though God dwelt there in his earthly glory. It was a place for hushed voices.

An intake of breath roused her from her reverie. She turned to find Drichan utterly transfixed. The expression on his face reminded her of Armoricus on their wedding night, though without the hunger. He had the look of someone who had suddenly found his heart's desire or had stumbled upon a place he'd long sought but only knew as mystery. She recalled their first conversation about his fascination with St Anthony and wondered if this was what he had been trying to describe.

"This is it!" he breathed as he dismounted clumsily. "This is it! Oh,

Domina, this is exactly what I came here to find. This is where I can offer up prayers and be at one with my God."

Even Cormac's translator seemed entranced by the hut. "This is a thin place," he whispered. "Not meaning to question your judgement, madam, but—are we fit to be here?"

Corotica laughed gently at them both. "As fit as anyone, I suppose. No one has lived here for almost thirty years. And the holy man never turned anyone away. I must say, it almost feels untouched by time."

"May I enter?" asked Drichan as he approached the beehive structure.

Corotica shrugged. "I don't see why not. Mind the door though. It must be rotten by now."

In fact, the door opened readily enough and seemed to have survived the decades remarkably well. Drichan removed his shoes before stooping through the doorway, as though he were entering a holy sanctuary rather than a long-forsaken hovel. She gestured to Aongus to enter too if he liked, but he shook his head. It occurred to her that the hut held a power for them both that she had never felt.

"Come and look at this," called Drichan, wonder in his voice.

Corotica dismounted and walked to the threshold. It was too cramped for her to enter along with Drichan, so she simply ducked her head through to see what had caught his interest. When her eyes had adjusted to the gloom, she began to see a remarkable sight. The hut was only just large enough for a simple bed, a chair, and a tiny pedestal that looked more like a pagan votive stand than an altar. But it contained a small cross and was draped in linen too clean to have lain there untouched for decades. Scattered around it lay a veritable trove of rubbish: clipped coins, hairpins, mouldy bread, strips of fabric, even a broken sword.

"People still come here in search of God," whispered Drichan. "These are their offerings. The very air in here feels saturated with prayers. Your holy man may be long dead, but this remains a holy place. He must have been a great saint."

Corotica was beyond astonished. Now that she could see the room better, it was clear that someone had been keeping the place tidy, though there were no signs that it was being lived in. The hut spoke of reverence, even love. As no one in her family had ever mentioned visiting, she could only assume that it had become a kind of covert shrine for the wider estate. People had come with their cares and concerns to this spot to plead and pray to the old saint in much the same way as they would have done as pagans to their Ancestors.

Much to Corotica's surprise, she found tears in her eyes as she stepped away from the hut. The shrine revealed something intimate about her father's people—like visiting dear friends after many years and accidentally discovering their trove of keepsakes. Their care spoke of something enduring, something stronger than the crumbling stones of the Roman forts or the fleeting power of kings. Drichan and Aongus might have sensed divinity in the little sanctuary, but Corotica was much more affected by something far more human. The shrine was not just a monument to a holy man. It was a reflection of the people who had tended it, who had left their offerings here in hope, grief or gratitude.

With light hearts, they had been drawn to the hut by curiosity. Now in reflective silence, they returned to the estate as pilgrims.

XVIII

"I think that it's time that we grab the bull by its knackers and have a proper talk about your future." Cadfan broached the difficult subject in his customary manner.

Ancarat was sitting next to him across from Ria, who had just put Ceridwen down for bed. "Please, dear, listen to what your father has to say."

Ria sighed inwardly but otherwise kept her face as impassive as possible. For weeks, her parents had seemed constantly on the verge of saying something momentous without ever actually saying anything. Just when she thought they'd come out with it, they'd just sigh deeply and look awkwardly around for something else to occupy them. And she had repeatedly caught them giving each other transparently meaningful looks in the way older folks do when they think they're being furtive. Ria had known right away what it all signified: her marital status had again become a concern.

She had lain awake in the small hours fretting about it. Despite her continued indifference towards Rhodri, she did acknowledge that their concern was valid. Now it seemed that they would never see Baglan again, the household had come to accept her as Ceridwen's mother. The child herself had taken to calling her "Mam", and in that small, tender word, Ria had found both joy and responsibility. But the fact that Ria was now her mother meant, in the eyes of many, that Ria needed a man.

And Rhodri, as everyone saw it, was the natural choice. He had a kind heart and a ready smile, and he doted on Ceridwen with a warmth that was hard to ignore. In her more charitable moments, she accepted his affection for Ceridwen as an emblem of his love towards her. Yet for all his goodness, Ria could not summon in herself the kind of feeling she had once known—that wild, unbidden passion that Brochfael had stirred in her heart.

Therein lay the problem: Ria now had a comparison. Six months earlier, she would have happily accepted the arrangements for marriage to Rhodri with hardly a second thought. But now that she had experienced the thrill of romantic love and knew what it was like to long for the touch of a lover, to hunger for his lips, she was wise enough to recognize that she didn't feel that way about Rhodri.

Ria wanted a man who excited her like Brochfael had, who knew how to make her heart sing, not only to satisfy her own needs but also (more importantly) to be a helpmate for raising Ceridwen. She knew that she did not have the patience to be both a doting mother and an affectionate wife if her husband could not enflame her desire to be both. Simply put, while Ceridwen made her want to be a mother, Rhodri did not in the least make her want to be a wife.

What made the problem worse was that she could think of no alternative. Why did men have to be so impossible? This was a question she asked herself regularly. To occupy herself during her chores, she often listed the qualities of those around her. What she wanted was a man with the virtue and wisdom of Armoricus, the bravery and easy-going nature of Meurig, and the youthful good looks of Aurelius. That man would suit her fine. But when she turned her cataloguing mind to the men on offer, she could only despair. There had to be more to life than endlessly repeating cycles of banter, gossip and conversations about livestock and the weather.

So it was with a desperate feeling of inevitability that Ria obediently listened to her father. "I know the past couple of months have been hard," her father was saying. "That business with poor Brochfael knocked you flat. I get that. Before the chick came into our lives, I was really worried about you. But you've blossomed as a mother. Makes me proud."

"It helps that she's such a sweetheart," added Ancarat. "You're a good mother, Ria."

Ria smiled dutifully but otherwise remained quiet. She wanted to wait and see how her father would approach the matter.

"You've grown into a fine young woman. Strong and capable."

"There is more sense in you, girl, than most anybody else around here," commented Ancarat.

"Ain't that the truth," replied Cadfan, but then he seemed to lose his train of thought. "You see, darling, part of my job is to think about your future. You've got a daughter now, and it ain't right for you to carry on alone."

Ancarat sighed loudly. "What your father is trying to tell you is that it's time you had a husband."

Cadfan scowled at her. "Woman, if you would let me speak without interrupting me all the time, I would have told her that myself."

"I won't marry Rhodri." Ria hadn't intended to put her decision so plainly. But now that she had spoken, she was sure she was right.

Cadfan gulped air like a suffocating fish. Before he could respond, Ancarat leaned forward and took Ria's hand. "Now, don't speak hastily, my dear. Hear your father out."

Ria shook her head. "I don't need to, mother. My decision is final. I'll not marry Rhodri."

"Why the hell not, girl?" demanded her father. "He's a good man. Honest, hardworking. He'll treat you right and get you with child easily enough too. What's not to like?"

Now it was Ria's turn to flush. "I don't love him, Father."

"Now, don't be so silly," replied Cadfan. "Love? Is that what this is about? Love's a fine thing, but it ain't the only thing that makes a good marriage. Tell me this: do you think Rhodri would be unfaithful to you?"

"No."

"Don't put too small a value on that," commented Ancarat. "Not in this world."

Cadfan continued. "Do you think he'll mistreat you?"

"Of course not. You know he's a gentle pup."

"And would he be a bad father to Ceridwen?"

Ria felt herself wilting under her father's interrogation. "No. He'd be a good father."

"Then what more do you want, girl?" Cadfan concluded firmly. "You've got a chance for a good life with a man who'll stand by you. Don't throw that away on some childish notion about love."

"It's not childish," Ria stammered. "It's knowing what I need to be happy. Rhodri is a good man. I don't doubt he'll make a good husband for some lucky girl. I'm just not that girl."

"Is there somebody else?" asked Ancarat. "Do you have a sweetheart we don't know about?"

Ria was surprised by how much that one question awoke the slumbering ache within her. She considered confessing her relationship with Brochfael, but immediately dismissed it, fixed now on not giving an inch to her parents. She would get her parents to accept her decision because it was her decision, not because they felt sorry for her. "No, Mother, there is no one else. A girl doesn't have to be already in love to have an excuse for refusing a man."

It was now her mother's turn to blush. She looked awkwardly at her husband.

Cadfan tried to speak in a tone of measured authority. "Look, Ria. Life is full of decisions we really have no choice about making. Some are good. Like you deciding to become Ceridwen's mother. Some are hard. Like committing your life to someone you hardly know."

"But I know Rhodri!" repeated Ria with a degree of exasperation.

Cadfan remained calm. "Yes you do, sweetie, yes you do. You know Rhodri, have known him your whole damned life. By your own admission, he's a good man, tender and handsome, who'll be a good father. By my account, this makes it an easy enough decision. In fact, girl, I look around us, and I can't see any better prospects. If I thought there was a better man, I'd make damned sure he would be your husband. I want nothing but the best for you."

"I think he'll make you very happy, Ria," added her mother, trying to mollify her feelings. "You'll come to see that soon enough."

"But I don't want to," exclaimed Ria with tears now in her eyes. "And I won't. You've always said that I can stand on my own two feet." She stood up from her couch for dramatic effect. "Well, Dad, I'm standing on them now. And I say that I won't marry Rhodri. I'd rather die an old maid than marry him."

"Now, you're just being difficult," yelled Cadfan, waking Ceridwen in the other room. "Well, like it or not, this decision's been made. Rhodri's already asked for your hand, and we've given him our blessing. You'll marry him, and that's that."

"Damn you," screamed Ria. "Damn you to hell, Father. You had no right to make this choice for me. None at all!" Never in her life had she said such a thing to anyone, least of all her father. Appalled by her own vehemence as much as by the news that her marriage had already been arranged, Ria grabbed her shawl and stormed out of the room into the frigid bite of the wet evening.

To her horror, she found Rhodri and his mother lurking outside the door. So certain had everyone been of her acceptance of Rhodri's offer that they had come to celebrate the betrothal. One look at their faces was enough to know that they had heard every word. While Rhodri's mother looked like an angry cat, he was clearly so shocked and dejected that she couldn't help but pity him. She almost reached out to him. Tears streamed down her face, the salt and the cold air biting her flushed cheeks. "I'm sorry. So sorry," was all she could say before rushing down the steps of the veranda into the rain and gloom.

She stumbled around the villa precincts, uncertain what to do. There was nowhere for a young woman to go on an evening like this to be safely alone. It would be too horrible and humiliating to return home. She dare not disturb Corotica who had returned from her journey with a terrible chest infection. She thought briefly about finding a dry place in the bathhouse or the barn, but both would be too dark, too cold and frightening. Not knowing what to do or where to turn, she ended up standing in the gentle rain, too tearful and disconsolate to care how wet and cold she was becoming.

"What on earth?" came an unwelcome voice a few minutes later.

She looked up to see Drichan emerging from the chapel. He ran over and threw his cloak around her. "Come with me," he ordered as he drew her by the hand towards the chapel. At first, she refused before quietly submitting. Her resistance had gone.

Once inside the chapel, Drichan left her sitting and shivering on a bench by the door as he lit the lamps from the perpetual flame that sat on the altar. A dim light filled the room; the shadows of the free-standing cross flickered against the plaster walls.

"Tell me what's happened," said Drichan as he pulled a chair next to her and sat down.

Ria's heart sank. She was too cold and weary to explain matters to Drichan. She didn't want a priest or even God at this particular moment. She just wanted to be alone. But she could think of no way to extricate herself. So she pulled Drichan's cloak more tightly around herself and replied flatly, "My parents want me to marry."

Drichan nodded, leaning back slightly, as if to absorb her words fully before responding. "I can understand that. You've come of age. Does the idea of marriage not appeal to you?"

"Not to the man they've chosen."

"Ah," replied Drichan sympathetically. "I suppose it rarely does."

She turned sharply towards him, her brow furrowed. "What do you mean by that?"

"Only that it seems to me that so often men choose, and women are chosen. Never the other way around. But tell me—what is it about this man you find objectionable?"

Her lips pressed together. There it was, the question that she couldn't seem to escape. "That's the problem," she said at last. "There's nothing to dislike about him. I know he's a good match. Sensible. But does that make me foolish for not wanting him?"

Drichan sighed. "That's not for me to say. But I understand your difficulty. It would be easier, wouldn't it, if he were unkind or unfit? Then you'd have cause. But it seems to me this might not really be about Rhodri at all. Tell me—do you think it could be about something else?"

Ria noted that she had not referred to her intended by name. So, even the priest knew about the proposal. She felt her anger rising again. "What are you trying to say?"

"Only . . . I mean . . . " stuttered Drichan. Then he seemed to gather himself together. "Don't be angry with me. Half the villa knows about the match. It's that obvious. What they don't know—what they can't know—is about your grief. What I'm asking is whether this is really about Rhodri, or if it's about Brochfael."

His words landed like an unexpected blow, stirring everything she'd tried to keep hidden. "What do you mean by that?" she snapped, and he flinched.

He folded his arms awkwardly, rubbing his hands up and down them as if to warm himself. Finally, he said, "The Domina confided in me before Brochfael's funeral. I know about your love. I know how hard his death was for you in particular. That's why I tried to comfort you, though I think I failed. I could never find an opening, a way to get you to trust me enough to confide in me. But I've prayed."

Her anger flared and faded in an instant. It hadn't occurred to her that Drichan might know about Brochfael, and the thought wounded her pride. Had the Domina betrayed her? Was everyone conspiring against her, whispering behind her back about Brochfael, about Rhodri?

But, looking now at Drichan, her heart softened. He was plainly ill at ease, a man fumbling in a field he didn't know how to tend, yet still determined to work it. "You may be right," she admitted at last, her voice quiet. "But does it matter?"

"How do you mean?"

"Only that the marriage has been arranged. I'm stuck. Shouldn't you be counselling me to swallow my pride and accept that Rhodri will be my husband and the father of my children?"

He regarded her for a moment, his expression thoughtful. "You've said it yourself—Rhodri isn't a poor choice. I think if you both try, it could work out well enough."

"Well enough," she repeated, the words hollow.

Drichan reached out, placing a hand on her shoulder. It was an awkward, clumsy gesture, but not without kindness. "If you're truly opposed, you might have other choices. Though they aren't easy ones."

Ria's curiosity piqued. "Yes?"

"The obvious one is to appeal to Armoricus. But given Rhodri's suitability and your family's wishes, I doubt that would succeed."

"And the other?"

Drichan hesitated, then said, "You could remain a virgin. Dedicate yourself to God."

Ria blinked at him. "What?"

"It would mean taking a vow," he explained. "Not as a way to escape Rhodri, but out of devotion. It's not uncommon. Though I imagine your parents wouldn't approve."

Ria laughed. "Yes, that would be drastic!"

"Others would undoubtedly see it that way. But they couldn't easily stop you if I supported your decision. I just mention it as an idea."

"And what of Ceridwen?"

Drichan shrugged. "Widows often devote themselves to God. I don't think it would cause trouble."

"Ha!" chuckled Ria. "Then I would be the Virgin Mother!"

Drichan's face turned bright red with embarrassment, and his stammered reply was unintelligible. The sight of him, flustered and out of sorts, made her laugh, draining away some of her ill-ease.

"Thank you, Drichan," she said as she rose, returning his cloak. The rain had eased, the steady drum fading to a soft patter. It was time to go home. She didn't for a moment take Drichan's suggestion seriously, but all the same, it was comforting to know there was an option. As she crossed the courtyard, the damp air fresh against her face, she smiled to herself. "Virgin Mother, indeed."

XIX

Aurelius tapped his fingers vigorously against his hip. He would have preferred to punch something.

He was leaning against the bookshelf in his father's office with his family crowded next to him. While his father was seated at his desk and his mother alongside him, everyone else was standing, which served only to heighten the tension. Although his father seemed collected, Aurelius noticed his right eyebrow flicking with agitation. His mother also appeared composed except that she kept twirling a loose strand of her hair with an index finger. Meurig was trying to pace up and down while Cunicatus shifted his weight from side to side. Only his grandfather, standing in the corner leaning on his stick, seemed unfazed by the discussion.

It was the first time they had gathered since his parents returned with heavy colds from Theodwald's estate. Armoricus, unshaven and pallid, had roused himself enough to provide a perfunctory account of their trip and to hear about the arrival of the refugees before confining himself to his bed to spend the next week shaking the villa with his coughs. His mother became similarly indisposed, though she recovered from the illness much sooner than her husband.

His father leaned forward on his desk and rubbed his hands together. He still didn't look entirely well. "I know this is hard for everyone. But my word is final. In this matter, at least, my word is also law."

Aurelius, standing with the restless energy of a horse champing at the bit, tightened his fist and tapped it against his thigh. His father had just reiterated his decision not to submit to the Irish but to allow their goods to flow westward. Aurelius burned with the conviction that such a stance was reckless, yet his father's authority seemed to him a stone wall that he could neither scale nor topple.

But where Aurelius seethed in silence, Meurig spoke. He leaned forward, his voice respectful but insistent. "Armoricus, you know I've always been loyal to this family. Whatever you decide will be as God's own law. But I can't accept your decision until we've talked it through."

"Especially when it's so foolish," added Cunicatus, always quicker than his brother to anger. "We can't stand alone. We need allies. You saw the hillforts being fortified. Even Theodwald knows what's coming."

Aurelius had been astonished by the news that one of the old hillforts was being fortified. The family based there was a surly pack of Silures, known for their quarrels and lawsuits. They had a prodigious appetite for other people's lands. His father had determinedly refused ever to do business with them. "You don't sleep with adders," his grandfather once said, "even when they're in the bed next to you." Yet here they were, preparing for what the future might bring, while his own family seemed paralyzed by indecision.

"I know my neighbours too well," replied Armoricus. "That they submitted to Cormac isn't surprising. They sniff opportunity."

Quercus, who had been listening quietly, growled his agreement. "Their lord is an arse and a fool. Always has been. As was his father, and his father before him. And Theodwald is a fool to trust him."

"But does my father have a choice?" replied Corotica, turning her head and shoulders to look behind her at Quercus. "Don't you think his siding with them is reason enough to think carefully about this?"

"Then you disagree with your husband?" asked Quercus with a devilish twinkle in his eyes.

"I'm not saying that, and you know it, you old rascal." She sighed heavily. "Anyone who claims to know the wisest course is either a liar or an idiot."

"Or both," interjected Meurig unhelpfully.

Corotica ignored him. "But we don't have to declare our intentions yet. Where's the harm in talking with our neighbours while we wait to see what happens? We need allies."

"Exactly," said Cunicatus. "My brother and I can continue to train our hands to fight, but they'll never stand up to a proper attack by warriors. We need to be in league with others, including the Irish who want to be our friends."

Aurelius could contain himself no longer. "You think we should bow to them?" he burst out, his voice filled with scorn. "What's become of this family? We're Romans! Rome doesn't treat with barbarians; she subjugates them! Besides, what's a protector but another name for a lord, even a king?" He spat the last word out as if it was bitter to the taste.

Meurig laughed loudly. "Wake up, cousin. Wherever Rome is these days, it's not here. It's not even close to here. You've seen the ragbag bunch of refugees coming here with your own eyes. That's all Rome is these days."

At that very moment, Muconius entered the office. Armoricus had asked the foreman to join them so he could finally address the needs of the refugees and hear for himself about their ordeals. Since the first groups had arrived, another dozen or so had made their way to the villa with their own tales of brigands and renewed Irish raids. The whole south coast now seemed to be in a state of disarray. And still there was no sign of Roman soldiers.

Muconius scowled at Meurig before bowing to Armoricus and saying, "Dominus, I am grateful for your family's generosity. It honours us ragbag refugees."

Armoricus rose from his seat and threaded his way through the others to clasp Muconius's hand. "I am sorry that I've not been well enough to greet you sooner. I hope everyone has what they need."

Ancarat had organized a battalion of women and men to knit warm blankets and cloaks while Cadfan had directed that shoes and clothing be found for all who needed them. It had been deemed safer to spread the refugees out among the tenant farms than to have a growing congregation of them encamped at the villa itself. Only Muconius had remained at the villa, employed by Cadfan as a foreman.

"Better than we dared hope. Your kindness won't be forgotten. But if I may—I couldn't help overhearing your conversation. And though it's not my place, I think you're right."

Armoricus arched an eyebrow. "You do? Why?"

Muconius shrugged. "You've no choice really. The authorities won't help; they've got the coast to pacify. You're on your own. The smart thing would be to take the Irish up on their offer. But how can you, and still call yourself a Roman? Sheep don't run to wolves for help because there are bears lurking nearby. Their only hope is to keep their heads low and pray that the bears and wolves kill each other."

Meurig replied, "It seems to me that when there are bears and wolves prowling, the one thing you know for certain is that the sheep aren't going to come out well unless they have a brave shepherd."

Muconius smiled like a cat with a cornered mouse. "Again, it's not my place to say, but perhaps what you all need is a shepherd."

"Cormac mac Urb?" asked Aurelius irritably.

Muconius shook his head. "No. Your father."

This caused a murmur among those gathered. Cunicatus replied first. "What do you mean by that?"

"I'm just a stranger here and you all know your own business. But it strikes me that you keep speaking of the Romans as though they're all somewhere else. But, of course, you're as Roman as they come. And what do Romans do best? They rule. So, rule. Demand to be made the magistrate here. Train a band of fighters. Backed by strength, the other families would acknowledge you as their protector. To hell with the Irish or anyone else."

Aurelius's eyes twinkled with ambition. He could see it now: his family's moment of greatness. They were Romans, after all—his was the only local family with senatorial connections. The gods had granted them the privilege and responsibility to govern. How could they expect them to bless his family if his father didn't shoulder that responsibility? Was this not their destiny?

His grandfather seemed to agree. "We didn't need anyone else's help the last time the Irish were here. We faced them down ourselves—I faced them down myself. Even when everyone else fled. We did it then. We can do it again."

All watched silently as Armoricus returned calmly to his seat and sat down. Corotica returned to her seat and the two exchanged looks that communicated something that only they understood. Then, unexpectedly, he chuckled.

"I shouldn't laugh," he began, "but your words reminded me of the

Gospel that we read the other day, when Peter urged Christ to turn away from the cross. Do you remember what he said?"

Though Corotica nodded, nobody answered his rhetorical question. Muconius frowned and began to look uncertain.

"*Get behind me, Satan,*" continued Armoricus. "That must have been pretty devastating for poor old St Peter. *Get behind me, Satan.* Well, Muconius, with all due respect, I say to you now, 'Get behind me, Satan.' It's precisely at moments like this that ambitious men reveal themselves. Perhaps that's how St Peter was. Perhaps he saw himself doing well when Christ came into his kingdom. I said to Cormac that I'm a man without ambition beyond the boundaries of my lands. I spoke honestly. I will not set myself against or over my neighbours. So, I'll decline your offer, Muconius. I'll not seek ambition beyond my lands. My duty is here. To protect my flock. Nothing more, nothing less. And you can be sure that I will do everything in my power to protect this flock even if the whole damned world becomes infested with wolves and bears."

Initially, Muconius's mouth dropped open, but he quickly recovered and bowed his head without saying another word. Corotica reached for her husband's hand, a gesture of solidarity. Quercus laid a hand on Armoricus's shoulder. Together, they formed a triptych of determination that increased Armoricus's stature. Nothing could have made it clearer that his words had become law.

But Aurelius felt only a sharp pang of alienation. How could his father allow this moment of greatness to pass? His father's resolve, his rejection of power, felt to him like a final failure. This was their moment, and it was slipping through their fingers. Rome's light was fading, but here—in this place—it could burn bright once more. And yet his father refused. And that would be their ruin. Aurelius was sure of it.

—

A shoot projected from the ice-gripped earth, a shock of green against a dull grey background. The sprout was hardly longer than Baglan's middle finger and gently arched towards the sun until it erupted into a delicate white flower that hung like a lantern above a scatter of frost. Baglan crouched, his knees protesting, and gently stroked its petals. A drop of water fell on his finger, which he held to his lips as though to savour the plant's budding life. While the snowdrops around it had all been trodden and crushed, it had somehow survived long enough to blossom: a prick of beauty amid ruin.

He felt his knees creak as he stood up, grabbed his satchel and made his way towards a line of carts loaded with lead ingots. He didn't understand much about the world. He'd never wanted to know more than how to tend his flock, look after his family and honour the gods. But he realized now how blind he'd been to the world's brutality, to the depravity of men. He had also learned how capricious the gods could be, that they delighted in tormenting a humble shepherd more than accepting his devotion. He had discovered how much the world was ruled by greed, that behind each lead ingot stacked neatly in rows on the carts lay good earth corrupted and decent men degraded. What he wouldn't give to be ignorant again.

As he was helping to load the heavy bars onto the carts, he caught sight of Potitus, deep in conversation with a foreman. Since their first meeting, he had come to enjoy his regular conversations with the compassionate man. Kindness was a language Baglan had once known intimately, woven into the fabric of his family life so thoroughly that it needed no name. Only through its loss had he come to appreciate its worth, perhaps also its scarcity.

Lost in thought, Baglan was slow to notice Potitus beckoning him. The foreman, a burly man whose bulk was matched only by his bark, gave a curt nod, allowing Baglan to approach. Potitus greeted him with a smile, brushing lead dust from his hands.

"Baglan! I am sorry not to have visited during the past couple of weeks. Business. I would advise you not to go into business in these troubled times, but that would be a cruel jest to someone in your predicament."

Baglan furrowed his brow at the comment but said nothing.

Potitus looked momentarily flustered, as though only realizing the inappropriateness of his greeting. "Yes, well," he continued awkwardly, "I suppose that brings us to the matter at hand."

"What matter?" asked Baglan.

Potitus turned to the foreman: a square, bald man from Hispania with a scraggly beard that made him appear like a warthog but with none of its graces. "I've been speaking to the authorities here about my need for a good shepherd. They've agreed to release you to me."

Baglan took a step back in astonishment. "They have?"

Potitus smiled kindly. "Well, you see, I'm one of the magistrates here, so they really have no choice. But I won't take you against your will. Will you come and work for me?"

"Certainly!" replied Baglan as though this development was the most natural thing to have happened. In truth, he was so overcome by events that he could think of nothing else to say.

Baglan noticed the Warthog looking slyly at his compatriots like a naughty boy. It was only then that he observed the small bag of coins in the man's hand. Money had obviously been exchanged.

"Then come with me," invited Potitus, taking Baglan by the arm and leading him briskly away from the yard. They walked at pace past the other workers and through the gates. Only when they had covered a good distance did Potitus slow and speak again.

"It's not as easy as it once was," he said.

"What isn't?" asked Baglan, still disoriented.

"Redemption, my friend. Redemption."

Baglan couldn't make head or tail of his companion's words. Potitus saw his confusion and laughed. "You're a free man now—or as free as one can be in these times. I've purchased your liberty."

"But, but why?" stammered Baglan.

"Let's just say that I value kindness more than gold—and infinitely more than lead."

By now they had reached the little town that had grown up next to the mines. It was the largest settlement that Baglan had ever seen, consisting of a small central forum surrounded by low houses with vividly painted plaster walls. A dry fountain lay to one side of the forum a few paces away from a large timber-framed building guarded by a statue of a robed woman, its fine quality somewhat diminished by the absence of her head.

People milled together in the forum or scurried between shops and booths while a few men armed with spears looked on.

"Welcome to Bonaven Taberniae. It's not much to look at, but it has been my family's home since we Romans first settled here. Come, my villa is this way."

As they entered a side street that rose gently to the south, Baglan suddenly stopped. None of this was right. He now knew Potitus to be a man of means and status. Why would such a man visit the mines, show kindness to the dregs of humanity employed there, and waste his own money to free someone like him? He had heard stories of how some Romans had a taste for unnatural relations, and he feared that his redeemer, with his delicate hands, might be such a one.

Potitus, noticing Baglan's hesitation, turned back. "Are you unwell? What's troubling you?"

"This!" Baglan exclaimed, gesturing wildly. "All of it. Why are you doing this? What am I to you?"

Potitus's brow furrowed briefly before his expression softened into a smirk. "You're not entirely wrong to question me. My motives aren't purely selfless. I do need a shepherd, and honest men are rare in these parts." He paused as he drew closer to Baglan. "I grew up playing in these streets, as did my father and his father and his father and so on going back three centuries. But as much as I love my home, I can see that it's a cesspool of humanity degraded and corrupted by those bloody mines. None of us is unaffected by them and what they have done and continue to do to anyone associated with them. Not even a magistrate like me can do much about that. But what I can do is save those who still carry a spark of humanity. That's what I've seen in you."

"But why me?" Baglan pressed. "There must be others more deserving."

"Not so many as I would like. Frankly, I wasn't coming for you today. I had someone else in mind. But as I arrived today, I saw you crouching down and admiring that snowdrop. I knew then that you'd listened to me. Let beauty sustain you, even in that wretched place. And that's no small thing."

Baglan's confusion deepened. "All because I stopped to notice a snowdrop?"

Now Potitus laughed loudly. "You say that like it's a small thing. Only a man with a shred of hope stops to delight in a delicate flower in a place like that. Remember what I said to you when we first met? 'While there's life, there's hope. Stay alive, and you'll find that hope will find you again.' Well, Baglan, you stayed alive, and like I promised, hope has found you again. Come, let me introduce you to my *familia*."

XX

Rusticella skipped merrily around Publius and their grandfather as they walked together down the lane towards the hamlet on a warm day that teased them with ideas of spring. It was the Nones of February, the day when the workers were roused from their winter idleness to start weeding the fields in preparation for the first crops. The villa buzzed with the happy chatter and laughter that began at dawn and would continue until late that night when everyone finally went to their beds. In that moment, all the troubles of the world seemed no more concrete than a nightmare after waking.

Yet their grandfather walked beside them in sombre silence, stick in one hand and a wicker hamper in the other. Publius knew why: it was the anniversary of his grandmother's death. Although his grandfather visited his late wife's tomb faithfully each month, on the anniversary of her death he would go to sit lovingly next to her with a meal that Ancarat had prepared for two. It was a pagan habit, of course. Publius knew that much. But not even the old priest was brave enough to stand in his way. Men responded to his grandfather's procession to the tomb by doffing their hats while many of the women curtsied.

What made this occasion different was that Grampa had invited them to join him. Never in all Publius's life had he ever taken anyone along for his visit. And no one had dared to intrude. Rusticella had at first demurred. But once it had been explained to her that her grandmother would not, in fact, climb out of her grave to share the roasted chicken with them, she agreed readily enough. As for Publius, he was honoured from the start, noting with some satisfaction that his elder brother had never been invited.

"Your grandmother," their grandfather said suddenly, his voice breaking the silence as they approached the small cemetery, "was quite a woman. Though a Briton, she was every inch the Roman. Far better read than I."

"Was she pretty?" Rusticella asked with the bluntness of her nine years as they approached the scattering of family tombs.

"Very pretty, my dear," replied Grampa with a smile that hinted at happy memories. "And she had a laugh that could fill a room and the sharp wit to silence it when needed."

They stopped before a stone plinth that had been erected for her. Unlike the other tombs, it was clean and set within a small perimeter of boxwood. On it were words inscribed in Latin:

> *MY BEAUTIFUL, FAITHFUL FLAVIA LIES HERE A DUTIFUL*
> *WIFE A LOVING MOTHER AND A VIRTUOUS MATRON SHE*
> *SANG WITH A BEAUTIFUL VOICE BUT VIOLENTLY TAKEN*
> *SHE NOW LIES SILENT*

With care, their grandfather spread a woollen blanket over the damp earth and invited them to sit. From the hamper, he drew out a roasted chicken wrapped in waxed cloth, a round loaf of bread, a flask of wine, and four small plates. Publius noticed that one of the plates was set aside and placed reverently at the base of the tombstone.

Publius studied the plinth and its carefully tended surroundings, picturing his grandmother as he'd always imagined her—a reflection of his mother, beautiful and kind, presiding over the villa with grace. He liked to think back to when the villa was more prosperous, when Grampa was running the place, and his own father was a child exploring the woods and hills, or grouching about his studies and daily chores. Looking beyond his grandmother's tombstone, he pondered the other tombs of his ancestors. Most of them had grown up at the villa like he had. Their memories had always led the way and Publius had always followed.

"I met your grandmother when I was about your brother's age," explained Grampa as much to himself as to his grandchildren. "My mother sent me to live for a while on her family's estate—a sprawling place with more workers than ours and your grandfather's combined. I hated it from the start."

Publius accepted the plate from his Grandpa and waited patiently for permission to eat. He sensed a ritual approaching. Rusticella did likewise but seemed fearfully fixated on their grandmother's plate.

"Your grandmother was a little girl then, not much older than you, Rusticella," he continued. "You have her eyes, her curiosity, too. She used to follow me around, full of questions. I'd tell her stories about our villa, about the hills and woods. She seemed to understand right away the difference between a humble farm like this and the grand estate her father owned."

Publius could imagine it vividly: his grandfather as a lanky boy, scowling under a tussle of black hair, trailed by a bright-eyed girl in a place so grand it must have seemed another world entirely.

"After I left, I didn't see her again for another twelve years. I'd forgotten all about her when my mother one day told me that her father and she had agreed that we should be betrothed. 'You'll be marrying into wealth and influence,' she told me, as though I cared about either. Floored me, I tell you. We were wed on a bright morning at the following spring equinox. She was radiant."

"Did you love her?" asked Rusticella. They were both still waiting for permission to begin eating.

"Hmm?" replied Grampa, having apparently forgotten that they were even there. "Oh, goodness me, my dears! Tuck in. Tuck in. Your grandfather can be an old fool at times. Don't let me keep you waiting any longer. No, wait. First ... " He raised the flask to the tomb. "To my darling Flavia, the best of wives and the most beautiful of women. I hope the good Lord is looking after you. I swore when I was a young man that I'd love you always. And now as an old man I can honestly boast that I have. I miss you dearly." With his tribute completed, he took a long draught of the wine before pouring the rest on the ground at the base of the plinth, which was stained dull red from previous visits.

After that Grampa seemed to brighten up and slip into one of his storytelling moods. While they ate, he told them about his childhood and what a bustling place the villa was in those happier times. "Come," he said when they had finished their meals. "Let's put all this stuff away and visit the others before we return home. Never does to neglect your ancestors. Without them, we wouldn't be. It's as simple as that."

"This is where it all began," he explained as he pulled away a strand of ivy from the largest but most dilapidated of the tombs. A great clump of colourful plaster broke away as he did so. "Proculus Rusticelius Fornax: your great-great-great grandfather. He was the first to come here from our ancestral lands in Armorica. He was a greedy, angry man—a tax collector who fleeced people of their money, took a local girl as a wife, and built the villa for a home."

"I don't like him," declared Rusticella, wrinkling her nose, before moving towards the next tomb.

"You're not alone," agreed Grampa. "Still, whatever we may think of him, his blood runs in our veins."

The next tomb was in better condition than the first, though much more modest in scale. Some of the words inscribed on a plaque mounted on the front were still legible, though again the years had not been kind to the plaster. Grampa knocked off an abandoned bird's nest with his stick and brushed away a broad patch of thick cobwebs.

"Gaius Rusticelius Rubus, my grandfather, though I never knew him. He was the youngest of Fornax's ten children. All the others died, were married off or moved back to Armorica. But Rubus stayed, taking over his father's licence to collect taxes. My father used to say that he only remained because he was sensitive to the sun, and the sun hardly ever shines here. But he didn't like the cold either, which is why he expanded the old bathhouse. The sun won in the end. When my father was your age, Publius, old Rubus stayed out in the fields too long and died of heat stroke."

The next grave marker was little more than a raised plaque, not much higher than Publius's ankles. Its plastered surface contained no words other than S. RUSTICELIUS SARCULUS. But it was well cared for and sat within a low boxwood enclosure next to a similar tombstone inscribed with the name of his wife Lucilia. Although in better condition, it seemed a humble companion to the other grave markers, even more modest than those erected for the other Rusticelii who had been buried there. Grampa stood quietly in front of his parents' graves for a while with his head bowed.

"And now we come to a great man, my father Sextus Rusticelius

Sarculus. The best damned farmer you could ever meet, a loving husband and a wonderful father. Publius, you can aspire to be nothing better than that. He turned this villa into something more than just a home—he made it a living thing. He could coax life from stone and brought out the best in those around him. He died too young. I was nine, and I miss him still.

"My mother was never the same after he died. She refused to remarry: the villa became her husband. I was never half the *paterfamilias* she was, and she never let me forget it. When I was old enough to take over, I had to fight her for control. I only won because she took your father to Armorica after your grandmother was killed by the Irish. She never came back. We placed her memorial because it didn't feel right for my father to be alone."

"Why wasn't a better tombstone made for him?" asked Publius.

Grampa laughed. "He probably didn't want even this. My father was a man who wouldn't give a fig for grandness. He dedicated his life to living beneath his station, which frankly isn't a bad ambition. My mother was from a humble local family whom he married solely for love. I think love was about the only thing that ever motivated him: love of his family, his people and his land."

Grampa retreated into a more reflective mood. As they started to make their way to the villa, Rusticella ran on ahead of them. A group of boisterous workmen was walking down the lane back to the village while Cadfan and Muconius stood in the field with another group of labourers. Hardly a cloud could be seen in the sky. Publius thought about all the people—the families and ancestors of everyone living here—except the refugees—who had worked, played, loved, argued, hated and died in his home. Some of them had been admirable, some wretches like his own forefather, Fornax. But all of them had called the villa home, and somehow each of their lives had helped to make it the place it was today. Publius didn't quite know what that meant, but he knew it to be true all the same. A strange feeling came over him that made him think of being very small, lying between his parents in their bed and listening to them tell him stories. It was a good feeling.

Without stopping, Grampa reached over and squeezed his hand. Publius looked at him, expecting him to say something. But his grandfather continued looking straight ahead. They walked along the lane without words, two links in the Rusticelian line separated by an intervening generation but joined together by their entwined fingers.

Omnia suffert, omnia credit, omnia sperat, omnia sustinet

XXI

An impenetrable fog hung heavy over the valley like a damp shroud, pressing down on the land and muffling the earth beneath it. It followed days of steady rain and a brief, fleeting breath of spring, as though the seasons themselves were caught between hope and despair. Corotica rode slowly homeward from a tenant farm, her mind preoccupied with the events of the past several months. The fog made it difficult to see, but the horse beneath her was sure-footed, and that comforted her as she passed from one patch of grey to the next.

Her thoughts were on the refugees—the pitiful stream of souls who had come to them, each with stories of ransacked homes, deserted estates, and the ever-present threat of brigands and marauding Irishmen. Over the winter, the villa had sheltered nearly seventy souls, though many eventually moved on, bound for Glevum and its promise of safety. For those who stayed, the villa had become a safe harbour. Corotica was proud of the way her *familia* had risen to the challenge. The women had taken the lead, setting up makeshift workshops where they mended clothes and blankets, made shoes and tended to the children. The men had devised an effective system for ensuring newcomers were harmless before directing them to nearby farms. It was a delicate balance, of course—too much sympathy could invite more trouble, too much distance could breed resentment. Yet for the moment it was enough.

Still, the strain was evident. Some men had arrived so broken by their ordeals that they drifted aimlessly, their eyes hollow, their hands idle, doing little but consuming the charity of others. Cadfan dismissed them as "freeloaders", but Corotica was not so hard-hearted. These men, robbed of purpose by grief and trauma, were as much victims as the women and children. Others burned with anger, their silence simmering with barely contained rage. Their bitterness spilled over to those around them, and they were harder to help. And some of the women, too, bore scars that went far beyond the physical—mothers who had lost children, women who could no longer recall their own names. Like rising flood waters, the encroaching disorder lapped at the shore of their island of tranquillity. The constant threat of it was gradually eating away at Corotica's *familia*. She felt powerless. They simply couldn't absorb the newcomers sufficiently to sustain the neighbourly society that had long been her responsibility and her pride. But neither could she turn them away.

Yet for all the strain, there was also a glimmer of hope. Many of the refugees possessed the skills that would be useful come spring: the knowledge of planting, of harvesting, of tending animals. Corotica knew that by summer, the villa could very well produce more than it had in many years. It was the short-term that worried her: the additional mouths were eating up supplies at such an alarming rate that some rationing had to be imposed. Those restrictions were now testing the hospitality of the *familia* more than Corotica cared to admit.

She was roused from her thoughts by the clap of approaching hooves from the direction of the village. Then she heard a rhythmic clanging of metal, and felt a sudden shiver run up her spine. She stopped and peered through the fog as her horse's ears flicked in response to the distant noise. There was no sound of danger—not yet. The voices she heard from the village were not those of panic or alarm, they were more like curiosity. Still, she spurred the horse forward, urging it towards the security of the villa.

When she arrived, she found Meurig and Cunicatus gathering men together. "Who do you think they are?" Corotica asked, her voice tense as she dismounted.

"Only two likely possibilities," replied Meurig, his face as unreadable as ever. "A detachment of auxiliaries, or Cormac. My guess is the former. But we'll see. I'm gathering the men, just in case."

Corotica nodded but felt her heart quicken at the thought of soldiers arriving, especially under such uncertain circumstances. "Should we be worried?" she asked.

"You'd better get to the house," Meurig replied, his tone firm.

Corotica hurried over to her husband, who was standing with Quercus and Aurelius on the veranda facing the lane. Armoricus calmly washed his filthy hands in a large bowl held by a servant and dried them with a towel before putting a toga over his long tunic. He squeezed her hand gently, as though bracing himself with her presence. "I was afraid you might come across them on the road," he said quietly.

"Do you have any idea who they are?"

"I've had no word of any visitors," replied Armoricus.

"You don't think they're brigands, do you?" asked Aurelius, his voice low and tentative.

"Not on horseback," replied Armoricus.

"Unless they're deserters," commented Quercus unhelpfully.

Aurelius's eyes widened slightly. "I hadn't considered that."

Before any further words could be exchanged, a man came running into the courtyard, breathless and dishevelled. "Soldiers, sir," he gasped. "About twenty of them. I think it's the tax agent."

Corotica felt the blood drain from her face. The tax collector. Here, of all times, when the larders were lean and winter pressed hard against the villa. She cast a glance at Armoricus, her husband, but his eyes remained fixed ahead. His jaw was set, his brow furrowed, as it always was when he faced an approaching trial.

A few minutes later the yard was filled with hoofbeats and the clatter of metal on stone. A small band of soldiers entered the courtyard, their breaths steaming in the frigid air. They were led by a man cloaked in fur, who sat perched unsteadily on a cart, his face pale and swollen as if he'd taken his fill of wine the night before. The wagon came to a halt between the barn and the fountain, and the man climbed down. He slipped on the icy cobblestones and caught himself against the wagon wheel, flinging his cloak aside to reveal a gold embroidered tunic and chains draped across his chest. He waddled towards the veranda, doing his best to seem unfazed by his undignified arrival.

Decimus Crassula. They knew him well: a man who wore his Roman name like a cloak to mask his British descent. He'd made his fortune as a tax collector, not by thrift or ingenuity, but by wringing the last coin from landowners. His indulgences were legendary, his greed unashamed. And now here he was.

"If ever there was a man anxious about our times, it's Crassula," muttered Armoricus coldly.

Crassula bowed deeply first to Armoricus and then to Corotica. He had a smooth, oily face that reminded her of an infant's, only pinched at the nose like a weasel. Ignore the eyes and the face combined intensity and innocence. But his green eyes were like a serpent's: cold and emotionless.

"Gaius Rusticelius Armoricus, greetings," he declared in a high-pitched voice and with a flourish of his right hand. "I trust you are well."

Armoricus nodded curtly. "Crassula."

"Domina, you look as fair as ever," Crassula continued, turning his attention to Corotica. "And Aurelius, my, you've grown into a fine young man. I hope you've not been indulging too much in Corinium. The city, as you know, has its pleasures."

Quercus snorted. "Get on with it, Crassula. I doubt you've come to make love to us."

"Charming as ever, Quercus," replied Crassula in an unctuous tone, though the twitch at the corner of his mouth betrayed him. He turned back to Armoricus, his smile thin. "But of course, we should speak privately. A warm room and a cup of wine would do much to ease our conversation."

Armoricus folded his arms. "I am an honest man, Crassula. I don't flatter and I don't deceive. Tell me plainly: have you come to demand payment?"

Crassula's smile faltered. "Rome's coffers must be filled," he said, in a more businesslike tone.

Corotica stepped forward. "And Rome owes its people safety, roads and peace. We have seen none of these. Our markets fail, our roads are treacherous, and the refugees we shelter go unaided."

"Without taxes, there can be no soldiers to ensure those things," Crassula countered smoothly, though his cheeks reddened. He turned to Armoricus. "If you cannot pay in coin, I can accept livestock or other goods in kind."

"Why now?" interrupted Aurelius, his voice steady despite the tension in the air. "Why not come in the autumn, when our stores were full?"

Crassula hesitated, his eyes darting away. "The timing of my visit is not your concern, young man," he said finally.

"Too dangerous, I imagine," Quercus muttered darkly.

Now Armoricus laughed bitterly. "Too dangerous, eh? Too risky to leave the safety of your walls? And now the authorities have come knocking for payment from you. Pity the person who can't pay his tax; pity more the collector who returns to his masters empty-handed."

Crassula's reddening face made him resemble an angry, fat rat. Corotica looked beyond him at the bored-looking soldiers. The rat had come with a full set of sharp teeth. She hoped her husband recognized that.

"Enough of this, Armoricus!" snapped Crassula. "It is late in the day and this weather is enough to put anyone in a foul mood. If you won't extend to us the hospitality of your villa, then at least allow us shelter in your barn. We can discuss this further tomorrow."

Armoricus held his gaze for a long moment, then straightened. "The field by the village is empty. Your tents will serve you there. My men will see to your horses. They, and only they, may rest here." With that, he turned and strode towards his office.

Corotica followed him, gesturing to the others to remain. She entered the office wordlessly, grabbed Armoricus's arm, and pulled herself into his embrace. "What are we to do? Paying now will ruin us."

Armoricus held her tightly while stroking her hair. "We don't have many choices," he said with a heavy sigh. "When the refugees arrived, we took a risk that we wouldn't have to pay the tax before the summer. We could seek a loan, but I've no stomach for the terms we'd be offered in times like these."

"We could pawn our silverware," suggested Corotica. "Your mother's jewellery would fetch a good price."

Armoricus shook his head. "No, I have other plans for that. Besides, I won't pay that man on principle, at least no more than we owe the State.

He's a thief, and I'll not see our children's inheritance squandered on his pleasures."

"He's got the men to take it by force."

Armoricus stepped back and leaned against his desk. "I'll make sure he sees we are not defenceless. Meurig and Cunicatus can drill the men in the yard tomorrow. Let Crassula understand that taking the tax by force will not be easy."

"You wouldn't dare fight them? That would only bring more soldiers down upon us."

"Not with everything else they're coping with," he replied. "Crassula is a coward. A show of strength may be enough."

"What if it isn't?"

"I see no other choice but to appeal over his head. The Bishop thinks highly of me and owes me a favour for taking on Drichan. I think he will act justly. Aurelius can go to Isca with our priest. Perhaps they can negotiate not just for us, but to get aid for the refugees. We just need to buy ourselves time."

"Why Aurelius?" Corotica didn't like the idea of her elder son leaving the safety of the villa.

Armoricus took both of Corotica's hands into his own. "He is restless and unhappy here, my love. We've both seen it. This crisis forces my hand, but the truth is, it's time for us to let our fledgling fly. We'll send him to Armorica with what little money we can spare. There, he can use some to finish his studies while keeping the rest secure for us until happier days."

Her breath caught. She'd known this day would come, but not like this. "Isn't that too drastic?"

"Perhaps. But I want him to stay with family. Besides, Britannia's future is uncertain. We must give Aurelius a chance to build a future for himself."

Now the tears began to flow. "What about us? What about here?"

Armoricus smiled affectionately. "You and I have always tried to be honourable and faithful stewards of these lands. Our whole life together has been committed to this place and to our people. You are the wisest *materfamilias*. I married well, far better than you did. Do you think we could ever leave?"

Corotica shook her head and wiped her eyes with her shawl. "No. This is where we belong for better, for worse. But what about Publius and Rusticella?"

"For the moment, they're safe with us. We'll see what happens in the months to come. If the Lord smiles on us again, then we'll continue to be good stewards for many years to come. If not . . . well, we'll cross that bridge when it comes."

—

"Do you ever wonder if St Anthony was tempted to go back home?" asked Aongus as he accompanied Drichan on his way back to the villa from Theodwald's estate. Since his first visit, he had been regularly visiting the estate as pastor, priest and spy. As a pastor he was attentive to people's needs: praying for the sick, burying the dead and catechizing the unbaptized. As a priest, he led the people in their prayers and offered them the holy mysteries. All this he did openly and with care for the benefit of both Theodwald's household and the trickle of refugees who flowed from the west.

Only Armoricus knew of his role as a spy. "All I need is for you to tell me what the Irish are up to and what Theodwald or his son think of it," he had said. "Don't ferret; only listen." Drichan had reluctantly agreed with the proviso that he would share nothing told to him by way of confession. Armoricus had accepted these terms, and so Drichan, who had come to be a hermit but served as a priest, now found himself a spy. *How unsearchable are your ways*, he muttered to himself.

"What was that?" asked Aongus as they began to climb a wooded slope.

"Forgive me," Drichan replied. "I was lost in thought. You were speaking of St Anthony?"

"Yes, I've become as fascinated by him as you are. There is something about his life that appeals to an Irishman like me. Anthony must have felt the pull of home, don't you think? I've lived long enough in my own wildernesses to know how strong that pull can be."

Drichan nodded. "The devil tempted Anthony with wealth, glory, even the care of his sister. Homesickness, perhaps, is another name for such temptations."

"And you?" Aongus pressed. "Do you think you'll return home?"

Drichan smiled faintly. "I came here to leave home behind."

Aongus and Drichan had regularly enjoyed conversations like this during the previous couple of months. Cormac's bard had remained in Theodwald's house as a kind of ambassador. *Probably a spy too*, thought Drichan. In fact, their friendship had probably begun as clumsy attempts to gain information from each other. Instead, they only ever discussed spiritual matters of no practical value whatsoever to either master. In the process, Aongus had come a long way towards faith. Drichan was sure of that, and he felt that his recounting of St Anthony's *Life* had been key.

Aongus laughed. "You don't strike me as the hermit type. You love conversation too much for that—fine conversation, the kind that doesn't happen on farms."

"Perhaps you're right. It is the conversations I miss most about my home, which is why I value our chats so much. And you? What draws you from place to place?"

"They say a bard's only home is wherever there are stories to be told, stories to be learned." Aongus paused, turning his gaze to the river Isca below. "I think your Christ enjoyed a good yarn more than St Anthony did. But he was reckless with them, wasn't he? Stories can entertain; they can teach; they can even persuade. But they're dangerous, too. Tell the wrong one, and you might find yourself on a cross."

"So you only tell the stories people want to hear? What of those that challenge?"

Aongus laughed. "I leave those to braver men than me. But I know this: to tell a meaningful story, you must first hear the stories people tell themselves. Theodwald wants comfort; I tell him stories that soothe his fears of death. My Prince dreams of greatness, so I fill his ears with heroes and wise kings. Stories are only as good as the ears they fall upon."

"And what story do you tell me?" Drichan asked, a spark of humour in his eye.

"Yours is a story I only listen to," Aongus replied, clasping his friend's hand as they parted ways beneath the old oak that marked their usual farewell.

About an hour later, Drichan reached the lane that led to the villa. He noticed an encampment near the village, which he assumed contained another round of refugees. But, when he entered the courtyard, he saw a line of horses being brushed down by some of the older boys and girls. Other hands were standing around talking earnestly with one another. Even the workshop and smithy were quiet. Drichan's thoughts immediately went to Cormac, but Aongus had said that his master was away in Demetia.

Despite his curiosity, he crossed over to the chapel. He had neglected his prayers that morning and now felt the need of them before he was thrust into the midst of new challenges. He tutted to himself as he entered the chapel; someone had allowed the perpetual candle to go out. He walked across the gloomy room to a small chest and took out a new candle, a flint lighter and a scrap of paper. A few minutes later, he lit a new candle and as he placed it on the altar, he sensed a presence enter behind him. To his utter astonishment, he saw that it was Aurelius.

In all the months Drichan had lived there, Aurelius had avoided the chapel, treating both it and him with an indifference that was probably meant to convey a degree of disdain but came across as awkwardness. Drichan thought of Aurelius as a supercilious youth like those he had encountered in Burdigala—a far cry from the practical gravitas of his father. Now the heir of the villa stood uncertain on the threshold, his gaze fixed on the altar.

"Does it matter?" Aurelius asked abruptly, nodding towards the flame. "The candle, I mean. Does it matter if it stays lit?"

Drichan considered his words. "In itself, it's a small thing. It won't bring rain or safety or change the world. But yes, it matters. In the darkness, we all need a light, however small."

Aurelius thought for a moment and then nodded. "Once, the candle in this villa burned for our *lares*, our household gods. It would have been my father's duty to keep it lit, and mine after him. Would it shock you to know I still have the figurines? I suppose you'd call them idols."

There was that familiar Aurelian challenge. But it lacked its usual edge, so Drichan let it pass. "My father kept ours too. He gave them saints' names but left them where they'd always been, next to the candle he kept lit until his death. I suppose I'm the first in my family to let that flame die."

Aurelius frowned. "It always does, doesn't it? No matter how hard we try, flames go out."

"What's troubling you, Aurelius?" Drichan could sense a story emerging. He prepared himself to listen.

"This place is everything to my parents," Aurelius said, his voice low. "They have devoted their lives to making this villa thrive in the backwaters of the Empire. Whatever name my branch of the Rusticelii has made for itself has been rooted in the soil beneath our feet. Mad, isn't it? Our family's fame extends no farther than forty or so miles, not even far enough to reach the nearest proper city. No one has ever written about our great men and women. Perhaps no one ever will. If a family's fame is like a flame, as I think it is, then ours has never shone very brightly.

"Ever since I first heard stories of the great men of Rome, I've had the silly notion that we could be like Julius Caesar or perhaps more like Vespasian or Diocletian, since they came from humbler roots. And the more I wanted that, the more I was ashamed of my father. He seemed content for us to remain inconsequential. Every time he has been given the chance to increase our fame, he has let it pass. He's like a farmer who insists on using his fertile soil for turnips rather than fruitful vines."

Drichan was about to defend Armoricus, but Aurelius, his attention fixed firmly on the candle's flame, continued. "I can now see that our flame must soon go out. The villa is dying. It's like an old man clinging to his past youth rather than face death. You can see it as soon as you see our bathhouse. I've always been able to see it, which is why I've always wanted to leave."

Drichan nodded. "Have you ever considered that your father and grandfather may have once felt the same way?"

Aurelius turned to him and frowned. "What do you mean?"

"Only that it's part of youth to want to leave. How can you discover who Aurelius really is in a place that has been so firmly stamped with the image of your father and grandfather? But could it be that the 'old age' you detect in this villa is just it waiting to be renewed in your image? Perhaps this villa is like the perpetual candle of old, kept alive by the care and attention of each new generation of Domini. Have you ever considered how your father might respond if he saw you beginning to value your home?"

Aurelius threw up his hands. "You're not listening to what I'm trying to say."

Drichan sighed. "Then tell me more plainly."

The boy settled back down and turned his attention back to the candle. "When I asked you about whether it was important to keep that flame going, I thought you were going to say that it gives hope. That's what flames do in darkness, isn't it? They give us hope that we can find our way. I never valued the flame that my home represents. It's such a slight and fading flame in a land long held by darkness. It was to another flame that I looked: the bright beacon of Rome, so bright that it has long cast its light even to here. What is my family but a tiny spark that has drifted off from that fire? But now I see that even the light of Rome is dying. I tried hard to pretend otherwise. But the last few months—"

"Have shown you more plainly what we've all felt in our bones? Rome herself is dying."

"At least, here she is," replied Aurelius nodding. "I realized that when the first refugees arrived. I waited for the authorities to respond, to take some action. But they didn't, haven't. Why? Because they're gone. When I was in Corinium, we often heard news about the Germans crossing the Rhine. Huns in the East. Rome is not now as she once was. She has grown old. Rome is like our villa but with one significant difference."

"What's that?"

"Honour. Though I've always disagreed with my father, I've always known him to be honourable. Perhaps the most honourable man in Britannia. No matter what, no matter the consequences, he always does what he believes is right. But Rome? I begin to see that Rome may die without honour."

Drichan frowned. "What do you mean, Aurelius? I'm not following you again."

Aurelius looked away from the candle as though awaking from a dream. "I'm sorry, Drichan, I've not told you why I'm here. My father sent me to fetch you. You see, yesterday, the tax collector arrived, demanding payment we cannot make. Despite doing nothing to help us or all those estates that have now been destroyed or abandoned, Rome still wants her money. The choice is ruin or defiance. Where is the honour in that?"

Drichan snorted. "Don't go looking to publicans for honour!"

Aurelius rose and made to leave. "Yes, yes. Of course, you're right. How foolish of me not to have realized that. You'll find my father in his study."

By the tone of his voice, Drichan knew that he had failed Aurelius. He hadn't really listened. The young man had been trying to tell him something, but he hadn't heard. He recalled his earlier conversation with Aongus. What was it Aurelius desired? Fame? Yes, but why? Because of his arrogance. Was that not obvious? But the boy who had just spoken to him was not the supercilious youth he had come to know. He was scared, lost even. Was that something new, brought on by recent experiences? It certainly seemed that way to Drichan. The young man he had first met had not had a drop of the vulnerability he had just seen. Had the tax agent knocked him that hard? Perhaps. But it felt to Drichan that the words Aurelius had spoken had come from somewhere deeper.

He returned to the altar and knelt, bowing his head in prayer. "Lord, give me the wisdom to see him as he is, not as he seems."

As he prayed, a memory surfaced—a play he had once seen in Burdigala. He had only ever gone to see a performance once since clergy were prohibited from attending. He had been drawn like Eve to the forbidden fruit by his curiosity. The actors wore grotesque masks, their features exaggerated to convey something about the characters they portrayed. Yet the masks had obscured more than they revealed. How often, Drichan wondered, had he failed to look past Aurelius's mask?

A story came to mind—the tale of Zacchaeus, the tax collector. Beneath his wealth and position, Zacchaeus had been a man desperate for redemption. And Christ had seen him for what he truly was, not for what the world believed him to be. What had the Lord said to him? *This day is salvation come to this house . . . For the Son of Man is come to seek and to save that which was lost.*

The candle flickered and, for a moment, Drichan thought it might go out. He crossed the room and placed it in its lamp, wondering to himself why he hadn't done that to start with. The flickering calmed and the light increased. *A light in the darkness*, he thought. *Hope.* Aurelius had spoken of it—a hope that seemed as fragile as the flame. And yet, it burned. *Salvation.* That's what Christ had given Zacchaeus. What Aurelius wanted was what all of them wanted: hope and salvation. But people didn't look behind his mask. Not just Aurelius's mask of haughtiness but also his father's mask of virtue. How could Aurelius, being the young man he is, ever live up to his father, being who he is? And so, Aurelius had turned to Rome, not because he thought himself superior to those around him, but because Rome gave him his story. Now that Rome was either too powerless to protect him or too dishonourable to appeal to his love, what was left? Where was Aurelius to find his hope and salvation now?

For that matter, where could any of them find hope and salvation in this dying villa on the edge of a dying empire? The Son of Man came to seek and save the lost. Had Drichan likewise been sent here to save the lost? Or was that just another story he was telling himself? He bowed his head, crossed himself and went in search of the Dominus.

XXII

Aurelius was sitting on the bench in the villa's orchard, trying his best to lose himself in the *Aeneid*. It was one of the older scrolls in the family's library and a little worse for wear. At some point the right-hand side had been singed, in some places badly enough to obscure the lines. Elsewhere, a child had scribbled over the text with charcoal before drawing what looked like a sheep. A sharp declaration read *Odi Virgilium*—I hate Virgil—inscribed by some forefather who had probably chafed against the demands of education. Each was the work of someone who, like him, had been made to study the *Aeneid*. He wondered who had loathed Virgil

Aurelius had come away from the chapel disappointed even more with himself than with Drichan. He had no idea why he had spoken as he had. He felt ashamed. Did he really believe some of the things he had said? He had heard himself expressing thoughts that he had never consciously entertained. Yet, he could not unspeak what he'd spoken.

He put down Virgil and studied the first blushing buds on an apple tree in front of him. He remembered planting that tree when he was Rusticella's age, part of a family tradition as old as the orchard itself. Every child in the family planted a sapling on his or her sixth birthday, each grown from the seed of a parent's tree—boys from their mothers, girls from their fathers. Aurelius's own tree now stood sturdy and tall beside the weathered, gnarled trunk of his great-grandfather's. Looking now at the orchard, it was hard to believe that his *familia* wasn't flourishing. If it held any symbolic value, then it ought to be marked by fruitful tranquillity. Well, in a way it was. But the orchard was also set within a decaying estate, just as his own *familia* was struggling to survive within a decaying world. How could they possibly succeed in that world?

The thought of Crassula gnawed at him with the bitter sting of disillusionment. Aurelius had so longed for Rome to rescue them, to demonstrate her power and authority to the lowlife brigands and grasping Irish, that it had never occurred to him that Rome herself could be one of the forces threatening his family. He felt like a sick man happy at last to see a physician, only to find that he had come to amputate his arms.

"There you are," came his mother's voice. "I've been looking all over for you."

Aurelius rose to greet her. "I've been trying to read some Virgil."

"On a wet bench?" she asked, raising a brow.

Aurelius wiped his hands down the damp seat of his tunica. "Well, yes, I suppose that was a bit silly. I was just enjoying the sun. Thank the gods we finally have some."

His mother frowned. "Your father wants you to join him before that spiteful tax man returns. There's much to discuss, and he wants you with him."

"Of course," Aurelius said, his stomach sinking at the thought of seeing Crassula again. He didn't want to have to look again at the money-grubbing face of Rome.

"Before we go," continued his mother, "there's something else your father and I have decided. Something I need to tell you first."

He turned to her, intrigued but apprehensive. "What is it?"

Her voice became thick with emotion. "He and I have long been reflecting on your future. Your grandfather has urged us to let you have your freedom, and we think that now, well, now it's both right and prudent to let you go. The world is changing. Only a fool would wager his family's fortune on the return of happy days. Your father and I can never leave this place, whatever happens. This is the only place where the world makes sense to us. Our lives and our love are sown into this soil. But you can leave. And more than that, you should. Your father is prepared to give you sufficient funds so that you can resume your studies elsewhere."

Aurelius blinked, startled. "Leave? You mean—?"

She nodded. "You'll go to Armorica. Our cousins there are powerful. Plus, they're safe from danger. You'll go first to Isca Augusta on an errand for your father and from there to Londinium to arrange passage."

His thoughts spun. Armorica? The very name conjured dreams he scarcely dared name any longer. The fear and doubts that had plagued him vanished in a surge of excitement. To go—truly go—meant escape from the toil of the fields, the gnawing anxiety of raiders, and the unending grind of survival. And from Armorica—from Armorica, he could go anywhere.

But when he looked at his mother's pained expression, the weeds of doubt began to spring up again. He could see she was trying to be brave, but her bravery somehow magnified rather than hid her distress. "How can I go?" he asked softly. "How can I leave you when there are so many dangers here?"

She reached up, brushing his cheek with her fingers. "We'll manage, Aurelius. We'll know that you are safe building a new life for yourself, for our family elsewhere. Perhaps we aren't meant to make any place a home for too long. It seems common for families to produce an heir whose heart belongs somewhere else. The need to wander takes hold of him and the family tree is transplanted. Your ancestors came from Armorica; perhaps you are being called to return. Or perhaps one day you'll come back to us, satisfied that you've seen the world. Who knows? None of us can see these things. But I will be happier knowing that you are both happy and safe. But come. We mustn't keep your father waiting."

Aurelius felt giddy as he and his mother re-entered the villa and crossed through to the veranda. There they found Crassula standing awkwardly between his grandfather and Drichan. Cadfan leaned against the railing with a scowl on his face and the accounts tucked under his arm. Labourers were making their way between the bathhouse and the barn or heading out in the fields with hoes and wheelbarrows of dung for fertilizing.

His father emerged, immaculate in his formal toga, an unusual sight. "Good," Armoricus said as they joined him. "We're all here. Let's go to the dining room and settle this."

Inside, the table was set with goblets of wine and an assortment of food. Armoricus took his place at the head, directing each of them to recline. Aurelius found himself between Drichan and his mother. Cadfan, his scowl now replaced with a look of intent, sat with his accounts at a small table by the wall.

"My wife has told me I owe you an apology," Armoricus began, addressing Crassula. "I was rude yesterday, and I am sorry for it. Your arrival was ill-timed, but that does not excuse my behaviour."

Crassula beamed. "Oh, Dominus, I could not be more pleased by your gracious words. I feared an unpleasant confrontation, but I should have known better. You are an honourable man. No one doubts that. So I meet your apology with my own."

Armoricus inclined his head in gratitude. "Thank you. I have asked Cadfan to bring our accounts, and Drichan, a close friend of your Bishop, will provide counsel. Now, let us discuss the matter at hand."

Crassula frowned profoundly as he nodded to Drichan. "The Bishop is a powerful man, a powerful man, indeed. Of course, he doesn't have to pay any tax, so I've had precious few dealings with him. Well, that's not strictly true . . . " He trailed off awkwardly.

Drichan replied, "Wait? You're not *the* Decimus Crassula?"

"I'm afraid he is," said Corotica. "But it would be unseemly for us to speak of that. My husband shouldn't have mentioned the Bishop."

Crassula took a deep draught of his wine and then replied, "It's all ancient history. But can we turn our attention to the matter at hand?"

As the others entered negotiations, Aurelius reflected on this opening exchange. It had obviously thrown Crassula off his guard. From time to time, the tax collector looked furtively across the table at Drichan, smiling awkwardly if eye contact was made before gulping his wine. As the negotiations continued, Ancarat and Ria refilled the goblets, Crassula's more frequently than anybody else's.

When the plates were cleared, Armoricus spoke again, his tone firm. "As you can see from our accounts, we can pay only half the tax. I will not bankrupt my tenants, nor will I entertain the idea of paying your cut. Our position here is vulnerable: the roads to the markets are unsafe, and until that changes, justice demands leniency. I accept that this isn't to your liking. We're at an impasse. But I'm prepared to appeal to the Bishop, who I trust will rule wisely."

Crassula flushed, his face a shade darker than the wine in his goblet. "The Bishop has no authority in this matter," he retorted, his words slurring slightly. "The curia will hear your case, if you insist. But I warn you that I would feel obliged to inform them of the additional manpower you have gained from other estates. From what I've seen, you have the potential to bring some of your fields back into production. It would all need to be re-assessed, of course."

"You scoundrel!" growled Quercus. "You know as well as we do those refugees are more burden than benefit."

"At the moment, perhaps. But the potential is there. I'm surprised they're not already clearing your northern fields. Very lax of you to leave them so idle."

Armoricus interrupted, "Thank you for outlining your case, Crassula, which I'm sure is not intended as a threat. I am content to present our case to the curia. My son will represent me, alongside Drichan, who will surely find support from the Bishop. I'm sure he'll be interested in hearing about this case from one of his own priests."

As the meeting concluded, Aurelius caught up with Drichan. "What was all that about the Bishop?" he asked.

"According to your father," replied the priest, "years ago, the Bishop charged Crassula with corruption, blackmail and the debauching of the daughter of a leading citizen. Only his patron saved him from ruin. Your father asked me to pretend to be the Bishop's favourite while he played up his own friendship. He thought it might unnerve Crassula. It seems he was right."

Aurelius stared at the priest with amazement. "So it was all a bluff? I never knew my father could be so cunning."

Drichan smiled. "Aurelius, if there's one thing I've learned here, it's that what you don't understand about your father is almost as much as he doesn't understand about you. But perhaps Crassula has given you the opportunity to change all that."

—

Baglan stood at the edge of a narrow field that lay behind Potitus's villa watching a group of boys kicking a ball around. Baglan had been given the simple charge of keeping an eye on them while the household servants undertook their spring cleaning. While the girls of the *familia* had been conscripted to help indoors, the boys had been ordered to muck out the stables, which they completed with remarkable efficiency. They had afterwards run into the villa to announce their triumph, spreading enough grime and stench to draw a fair stream of profanity from the headmistress before being turned outside again. Now, they ran wild. The smallest and youngest of them was named Patricius, the grandson of Potitus, who flailed around after the older children with the awkwardness of a child still learning to use his legs. There was something of Brochfael about him, which drew Baglan to him from the start.

When he had first arrived, Baglan had found the household's personalities difficult to navigate. It was not just that some of the servants and hands were good people while others weren't but that so many of them could be either as circumstances demanded. They had all been trained so thoroughly to reflect the personality of whomever they were serving or helping that they had forgotten who they were themselves. When Potitus was on site, the villa functioned happily enough. But when business took the Dominus elsewhere, the household felt adrift, swept by unseen currents of anxiety and discord. That he didn't yet understand.

The cause for the villa's split personality was Patricius's parents. His father Calpurnius was a humourless decurion, entirely lacking in the gentle warmth and wisdom of his father Potitus. Baglan had learned quickly from others that Calpurnius objected strongly to his father's habit of redeeming people. He was supported in this view by his cadaverous and prematurely grey wife, Vibiana, who reminded Baglan of the wailing female spirits that haunted folklore. Her face seemed permanently drawn into lines of disapproval, and she had the personality to go with it. It was as though she had donated all human warmth and vivacity to her son at his birth and had been left as dry as old bones.

"My *familia* is an odd thing," mused Potitus a few days after Baglan's arrival as they had walked out to his country villa a mile or so outside of Bonaven Taberniae. "Poor Calpurnius never really recovered from his mother's death. And I suppose I didn't do enough to help him with it. Strange, isn't it? We can be so quick to help others but neglect our own."

Baglan had said nothing, unsure how to respond. He wasn't used to such candour from a patrician. He sensed that his new Dominus was the sort of man who could only see people as people, as though their rank, family and influence were of no more consequence than the colour of their hair. It helped that he liked to talk.

Potitus sighed. "Forgiveness is much the same. I don't think he's ever forgiven me for her death. And I—well, I can forgive him for bringing that hag into the family. But what I can't quite forgive is the way they both neglect Patricius." His mouth twisted in a wry smile. "I may shock you, Baglan, but at times I think that when they copulated, they found both the experience distasteful and the consequence unpleasant. Thankfully, God blessed Patricius with a nature that seems as impervious to his parents as the sun is to frost."

Baglan had shifted uncomfortably, looking for a safer topic. "How did your wife die?" he asked at last.

"Not well," replied Potitus with a frown. "A rusty nail—a small thing, really. But infection and fever followed, and then pneumonia. She was gone before I could understand what was happening. At the time, I was devoted to the god Lugus Mercury. I gave offerings, wealth beyond imagining, all in the hope of his favour. But when my wife died, I found my god as capricious and comfortless as the wealth I had hoarded."

Baglan nodded, thinking of his own loss. The gods, he had learned, did not care. Neither, most often, did people.

Potitus continued, his voice low. "It was the Christians who showed me kindness then. I had thought them fools, easy prey for charlatans. But they . . . well, they surprised me. In them—no, in their God, I found peace, I found purpose."

Baglan sighed inwardly. He had heard this story before: the weak and grieving preyed upon by smooth-talking Christians. "So you became a Christian," he concluded matter-of-factly.

"I did," Potitus said with a laugh. "In fact, I became a priest."

Baglan gasped. "By the gods, you're a damned priest?" He would have been hard pressed to say anything more likely to offend in such a short outburst.

Potitus clapped him on the back, still laughing. "Don't look so scandalized! You sound just like my family did then. Yes, a priest. And my whole household, too, is Christian. Had you not noticed? No? That depresses me very much."

A thought occurred to Baglan. "Is that why you visit the mines? To win converts?"

Potitus' smile faded. "You are a cynic, aren't you? Well, I suppose you have every right to be. Hard lives can make for hard hearts. I go because my family's wealth was built on those mines. The suffering and degradation there are woven into the fabric of my *familia*. I would gladly atone by giving all my wealth for the care of the unfortunate. My son is naturally opposed to this idea. But I can . . . I can try to ease the suffering. I make no demands of those I help. Faith, like love, must be free or else it's no faith at all."

"Why are you telling me all this?" asked Baglan as they reached a wide meadow, hedged in by hawthorn and filled with grazing sheep. It sloped up gently towards a modest villa that looked out over the town, mines and northern slopes.

"I wanted you to know how things stand before I ask you a favour."

"A favour?" replied Baglan incredulously. "I'm but a shepherd and you a Dominus. Just tell me what you need."

Potitus shook his head. "No, a favour. In fact, two. The first, I think you'll like: I want you here at my villa rustica looking after this flock you see now, plus the rams in the next field over. My shepherd is too old to do the job anymore. I'd like to see what you can do. If you're half the shepherd I think you are, the position is yours."

Baglan turned to look at the flock, casting his expert eye over them. There were around fifty ewes gathered on the far side of the field munching grass, while roughly the same number of lambs—about a month old by the look of them—gambolled playfully among them. It was a good flock, healthy and thriving. In the sunshine and gentle breeze, it was a scene to lift any heart, but for Baglan it stirred something deep within him. In the bleak existence of the mines, he had given up all hope of returning to anything like a semblance of his former life. Now, thanks to Potitus, he would once more be as he ever had been: a simple shepherd. *While there's life, there's hope.*

"What of the second favour?" he asked cautiously.

Potitus turned to look back down towards the town. "I want you to keep an eye on my grandson Patricius. My household in town does the lad little good. I want him up here in the pleasant countryside, learning how to be a proper man. His tutor will continue to be his day-to-day guardian. But I want you to give him a taste of shepherding. He needs to know the land, the animals. He needs to grow into a man who can care for his own."

Baglan furrowed his brow. "What could he learn from me? Surely, he'll have his own people like me to tend his fields."

Potitus's eyes darkened. "I shudder to think what lies ahead for his generation. I want Patricius to know how to be a dependable husbandman. I want him to know how to look after the beasts of his fields as well as the people of his *familia*. I don't want him to be like his parents. I want him to be a good shepherd."

For a long moment, Baglan said nothing. Bittersweet memories of days spent in the fields and on the hilltops with Brochfael flooded his mind. He realized he had not thought about his family much during the previous few weeks, and guilt stung him. His son's body would by now be riddled with worms if it hadn't been dug up and dragged away by scavengers. His wife and daughter could be anywhere, if they even still lived. How could he even think of happiness and contentment? He had failed them all. There should be no redemption for the likes of him.

Yet, even as his heart choked with remorse, anger and resentment, it couldn't resist leaping at Potitus's offer. How could he turn down a return to days out in the open, caring for a happy, healthy flock with a young boy at his side, seeing the wide world through his eyes? If the gods weren't, in fact, going to destroy him, perhaps he now had a chance to make a new life. He turned to Potitus and extended his hand.

"I'll do it," he said.

Potitus smiled, his grip firm. "Good. Come, let me show you the rest."

The flock bleated loudly and scattered as they walked towards the villa. The lambs trailed behind them before latching greedily for security onto their mother's teats. Baglan watched them, his heart light. Perhaps, in tending this flock, in guiding the boy, he might find a measure of redemption. He might even begin to forgive himself as well.

XXIII

It was the farthest Publius had ever walked.

He had not meant to go so far from the villa. His disobedience had not been wilful, or at least not entirely. He had only intended to stand once again in the depths of the woods where the fructifying aromas of spring could tickle his nose. But he'd been so captivated by his surroundings that he was hardly aware of where his feet were taking him—or so he told himself.

Yet Publius couldn't bring himself to turn back. Whatever the risks he was taking, the thrill of standing high upon the side of the mountain rooted him to the ground as firmly as the gnarled, budding hawthorn at his side. He had never seen his world from such a height. It felt impossible, even shameful, not to enjoy it properly now that he was there.

His homeland stretched out in front of him like broad carpet, woven with a thousand shades of green dotted with wintry purple and brown. Most of it was forest: deep woodlands, ancient beyond reckoning, which undulated over hills and blanketed valleys. Here and there, fields and meadows had been carved out of the canopy, their precision orderly and unnatural. He could just make out his family villa and some of the surrounding farmsteads, like islets in an ocean of dark trees. Except for the fields and the occasional meadow, only the highest hills and the mountains around him were exposed to the sun. These were wrapped in thick turf or bristled with the early tendrils of bracken.

Publius watched a red kite, almost at eye-level, motionless in the air with its beak aimed downwards. The bird was near enough for him to see the wind coursing through its red and grey feathers. Then, with a sudden curl of its V-shaped tail and a backward sweep of its wings, it plunged. For a moment, its shape was perfectly silhouetted against the sky, the rusty plumage of its chest exposed fully to Publius's view. Just as it was about to crash, it swooped with its talons stretched forward to snatch up its prey. It shot across the ground like an arrow and vanished into the woods.

Publius delighted in the kite's utter freedom. He had studied wild creatures enough to know and appreciate that freedom. He grasped that it was rarely safe, hardly ever without risk. He couldn't imagine facing death as often as a rabbit, mouse or deer. And yet, their mortality liberated them. Fighting, fleeing, foraging, sleeping—it was all one for them, and that made them freer than any person Publius had ever met.

It occurred to him that his *familia* now knew danger in the same way that animals do. Threats of death crowded around them like prowling predators in the woods. But unlike animals, they were shackled by their fear. Dread kept them from being free. When he thought harder about it, his only conclusion was that people thought about the future in ways that animals couldn't. Humans might be smarter than animals, but they were also less free. That seemed like a heavy price to pay. He thought of Lupus and Flox running wild in tall grass, leaping and pirouetting in joyous abandonment to the present moment. He had never seen a human live that way, unburdened and utterly free.

Publius had now been away from the villa for too long. It was not uncommon for him to be out of sight for a while without really being far away: lost in his own thoughts in the hayloft, catching tadpoles in the pool, or playing with friends in the village. But if someone had seen him slip into the woods, then people would be searching for him by now. It was at least three miles back to the villa, and he had not travelled quickly. In fact, to his dismay he saw that the sun had descended more than he had realized. He would need to run not to miss supper.

Even so, he found it hard to turn away from the beckoning heights. He stopped at the forest threshold, sensing more than considering the liminal space that divided the sheltered woodland gloom from the open sky of the mountains. For him, the edge of a forest was a magical boundary not unlike the threshold of the villa's chapel or border of a graveyard or, for that matter, the doorway into his parents' bedroom. He didn't know why it felt that way—perhaps it was nothing more than a feeling of moving from light into shadow, from the two dimensions of field and meadow into the three dimensions of woodland. *Never forget to look up*, his grandfather had once told him. *You miss half the marvel of a forest if you never look up.*

But there was something else that imbued the forest edge with mystery.

In the woods, Publius could feel the long age of the world lingering in the knotty limbs and grasping roots of trees. The pungency of the loamy soil, thick with the decaying leaf fall of the previous autumn, communicated it to his nose, just as the silence of the woodscape did to his ears. You couldn't help but feel at least half-wild in a place like that.

Once into the trees, Publius picked up his pace, happy that the steady downward slope made it easy to wend his way back home. As long as he didn't stray down the western side of the hill, he would come out at the stream that ran past the villa or across one of the satellite farms. With nothing to worry about, he could fully enjoy the freedom of the run. He could be wild.

About half a mile away from the villa, he came upon a glade he knew well. He was not too far from home. But before he could step into it, movement caught his eye. There, in the shadows, stood the stag. Publius knew it at once, recognized the proud angle of its antlers and the heavy strength of its neck. It took him longer to see that it wasn't alone. Nearby, partly obscured by a branch of ash, stood a doe and a young buck. Publius paused, unsure how to feel. He had conjured up such an impression of the stag as a lone sentinel of the woods that he couldn't quite adjust to the idea that it was, in fact, a family man.

A faint sound reached him then, barely audible, causing the three creatures to raise their heads, ears flicking and noses sniffing. It came again—still too distant for Publius to tell what it was—and this time the deer reacted by moving into the glade. They didn't run or panic. They must have gauged that the noise posed no immediate threat. All the same, they moved steadily in the opposite direction. Publius knew they had seen him. But not once did they look in his direction. He felt like a supplicant refused a priestly benediction.

Then he heard the sound again. It came from the direction of the stream that ran down past the villa. He realized then that it was a cry, the voice of a woman in distress. Only this time, it was joined by the deeper tones of men. He sensed danger immediately, attuned to it instinctively like the stag and its family had been. Unlike them, though, Publius didn't move away from danger. Someone needed help. He was sure of it just as he was certain that no one else would be near enough to hear or respond.

If the stag was now preoccupied with being a mate and father, it was Publius's duty to serve as the lone sentinel of the woods. He didn't understand how this could be, given his youth and slight, boyish frame. But he accepted the weight of responsibility like a king his sceptre. His day in the wild had charged him with the wonder of the world. And the freedom of it gave him courage. He ran towards the cry.

—

"Surely, the Lord did not intend for Adam, in his innocence, to be wearied by his labour. The first man was not made for toil as we now know it—backbreaking, endless and worry-laden. No, his work in the garden must have been of a different kind. We have seen, have we not, how some among us find their greatest joy in the work of their hands? They experience such delight that it feels much worse to be called away from that work than to keep at it. I've seen for myself how such joy can make the many one, fused together into one body, as though all are one farmer tilling one field."

Drichan stood on the chapel steps, his voice strong yet tinged with emotion, delivering his final sermon before setting out to meet the Bishop. With Ceridwen fidgeting at her side, Ria stood with the other members of the *familia* listening to his words intently. Like most of the others, she assumed that they would never see Drichan again. Once he had left this place, had left *them*, he would never return. Why would he, once he was secure in the comforts of the city again?

Drichan's homily continued: "If we find even a glimmer of joy in our work now, imagine the exhilaration Adam knew in those first days. The earth did not resist his touch; the sky did not withhold its blessing. There was no weariness then, no struggle—only an exhilaration of spirit, for Adam's labour was not his alone. He knew his strength and skill came from the Lord, who laid the soil, planted the trees, and formed the beasts of the field, and directed them to be fruitful and bountiful. Paradise was not idleness; it was the flourishing of God's handiwork under the hands of man.

"But that Paradise was lost. For us, tilling is toil. You farm by the sweat of your brow. You know why. It was the serpent—the Devil, crafty and cunning. And Adam and Eve, tempted by his diabolical whisper, tried to reach beyond their bounds. They tried to become as gods. And so, in their pride, they were cast out, leaving us to labour in sweat and toil. Thorns and thistles are the marks of their fall, but we bear them still. Now, in the sweat of our faces must we eat our bread until we return to the earth from which we were taken."

He gestured to the villa and the fields beyond. "And yet, here is our Eden. Our labour has brought fruitfulness to this place. We thank God for it. But can you see the Devil prowling nearby? He approaches us in the guise of the wicked Irish, the lawless brigands, a distant and uncaring Rome. We can plainly see God's judgement upon the world. But we must be aware too that the Devil can come in a more cunning guise: in the darkness of our own hearts. His sweet suggestions lead us to envy our neighbours, lust after beautiful people, gossip maliciously, scorn those who come to us in need, and worship false gods. Guard your hearts, lest you lose this home, this abundance, this Paradise to the same cunning that undid the first man."

The congregation murmured its approval. Drichan had matured during his time with the *familia*. Ria recalled her earlier annoyance with him, when she was convinced that he had feelings for her. But over the months, her irritation had softened. She began to see a kind of holiness in his struggle, a sincerity in his missteps that gave heft to his words. The man was undoubtedly flawed, yet he never gave up or complained; perhaps that was the greatest testament to his faith. Now, as he prepared to leave, she realized she had grown fond of him.

After their conversation about her possibly becoming a consecrated virgin, Ria had returned home to face the ire of her parents. Instead, she found them silent and sulking, as though they had settled for a sullen siege rather than a continued frontal assault on her rebellion. They had not again mentioned the disagreement or even the prospect of marriage to

Rhodri. She wasn't even certain if the matter had been dropped or if they might one day casually mention that the wedding would be that very day. It was a clever tactic—the longer this state of affairs continued the more she missed their happy company and the more she questioned her own obduracy. Had it not been for Ceridwen, they may have prevailed—Ria had the cussedness to defy the attacks of the Devil but not the stamina to endure a long siege by her parents. But Ceridwen met her need to love and be loved, and this strengthened her resolve.

Ancarat was the first to relent. Her grandmotherly love for Ceridwen required at least the façade of domestic concord. That demanded a degree of hypocrisy that she couldn't sustain for long, and so the pretence of harmony eventually became the reality. Her father took longer to thaw. Ria's refusal had wounded his pride in front of people under his authority, and he could see no way of conceding to his daughter without appearing to be a weak master of his own household. But, over time, he allowed enough warmth to seep back into their relationship for their bonds of love to hold, even through the strain.

As the congregation dispersed, Ceridwen ran off to play with the other children, leaving Ria free to enjoy her own company for a couple of hours. The afternoon was so fresh and warm, so alive with the quiet promise of spring, that she couldn't help feeling something of the exhilaration of spirit that Drichan had mentioned in his sermon. Not even the hungry leer of the sinister tax collector could ruin her mood as she made her way past the barn into the fields. Her heart longed for the scent of the springtime woods.

Since it was still forbidden for anyone to visit the woods alone, she took a circuitous route to the far side of the river where a path lay hidden among the trees. The forest floor was alive with new growth—wood anemone, celandine and violets pushing through the damp earth. Though they had not yet flowered, their shoots were enough to signal the season's renewal. In a week or two, the ground would burst into colour and the sharp tang of wild garlic would scent the air. Ria resolved to ask the Domina for more freedom to wander when spring reached its fullness, perhaps under the protective eye of their newly formed militia. Surely, the beauty of the woods would soothe any anxious soul.

She removed her sandals to cross the icy river. The cold gripped her feet, but she welcomed the sensation, feeling alive and awake. On the far bank, she approached the old beech tree that she had visited regularly since she was a girl. Its smooth, ash-grey trunk rose like a guardian, unchanged by the years. She wrapped her arms around it, pressing her cheek to its powerful sinews, as though greeting an old friend. She pictured herself coming there at various stages in her life, in every kind of mood, preoccupied with the weight of inconsequential things that had mattered to her more than anything else. It struck her that though she had grown now into a woman, the old beech remained unchanged. Beneath its sprouting canopy, she felt as small as she had as a girl, and she felt secure.

Settling into her old spot among the roots, she watched the life of the forest unfold. Two chiffchaffs flitted through the undergrowth; the river murmured its timeless song. Here, within the tree's shadow, the weight of her cares lifted. The world stretched beyond past and future, resting in a stillness she could not name but felt deeply. *How good this place is*, she thought. The melody of blackbirds and thrush seemed to sing out her thoughts.

Ria's reverie was shattered by the faint murmur of voices carried on the wind. At first, she felt only irritation—who dared disturb her refuge? But then she felt afraid. Instinct drove her to hide, and she slipped behind a cluster of holly, crouching low where the leaves pricked her skin and the earth's damp smell filled her nose.

" . . . thought him insufferably sanctimonious," came one of the voices: nasal, lisping, and altogether unfamiliar to Ria.

But she knew the second. "He's old school, that one. A man out of tune with these times. Blind, too. He can't see how this world is turning." It was Muconius.

Sure enough, the one-armed man came into sight, walking next to a man Ria now recognized: the tax collector.

"It's every man for himself these days," continued the veteran. "Loyalty won't get you nothing but the grave, and it sure as hell won't grow back an arm. You have to do what it takes to survive."

"So cynical, Muconius. One might almost believe you'd forgotten what it means to serve under the eagle," teased Crassula as they stopped beneath Ria's tree. They stood in profile to her, facing towards the river.

"That eagle left me with one arm and nothing but a handful of coins to show for it," Muconius shot back. "I've learned my lesson well enough."

"My heart bleeds," replied the other man sarcastically. "Now, can you please explain why you have dragged me all the way out here?"

"Looking after myself, that's why. I've heard from the others that the Dominus disrespected you. He thinks you're a snake. And I'm not surprised."

"You're not?" squeaked Crassula indignantly.

Muconius chuckled. "I'm not saying he's right. Only that Armoricus thinks himself better than people like you and me. He's not like other masters I've worked for. Oh, he's arrogant like them, but he doesn't care about status. I suppose it comes from his sense of virtue. Yes, that's it. Virtue. And that I can't take. It makes him insufferable. Folks just pretend to adore him. I suppose they once did. But now? They think he's lost the plot, that he can't handle all the pressures around him."

"That doesn't surprise me," replied Crassula. "I've always thought him a buffoon, and there's nothing worse than a sanctimonious buffoon. I'll get him, though, even if he has got the protection of the bloody bishop."

"I knew you'd feel that way," replied Muconius. "What if I told you that I might be able to help you? What if I told you that Armoricus has plenty of money to pay his tax? What if I told you that right now, you're standing not too far away from it?"

"What do you mean?" asked Crassula suspiciously.

Muconius chuckled. "That got your attention, didn't it?" He licked his lips and then grinned. "Whole new horizons open up when you start a sentence with 'What if'. What if I still had two arms? I sure as hell wouldn't be in this shithole. What if I didn't break my girlfriend's neck for disrespecting me? I'd still be enjoying the good life on a villa near Verulamium. What if the Irish hadn't ransacked the villa down south? I'd still be a steward doing whatever I wanted with the lowlifes working the fields. So I'm just asking what if I told you how to cheat Armoricus? How might I benefit from sharing such juicy information?"

The tax collector's voice trembled with his need to know. "Are you telling me that he's buried some of his treasure? Is it around here?"

Muconius shrugged. "I'm just speaking in hypotheticals, of course. What if I knew where the treasure was? What if it was buried right here?" His voice turned sly. "What if I needed a partner?"

Crassula's eyes gleamed with a hungry light. "And what would this partner of yours owe you in return?"

"A job," said Muconius bluntly. "There's about enough buried here to pay what you're owed plus some left over for me. I could take the whole lot myself. But how the hell would I go anywhere with it? Even if I had a horse, I can't ride worth a damn. I can't carry it, one-armed as I am. In any case, I'd just be robbed along the way. What I need is employment. Not much work out there for a one-armed veteran. But I've got a knack for finding things people would rather keep hidden. I could be useful to a man like you."

Crassula began to pace along the path as he considered Muconius's words. Ria's heart raced. She knew enough now of the threat they posed— not just to Armoricus, but to all who depended on him to hold this fragile *familia* together. She grew impatient for them to move away so she could go report their treachery to Corotica.

Finally, the tax collector asked, "What possible use would I have for a cripple?"

"What I've lost in having a second arm, I've more than made up for in wits. I can be a devious son-of-a-bitch when I have a mind to be. I think you can too. But you don't have the devil in you like I do. You're too refined for that. In these lean times, what you need isn't someone trained like you in the art of rhetoric. All the fine words in the world ain't going to get people to cough up what they don't think they have. But put the fear of the devil into them? Oh, what people won't do to escape him!"

"So, you want to be my heavy?" replied Crassula cautiously.

"Not exactly—one arm thing again," he said waving his arm in front of

Crassula. "Most of the fat cats have something in their background they want to keep hidden. A tart on the side or maybe a liking for little boys. Something like that. I have a talent for finding things out—like where buried treasure is. As I see it, these days lend themselves to a nice bit of extortion. Let the devil loose and you, my friend, will be rich. I promise you that."

They struck their bargain with the same ease that a snake strikes its prey. Ria, watching from her cramped hiding place, knew she had to act. But before she could slip away, Muconius turned sharply. "Hold on," he muttered. "Nature calls."

He began walking towards the holly. Towards her.

Panic rooted Ria to the spot. She willed herself to move, to flee, but her legs refused to obey. Muconius stopped just short of the holly bush, fumbling with his garments. The sound of water and the acrid stench of urine provoked a groan of satisfaction. His face was relaxed, his guard down—and then he saw her.

For a moment, their eyes locked. His, widening with surprise and then narrowing with calculation. Hers, wide with terror. "Well, well," he said, his grin like a wolf's. "What have we here?"

Ria tried to flee, but Muconius's hand shot out with startling speed. He fixed her arm with an iron grip and jerked her closer. The pain of his hard fingers pressing on her wrist was so intense that she screamed, her voice tearing through the stillness of the grove. But then she recalled that Muconius had only one arm and that if she could somehow break free, she might yet escape.

"Crassula, give me a hand!" he called as she squirmed and beat hard with her free hand against his arm.

Crassula skipped over surprisingly quickly for his size, and took awkward hold of Ria's free arm with both his hands. The hungry look in his eyes and the sheen of sweat on his smooth face filled Ria with disgust.

She screamed again, twisting with all the strength her young body could muster. For a moment, Crassula's grip loosened, and she thought she might break free. But Muconius suddenly struck her hard across the face with his open hand. The blow landed like a rock, sharp and cruel, and it left her reeling. She stood still, dazed, as hot tears sprang to her eyes. The world around her blurred—trees, river and sky melting into a single, indifferent haze.

"A fine catch we've got here," Muconius said, his grin as sharp as the knife he drew from his belt.

Ria swallowed hard, her mind spinning with fear and pain. She tried to gather herself, to think of something that might disarm them. "You know who I am," she said, her voice steadier than she felt. "Let me go, Muconius, or you'll regret it."

His grin widened. "Oh, I know who you are, sweetie. Oh, yes, I do." He drew closer, the blade glinting between them. "Now, be still, or you'll see just how sharp this knife is."

Before Ria could reply, Crassula spoke, his voice uncertain. "Who is she?"

Muconius did not take his eyes from Ria as he answered, savouring the moment. "She's the steward's daughter. Ria's her name. And a lovelier piece of meat you won't find here at the villa, though she likes to play coy. Don't you, my love?"

"Were you following us, girl?"

Despite the pain in her head and the sound of her heart beating loudly in her ears, Ria held her chin high and looked them both squarely in the eyes. "No, I wasn't following you," she said, her voice sharp. "This is my place. I've been coming here long before either of you ever came to this villa. Let me go!"

Crassula frowned, stepping closer. "But you heard us, didn't you? Heard too much."

"No, I didn't," Ria shot back too quickly, her words tumbling out in desperation. "The river—it's loud. I couldn't make out what you were saying."

Crassula's expression darkened. He looked at Muconius, who only shrugged, then back at her. "I don't believe you," he said slowly. "No. I think you're lying."

With another desperate effort, Ria pulled free of Crassula's grip. But Muconius was too fast for her. He kicked her feet out from under her. With another scream, she fell hard to the ground. Muconius handed his knife to Crassula, pulled her up roughly, and locked her firmly against his body. She struggled vainly to break free but after a few seconds gave up. She was so frightened that she couldn't think clearly. She would say anything—do anything—to escape these two devils. Her heart pounded in her ears.

"You like her, don't you?" Muconius taunted Crassula, his voice low and ugly. "She's got spirit. And soft, too." He leered, his movements vile and deliberate.

Crassula's eyes gleamed with a devilish hunger that turned Ria's stomach. "Yes," he said, almost to himself. "She's . . . perfect."

Muconius's voice turned thoughtful, almost playful. "Here's what I think," he said. "No one probably knows she's here. That puts her entirely at our mercy, doesn't it? And we can't risk her running back to tell anyone about our little meeting." He paused, letting the words sink in. "What do you say to that, girl?"

Before she could answer, Crassula suddenly reached out and tore away the top of her tunic. Muconius's arm kept it from falling down altogether, but she felt her left breast spill out. Trembling, she tried her best to use her free arm to cover herself.

"Hold on, hold on, Crassula," Muconius warned as he pulled Ria back a step. "We need to think this through. She's not just some saucy tart for us to treat any way we like."

"Never mind that," replied Crassula. "I want her. I want her now."

"I can see that, you randy toad!" chuckled Muconius. "But how far are you willing to go?"

Crassula reluctantly tore his gaze away from Ria to look at his companion. "What do you mean?"

"Before we have a bit of sport with her, we need to decide what to do with her afterwards. I can't see how we can let her go. But I reckon that if no one knows she's here, they'll assume brigands are to blame."

"Please," she whispered. "Please. I won't tell anyone. Just let me go."

Crassula reached out, his fingers brushing her arm with a grotesque tenderness. "Shhh," he murmured. "Quiet now. I'm afraid it's too late for bargaining."

Ria screamed, the sound tearing through the forest, and in one swift motion, she twisted and drove her elbow into Muconius's ribs. His grip loosened, just enough. She turned her head and sank her teeth into the soft flesh of his arm. She bit down hard, tasting blood, warm and metallic against her tongue.

Muconius roared, losing his grip, and Ria stumbled free. She felt Crassula grab hold of her hair and saw him lurching towards her when something flew by her head. Crassula dropped like a heavy sack of grain and lay motionless on the ground.

"Run, Ria, run!" came a high-pitched voice.

In her confusion, Ria nearly stopped to see who had thrown the jagged stone that now lay next to Crassula. But fear and instinct drove her forward just in time to elude Muconius's swipe at her. Holding her torn tunic against her chest, she sprang down the path towards the villa. Out of the corner of her eye, she saw another stone arc and heard it strike its target.

"What the hell?" yelled Muconius. "You little bastard!"

As she escaped, Ria glimpsed Publius standing on the slope that rose behind a dense wall of brambles. He hurled one last rock that struck Muconius square enough to send him stumbling with a curse. It gave her all the time she needed. Forgetting about her modesty, she ran, her screams piercing the woods, her feet flying over the path. She did not stop until she collapsed, sobbing, into the waiting arms of Meurig and others. The forest's shadow fell behind her, and with it, the grip of the devils who had invaded her paradise.

XXIV

News of a great battle reached Bonaven Taberniae.

Baglan was moving the sheep to another field after three days of rain. The rain-soaked earth at the gate clung thick to his boots, a slurry of mud and manure. Once the flock had passed through, he cut two flowering branches from the hedge and laid them by the fence. "Blessed be your name," he said in a soft voice.

Patricius was perched on the fence safe above the muck, his brow furrowed as he watched Baglan. "Why did you do that?"

Baglan saw a thin, bald man across the field approaching as he swung Patricius down to the ground. "A token for Silvanus Sucellos," he said. "An old habit. Shepherds and farmers have long given him thanks for his care. I see your grammarian is coming. I didn't think you had lessons today."

Patricius frowned deeply. "I don't. I shouldn't. Please don't let him make me study today. I want to be with you out in the fields."

Baglan smiled. "I'd like that too. Cheer up. He may be here for other reasons. Come. Let's not make the poor man walk all the way down the hill to meet us."

Patricius took Baglan's hand and reluctantly followed. The tutor waved to catch their attention, though he would have been hard to miss in the empty field. Baglan felt sorry for the man, who was too kind to be a disciplinarian. He had been entirely fazed by Patricius's reluctance to apply himself to his books.

"Why do you worship the old gods?" asked Patricius, reminding Baglan yet again of what an inquisitive child he was.

"You don't approve, my young master?" he replied in jest.

"My mother and father wouldn't. They say that people like you will go to hell when you die."

Baglan nodded. "Yes, that's what Christians believe. It may be so."

"Aren't you scared?"

Baglan laughed. "I've seen the devil too many times to be frightened of him." Then he snorted. "But that's just silly of me. You should listen to your folks and not tempt the devil to make your life harder than necessary. I'm like an old sheep who can't change the route he walks every day in the fields."

Patricius was quiet for a moment, then said, "Maybe you're helping them."

"The gods?" Baglan asked, surprised.

"Maybe the old gods are like my tutor: they try hard but just aren't very good at what they do. So no one worships them much anymore. I bet that makes them sad."

Baglan stopped and looked the boy in the face. "You are a wise soul, my little friend."

Patricius shrugged as though his thoughts were obvious enough. "Grandfather says we should befriend lonely people. Maybe it works for gods too. Maybe Silvanus is sad because fewer people pray to him anymore, and that's why you gave him the branches—to make him feel better."

Before Baglan had a chance to reply, the tutor called, "I bring news. A great battle to the north—near Bannium. Prince Cormac mac Urb has won a mighty victory against the Irish!"

Baglan frowned. "Bannium is near my old home. But Cormac—that's an Irish name, isn't it?"

"Yes," the tutor replied. "His father was made sub-king of Demetia by Magnus Maximus. He's friendly to us—or so we hope."

Baglan frowned. "We've now sunk so low that we must rely on the Irish to protect us from the Irish."

"Yes. I take your meaning. *Quis custodiet ipsos custodes?* Who will guard the guards? I'm afraid that's the world we live in now. If the news is correct, however, we can be doubly thankful: first, that the friendly Irish won (thanks be to God) and second, that, be they friend or foe, only Irishmen were slain. Let them kill each other, like barbarians have always done, and leave us alone."

With that, Baglan could only agree. Still, it troubled him that a battle could be fought so close to his old home. He had no idea who Prince

Cormac was or what he might be like, but his presence could only bode ill for Armoricus and his *familia*. Baglan felt an impulse to return home.

Patricius looked worried. "Are we safe here?"

The tutor gave a sardonic smile. "Safe? Who's ever truly safe? But with this victory, we shouldn't need to fear raiders for a while."

Baglan muttered. "That only leaves thieves and brigands."

The tutor nodded. "Yes, but our soldiers can handle them."

Baglan thought of the soldiers who had scowled at him when he arrived in Bonaven Taberniae. "And who, I wonder, is guarding the guards?"

———

News of the great battle reached Corotica at the villa on an otherwise uneventful morning. Armoricus and Cadfan were out with the men reclaiming two fields that had lain fallow for many years. After three days of rain, they would return as black as coal with moods to match. Rusticella was asleep on a couch across from where Corotica was mechanically working her drop spindle. Outside, she could hear the dull smack of arrows striking targets and the clash of wooden swords. Despite everything the winter had brought them, she sensed that the villa was coming back to life. All the sounds were as they should be and the routines as they ever had been—only the future remained shadowy. Such was the tonic of that moment that there was not even a hint of the clutching tightness in her chest. She had momentarily escaped her nagging anxieties.

This calm broke with the clatter of a galloping horse. A rider's shouts cut the air, startling Rusticella awake. Corotica set her spindle aside, rising with deliberate calm. "Stay here, pipit," she told her daughter, brushing a hand over the girl's hair. "I'll see to it."

Outside, she nearly collided with Ria on the veranda. Beyond her, a small crowd had already gathered, drawn from the bathhouse and the barn. In their midst stood her brother, Tewdrig, beside a fine roan horse. Dust rose in the slanting sunlight as workers paused their work to listen.

"Tewdrig!" Corotica called, her voice bright with surprise. "What brings you here?"

"News, sister. Great news. Two days ago, Prince Cormac defeated a band of Irish raiders. Their lord has been captured and taken to Moridunum. Some of our own men were in the fight."

The announcement was met with cheers from the gathered men and women. Corotica, though, remained composed. "Where was this battle?" she asked.

"Ten miles south and west. The rains made the ground treacherous, but our prince used it to his advantage. God be praised, he believes we'll have peace for a time."

Corotica nodded, her mind working behind her still expression. She noticed Tewdrig's possessive tone when he spoke of Cormac as "our prince". Victory would strengthen the Irish prince, she thought. Such a man would not be resisted easily now. But this was not the time for such reflections. "Then we must celebrate," she said. "Armoricus is still in the fields, but he'll return before evening. We'll prepare a feast."

But Tewdrig's face darkened. "There's more," he said. "I wouldn't have come myself for the battle news. Sister—our father is dying. I've come to bring you to him."

Three hours later, Corotica knelt by her father's bedside, Tewdrig and Gwladys standing across from her. When she had first crouched by his bed and covered his folded hands with her palm, he had hardly seemed to be alive. His shallow breathing suggested that his spirit was already drifting away from the world. Corotica took his folded hands in her own, the roughness of his palms familiar even now.

"Father," she said softly. "It's me, Corotica."

His eyelids fluttered at the sound of her voice and his breathing strengthened. He took her hand into his own and squeezed it weakly. A flicker of a smile came to his face as he opened his eyes to look at his daughter. "I knew you would come, my ever-constant Corotica," he said in a surprisingly clear voice. "And I daren't meet my Maker without your permission first."

Corotica's laugh caught in her throat, breaking into a sob.

"No tears, my girl," he said gently, squeezing her hand. "I've lived a long and good life. Soon I'll see your mother again. Though what she'll make of me, as old as I am, God only knows."

"If she's been looking down on you all these years, I imagine she'll give you a good talking to," replied Corotica. "Though I seem to remember that she never could resist your charm."

Theodwald winced in pain and for a moment seemed to fall back into a light sleep. Corotica stroked his arm, feeling the tension in his body ease as the pain subsided. "Rest, Father. Just rest."

He opened his eyes again as though startled from his sleep. "No, no. Not yet," he stammered. "There are things I must say, while I have the strength."

"Why don't you rest first?" suggested Gwladys.

"Because there may be no second chance," he replied. "What I must say, I must say now. My oil-lamp runs dry. God give me the fire to burn a while longer."

He fell silent for a few seconds, gathering the strength he needed. "I have seen much since I was a boy on the banks of the Rhine: honour and deceit, love and hatred, war and peace. I have also seen the violence of this world. I rode with Magnus Maximus and stood in battle with Count Theodosius. I have felt the bloodlust of sword-strife—known also how it turns men into beasts.

"The Romans call us barbarians. Perhaps we are. I have never cared for the refined ways of your husband's people, Corotica. Fine manners are like glory: glitter cast upon dust. I have known great men of state and the meanest of soil-tillers, and I have known honour, deceit, love and hatred in them all. Peace . . . peace . . . "

Corotica saw Theodwald's eyes grow glassy. She wiped his brow with a damp rag. As she did, his gaze focused again on her and he smiled affectionately.

"Peace. For many years, I sought only peace," he continued. "I tried to teach it to you and Tewdrig. I wanted you both to live without fear or hatred, to fashion this land into a place where the blade was used only on the soil. But I forgot a hard truth. The world bends towards judgement. And the ruin of it now condemns us."

The room was silent, save for the rasp of Theodwald's breath. When he spoke again, his voice was quieter, more intimate. "I've done what I had to, for peace. Corotica, your husband is a better farmer than I ever was, but his righteousness blinds him. He thinks the world will reward his virtue, that the land will protect what is good. But no man can stand upright against the storm that's coming. To endure, you must bend."

Theodwald's body convulsed with a hacking cough. He looked at Gwladys and croaked, "Water." She handed him a cup, which he sipped clumsily. Then he closed his eyes and sighed deeply. "Your husband will never bend. There is too much of his father in him. But not even Quercus in his most stubborn youth could remain upright in the storm that's coming to Britannia. Armoricus may be a better farmer than I, but I am more far-sighted. I can see that what we hold dearest—our family, the lands we cultivate, the animals we husband, and the old stories we tell our children—these will weather the storm because they are true and good. If God's judgement is only against evil and falsehood, then they will endure. I see this as clearly as I see anything. That is why there's no compromise I would not make to ensure my people endure. There can be a peace of the land even amid the ruin of the world. I've done what I've done to ensure that our story continues to be told."

"What have you done?" breathed Tewdrig, speaking now for the first time. Corotica looked at him and saw fear in his eyes. He had suspected something, had dreaded its revelation.

"I've made Prince Cormac heir to these lands," he said. "In return, he's sworn to protect them, to lease them to our family in perpetuity. You'll hold the land, Tewdrig, but his strength will guard it. It's the only way to keep peace."

By the time that her father had finished speaking, Corotica had shifted her attention to her brother. His face had turned a deep red and his glare held a hostility unlike anything she'd ever seen in him. Gwladys buried her face in her hands and wept. Corotica had never known her father to be deliberately unkind, but the timing and manner of this disclosure was as cruel as it was tragic. In the waning moments of his life, her father had tarnished a lifetime of fatherly love.

"Why? Why? Why?" pleaded Tewdrig, each note growing sharper.

"For the sake of peace," her father replied in hardly more than a whisper. Tewdrig took his wife's hand and without even looking at his father marched out of the room.

"I could do no other," croaked Theodwald as he looked on his son for the last time.

Corotica took his hands again into her own, leaned over and kissed them, bathing them with her tears. There was nothing to be said. Whatever story he had told himself had not survived its utterance. Now, she could only remain by his side, silently bearing with him the tragedy of that moment. She felt no anger towards him. She could not even be disappointed in him. All that remained was love: a love that gave wings to her prayers.

Theodwald quickly slipped into a coma and a few hours later drew his final rasping breath. A man whose entire life had been devoted to his people and to his family died with no one by his side other than Corotica. Only later, did she come to realize that his desolation, borne wordlessly in his dying hour, was his final and most enduring gift. The reed had bent painfully low, but in bending it could now endure the coming storm.

—

Ria was even more amazed than her parents by how little the attack in the woods unsettled her. Though she had returned shaken and distraught, the moment she crossed the familiar threshold of the villa, something within her grew calm. In the quiet of the household, she described what had happened with a strange detachment, as though it were another woman's story, and not her own.

"Really, it was nothing," she had reassured Armoricus, Corotica, and her parents.

All the same, their mood had quickly turned to thunderous outrage as she recounted how the two men had assaulted her and threatened worse. This had given way to wordless astonishment when she spoke movingly of her debt to Publius's bravery. Even amidst this range of emotions, she had reflected about how her story would long be recounted to the enduring credit of Corotica's boy.

"Really, it was nothing," she had assured them again.

Despite her calmness, the incident had set the whole household ablaze with activity. Cunicatus rounded up a dozen farmhands to search for the culprits while Meurig gathered the militia to keep an eye on Crassula's encampment. Armoricus, Quercus and Cadfan looked for the still-missing Publius, fearful that he might have fallen into the hands of Muconius. Meanwhile, Corotica and Ancarat smothered Ria with love, bundling her up on Corotica's own couch and insisting on checking her over for any harm. Though their attention and loving words embarrassed more than they soothed, Ria had accepted both gracefully.

It was during this flurry that Publius wandered into the courtyard, looking for all the world as though he'd simply lost track of time. If he thought he could pretend that nothing out of the ordinary had happened, he was immediately disabused of this notion. A great maelstrom of voluble women had swept him up and showered him with tearful kisses and bosomy embraces. Dazed and half smothered, he had staggered more than walked onto the veranda, only to be enshrouded by his mother's embrace and praised to the skies by his father. No one thought to ask him why he had been out there in the first place. When he looked at Ria, he blushed deeply and lowered his eyes, recoiling from the extravagant praise.

"Brave Publius!" she exclaimed, hugging him tightly, and though her embrace was full of gratitude, it only seemed to deepen his mortification.

The furore had died immediately when Cunicatus and his men returned with a dazed and bleeding Crassula in tow. The gash on his forehead was deep and wide, more like a crater than a cut, and was perfectly centred in an enormous purple welt that covered most of his forehead. Publius's aim had been as true as the blow was effective. The *familia* greeted the tax collector with a menacing silence that gradually became a hiss of low, angry voices. Only when the band had reached the courtyard did they let loose their fury and outrage fully, hurling abuses like more sharp stones at the addled Crassula. They might as well have saved their breath for all that the man was aware of his surroundings. Not even Armoricus's wrath, unlike anything anyone had witnessed from him, could cut through Crassula's confusion. In the end, he was taken to an empty storeroom and locked inside where he groaned loudly about his aching head.

On the morning after his return, the centurion of the auxiliaries came to meet with Armoricus. While sympathetic, he laid out the limits of their power. Crassula, the man explained, carried the authority of Rome itself. Any harm done to him, no matter how deserved, would bring punishment to the *familia*. And so Crassula would have to be released.

"Besides," concluded the veteran soldier with a wink, "she's only a maid. You've probably had a turn with her yourself. By the gods, the man got knocked out by a boy! A humiliation like that is punishment enough, I should think."

Armoricus made it clear that he did not, in fact, think that at all. But there was little else he could do. Although Meurig and Cunicatus wanted to assemble the villa's militia as a show of force, such a mutiny, however justified, would only have ended badly. Besides, what would violence actually achieve? They could not very well sentence Crassula themselves and they certainly could not punish him, however much he deserved it. They were powerless and, therefore, must let him go.

Ria accepted this as a matter of course. "Really, it was nothing," was her way of expressing her own powerlessness. She understood the world into which she had been born. Within the *familia*, she enjoyed a status determined in part by her role as Corotica's handmaid and by her relation to Cadfan and Ancarat, but mainly by the respect and affection in which the others held her. Her place within the *familia* was as assured as it was fulfilling. But the moment she stepped beyond the boundaries of the villa, she became as nothing. Crassula was a man of substance while she was only a simple woman to whom such high-minded ideas like justice and honour were entirely blind. Her liberty, even her worth as a person, was circumscribed by the same boundary stones that marked the limits of her home. Here in the villa, she was Ria; everywhere else in the world she was no more than a serving girl to be used by powerful men as they saw fit.

All the same, Armoricus was not about to let Crassula depart casually. When he confronted the tax collector, his voice rang out like thunder across the courtyard, every phrase a blow, every syllable a lash. Everyone in the village must have heard him. Ria, watching from a distance, almost pitied Crassula. Almost. She remembered too well the way his eyes had devoured her, the hunger and cruelty in them. And though her master's words could not undo the wrong done to her, she prayed they would at least carve a warning into the man's heart.

Afterwards, Crassula was cast from the villa like Satan out of heaven.

The next day, rain began to fall, soft at first, then steady and relentless. The roads turned to mud, the fields lay sodden and the work of the farm came to a halt. For three days it poured, hemming the household indoors, where tempers flared and spirits soured.

"This rain is as miserable as the rest of the world," Cadfan muttered, shaking the water from his coat as he returned from the fields.

"It's a cleansing rain," Ancarat replied, her hands moving steadily over her knitting. "God is washing the filth away. You'll see—when the sun comes, it'll feel like a fresh start."

"God, I hate it when you're chirpy," grumbled Cadfan.

But Ria found herself unable to share in her mother's hope. Each night, her dreams were haunted by Muconius—his shadow emerging from the dark with flashing eyes and the look of the devil. She would wake feeling the strength of his arm against her chest and the smell of his breath in her nose, as though he had actually come to her in her sleep but had escaped before she woke. When she looked out into the misty rain, she imagined him lurking in the dark woods, watching her with Crassula's depraved leer. In her weary mind, the two men merged into a single devil: violent, twisted and perverse. If only they knew of Muconius's whereabouts, she could find peace. Instead, his very absence made him ever-present.

When the rain finally broke and sunlight spilled over the land, there was a collective sigh of relief. The fields shimmered with promise, the animals shook the wet from their backs, and the villa hummed again with the rhythms of ordinary life. Even Ria felt some of that lightness, enough to tie her apron around her waist and step out into the day.

She was heading towards Corotica's room when the sound of hooves shattered the quiet. A rider, dressed in the colourful garments of a Silurian nobleman, galloped into the courtyard. Ria barely had time to recognize him—Tewdrig—before Corotica appeared behind her, her face breaking into a smile.

"Tewdrig!" she called with obvious pleasure. "What brings you here?"

The man's answer sent a ripple through the household: Prince Cormac had triumphed over the Irish. Cheers rose, and people clapped one another on the back. Ria knew that the Dominus didn't hold Prince Cormac in high esteem—and she couldn't work out how he could be Irish and yet not Irish—but she assumed that even he would greet this as happy news. But then she noticed Quercus growl and stamp his walking stick hard against the ground before turning back into the barn. She realized the news was not uncomplicatedly welcome, though she didn't understand why.

And then came another revelation, one that stilled all chatter: Corotica's father was dying. Ria watched as her mistress's expression faltered, her composure slipping only for a moment before she called for her horse.

"Find my husband," Corotica told Ria. "Tell him I've gone to my father, and tell him to keep Aurelius here until I return. I must say goodbye."

Ria held her hands to her mouth and nodded. "Go safely, Domina."

As Corotica and Tewdrig cantered out of the courtyard, Ria hurried down the lane and across the broad meadow towards Fox Field. The sodden ground squelched beneath her feet. She felt the cold groundwater covering her toes and the irritating tickle of the wet grass against her calves. The world felt fragile, as though one more jolt might shatter it entirely. And then, as she neared Fox Field, she saw him. Muconius stepped from the shadows, his single arm marking him unmistakably. He said nothing, only stared at her with a grin that chilled her blood. Slowly, he raised his hand, palm parallel to the ground, indicating someone small, and then drew his finger like a knife across his throat.

Ria's breath caught. She understood his meaning, as clear as though he had spoken aloud: Publius was in danger.

And then Muconius was gone, swallowed by the trees, leaving her standing alone in the damp field.

XXV

"How goes your study of the *Aeneid*?" Armoricus asked Publius as the two of them sat on the old beech log above the villa. Rusticella was twirling in circles a few feet away as she endlessly repeated a nursery rhyme. Flox and Lupus stood at attention in front of them, patiently waiting for his father to throw a stick again. Nearby, three men with spears stood sentry.

"Fine," Publius answered, not meeting his father's gaze. Since his own small adventure in the hills last autumn, the tales of Aeneas and his Trojans had seemed less compelling. What was the use of reading about faraway cities and long-dead heroes when the woods and streams held more life and mystery than any book could describe?

"You'll like Livy better," his father said with a smile. "There's a story in his histories about Romulus and Remus being nursed by a she-wolf. Did you know that? I sometimes wonder if you were nursed by one yourself, half-wild as you are. I should ask your mother."

Publius frowned. His father's teasing always perturbed him. "I want to go hunting with Meurig," he muttered.

Armoricus laughed. "Don't we all, boy! We'll go, you and I, when the time is right. It's been too long since we went out together. But tell me—do you know why I make you study Virgil and Livy?"

"To learn," replied Publius without enthusiasm.

"Well, yes," said his father as he finally threw the stick. "But it's what you're learning that's important. What has the *Aeneid* taught you so far?"

Publius's frown now became a grimace. His father always asked these kinds of questions, and the answers always seemed just out of reach, like the shadows at the edge of a lantern's light. He tried to think of what would satisfy his father. Finally, he said, "It's about where we Romans came from."

"That's right," Armoricus said, nodding. "It's the story of how we came to be who we are. And it's important to know that, to see how our story fits into the larger one. Our life here, on this land, is part of something that began long ago and far away. Do you see?"

Publius nodded hesitantly, though he didn't entirely. "What about Mamma's story? Where did the Silures come from? Not Troy?"

"No, not Troy," replied Armoricus as he threw the stick again and tried to wipe the dogs' drool off his hand. "Perhaps they've always been here. Perhaps their stories go back to the days of Adam. Or perhaps they've forgotten their beginnings. That happens, you know. A people can lose their stories, and when that happens, they lose themselves."

"Like we came from Armorica?" offered Publius. He wondered what the land across the wide sea was like. He couldn't really imagine the sea.

"Yes, like Armorica, though our family came from northern Italia before that. Did you know that? Grampa once had an old sword that it was said belonged to an ancestor who fought alongside Caesar at Pharsalus. Whether that's true, I don't know. The Irish stole it in any case."

Publius thought for a moment and then asked, "But, Pappa, why do we need to know where we came from?"

"It matters," Armoricus said, "because to honour our ancestors, we must remember them. That's why you must study the *Aeneid*, as your brother did, as I did, as my father before me did. It's what every proper Roman learns. Imagine that—boys and girls all across the world, reading the same stories, learning the same lessons."

Publius shrugged, unimpressed. "But if we're all learning the same old stories where will new stories come from?"

Armoricus smiled at that. "Ah, but that's the wonder of it. New stories grow from the old ones, just as the crops we plant grow from the seeds we save. Where do you think the seeds come from, hmm? Without the old stories, there would be no new ones. And when people retell the old tales in their own way, the stories live on. They branch out, like trees in a forest, each unique but all rooted in the same soil."

"Like Cadno fighting the Romans?'" Publius said. The stories of Cadno, the local folk hero, filled the evenings at the villa when the fire was high and the shadows deep.

His father nodded. "Yes, that's good. There are many more stories about Cadno than any man, even a hero, could ever have lived. But however strange and wonderful the tales might be, it's always the same Cadno.

That's how you know a story is worth keeping—it keeps growing and growing, no matter how many winters pass."

Publius liked that thought. It was as though the stories themselves were alive, taking root in and sprouting in the minds of those who retold them.

His father continued as the dogs began to whine. "But stories can also be lost. Do you see that hill over there, where Empress Oak stands? Look closely—you can just make out the faint ring of a fort that once stood there. Think of the people who lived there, who built their homes and raised their children. We know nothing about them now because their stories have been forgotten. I suppose we truly die when no one remembers our stories any longer."

Publius frowned again. "Maybe that's when new stories really begin," he said. "Mamma's people have forgotten their oldest stories, but they still tell new ones."

Armoricus looked at his son, a spark of surprise and pride in his eyes. "I had never considered that," he admitted. "Yes, perhaps new stories can also come from elsewhere. You and I can't read the *Aeneid* like our ancestors did because we know that the old Roman gods don't exist. And we have new stories—the Gospel ones that Drichan tells us. Our stories are changing into something new."

Publius hopped down from the log and picked up two sticks, which he threw in opposite directions for the dogs. Lupus and Flox looked confused for a moment before Flox bounded after one of them, closely followed by Lupus, who was too stupid to realize he could have run after the other unchallenged. Rusticella skipped away to retrieve it for the dogs.

"Pappa, do you think our stories will one day be forgotten?"

"What do you mean, son?" he asked before waving at Corotica who had just come through the boundary hedge and was making her way towards them.

"If stories can be forgotten, like those of the people who once lived in the old fort, then perhaps our stories won't be remembered one day. All the good things we do forgotten."

"The bad things, too."

Publius thought for a moment and then asked, "But does God

remember them? He must. God must remember all the stories. Even the ones we've forgotten."

His father laughed as he stood up from the log. "I suppose he does. Perhaps when we go to heaven, we'll get to hear all the stories. Perhaps that's how we'll become wise and good. We'll know all the stories."

By now his mother had reached them. Rusticella had run out to greet her and the two walked the rest of the way hand in hand. Publius saw that his mother's cheeks were wet and her eyes red and puffy. He felt a little embarrassed, but his father took her into his arms and hugged her tightly. Rusticella insinuated herself between their legs, but Publius crouched down next to Lupus and rubbed his chest. Flox was too busy chasing her tail to notice anything else.

"Children," Corotica said, her voice steady despite her tears, "I have sad news. Your grandfather Theodwald has died."

Rusticella began to cry, clinging to her mother's skirts, but Publius only nodded and kept scratching Lupus. He felt the sadness settle in his chest, heavy and strange, but no tears came. He wanted to weep, for his tears to honour his grandfather, but he couldn't make himself cry. He hoped that maybe later the tears would come. It occurred to him that when his grandfather died, so did all the stories only he knew. That was a very sad thought.

The family walked together hand in hand back towards the villa. The dogs ran before them, luxuriating in the soft breeze as they chased after crows and field pigeons. The sun was low behind them, its long rays stretching across the fields to pick out objects with long shadowy fingers pointing towards the rising moon. The landscape seemed to be moving, as though everything was flowing eastward towards the night that was coming to greet them. Publius thought about his conversation with his father and wondered if the death of his grandfather was the ending of a chapter. Or perhaps it was the beginning of a new one. He couldn't tell. As he looked at his home, now coming to life with pinpricks of warm lights, he decided that whatever his own story was, it only made sense here among the other stories being written and retold. He imagined the villa being like one of Drichan's books, containing between its covers and on its pages everything he really knew.

—

"Let me see if I've got this straight," said the Bishop with an air of incredulity. "That snake Crassula came to you . . . how many months late, did you say?"

"Six," replied Aurelius, who sat next to Drichan at the Bishop's writing desk.

"Six months," the Bishop repeated, shaking his head. "He arrives with a veritable army at his side, demands taxes he was too lazy or too craven to collect on time, and then attempts to ravish one of your maids? Have I missed anything?" A vein running along the Bishop's left temple throbbed prominently.

Aurelius hesitated, then added, "He might have succeeded if not for my brother. Publius knocked him cold with a well-aimed stone."

"Like David and Goliath," offered Drichan.

The Bishop snorted. "Crassula is many things, but Goliath he is not. Still, I take your point." He fiddled with his silver pectoral cross absentmindedly. Drichan was struck by how much he had aged during the previous nine months. His healthy complexion had drained to a bluish tinge. Dark circles under his eyes accentuated his drawn and pallid cheeks. But his voice remained as strong as ever and his presence lacked little of its customary command.

"I must tell you that Crassula came here—it must have been straight from your villa—with an altogether different story," he said, his words clipped with frustration. "He spun a tale about your father refusing to pay taxes and attacking him outright. Enough of his auxiliaries are backing his story to lend it some credence."

"That's preposterous!" exclaimed Aurelius. "How could my father, with no armed guard, have overpowered a man surrounded by his soldiers?"

The Bishop raised a hand, calming the outburst. "Precisely. Crassula's reputation is well known, as is your father's. Fear not—I will speak in his defence. Still, there are those who will see the unpaid taxes as proof of your father's contempt. In these straitened times, tax collection has become a touchy subject."

Drichan glanced at Aurelius, whose posture relaxed at the Bishop's assurances. Yet a sense of unease lingered. If their case seemed straightforward enough, the politics of the court did not. He wondered what falsehoods Crassula was spinning to other members of the curia. Would they believe him?

"What of the girl?" the Bishop asked after a pause, his voice quiet. "Is she well?"

Drichan straightened in his seat. "I believe so. Crassula was not alone in his intent—a man we had taken in as a refugee betrayed us. If not for Publius . . . " He shook his head, the words trailing off. "But she is strong and has loving parents. She'll be fine."

"I'm relieved to hear that. I presume there's no consideration of making a formal accusation."

Aurelius sighed. "No, for the same reason that Crassula was allowed to leave of his own free will. To accuse Crassula of such a crime would pit a maid's word against that of a Roman official. And there is the matter of jurisdiction. Prince Cormac lays claim to Garthmadrun."

At the mention of Cormac, the Bishop's eyes narrowed. "Tell me everything," he said, his voice sharp.

In response, Aurelius and Drichan informed the Bishop of Prince Cormac's claims, the allegiances he was forming, and the villa's exposed position. The prelate seemed unsurprised by the news but asked searching questions about the Dominus's intentions. Aurelius and Drichan answered as honestly as they could, neither daring to dissemble in the Bishop's presence.

When they had finished their report, the Bishop rose from his chair and walked over to a large silver box etched on each side with the likenesses of three men, presumably the Apostles. Because the box was narrow, the figures looked more like grim dwarves than Iesu's original followers. Each had an oversized hand raised in benediction. A votive candle burned dimly next to the reliquary.

"This contains the relics of the saints Julius and Aaron," he said, gesturing to it. "Martyrs of our faith. Julius was a Roman soldier, Aaron a Jew—two men united by their Christian faith for which they were executed. Well, there are hardly any more soldiers than Jews in this part of Britannia today. But we hold fast to their faith. If there's any hope for us, I believe that faith must unite the Irish with us. Your little church may one day be key to their conversion. I will pray daily that God blesses it."

He sounded weary. Drichan sensed it was a fatigue of the soul as much as the body. He sensed that the Bishop had endured some great spiritual trial that had left him grievously wounded. *He is dying*, reflected Drichan.

As though hearing his reflections, the Bishop turned and said, "Thank you for coming, Aurelius Rusticelius. I will do what I can for your father. Speak to my deacon on your way out—he'll arrange for your travel to Armorica. God be with you."

Aurelius rose, bowed and left the room. The Bishop motioned for Drichan to remain.

"I'll speak plainly," the Bishop said, sinking into his chair. "When we first met, I doubted you. You were timid, uncertain. Yet here you are, grown into a priest of resolve. I see it in the way you carry yourself now." He paused, his gaze heavy. "But I am not well, Drichan. You see that, don't you?"

Drichan hesitated, then nodded. "Yes, my lord."

"Those demons you once obsessed about have been hard at work on me. Everywhere, things fall apart. Pagans harry us from all directions while Rome looks elsewhere. I nominally remain bishop of all the lands west of here. But like the governor, my actual authority extends no farther west than about twenty miles. Many of my clergy have fled east or across the channel to Dumnonia or even to Armorica. Despite what I said earlier, Prince Cormac and his father can do whatever they damned well like. We haven't the means to stop them. Only Glevum has a field army, though it's better dressed than drilled."

The world really was unravelling at an alarming rate. "Is there no hope of relief from Gallia?"

The Bishop shook his head. "None. At least not unless there is a great victory over the Visigoths and Rome decides to intervene in Britannia again as it did under Count Theodosius." He paused to rub his eyes. "But I didn't ask you to stay to discuss politics. I wanted to tell you that I've decided to leave Isca Augusta."

Drichan nodded, assuming that the Bishop was referring to his long-anticipated move to Venta Silurum.

"I am going to Gallia."

"Gallia?" Drichan's voice rose in surprise.

The Bishop grinned like a naughty boy. "That won't surprise you half as much as my reason. Have you heard of St Martin?"

"Certainly. A holy man like St Anthony." Drichan had been tempted to join those who followed Martin by dedicating themselves to live together in prayer and poverty. But St Anthony's *Life* had convinced him that his was a more solitary vocation.

"He came to me in a dream," began the Bishop a little sheepishly. "I had been growing increasingly agitated by the plight of the faithful under my care. I'm powerless to help them. Then, about three months ago, I felt a terrible pain in my chest, like I had been caught in a crushing vice. I collapsed. I lay close to death for days."

"How dreadful!" interrupted Drichan earnestly.

"I'm not telling this to you to gain your pity, boy," replied the Bishop with some of his old vigour. Then he rubbed his chest and smiled. "My apologies. Old habits die hard. As I was saying, I was so near to dying that I could almost lay my head on Abraham's bosom. But then the blessed Martin appeared to me in a dream. He came dressed as a soldier but wearing half a cloak wrapped around his shoulders like a shawl. He told me that I would not die until I had been blessed by the poor. I believe God is calling me to Martin's community. There, I hope to find the blessing I need to meet my end in peace."

Drichan was so astonished by this news that he hardly knew what to say. The question he eventually asked seemed entirely inadequate to the moment. "When do you plan to leave?"

"As soon as I can put my affairs in order," replied the Bishop. "Certainly within a month."

The room fell silent. The Bishop's weariness seemed to deepen, his words heavy with resignation. Drichan, too, felt the weight of the world pressing against his chest.

"Join me," the Bishop said suddenly, his voice soft but commanding. "There is no future for you at Armoricus's villa. I suspect there's no future for them either. Rome retreats, never to return. This land grows dark, Drichan. Let me save you while I can."

Drichan shook his head. "I can't abandon my calling. The villa is my home, my house of prayer. The people there need me."

The Bishop sighed. "Perhaps you're right. Yes, you must serve where God calls you, be that to the few or the many. But I fear for you, Drichan, as I fear for others under my charge. It weighs on me heavily. We're all like chaff before the wind, blown in too many directions to be gathered and saved. 'Ransom the captives,' our Lord commanded us. But not all the gold in the world could buy back those taken across the sea to Hibernia. Allow a dying man to save you, Drichan. Again, I ask—come with me to Gallia."

"How can I go back to Gallia, my lord?" exclaimed Drichan. "I left there to become a hermit here in Britannia. That you know. You once mocked me for it."

"For which I am sorry. I see now how much I was sick with pride. What a sinner I am."

The despair in the Bishop's tired voice was palpable. There was no hope in the Bishop's eyes, only the expectation of death. So instead of replying to his request, Drichan asked, "Why? Why do you think God is allowing this to happen?"

The Bishop drew in a long breath, his voice becoming steadier now. "Rome was built on a lie. Not greed or violence or pride—those are only its fruits. The root of that lie is the belief that man can outrun death. All our greatest men—Caesar, Cicero, Augustus, even Theodosius—spent their lives chasing that falsehood. They foolishly thought that power and wealth could shield them from the shadow. In that pursuit, they seized from others what they could never truly keep. But a lie, Drichan, is not the opposite of truth. Truth is a thing, a divine and beautiful thing. But a lie? It's nothing—a hollow absence. You can't build anything enduring on something that's not there. It's like building a house on a hole. Rome was never eternal because her foundations were planted on an empty lie. So, she dies."

Drichan, subdued by the weight of the Bishop's words, asked quietly, "Then is there no hope for us?"

The Bishop looked at him, a tired yet gentle resolve in his eyes. "There is always hope. The seed doesn't grow unless it falls to the ground and dies. I think your Armoricus knows that truth, as every good farmer does. Perhaps life, to be free of death's shadow, must first pass through it. Perhaps all our mighty works are decaying like last year's crop to ready the soil for something new. We see the decay, the ruins. But perhaps this is only the first breaking of the ground for another planting."

Drichan had always known the Bishop to be a great man, a true patrician who knew how to command. He had tried to defend the good by fashioning power into unquestioned authority. Now, he had begun to shed that power like a dying man divesting himself of all his worldly goods. The Bishop had always been great; no one could deny that. Now he was becoming holy. Drichan's heart sank with that acknowledgement. He was defenceless against such sanctity. He knew then that he could not say no. He would go to Gallia with his Bishop, though he wished with all his heart to see the villa—his home—once more.

—

Bile was rising in Aurelius's throat as he struggled to focus on the task at hand rather than on his nerves. Only as he approached the curved row of benches on which sat the remnant of the great and the good of Isca Augusta did he realize what a formidable responsibility his father had laid on his shoulders. Aurelius could still see the firm resolve in his father's face as he'd said, "You will speak for me." And so here he was, the family's future resting on his words, with the weight of Rome and all her faded grandeur pressing against him.

The proceedings were held in the old assembly hall, which now bore the scars of long neglect. After the departure of the legion, the civilian population had gradually migrated to Venta Silurum or other destinations, leaving only a rump of citizenry, mainly the local elite and their dependents. *What a difference a legion would make now*, Aurelius mused as he waited for the proceedings to begin.

"Aurelius Rusticelius, we greet you," intoned the president of the assembly. His self-indulgent corpulence reminded Aurelius of Crassula except that his eyes were round and friendly. "Do you understand the charge made against your father by Decimus Crassula?"

Aurelius took a deep breath and replied, "I do. And I give my thanks, and that of my noble father, to you and this council for granting me the opportunity to speak."

"Proceed, then," said the president.

"My father, Gaius Rusticelius Armoricus, is a man of integrity, whose life has been a testament to service and virtue," Aurelius began. "That he should be accused by a man like Decimus Crassula—a man whose greed and corruption are as well-known as his depravity—is an insult not only to my family but to the very ideals we claim to uphold as Romans."

Crassula shot up from his bench, his jowls quivering with indignation. "I object to this slander!" he shrilled.

The president raised his hand until Crassula had resumed his seat. He turned back to Aurelius. "I would advise you to temper your remarks. This court knows of Crassula's venality well enough."

"Because it shares in at least half his vices itself," muttered a well-groomed young man on the far left who was clearly finding the proceedings amusing.

The president glowered at him. "Yes. I mean, no. We are here . . . we are here to deliberate on your father's refusal to pay the tax owed to us and the charge that he resorted to violence to prevent our tax agent from performing his duty. However, the Bishop has already spoken eloquently in his defence. We also understand from him that, far from your father treating Crassula violently, it was in fact Crassula who attempted to rape one of your mother's handmaids. What say you? Can you present evidence for this charge beyond the words of a female servant?"

Aurelius looked with surprise at the Bishop, who was sitting to the right of the president. Seeing his confusion, the Bishop spoke up, "Please, Aurelius, tell the curia what you know. I have testified to this council that no formal charge is being made against Crassula. Nevertheless, the incident is consistent with his known behaviour and explains the injury to his forehead."

"I object again!" Crassula shouted, his face contorted with rage. "These are baseless accusations meant to distract from the real issue—your father's refusal to pay what is owed!"

The president waved him off with growing impatience, and another voice broke in—from a magistrate, whom Aurelius vaguely knew to be the owner of a large estate a few miles north of the city. "Let us not ignore the wisdom of Cicero," the man said, his tone measured but sharp. "In cases where evidence is scarce, the character of those involved must guide us. We know the kind of man Armoricus is, and we know the kind of man Crassula is. Do we need more?"

"But this is not a debate about character," countered another, an older man whose voice carried the authority of years. "It is a matter of justice. Taxes must be paid, or the whole foundation of our society crumbles."

The Bishop raised a hand to speak again. "Justice," he said, "requires truth. And truth is often revealed by the fruit of a man's life. As our Lord taught, a good tree cannot bear bad fruit, nor can a bad tree bear good. Armoricus has lived a life of honest labour and honour. Crassula, by contrast, has sown nothing but corruption and malice. Let us judge this matter accordingly."

The room fell into a low hum of debate, voices rising and falling like the wind through a forest. Aurelius felt extraneous to their deliberations. He kept expecting the president to call the meeting back to order and ask him to resume his oration. It was Crassula who finally brought an end to their chatter.

"Honourable gentlemen," he said. And then more loudly, "Honourable gentlemen. Please, please, listen to me. Thank you. I knew the Bishop would be intemperate in his remarks about my character; the gods know I have long endured his animus towards me. I accept that by his lofty standards, I may seem a man of vice, even (to use his language) a sinner.

But I make no more excuse for enjoying the fruits of my labour than any of you do. We are men of the world, are we not? I don't pretend to be a Christian. I keep with the older gods. His god speaks of fruit. Well, I enjoy the fruits of my labour, as any man would. Can you claim to do otherwise?

"As for Armoricus," he continued, his tone sharpening, "you say he is more honourable than I. That may be. His opportunities for dishonour are few and far between. Indeed, he is no better than the hill tribes he admires. We know that such men may be good—we might even say *solid*—after a fashion. But we also know that such men scorn us whom they deem womanly, corrupted (as they see it) by urban decadence. I put it to you that Armoricus is precisely such a man. He scorns the Roman way of life, scorns us, his peers. He refuses the tax not out of necessity, but out of disdain. He thinks us weak, unworthy of our positions. If you let his defiance go unpunished, others will follow. We will lose not just the tax, but our authority. And then we will deserve our ruin."

The room erupted in a cacophony of voices. Aurelius stood dumbstruck as some shouted "Hear, hear!" while others bellowed "Shame, shame!" The Bishop tried to raise his voice above them all by roaring, "May I remind the room? May I remind the room?" But he could get no further. All the while, the visibly distressed president kept shouting "Order, order, order" to a room beyond any semblance of order. Crassula just smiled, clearly pleased with the effect of his slanderous speech.

Aurelius stood motionless, watching the scene unfold. He felt the truth of Crassula's words, twisted though they were. His father did disdain the corruption of Roman society. He did live simply, stubbornly, refusing the luxuries that others saw as their right. Aurelius could see the cunning in Crassula's approach. The great men of Isca Augusta, reduced now to little more than their status, could easily overlook Armoricus's supposed attack on Crassula. They could even pardon him for not paying his tax. What they could never forgive was his virtue.

Aurelius realized, with a cold certainty, that the council would rule against his father. They would side with Crassula, not because they believed him or even liked him, but because they feared what his defeat might mean for their collapsing authority. Aurelius could feel Rome fading into the distance like an eagle flying towards the setting sun. He could still go to Armorica. He had enough funds from his parents to begin laying the foundation for a new life away from Britannia with all its violence, greed and decay. He knew now, however, that if that had ever really been a choice, it had depended on a peace and prosperity unknown for longer than he'd been alive. He had clung obstinately to Rome's final glory only to discover that he was living out her eulogy.

He turned away and walked quietly towards the exit. As he neared it, Drichan fell in beside him. The two men exchanged no words. There was no need. They both knew what they must now do.

They were going home.

XXVI

"We need to round up the year-old shearlings," explained Baglan as he and Patricius walked from the villa towards the barn. A group of men and women armed with clippers were waiting for him. "I'd have liked to shear them all, but with all this cold and wet, we'd better leave the main flock for another few weeks. We don't want to risk their getting pneumonia."

"Why the shearlings, then?" asked Patricius as Baglan handed him a crook.

"They grow faster without their wool," replied the shepherd. "We do them first, then the rest of the flock, and then we start moving the flocks into the hills. In about a month, my lad, you'll trade your grandfather's fine villa for the proper life of a shepherd in a *hafod*." A grin spread across his face as he added, "Oh, how I've missed it!"

The boy's eyes sparkled. "Can I learn to be a proper shepherd there?"

Baglan laughed and slapped the boy gently on the back. "Patricius, my eager little master, you'll have no other choice."

Baglan and the men herded the sheep back to the barn. There the shearlings were separated from the rest to be shorn completely of their thick coats, while the ewes were crutched and wigged, leaving their faces and hindquarters closely shaved. The sheep raised a horrendous din that was answered by the flock left out in the fields. Baglan could see that the hands knew their work, but he detected little joy in it. They were manhandling the poor creatures as though punishing them for daring to grow fleece.

He turned to Patricius and said loudly enough for the others to hear, "You know what sheep appreciate? A good song. Shall I teach you some of the old shearing songs from my home?"

Without waiting for an answer, Baglan began to sing. His tenor voice was as clear as a bell and as rich as a harp. He began with a soothing lullaby sung by his people from time out of mind to comfort both man and beast. All the workers knew it from the cradle, where their mothers had sung them to sleep, or from the hearth, where they evoked from the darkness bright scenes from a forgotten past. As the workers joined in, their shearing became proper teamwork, and the joy of their work settled the flock. Watching the hands, Baglan took a deep, satisfying breath and quietly thanked the gods.

The next few weeks were a blessing. Baglan worked tirelessly with Patricius almost always by his side. Only during the wettest days did the boy complain about the tasks he was given. Otherwise, he followed Baglan around like a lamb its mother, bombarding him with questions about sheep and farming or pestering him for stories from the olden days. Baglan found in Patricius a mind far sharper and more curious than his own but tempered by a guileless wonder that made all his old knowledge feel somehow new. He could imagine the boy growing up to become one of those saints that Christians venerate.

As Midsummer's Day approached, they gathered the flock and moved them into the richer fields higher up in the hills. There the grass was thick and tussocky and the views long and dramatic. They were led to the *hafod* by the steward, a gruff veteran with a thick, peppery beard, who helped them unload the supplies from the donkeys before turning back for the villa. Potitus had given his permission for Patricius to live with Baglan for much of the summer, though he insisted on their taking a guard along with them as well as three of his prized wolfhounds.

They shared the one-room *hafod* with the guard, a taciturn man who drank too much and snored too loudly. During most days, he'd hunt in the woods that girded the hills or slink back into town to find his mates in one of the taverns. But neither Baglan nor Patricius minded. They felt safe enough on the secluded slopes and much preferred the guard's absence to his sullen presence.

Baglan taught Patricius how to tend and guard the flock. Though wolves were uncommon, they were not unheard of, and the hounds— keen-eyed and quick-footed—were invaluable in keeping the sheep safe. Baglan grew confident enough to leave Patricius with the flock, trusting the boy and the dogs to watch over them while he repaired and improved the sheepfold. Once it was completed, they were able to gather the flock in at night or when they wanted to go down into the woods to set traps for hares or hunt roe deer.

Late evenings were the times that Baglan loved best. The long summer days gave way reluctantly to the night, freshening the air with a comfortably cool breeze and pigmenting the skies from a celestial palette of reds and pale yellows. Long and lazy dusks on dry evenings gave them time to lounge by the fire with the hounds hunkered drowsily at their side. Patricius listened raptly, wrapped up in a woollen blanket, his eyes wide with wonder as Baglan spoke of the Ancestors, whose spirits dwelled in the hills and woods around them.

Baglan paid tribute to those Ancestors as he did his daily work. Though he'd lost faith in their divine potency, his homespun piety was too deeply ingrained for him to abandon. Patricius observed his devotions, but rarely asked him about them. When he did, Baglan invariably struggled to explain their purpose. They were habits learned from his own father and mother who had inherited them from their parents. He knew each and every one of them to be important, but it had never occurred to him to ask why. Perhaps they were precious simply because they were valuable enough to have been handed down from generation to generation. By venerating the Ancestors, he was honouring his own forebears.

The one exception to Patricius's lack of curiosity was Baglan's morning observance. Each day after rising, he stood at the *hafod*'s threshold with a damp clump of mistletoe he'd cut loose with a knife and purified in a nearby waterfall. Then he solemnly flicked droplets in all four directions as he softly chanted:

> *The Ancestors be with me,*
> *The Ancestors before me,*
> *The Ancestors behind me,*
> *The Ancestors beneath me,*
> *The Ancestors above me,*
> *The Ancestors on my right,*
> *The Ancestors on my left,*
> *The Ancestors when I lie down,*
> *The Ancestors when I sit down,*
> *The Ancestors when I arise.*

Only then would he go check on the flock and start his morning chores.

"Why do you do that each morning?" asked Patricius one day. "Is it a spell?"

Baglan shook his head. "No. It's more like a prayer. A prayer to the Ancestors to protect us during the coming day. We call it a breastplate. Reciting it each morning is an ancient custom of our people. It helps us to remember that the Ancestors are everywhere."

"And do they protect us?"

"I once thought so," replied Baglan. "I don't know anymore. But it doesn't hurt to remember them."

Patricius screwed up his little nose as he thought hard about Baglan's words. "What if the Ancestors are like my own mother and father?"

Baglan could think of no response to this.

One day, Potitus rode up from the town to spend the afternoon with them. He arrived with a few supplies, but also with a lavish lunch of freshly baked bread, cheese, dried meats, garum and wine. They spread the feast beneath the shade of a great chestnut tree that stood between the *hafod* and the edge of the forest and Potitus updated them on local news and gossip. Thanks to Prince Cormac's victory, the road to Moridunum was entirely clear for trade while even the road eastward to Venta Silurum was safe enough for armed convoys. There was hope that a degree of prosperity might return since both cities desperately needed the lead from their own mines.

Baglan listened with half an ear, his attention wandering to Patricius, who was playing an imaginary game that he couldn't work out. The boy's face was alive with concentration and joy. It was unseasonably cool but a breeze, gentle and warm, hinted at better weather to come.

"I have other news that will interest you," said Potitus. "Two days ago, our soldiers returned with a little wild man they captured during one of their patrols."

Baglan gasped. "Gwas?"

Potitus nodded. "I believe so. They found him lurking in the woods nearby. When they went back to search for others, they found his hut—a crude thing—and what looks to be a shrine beneath an ancient yew tree."

Baglan had long since stopped wondering what had become of the old man. And now here he was, not far from them all this time. What had drawn him to leave the Stone?

As though reading his thoughts, Potitus explained, "They caught him with a sack of stolen food. I think he's been here since you arrived."

"You think he followed me here?" asked Baglan, astonished.

"You'd know better than I. Is he a druid?"

Baglan shrugged. "There haven't been any druids since time out of mind. But he may think himself one. Or he may just be mad. Either way, he saved my life once. I'd hate to see him come to harm. What will happen to him?"

Potitus's expression darkened. "What do you think? He has been sent to the mines."

Baglan's breath caught. "The mines? But that will be the death of him! How can they send someone his age, in his condition?"

"They can do as they like to a thief. I'll see what I can do to ease his captivity. But whether he's a true druid or not, people believe he is. They won't tolerate his release."

Unbidden, memories returned to Baglan of that day when he had lain wretched and bereft of hope in the small wood near the Stone. It was Gwas who had found him and tended him, who had saved him from despair. And how had he repaid him? Only with complaint before abandoning him. The image of the Stone sprang to mind, and the uncanny sensations he'd experienced on that mad, strange solstice. He felt those memories begin to dredge up a well of emotion, which he thought he'd sunk too deep to bother him again. Yet, as it came to the surface, he understood that he couldn't really leave the past behind him until he'd repaid his debt. He saw plainly what he had to do.

He took a long breath and said, "I must try to free him."

Potitus smiled. "Of course, you must, my friend. And I will help you."

—

Many had wept alongside Corotica when Aurelius and Drichan had set out for Isca Augusta. Everyone had assumed that it was a final departure.

Few were terribly grief-stricken to see Aurelius go. Instead, they wept for their Domina but also for the responsibility that her son and their priest carried. They knew that the welfare of their home depended on the bravery and eloquence of those two men. They prayed that Crassula would be confounded by Corotica's elder son as he had been by the younger.

And so it was with no small confusion that they greeted the two men back so soon. Drichan could see the concern in their faces as they approached the villa; the urgency of their questions pressed on him heavily before any words were spoken. He was glad to be back before the end of the Paschal season. He had keenly felt his absence from his flock, unable to celebrate the Eucharist on Pascha itself, to call to their mind Christ's victory over death, the final failure of darkness to overcome the light. He had time now to give them Christ's Body and Blood before the fifty days of the Paschal season were complete. He planned to visit Tewdrig's estate as well.

This eagerness to return to his pastoral duties salved the guilt he felt in abandoning the Bishop. He thought back to the painful meeting of the curia when he had watched Crassula coax enough magistrates to support him. The once unassailable Bishop has been deftly outmanoeuvred, and the defeat diminished him. The Bishop he knew of old would have caught wind of Crassula's machinations and used resentment among the magistrates to his own advantage. The Bishop hadn't perceived how people facing ruin often comforted themselves by destroying the righteous—how "hosanna" too swiftly became "crucify him".

When Drichan had informed the Bishop of his decision to return to the villa, he had done little more than nod. Drichan had found him alone in his unlit chamber, staring at the reliquary without really seeing it. What could he have said? It was as obvious as it was tragic that his vision to go to Gallia, to become a disciple of St Martin before he died, was nothing more than an old man's dream. The journey would have taxed his health to breaking point even before the council meeting. Shattered as he now was by his failure to protect Armoricus, the Bishop had not the strength even to start.

"His world is passing," the Bishop's deacon commented as Drichan left the episcopal palace. "I fear the future lies with men like Crassula."

But, thinking of Prince Cormac, Drichan replied, "No. The future doesn't lie in any of our hands."

"You believe these are the end times?"

Drichan shrugged. "For the world? No. But for us? Perhaps they need to be."

The formal decision of the curia arrived just before their departure from Isca Augusta. The magistrates had authorized Crassula to return to the villa with a cohort of thirty soldiers to collect the tax. The debt had been reduced and the deadline for payment extended until the Ides of July—gestures of supposed mercy—but neither Drichan nor Aurelius were fooled by the council's supposed magnanimity. It was offered more to assuage their guilt than to help Armoricus, and, in any case, there could be no doubt that Crassula would use his mandate for revenge.

Yet, as the villa came into view, its familiar sights, smells and sounds unfolded before Drichan like a long-remembered hymn. Their journey to Isca Augusta made him realize how much this place had become his home. It was where he made sense, where his life made sense, where everything made sense. Here, he belonged. Here, he understood himself as part of something larger, a tessera in the great mosaic of the *familia*. However cracked or faded the actual mosaics of the villa might be, the living mosaic of the people he'd come to know remained whole, its beauty undiminished.

The courtyard greeted them with its own familiar tableau. Armoricus was wearing his straw hat and leaning on a hoe caked with mud. If he was concerned about his son's return, he did not show it, nor did Quercus who stood by his side with both hands resting on the rounded head of his walking stick. Drichan couldn't tell if it was concern, joy or a combination of both.

"Aurelius, my son," greeted Armoricus. He stepped forward to grasp Aurelius's horse's bridle. "We had not expected to see you again so soon." Drichan noticed the slightest pause before the final two words.

Without a word, Aurelius dismounted, embraced his astonished father, and sobbed.

They retreated into the living room where Aurelius soon regained his composure and related to his family all that had happened in Isca

Augusta. Drichan added his own account, speaking especially of his conversations with the Bishop. Last of all, Meurig shared what he had learned in the taverns—soldiers from Isca who harassed landowners or stripped abandoned estates of anything valuable.

"Everyone has become a brigand," he concluded.

Armoricus wanted to know everything: what they had seen on their way to and from Isca, any scraps of news or rumour, and information about specific magistrates. Quercus grumbled about the curia's dissolute state and swore violently about those whom he had considered friends or allies. Through it all, Corotica sat silently, watching Aurelius closely.

When at last all had been said, Armoricus leaned back, his voice weary but resolute. "This changes little. In the immediate future, I mean. We knew it was likely that Crassula would return with more soldiers than before. I'm relieved that we have until the Ides of July to prepare. That is almost two months from now. Much can happen between now and then."

"Like what?" asked Aurelius incredulously.

"An appeal," suggested Quercus. "A letter to the governor or better yet, a personal visit to him in Corinium."

"It's worth a try," replied Armoricus without much conviction. "But I'm not hopeful. What is a remote villa to a man who must be up to his eyeballs in crises?"

"But that's hardly sufficient for setting our minds at ease," said Corotica. "Does two months give us time to harvest enough produce to pay the tax?"

Armoricus rubbed his cheek thoughtfully. "Whether we do or not is immaterial. Crassula won't be coming back to collect taxes. We'll be entirely at his mercy."

"There's another option," ventured Meurig.

"I know," replied Armoricus. "Some would say it's our only way. But to take it will lead to the death of this place as assuredly as Crassula's return."

"Cormac," muttered Quercus.

"Why not?" asked Meurig. "Tewdrig has already come under his protection."

"His lordship, you mean," countered Corotica. "Don't forget that my brother is no longer the master of my father's estate, only its steward."

Meurig held out his hand in appeal to Armoricus. "Surely, he would not demand the same here. Armoricus is already the Dominus. And God willing, he has a long life ahead of him yet. Do we have a choice?"

Armoricus sank heavily onto the couch and rubbed his eyes. For the first time, Drichan noticed a sadness in them. Corotica moved behind him and started to rub his shoulders. But he reached up and placed his hand on hers, looking up at her with such fondness that Drichan could only smile.

Turning back to the gathered company, Armoricus said, "Meurig is right. We must appeal to Cormac. But I will not accept his lordship. Whatever authority they may claim, Cormac and his father have little understanding of what it means to be Roman. They are warriors first and always. For them, life is war—for plunder or to defend themselves against their enemies. To submit to him is to bind ourselves to the sword. He will demand not only our goods but our sons as soldiers. And those under his command—violent men—will want our lands, our goods and our beautiful women. What could they demand that we could refuse?"

The silence that followed weighed heavy on them all. Drichan could see it clearly: the choices before them were all paths to ruin, whether by Crassula's hand or Cormac's. Perhaps these were indeed the end times. Perhaps the ruin of Britain had come.

But now Quercus asked, "What then? You said you would appeal to the Irish prince but not accept his lordship. What do you intend?"

Armoricus sighed. "God only knows. We will try to do the Roman thing and buy his protection with coin and guarantees that our goods will flow westward. I hope that will be enough."

As the discussion continued, Drichan sat quietly, turning their predicament over in his mind. The Bishop's words echoed within him: the faith had made brothers of Aaron the Jew and Julius the Roman soldier. Faith. Faith had given them a new story, a new way of understanding themselves. It had given them something to share: a common purpose, a common way of looking at things. Was that not what this fractured world needed—a new story, something that could bind Roman, Briton and Irish into one?

His earlier conversation with Aongus about the power of stories came to mind, and with it the seed of an idea. The Irish bard was the key. It was not armies or governors or even gold that would save them. It was something far simpler, and yet far more enduring and profound.

They needed a new story.

XXVII

Publius and Rusticella walked side by side, each clutching kindling for the construction of the Midsummer bonfire. Determined to prove himself, Publius was valiantly carrying as many branches as his little arms could manage, his face tight with the effort of holding them all. Rusticella, ever practical, had chosen a single, stout branch that she dragged along behind her, its end bouncing and catching on stones in the path.

"You could have carried more, you know," Publius grumbled, struggling to balance his unwieldy bundle.

"And you could have carried fewer," she replied before running ahead with her branch bumping along the ground like a plough on rocky ground.

A couple of men from the villa militia accompanied them. Neither of Armoricus's children knew why they were being constantly chaperoned nor why their freedom to roam had become so constrained. Publius felt increasingly like a caged bird. He missed the days when he could vanish into the woods, running wild among the trees, pretending to be a hero from one of his favourite stories. Twice he'd tried to sneak off, only to be caught and marched back by villagers who all seemed to be conspiring to ruin his fun. Each time he'd asked why he wasn't allowed his freedom he'd been met with the same maddening response: "It's for your own good."

He couldn't understand it. Everything had changed since he'd rescued Ria, though he couldn't see how that could have anything to do with his sudden confinement. Not even Meurig would explain, though he did try to make amends by taking him hunting a couple of times, though again in the company of armed men. A few weeks earlier he would have gone with Meurig alone.

He only just managed to reach the growing woodpile without dropping any of the branches. The pile of wood lay about fifty yards down the slope from the bathhouse, near the stream. Riderch the carpenter and Owain the blacksmith worked together to erect the conical frame of the pyre. It would stand almost twenty feet high and twenty feet wide when they were done. Around them, a throng of men and women sorted the kindling, handing on the larger branches for the frame or bundling small branches into faggots. Young children scurried playfully amongst the workers while older ones looked on resentfully as they grudgingly helped the adults. A happy hum of conversation and laughter filled the air.

"Publius, Rusticella," came their father's voice, calling from the edge of the barn. He stood beside Cadfan, who held two large clay jars covered with muslin.

"Excited about Midsummer?" asked Cadfan when they arrived. They both nodded eagerly. "Don't tell anyone, but I hear the bees have made a lot of honey. You know what that means?"

"Honey cakes!" they both squealed.

"Take this to your mother," said their father, as Cadfan handed them a jar. "Careful now, they're full. And walk carefully—no running."

"What is it?" asked Publius, looking curiously at the jar.

"Fresh milk." He winked at them. "I think it might be for some of her honey pancakes. Now run along. And make sure you don't wander off."

The promise of pancakes was all the encouragement they needed. They carried the jars back to the kitchen as carefully as if they held treasure. They slowly climbed the steps onto the veranda and edged their way along the walls of their house to avoid the swift traffic of people too busy to notice two children.

"There you are!" exclaimed Corotica as they entered the kitchen. She was standing at the far end of the kitchen table, her arms and apron dusted white with flour. Ancarat and five other women stood beside her. The tabletop was covered with bowls, rolling pins, and globs of honey beneath clouds of flour. Flox and Lupus, each with white noses and hair matted with honey, sat beneath the table in a state of quiet ecstasy. A line of honey cakes stacked in pyramids five rows high ran down the middle of the table. The aroma was divine.

"Thank you, my loves," welcomed their mother as one of the kitchen maids took the jars from them. "Have you both been having fun?"

"Oh yes, Mamma!" chirped Rusticella as she hopped up onto a stool near the hearth. "I carried lots of sticks for the bonfire."

"I carried way more than you," replied Publius. "As many as my arms could hold. But you never took more than one each time."

"But mine were better. Owain told me so. You just picked up any old sticks. I bet they don't even use half of yours."

"Will too."

"Shush, you two," ordered Corotica. "Rusticella, you stay here and help us make honey cakes. Publius, would you please go find your brother? I think he's in the living room. Ask him if he'll go check the candle in the chapel. I promised Drichan we'd keep it lit while he's away at your uncle's home. Come straight back here when you're done. I don't want you wandering off."

As Publius turned to go, Ancarat handed him a small honey cake. "A treat for my brave little helper."

"You'll spoil my child," clucked Corotica with an affectionate smile.

Publius thanked Ancarat and turned to go through the door leading to the living room. Once outside, he stopped to eat the cake, savouring each bite. He loved the taste of honey more than just about anything. Normally, it would have been covered in almonds imported from the Mediterranean. But the women had made do with cobnuts harvested from their own trees. Publius decided he liked them better that way. He licked his fingers clean before heading to the living room.

Instead of his brother, Publius found Ria dusting the surfaces. An intimacy now bound them together that tied his tongue and made him feel that he ought to be somewhere else. He heard people say how indebted she was to him for rescuing her—and she behaved that way herself—but it wasn't a feeling he had at all. It seemed to him that Ria was too beautiful and kind to be beholden to anyone. He wished he knew how to free her of it, but he didn't.

"If it's not my little hero," she greeted him happily, proving that she could not read his thoughts. "How are you today?"

"Fine," he managed, shifting on his feet.

"Have you been helping with the bonfire?"

"Yes," said Publius. But he felt he ought to respond with more than a single word, so he added, "Mamma told me that a bard might come back with Drichan to sing songs."

"They say he's Irish. Fancy having an Irishman come and sing for us!"

That was news to Publius, and he didn't know what to make of it. One might as well try to cuddle a wolf as invite an Irishman to sing for them.

"Do you know where my brother is?" he asked. "Mamma wants him to check the chapel candle."

"I saw him and Meurig by the bathhouse. Do you want me to go with you?"

Publius shook his head, tired of being treated like a child. "No. It's only across the yard. I can find them on my own."

Ria placed her hands on her hips as she considered the situation. "All right, Publius," she said at last. "But you go straight to the bathhouse. If you can't find your brother, come straight back here to me. Promise you won't go wandering off."

"I promise," replied Publius, trying to hide his exasperation.

He found Aurelius sparring with Meurig outside the carpentry shop, each armed with a wooden practice sword. Aurelius had never shown much interest in being a soldier, preferring instead to loaf around reading books or take his horse out for a ride. He didn't actually know what his brother enjoyed doing. It certainly wasn't farming. It had long seemed to Publius that Aurelius yearned to be important without having to do anything much that anyone actually valued. But now that he watched his brother practising with Meurig, he wondered if there was more to him than he'd thought.

When they paused for a drink, Meurig spotted him. "Hello, Publius. I thought you were helping with the bonfire."

"I was. But Mamma sent me to fetch Aurelius. She wants you to check the chapel candle."

Aurelius rolled his eyes. "Can't she send one of the servants? I'm busy."

"When did you start sword fighting?" he asked his brother.

"We were made to practise when I was in Corinium. I thought it would be useful to take it back up. It's good exercise."

Publius reached for Meurig's sword. "Will you teach me?" he asked. "I want to be a warrior, like Cadno."

Meurig laughed. "Of course! I think you'd make a fine warrior."

"Look, Publius," interrupted Aurelius. "I was hoping to practise more with Meurig. Would you mind checking on the candle for me?"

Although Publius wanted to get back to helping with the bonfire, he agreed reluctantly. As he started towards the chapel, he was unsurprised to hear Meurig call after him, "Don't go wandering off, Publius. Get straight back to the bonfire when you're done." He pretended not to listen.

He found the candle in its lamp nearly burned out. The molten wax in the cupholder glowed golden in the candlelight, reminding him of the globs of honey on the kitchen table. He retrieved a replacement in a small cabinet near the altar and carefully lit it from the other candle. Hot wax coated his fingers, and he stopped to strip it off and roll it into a ball. Drichan's Gospel book lay open on its stand in the centre of the altar. Publius flipped through it, admiring the ornate script and wondering how long it must have taken to fill its pages. Then he turned to leave.

As he stepped back out into the sunlight, a shadow fell across him. He turned to find Muconius by the corner of the chapel where nobody could see him. He grinned at Publius with a malice that chilled him to the bone. In his hand was a knife. Publius froze, his legs trembling. Now he knew why everyone had been worried about him.

"Don't you go wandering off," mimicked Muconius with a snicker. Then he ducked back around the corner of the chapel. By the time that Publius had the nerve to go look, he was gone.

—

"It's yours if you want it," said Tewdrig. "My father's will is clear. All he asks is that you pray regularly for his soul."

Drichan sat with Tewdrig next to the smouldering hearth in the great hall while men and women bustled past them preparing the evening's feast. He had commended Theodwald's soul to his Lord on the previous evening in a funeral unlike any he had ever conducted. He had processed immediately behind Tewdrig to a massive pyre erected in the centre of the estate. The deep drone of the men's melodic hum had caused the hair on his neck to stand.

Drichan thought that the funeral pyre looked too much like an altar for a Christian funeral. He was reminded of the story about the competition between Elijah and the pagan priests of Israel and briefly worried that he might be expected to call down fire from heaven. He wondered how God would resurrect a new body for Theodwald out of the ashes of the old. *With God all things are possible*, he thought to himself, grateful for that verse to explain anything otherwise inexplicable. *With God all things are indeed possible*. He held tightly to that assurance as he thought about the dangers that now encroached upon them.

Though he had said some prayers and preached about the resurrection of the dead, he knew he was largely extraneous to the proceedings. His sole purpose was to provide a Catholic veneer to an otherwise thoroughly pagan, thoroughly Germanic funeral. Once lit, the pyre became an inferno that roared with a ferocity unlike anything he'd ever heard. There was no escaping its scalding heat on a night unusually sultry for that time of year. Its smoke rose in a thick pillar towards the darkening sky as though bearing Theodwald's soul straight to heaven. Drichan couldn't help but admire the effect. It seemed to symbolize the upward movement of the soul better than the Christian practice of burial—that is, if Theodwald's soul was indeed being borne to heaven by angels. He prayed hard that it was. Theodwald had been kind to him.

"Do you want it?" Tewdrig's words cut through Drichan's thoughts.

"Yes, yes," he replied too hastily. "My apologies, Tewdrig. The hermitage is all that I could have hoped for. I accept it with thanks and will certainly continue to pray regularly for his soul. I'm sorry for my distraction. Much has happened of late."

"To us all." Tewdrig's words were delivered impassively and yet Drichan knew them to mask deep feelings.

"What of you, Tewdrig? Will you stay here?"

"Yes," he replied. "Prince Cormac will honour the terms of my father's will if I swear an oath to him as my lord. Gwladys's father has agreed to do the same in exchange for Irish protection. Cormac is now lord of all Garthmadrun, though he came to us claiming only to be our protector. What can we do? We're on the cusp of a violent age. The future belongs with men like Cormac, not like my father, Armoricus, or even me."

"Rome may yet return," assured Drichan without conviction. "She did the last time the Irish sought to conquer our lands."

Tewdrig spat into the hearth. "If you believe that, Drichan, then you are indeed a man of faith. I have stopped hoping for the eagle of Rome to swoop to our rescue. It has grown fat and feeble. Yesterday you preached about the resurrection. You said that even from my father's ashes, mingled though they are with the ash of his pyre, God would raise up a new body completely unlike the old one. I must accept what you say, though I can't see how it can be. But perhaps the same is true for my home. All is now turning to ash. But perhaps one day, a hundred or more years hence, a new peace will come. I will never see it, but perhaps my children's children will. It is for them that I will bend the knee to Cormac."

"We do what we must to protect our homes, our children," replied Drichan.

The next morning, Drichan and Aongus walked together out to his new hermitage, leading a donkey that jingled with an assortment of tools. Two armed men accompanied them, though they weren't necessary under Prince Cormac's growing dominion. Almost as soon as Drichan had crossed the Isca, he had sensed a security that didn't include the villa.

"What do you make of Armoricus's plan?" he asked after he had recounted recent events to Aongus. It was a risk to share such matters with Cormac's bard, but Drichan trusted him.

"I think Cormac will scoff at it. My prince is not so desperate as to bargain for food, though your horses might tempt him. His father's lands now stretch from here to the western sea, encompassing the whole upper valley of the Isca. Soon, they'll extend even farther east. Armoricus will be trapped between the mountains and our lands. How long before he's forced to submit? And if the Romans are mad enough to help my lord by taking all Armoricus's money, then so much the better."

Drichan nodded. "But what if Cormac could be convinced to help

Armoricus in a way that preserves his honour and dignity? And what if we could convince Armoricus to accept Cormac's authority?"

Aongus raised an eyebrow. "What are you suggesting?"

"Remember our conversation about the power of stories? For a long time now, our people have been trapped in an old tale of endless strife: Romans conquering Britons, the Irish raiding Romans, Romans beating your people back into submission, and so on. In that story, there's no honourable way for Armoricus to accept Cormac. In that tale, Cormac can only see Armoricus's villa as fresh territory for him to grasp. What we need is a new story, one that binds us together as one people. Out of the ashes of the old, something new must rise or else the coming age will be dark for us all."

Aongus smiled with a twinkle in his eyes. "Now that would be a fine story to tell, wouldn't it?"

"A necessary story, too," continued Drichan. "Look, all people want is a place to call home. Even a warrior like Cormac longs to return home when he's away conquering new lands. The people here just want their home to be safe and prosperous. They're of this land. And this land's stories are older than any of us. They are written in the hills, the rivers, the woodlands, the fields. Their stories know nothing of our boundaries. They can't be overcome by the strength of arms. Even Rome's might could not erase them. We conquered a people but not their stories; we took away their lands but never their homes. And this will remain their home long after our bones have dissolved into the damp earth."

"Fine words, Drichan. You could almost be a bard," laughed Aongus as the old Roman fort came into view.

Drichan recalled his friend's amazement when they first saw the derelict Roman fort. "If even something like that couldn't endure, what hope does your prince's new territory have? If he wishes to leave a legacy, then he must achieve what Rome never has."

"What's that?"

"He must make this place his home. He must love it as his own." Drichan paused as a thought suddenly occurred to him. "Aongus, my friend, I suppose what I'm saying is that Cormac must become like Armoricus."

Finally, Aongus understood what Drichan was intimating. "You need my skills as a storyteller. You want me to tell that story."

"Precisely. Only you can tell the stories that will bind Cormac to this place. But it's more than that. You must tell him the tales that bind him to this land. Stories of its people, its beauty, its enduring spirit. But more than that, you must tell our people's stories that'll teach them to dream dreams, to see that whoever we are—Briton, Roman, Irish, native or refugee—our future is bound up together. You can tell that story to Cormac. You can tell that story here. You can begin to tell that story when you come to sing for us at Midsummer."

Aongus looked thoughtful. "A tall order. But if it can be done, it would be a tale worth singing for the ages."

They finally reached the quiet of the hermitage. In the green of summer, it was a place transformed from when they had visited it in the winter. Now it reminded Drichan less of the Holy of Holies than of Paradise. But perhaps the two were one. If God's glory dwelt in the Holy of Holies and the Lord could go for a stroll in the Garden of Eden, then God could be present here also. Drichan would become Adam; he would become the high priest tending to the needs, the joys and the pain, the confusions and delusions—the soul—of these people. He at last understood his vocation. He at last knew his place.

He turned to look at Aongus. "I will preach that story, too. And I'll preach it from this place. This shrine is the soul of Garthmadrun; its Holy of Holies. For a long while it has stood derelict and yet it remains sacred, as we saw from the offerings the people still make. What this place lacks is someone, like Adam, to tend and keep our people's prayers like a farmer his crops. I can do that. I now know that I must. That is what God has been calling me to do, to be. I can become a saint. All I need is a miracle."

"How will you perform that?"

Drichan's smirk masked the gravity of his purpose. "By baptizing your prince."

XXVIII

The fields had their own language, and Aurelius was just beginning to hear it. He walked the rows of barley in the grey hush before dawn, the earth damp beneath his sandals. The stalks whispered as he passed, brushing against his hands and leaving them damp with the morning's dew. The air smelled of turned soil and the faint sweetness of ripening grain, and the first notes of birdsong reached him from the hedgerows. For Aurelius, the land felt charged with something new, as though it held a life he had never noticed, a voice he was only beginning to understand. That voice stirred in him an awakening, like seeds long dormant breaking open at last under the rain.

Aurelius had discovered his home.

He watched his father instructing a small gathering of workers on the nearside of the adjoining field. For the first time in his life, Aurelius wished he were more like him. The court hearing in Isca had allowed him finally to see his father's character clearly and admire as virtues the very traits he used to mock to his friends. Yet admiration alone couldn't bridge the distance between them. Aurelius resolved to prove himself worthy of his father's respect and establish his place in the family, which amounted to the same thing. And he would begin by sharing in the work of the villa.

That morning was the first time since he was a child that Aurelius joined in tilling the soil. He hacked at it with a hoe, his strokes uneven, his rhythm unsteady. The work was harder than it looked; the muscles in his arms and back protested with each stroke. The soil turned reluctantly, clumping and clinging to the blade, and sweat beaded on his brow despite the cool air. Yet the rhythm of the task, rough and uneven as it was, began to loosen something in him. As he worked, his thoughts wandered back to his return, to the moment when he had buried his face into his father's shoulder and sobbed, as though his old self was being shed through his tears. That moment of surrender had marked the beginning of something new—a breaking open and a planting, though he had yet to see what might grow.

The tilling was simple and repetitive enough for his mind to wander freely. As he began to see how small and foolish his dreams of Rome had been, he struggled to cling onto something else that was solid and sure. In a world unravelling—where Rome itself seemed to be crumbling under its own weight—what was someone like him to do? The answer, he realized, lay in his father's quiet insistence on tending their small corner of the earth.

His grandfather's words, a line from Virgil, came back to him: "*All things by nature are ready to get worse, lapse backwards, fall away from what they were.*" How prescient the poet had been, speaking of decline even from the heights of an empire at the apogee of its splendour. Aurelius saw clearly what he had not before. If even Rome's legions couldn't stem the tide of chaos and disorder, what hope was there for a single man? And yet he began to see more clearly that this was what his father had been trying to do all along. He had staked his life on this patch of land, not out of blindness to the wider world's disorder, but out of wisdom born of humility. The good life, Aurelius began to understand, was not found in chasing distant glories but in tending to the small, tangible things—family, land, home. Perhaps that was what the Christians understood with their talk of loving their neighbours as themselves, that there cannot be a true love of oneself apart from loving one's neighbours.

But here, Aurelius found himself at odds with their teaching. Could a man love his neighbour without hating his enemy? He thought not. Love, he reasoned, demanded defence, a fierce loyalty that could not coexist with softness towards those who threatened what he held dear. How could he love those who sought to destroy his home, his family? The very idea seemed a betrayal. And if that were true, then could he really exempt Rome, which, in the guise of Crassula and the curia, sought now to harm his family?

That last question haunted him throughout the day. He felt like a man whose dearest love turns out to be a harlot. His bitterness towards Rome threatened to overwhelm him—it was by the exacting standards she had taught him that he now condemned her without pity. Only in his parents and his grandfather could he see those ideals manifested, which bred in him a fierce filial loyalty as naïve as his worship of Rome had been.

In the days that followed, he committed himself totally to his father and his *familia*. He worked with an intensity that bordered on desperation, and his whole body ached from the unfamiliar demands. Shame for his former arrogance drove him to push harder, to sweat more, to atone. In the evenings, he joined the militia for drills, the clap of wood and the bark of commands filling the yard. He practised with a ferocity that unnerved others, throwing himself so completely into their sparring that few wished to be paired with him. When he wasn't working or training, he kept to himself, retreating into his thoughts as if they were a fortress. Words felt too fragile, too slippery to hold what he wanted to say. He believed his actions would be enough.

But they were not. The people around him saw only hardness, the sharp edges of a man who seemed more intent on proving something than on belonging. His labour, though earnest, did not draw him closer to the *familia*. Aurelius remained as much a stranger to the *familia* he now loved as when he had rejected it.

"Give him time. Give him plenty of time," he overheard his mother say to his father one day. "He's only a young man and this world can be very hard for someone like him to work out."

"I don't doubt his intelligence or even his love," his father replied. "But that boy still hasn't learned kindness. I'm not sure he ever will."

Aurelius froze, the words landing like a punch. *Kindness.* The word hung in his mind, foreign and sharp. He clenched his fists, anger and resolve twisting together in his chest. He would prove his father wrong. He would show him how great a man he could be and how worthy an heir he really was.

—

Ria had reached a decision: they would celebrate Midsummer's Day as Ceridwen's birthday. She couldn't recall the exact moment she'd had the idea, but she knew it had been growing steadily, like the wild violets that crept up around the edges of the courtyard. Ceridwen had no birthday of her own, no date tied to memory or certainty. Ria knew only that she'd been born in summer, perhaps three or four years ago, before tragedy made her an orphan and sent her into Ria's arms. The solstice seemed fitting, as bright and full a day as any to designate Ceridwen's *dies natalis*.

For the occasion, Ria had embroidered the hem and neckline of Ceridwen's tunica with intricate scrollwork made of four parallel threads that symbolized the members of her family. Cadfan had built her a model of the villa that could be populated by little fabric figures that Ancarat had stitched to look like the principal members of the *familia*. She had even included Flox and Lupus. Ceridwen would wear her dress to the party, but her gifts would be a surprise.

A brilliant sunrise announced the arrival of Midsummer's Day with a promise of a fine, nearly cloudless morning. The sun was greeted by some people at the feet of Empress Oak. They wrapped the tree in garlands and danced merrily in circles. A few old-timers took the risk of climbing even further into the hills where they could welcome the rising sun without any obstructions, pour out libations of wine to the sun god Luga, and offer prayers for his protection. Both groups then scurried back to the villa to attend the Eucharist. At Ria's request, Drichan included a special prayer for Ceridwen, which pleased the girl mightily.

As there was much work to be done to prepare for that night's feast, they celebrated Ceridwen's birthday immediately after the Eucharist. Ancarat spread a cloth on a table in the orchard, and placed cups for the milk. Ria's father fetched chairs from the workshop, muttering good-naturedly about how he'd not raised his daughter to throw parties like some grand lady. Finally, Gwen and Rhodri arrived together, the latter with a loaf of bread still warm from the hearth. Rhodri was there at Ceridwen's special request, which Ria couldn't refuse. There remained enough awkwardness between them to make his presence at the party unwelcome. She knew that her parents still held out hope that she would see sense and accept the young man, especially as she scarcely seemed interested in anyone else.

But she pushed her own feelings from her mind as they gathered around the table. Ceridwen perched proudly at the head with a laurel of daisies crowning her head. Her delight spilled over in her laughter as she was presented with her birthday gifts. Cadfan's model of the villa was unveiled first, its tiny wooden rooms crafted with care, a labour of love. Ancarat's dolls came next. Ceridwen squealed with delight, setting the figures in their places and mimicking the voice of each member of their household. *This is my family*, Ria thought to herself with a sense of such contentment that she was almost willing to include Rhodri. In fact, she was beginning to suspect that something more than friendship existed between him and Gwen. Or was that wishful thinking on her part?

"She's a ray of sunshine," commented Ancarat after they had consumed their fill of honey cakes and fresh milk. "She reminds me of you at that age. Sweet as can be."

Cadfan scoffed. "Your memory's as crooked as an old fence, woman. When Ria was that age, she'd sooner be up a tree than sitting quiet with dolls."

"Aww, don't be so mean," said Gwen. "Butter wouldn't have melted in Ria's mouth. I remember being jealous of her, sweet-talking everyone into doing what she wanted."

"As I said, just like Ceridwen," chuckled Ancarat. "I bet she'll grow up to be just like you, Ria."

"I hope she grows up to be better than me," replied Ria. "She's had a rough start, but she's found a family. That's more than enough."

As soon as those words left her mouth, Ria's thoughts wandered unbidden to Brochfael, to the anniversary of their courtship marked by the solstice. That memory brushed against her lightly now, its sharp edges worn smooth by time. She watched Ceridwen pretend that the Armoricus doll was giving orders to the Cadfan one. What would her life be like now had Brochfael not been killed? It was an unanswerable question. She couldn't disentangle the love she had gained by becoming a mother from the horror that made that love possible. She told herself often that she would give it all up in a heartbeat to bring Ceridwen's family back from the dead, but deep down she knew that was a lie. She had not the heart to wish away her own blessing.

"Life really does have a way of working out, though," commented

Cadfan, as though reading her thoughts. "I think it's a sign of a good home that when bad things happen there's always good folk to help make them right. At least as right as can be. If the rest of the world worked that way, we'd all be as fine as frog's hair."

"There's too much hate out there, though," said Rhodri, joining their conversation for the first time. "Hate is what killed her family. And hate's still out there, walking free. That Muconius—he was seen down by the river again. Why can't anyone catch him?"

Ria recoiled at the mention of the man from her nightmares. Muconius's menace had only grown since he had threatened Publius by the chapel. In the days since then, he'd been spotted a few more times, but never at a time or place where anything could be done about it. People had the feeling he was letting himself be seen.

"And to think that man used to come into our home," said Ancarat. "I wish he had choked on the bread I used to make for him."

"Goes to show that trying to make things right isn't always the right thing to do," suggested Gwen. "Maybe . . . maybe the others were right. About the refugees. Maybe we should have told them to keep moving."

"No," replied Ria firmly. "Trying to do the right thing can never be wrong, even if it ends wrong. As I see it, it's the intention that counts. Each of us can intend the right thing even if we can't always do it well or at all. And it's not our fault if other people make the good we intend bad."

"You sound like the priest," laughed Rhodri. "Are you thinking about becoming a holy woman?"

Ria flushed with annoyance. She recalled Drichan's suggestion after she had fled from Rhodri's proposal and felt it wrong that he of all people should now make a jest of it, even in ignorance. She forced herself to push past her irritation. "I've seen enough to know this much: the world needs more kindness, not less."

Rhodri shrugged. "Kindness won't stop a man like Muconius or Crassula, or the Irish or whoever it was that murdered Ceridwen's family. That's what strength is for. I suppose that's why tillers of the soil like us also need people like Meurig and Cunicatus. Without them, we'd all be in trouble."

"I could always do with a strong man like them," interjected Gwen with a wicked grin.

This time Ria did see the look. When Gwen had spoken, she had glanced at Rhodri, and he at her. She was pretty certain then that the two had begun to court. She was glad of it and thought she would press Gwen for details when they met that evening at the bonfire.

Ancarat handed Ceridwen and Rusticella's cups down to them. "Finish these up, girls. We need to clear up and get started on our chores."

As the others rose from their seats to help clear away the tables, Ria asked, "Do you really think we depend on people like Meurig and Cunicatus?"

"Seems pretty obvious to me," replied Rhodri. "Where'd we be now without them?"

"I wonder sometimes," said Ria. "It seems to me that it always comes back to who's the strongest. Why is it strength that's most important? Why not love and kindness?"

"That's just girl talk," laughed Rhodri. "Love and kindness won't protect you against evil men. They didn't help you . . . " He trailed off after Gwen shot him an evil look.

Ria clucked. "That's not what I'm saying. I'm not talking about the world. Who am I to talk about the world? But look at our home. People here are good folk. We've got some bad eggs, but we mostly look after each other. Why is that? It's not because the Dominus is a strong warrior or we're afraid of Meurig and Cunicatus. People here are simply good, honest folk."

"Yes, but we all know each other," said Cadfan as they started towards the door to the kitchen. "Hell, we all go back generations here. We've learned to rub along with each other. And everyone knows that they'll get a boot up their arse from me if they misbehave."

"Oh, Dad, you know that isn't true," replied Ria as she put her arm around her father. "I wonder if the problem in the world is that there are too many strangers and not enough neighbours. Neighbours seem to get along somehow, even when they don't get along, if you get my meaning. It's harder to be too unkind to people you're stuck with."

"Fat lot of good any of that does us," grumbled Cadfan. "No one can know everybody, which is why I say that we should just try to do what's right with the people around us and to hell with everyone else. All you can do is hope other folk have good folk looking after them."

"You all are just a barrel of fun at a party," laughed Rhodri as he made to leave. "I'll make sure not to spend too much time with you at the feast tonight!"

Ria watched Gwen skip over to Rhodri's side as he left. Ancarat leaned over to her. "I think those two are sweet on each other," she said with a conspiratorial tone. "That must be a relief to you."

Ria nodded. "But not for the reasons you're thinking, Mamma. I'm just glad they've both found someone."

"And what about you? When will we find someone for you?"

Ria nearly knocked the plates out of her mother's hands as she turned and hugged her. "With good folks around me trying to do what's right, I'm sure to end up with someone eventually, whether I like it or not."

"Don't you want a man?" asked Ancarat.

Ria chuckled. "Oh, Mamma, you never stop. All I can say is that I don't not want a man, if you get what I mean. But I'm in no rush to find one either. I'm learning that I can stand well enough on my own two feet." Then she added, "As long as I have the mighty Publius keeping an eye out for me!"

"I just don't want you to be lonely."

Now Ria really did laugh. "Mamma, if there's one thing you don't have to worry about, it's my being lonely. Who could ever be lonely here? As Daddy says, there's too many good folks looking out for me. I'll be just fine."

Feeling happy with the world, Ria went to find the Domina and start the jobs she knew had to be done for the feast. Rhodri was right, there was too much hatred in the world. There wasn't much she could do about that except make sure she didn't add to it herself. She realized then that one of the things she loved about her *familia*, thanks in no small part to Corotica and Armoricus, was that it wasn't adding any hatred to the world.

If God was keeping a ledger for the villa's morals like her father did for its production, then she had no doubt its credit was excellent.

She decided that that was about as much as anyone could hope for. She just hoped it would be enough to see them through a world that seemed to lack the sense to do the same.

XXIX

"I thought we were staying all summer," complained Patricius. "I don't want to go home."

"It won't be for long," reassured Baglan as he adjusted his hat to block out the hot rays of the sun. "A few days. A week at most."

"But why?"

"There's a debt I must repay." Baglan thought again of poor Gwas, captive in the mines. He had feared that the little man would die before he could rescue him, but Potitus had assured him that he still lived.

"Won't Grandfather give you the money? Have you asked?"

"It's not that kind of debt."

"What kind is it?"

He sighed and knelt down to meet Patricius's gaze. "A debt of honour," he explained. "I owe my life to a kind and holy man who once saved me. When I was near dead, his kindness brought me back to life. Doesn't your Christ command everyone to do to others as you would have them do to you? Well, that's what I must do."

Patricius tilted his head, considering. "Can I come with you, then?"

"No, lad," Baglan said, resting a steadying hand on the boy's shoulder. "Look, I won't be gone long. You'll be safe at home with your parents. When I'm back, we'll fetch some supplies and be back up on those hills with the whole summer ahead of us. Besides, you'll have the Midsummer festivities to enjoy. That'll be something, won't it?"

"I suppose," muttered Patricius in a tone that suggested that he did not, in fact, suppose.

A couple of Potitus's farmhands arrived a little later to tend the flock while Baglan and Patricius were away. Baglan grabbed his bag of supplies, attached it to the end of his crook, and flung it over his shoulder. "Let's get going, Patricius. It's a fine afternoon for a long walk."

The two chatted contentedly as they made their way through the high bracken and down the wooded hillside towards the town. An hour or so later, they found Patricius's grandfather chatting with a group of men in the street outside the doors of his villa. When Potitus saw Baglan, he stepped away from his companions to embrace his grandson. Baglan tried to make light conversation with Potitus to mask his unease, but he suspected that Patricius was too perceptive to be fooled by their banter. A few minutes later, a small, wiry man covered in tattoos arrived and gave a nod to Potitus.

"It's time," he said. Then he looked at Patricius. "Run along inside. Supper should be waiting."

For a moment, the boy hesitated. Then, as if sensing the weight of what lay unspoken, he turned and threw his arms around Baglan. The embrace was fierce and quick, and it nearly undid him.

Baglan stooped down and returned the hug. "I'll be back before you know it. You behave yourself in the meantime. You've become quite the shepherd these past weeks. I've not told you that before, and maybe I should have. I've been remiss in that—saying what needs saying. I didn't tell my old family how much I loved them often enough. I don't think I ever told my boy how proud I was of him. But you, Patricius—you've all the makings of a fine shepherd. You can't say fairer than that. I don't expect you'll become one—you'll be the master of this fine villa—but I think if you look after your people like you do the flock, you'll be a good man. I may not be your daddy, but I'm proud enough to be. Now, get yourself inside. I'll see you soon."

Baglan thanked the gods that Patricius obeyed without looking back.

The plan to rescue Gwas was a simple one based on an assumption: that the guards and workmen would not be able to keep away from the festivities that evening. It was the longest day of the year—a day not to be ignored—and the lure of wine, music and women would be too much for them to resist. It wasn't a foolproof plan—far from it—but it was the best they had.

"My guess," said Potitus after Patricius was safely indoors, "is there'll be only a few sullen guards left by nightfall. The rest will be at the party."

The small man nodded. "That's usually what happened when I worked up there. A few of us used to sneak down after dark for a drink too. Half of those that stay behind will be drunk."

"This fine fellow is Brutus," explained Potitus as they began to walk together down the street. "He used to be a guard at the mines. But he became a Christian and afterwards felt that he couldn't continue working up there."

"Hard to love your neighbour when you're working him to death," he explained.

"What do you do now?"

"Flower arranging," he replied matter-of-factly.

As they entered the forum, they were immediately swallowed up by a crowd of people, many of them already visibly drunk, milling around food stalls or gathered in noisy groups by the unlit bonfire. "I'll go first, as though it's a routine visit," shouted Potitus over the din. "I'll try to find where your friend is kept. You and Brutus wait by the wagons near the tannery. You don't actually need to do anything, Baglan, but wait here. If Gwas is locked up, Brutus can break him out."

"No," replied Baglan. "I think it best if I come. Gwas knows me. I think he's more likely to come quietly if I'm around. But I might say the same thing to you, Potitus. You've got too much to lose if things go wrong. Just tell me where he is, and I'll go alone. This is only my risk to take."

"Don't be obtuse," replied Potitus. "How could I let pass the opportunity for a dignified Roman priest to help rescue a mad druid? I do rather hope news of this somehow gets back to my son and his wife."

As no traffic was going up the street in the direction of the mines, they decided to split up earlier than planned. Baglan and Brutus loitered by a cistern for a few minutes while Potitus continued ahead. Once he was far enough in front for no one to associate them together, they continued walking until they reached a jumble of discarded waggons near the tannery. They crouched down in between two of these, though it was hardly necessary given how empty the area was.

The din in Bonaven Taberniae swelled to a crescendo as a bright flickering glow began to grow from the forum. Baglan offered his own prayer of thanksgiving to Luga for providing such an auspicious moment for him to repay his debt to Gwas. He thought about the lonely Stone and wondered whether it was returning to the stream to drink. He hoped it was, and that the power he had felt within it would extend across the intervening miles to bless him. If the old gods still had any strength left in them, he needed it tonight.

"Our supposition has proved true," said Potitus when he finally returned. "There are hardly any guards. Most of the workmen seem to be in town and the ones who remain are either under lock and key or too poorly to join the revels. Two of the guards I spoke to were already in their cups."

"What about Gwas?" asked Baglan. Brutus waved his hand for them to duck down as two men walked down the street past them.

"Two fewer for us to worry about," whispered Potitus. "That leaves only four or five. I couldn't find Gwas, not without being obvious. I'm afraid we can't even be sure he's alive."

"What now?" asked Brutus.

"That's up to you, Baglan. Do you still wish to go through with this?"

"Yes. I owe it to Gwas to try, whatever the consequences to me."

"Just to make sure you understand what those are: if you're caught, there'll be little I can do to help you. Are you willing to risk that?" asked Potitus.

"I am."

"Then, my friend, this is where we part ways. I will station myself on the road to delay anyone who might be returning to the mines, though there's little likelihood of that happening soon. You and Brutus know the layout well. Here's where I found the guards." Potitus drew a diagram of the compound in the dirt with a stick. "They didn't seem to be patrolling, so they'll probably still be there. You'd better get going now. Whatever happens, Baglan, you have a long night ahead of you. God be with you."

Without further word, Potitus walked back out onto the street. The sun was now yielding slowly to a crimson sky. *A shepherd's sky*, thought Baglan.

Potitus signalled that all was clear, and Brutus led Baglan around the waggons and across the tanner's yard towards the low boundary walls of the mines. They clambered over this with ease and scurried into the shadows of one of the outer buildings to listen for any indication of an alarm. But the precincts remained quiet except for a soft moaning coming from one building and the distant sound of two men singing somewhere near the headquarters.

"Where do we start?" whispered Brutus. "We'll have to be careful or we'll raise a din if we go into the wrong place."

"The medical building," Baglan replied. "If he's injured, that's where they'd put him."

"Agreed. Let's take the long way around the workmen's quarters. There's less chance of being seen that way."

They crept around the back of the first building, stopping at the corner to listen before dashing into the shadows of the next. Inside, they could hear the sound of stabled horses as well as a couple of men playing knucklebones. It was only then that Baglan had an alarming thought about the dogs. They hadn't considered the guard dogs, which would almost certainly realize their presence before they reached the medical building.

When he pointed this out to Brutus, the little man smiled. "We forgot to mention that I was in charge of the hounds when I worked here. Don't you worry. They'll know me."

"I really hope you're right," breathed Baglan as they continued on their way.

They reached the rows of workmen's barracks without incident and moved quickly along the rear of these with little fear of being seen. Only when they reached the final one did they crouch down again and listen. A few seconds later, two men walked by, but they were too preoccupied with their conversation to notice them in the shadows. Once they were far enough away, Baglan and Brutus walked briskly across the wide avenue and ducked down behind a pile of slag. Baglan's heart was racing, and he felt a growing urge to relieve himself. *Calm yourself*, he thought without any sign that his body might be listening.

They reached the medical building. Though the sun had not yet given up its light for the day, it was now dark enough for them to move more cautiously to avoid tripping over unseen obstacles. The hairline curve of a waxing crescent moon hung beneath the first stars, hardly shedding any light for them to see by. Few lamps had been lit except at the doorways of each building and in the central square. It wasn't long before they would be in almost complete darkness.

They found the back door of the medical building unlocked. "I'll wait here while you go inside," whispered Brutus. "If Gwas is in there, he's unlikely to be chained up. But get me if he is. I'll knock twice on the door if I hear someone coming."

The air was ripe with the smell of unwashed bodies and damp straw. The faint sound of breathing marked the presence of the injured and sick. Baglan moved carefully, his hands groping in the darkness along the rows of beds. He knew there to be around twenty—ten on each side—but he had to go by sound to know which were occupied. How he would find Gwas among them, he did not know. Yet, he moved forward, determined hope pulling him onward.

He had reached the first occupied bed when a deep, baritone voice rose outside, cutting through the stillness like the first bird of morning. He stopped, breath held. The voice was weaker than he remembered, weak and thin, but unmistakable. Gwas. Baglan quickly slipped back out and quietly closed the door behind him.

"That'll be your friend, I reckon," murmured Brutus. "He must be over by the headquarters."

Gwas's voice carried through the air, rising in song—an elegy for the sun so old that it seemed drawn from the land itself. Baglan knew it well; he had sung it many times himself to mark the turn of the year, the moment when the days, having stretched to their fullest, began their slow, reluctant retreat into darkness. As Gwas's voice strengthened, Baglan felt the past and present merge into one. The elegy grew, joined by other voices from the encampment—first hesitant, then sure, until it became a chorus that filled the air, its sound echoing along the alleyways. Nearby, Baglan and Brutus saw two guards, too drunk to stand steadily on their feet, giving full voice to the hymn as they faced towards a westward sky where the last smudge of red was now fading to black.

By the time they found Gwas, the sun had set and his elegy had ended. He finished it abruptly in mid-verse, as though his rhapsody had been the haunting chords of the dying rays, a surrender to the encroaching darkness. For a long moment, the silence seemed immense, infinite, stretching upward to the stars that had begun to appear in the night sky. But then Baglan realized that he was wrong. Gwas's elegy wasn't a surrender at all—as he was singing, the raucous hum of the town's revelry had been growing louder. He may have bidden farewell to the waxing daylight, but his song seemed also to welcome the riotous joy of the night. Day and night, light and darkness—not adversaries but companions, bound in an endless turning that Baglan knew to be the world's soul.

They found Gwas chained to a post near the latrines, beyond the headquarters. He was so small and frail that they would never have found him had his song not drawn them to him. He lay curled up like a scrawny cat, muttering incoherently to himself. It was too dark for Baglan to see him clearly, but he could tell that he was in poor shape. He seemed more like a child's forgotten toy than the man Baglan remembered.

Brutus crouched by the chain, working quickly to unlock the manacle around Gwas's ankle. Baglan knelt beside him and spoke softly. "Gwas, it's me," he said. "You saved me once, in the wilderness. I've come to repay that debt. I've come to rescue you."

But Gwas's rambling mutter continued uninterrupted. He seemed oblivious to them, lost in a fog of exhaustion and madness. He was so frail and pitiful that the guards hadn't bothered to secure him firmly. Brutus freed him quickly and lifted him gently into Baglan's arms. He was shockingly light; little more than bones inside a thinly stretched bag of skin. Gwas stirred faintly but gave no other sign of comprehension.

They returned to Potitus unnoticed. The din of the Midsummer's festival was so loud that there was no need for them to be particularly cautious. All the same, they spoke little as they skirted the northern boundary of the town, keeping well away from the fort until they came to a small stand of beeches above the river that marked the boundary of the wilderness. Beyond in the darkness lay the broad expanse of the bog and beyond that the old road that Baglan had followed to Bonaven Taberniae. There, a donkey with Baglan's supplies was waiting for them.

"This is where we say our farewells for now," said Potitus as Brutus helped Baglan secure Gwas to the back of the ass. "I hope your friend recovers. But are you sure you don't want to bring him back to my villa for proper care? It's safe enough."

"Thank you, but no. I think I know what he needs. And I'll take him there, though I fear it may already be too late." He paused, as he considered what he must do. "Tell Patricius—tell him that I may be gone longer than I planned. Gwas needs me now, and I'll stay with him for as long as I must. But I'll return. Assure him of that."

Potitus stood silently for a moment, studying his friend in the darkness. "Do what you have to, Baglan. Keep safe. Remember the road is now being used by brigands and thieves. Watch yourself."

"I will," Baglan replied. He hesitated, then added, "Thank you for everything. I have always known the kindness of my own people. But you—and Gwas—have taught me something even better: the kindness of strangers."

Potitus embraced him. "Without such kindness, there could be no friendship. Whatever God wills for us, Baglan, remember this: we will always be friends."

—

Corotica found her husband resting against the old beech log at the edge of their land, his straw hat pulled low over his eyes, the short crook still in his hand. His head was turned away from the hustle and bustle of the villa towards the eastern range of the mountains. She had known he would be here; it was his refuge where he could steady himself before the heavy weather of socializing.

"It's almost time," she said as she nestled herself next to him. Only then did she notice the two men with spears standing guard in the shadows of the woods. Their silent vigilance was a reminder of how much had changed. Once, the idea of guards hovering nearby would have been unthinkable.

"I know," he sighed. "It looks to be a fine night for it. Even from here, I can smell the ox turning on the spit."

They sat in a loving wordlessness for a few minutes before Armoricus said, "I've been thinking about last year's festivities and how different the world was then. No, that's not right. The world was the same then as I suppose it always has been. But *our* world was different. I wonder what it will be like next year."

Corotica detected her husband's mood, not quite despair but near to it. She leaned her head gently against his shoulder. "Whatever comes," she said, "you'll see us through it. You always do."

He didn't respond to her confidence but instead said, "I've been watching the way the sun lights the old hillfort. I didn't tell you, but I went up there the other day."

"You shouldn't have," interrupted Corotica. "Not with Muconius still lurking."

"If I run into that man, I'll deal with him," he replied with some of his old assertiveness. "But the odds of him finding me in the woods are slim enough. I felt I had to go."

"Why?"

"I've been thinking about stories," he said. "I was talking to Publius about the people who used to live in that hillfort, how their lives and stories have been swallowed up by time. It got me wondering about us— our home, our *familia*."

Corotica chuckled. "You do fill that boy's head with strange notions. No wonder he's so fanciful."

"I've built my life on the idea that my duty is to this place. To care for it, preserve it, honour it in the way my forefathers did. I've cared for the soil, the animals, the fields. But I mainly left the welfare of the members of our household to you, not least because you're so much better at that than I. I've always imagined our place to be like an island—perhaps too much so—detached from the mad world out there. Virgil's *Georgics* is a bit like that:

> *The farmer who works the soil with his curved plough;*
> *This is the work he does, and it sustains*
> *His country, and his family, and his cattle,*
> *His worthy bullocks and his herd of cows.*

Nothing there about maintaining roads or trading or buying slaves like you find in Cato the Elder or even Varro. I suppose I've never been happy with running a farm—I've always aimed higher. I've wanted to create paradise."

"You've done a fair job at being Adam."

"Maybe," he replied, still lost in his thoughts. "But perhaps like him, I've been too eager to play God, at least the God of this place."

"What are you trying to say, my love?"

"I'm not sure I know," he admitted. "That's why I went to the hillfort—to look for answers, though it may be madness to look for answers among ghosts. At first, standing there, all I felt was futility. Places like that make the world seem so ancient. Drichan says it is, that we're in the sixth and final age of a tired, old world. But it doesn't feel old to me. It never feels that way to a farmer, I think. The world I know is always being reborn. Winter yields to spring and dead earth returns to life with the bounty of the new year. I never needed Pascha to teach me that. I've always known it."

He paused, his voice quieter when he spoke again. "The futility I felt wasn't in the land. It was in us. The world is forever young. But what we build—our cities, our empires—those grow old. They crumble. Like Rome."

Corotica could feel him turning something over, working his way towards a conclusion. She stayed quiet, resting against him, letting him speak in his own time.

"On the way back, I passed Empress Oak. What a tree she is! For generations, people have worshipped her, offered prayers and gifts at her roots. Less so, perhaps, now that we've all become good Christians, but there are enough offerings there now to cause Drichan sleepless nights, if he only knew. I suppose when that tree was still only an acorn, the people who lived in the hillfort were still remembered. Stories were probably told about them, maybe even some of the same stories its occupants told themselves. That was long before we Rusticelii arrived. Maybe before Caesar himself came to Britannia. And yet, for all that, she's just an oak. She has no mind, no soul. She blesses no one, except by being herself—by growing, reaching for the sun, scattering acorns for the next generation. She does what an oak does. And I envy her for it."

He turned to look at her. "And that is where I found my answer. I've worked hard to ensure our future, a future that now seems impossibly remote. I've worried too about honouring our ancestors by ensuring that they're remembered by future generations. But neither of those things has ever been in my hands. Like Empress Oak, I can only be who I am, can only do what God has placed me here to do. I see now that the virtue I have always sought for myself is not a tool, not a means to an end. It's the thing itself. It's more like the crops we raise. What I'm trying to say is that I now realize that the good life involves nothing more than simply being good, by which I mean loving the people and the place that is ours now. And when you see that, you see also that so much of this world's evil is rooted either in fearing loss or the future. We find it hard to understand that it's the nature of the past to be lost and of the future to elude us. But whether we live our lives well or badly, people will always go on being people, no better or worse than people have always been."

She frowned slightly, not yet convinced. "But doesn't that make it all futile? If it doesn't last, if none of it matters in the end—what's the point?"

"That's the mistake we make—thinking there has to be some grand purpose for us to pursue. Rome has always claimed to civilize the world. We've justified our wars, our conquests, by saying we bring a better way of life. But what has it come to? Rome is falling, at least here in Britannia. And I don't think much of what we've done will endure."

His gaze drifted back to the hills. "But then I asked myself: are the cities we've built, the armies we've raised, really more important than what we've nurtured here? I don't think so. I can imagine a world without Rome, but not a world without the love we've known here—between us, with our children, our household. *That* love, *that* care—that's what makes a good life. Knowing that I've never done anything other than try to sustain that love is sufficient. I need nothing more. That for me is the good life; that is what it means to be not just blessed but also a blessing to others. I think you, my wise wife, have always known that better than I."

As her husband spoke, Corotica felt how full her heart was with love for him: this good and honest man. Now she saw the truth in his words, the beauty of it. It was the foundation for their own love as well as the care they'd shown for their home. Armoricus's love was strong enough to make the villa a home for everyone who belonged there. She could see now that the villa was their home only because his expansive yet quiet love had made it so. And his love for her was such that it freed her to love others better than she would have otherwise. Armoricus and she had not just known the good life, they had built it together. That was all the paradise either of them needed.

The Villa

The villa pulsed with life, a heartbeat of song and laughter carrying over the fields. Men and women, boys and girls, the young and old (and quite a few dogs) greeted Midsummer's Night with the kind of unrestrained revelry that blooms from the soil of hardship. Musicians strummed, thrummed, banged and blew one lively tune after another, with all the crude talent of a small village but with the zeal of a street party.

Amid the happy throng roared the great bonfire. Flames leapt into the night, sending sparks spiralling upward like fireflies joining the constellations. The heat rolled outward in waves, forcing the crowd to keep their distance until the blaze waned enough for more wood to be added. Its light played upon the villa's walls and the fields beyond, illuminating the scene with a flickering glow that seemed to pulse with the music and laughter.

People danced and cavorted to the music; some tunes had them dancing in wide, jubilant circles around the bonfire, and some folk dances had them whooping and laughing while Cadfan or even Quercus called out the movements. At other times, couples paired off to whirl together, their movements full of energy if not always grace. In quieter moments, the crowd gathered in clusters, leaning close to share stories, sing along with a ballad, or simply sip from mugs of cider.

The villa had not seen such a Midsummer's Night in years. The winter's influx of refugees had swelled the household; it wasn't until people had started to wander up from the hamlet and the surrounding tenant farms that they realized how large the household had become. Thankfully, many brought gifts of food, adding to the feast that Ancarat and her kitchen had worked tirelessly to prepare. Cadfan, ever practical, had anticipated the crowd and arranged for two oxen to be slaughtered and roasted over slow fires. Their rich aroma mingled with the sweetness of cider and the woodsmoke of the bonfire.

That night, too, the *familia* came together in countless encounters. Labourers, who usually grumbled about the weather or stubborn livestock, renewed friendships with ribald jokes, good-natured ribbing and the swell of laughter. Women, who had quarrelled over trifles days before, now banded together to mock their menfolk for their clumsy feet or to encourage with lewd enthusiasm their girls to pursue shy suitors. The old men sat around telling the same old stories as though they were new ones while the elderly women reminisced about when they were young. Young lovers danced to exhaustion before retiring to dark corners to make love with sweet words and kisses just as their parents and grandparents had done in their time. Even the dogs seemed to share in the merriment, darting between groups of dancers, tails wagging furiously.

At the height of the festivities, Aongus was finally invited to perform. The change in the mood was palpable as he stepped into the firelight. The crowd grew quiet, greeting the Irish bard only with soft murmurs and ragged clapping. But Aongus was no amateur minstrel brought in only after drink had softened the audience. He had entertained lords and kings and performed at more festivals than he could recall. It was not for nothing that he was a renowned bard, a teller of tales and a weaver of words. He took their suppressed hostility in his stride.

When he began to sing, his voice was to the ears like honey to the tongue. None could long resist its practised beauty which, like magic, charmed them all, seducing them with and into his words. He began with their songs—ballads and elegies everyone knew well. Hearing an Irishman sing their own stories with beauty and reverence captivated his audience. He demonstrated in song after song that he had not only taken the time to learn their ballads, their elegies and their epics, but he had also respected their stories enough to apply his own skill to their retelling. And he sang them all in their own tongue.

As he sang, Aongus began to weave new threads into the old fabric, eloquently blending Roman, Silurian and Irish stories. His songs never invoked the great Romans, Silurian heroes of old, and definitely not the prowess of the Irish. Instead, he sang of the quiet dignity of those who tilled the soil, tended flocks and carved their existence from the land. His themes were timeless: the turning of seasons, the cycles of planting and harvest, the hearth and the home. He sang not of glory but of the goodness found in humble work, the joy of honest labour, and the enduring bond between people and the earth. He sang their lives back to them, and they received it as tribute more valuable than gold.

The crowd swayed with his melodies, laughing and weeping in turn. Aongus touched something deep in them, drawing out yearnings and cherished hopes, and awaking possibilities that none had dreamt of. His performance ended with his extending his hand to Corotica and Armoricus to partner for a dance, an invitation they could not refuse.

When Aongus bowed at last, the crowd roared their approval, stamping feet and whistling. In that moment, all grudges and suspicions fell away. The Irish bard, once a stranger, had become a friend. It was the climax of a Midsummer's Night that none of them would ever forget.

And so, under the endless sweep of the night sky, all the troubles of the world were banished, even dispelled. Time itself could have little meaning in festivities almost entirely untouched by it, where the ghosts of their ancestors would have felt entirely welcome—and, indeed, were welcomed in the memories shared and the toasts offered to them. It was a moment when the old felt young again, and the young could sense themselves living out memories they would one day recount in their dotage. If the villa had been alive, she would have purred like a nursing cat or clucked like a hen with her gathered chicks. In fact, in the joy of that community, she came to life—and that life was the love of her people.

XXXI

The attack early the next morning was as swift as a falcon's strike and just as deadly. It began with fire.

Despite the late night, Drichan had risen at dawn to welcome the morning with his daily devotions. He walked half asleep from his doorway onto the veranda and down into the courtyard. The villa still slept. The only sounds were low voices in the barn and the gentle snoring of a farmhand slumped fast asleep against a bale of hay outside the bathhouse. Something flickered at the edge of his vision—a shadow that didn't belong—but he paid it no attention as he turned towards the chapel.

The sanctuary light glowed brightly in the gloom of the chapel as he approached with a taper with which he lit a series of lamps. The darkness gradually faded into a soft orange ochre, revealing the small altar and the desk on which his treasured books lay. He didn't feel much like praying that morning and had to resist the urge to say a perfunctory paternoster and slip back into bed. Who would know except his Redeemer?

He opened his psalter and grudgingly began to recite Psalm XVII:

> *I will love you, O Lord, my strength:*
> > *The Lord is my firmament, my refuge, and my deliverer.*
> *My God is my helper, and in him will I put my trust.*
> > *My protector and the horn of my salvation, and my support.*

God was indeed their fortress, the one who would deliver them from their enemies and uphold them by the strength of his arm. Though the *sorrows of death surrounded them, and the torrents of iniquity troubled them*, God would always be their strong helper.

The words, like the rising light, were slow to pierce his weariness. His mind wandered back to the Midsummer's festivities. Aongus's eloquence had lit a spark, one Drichan hoped to fan into steady flame with a sermon he had been preparing on the *Nunc dimittis*. The call to be a "light to lighten the Gentiles" might seem grandiose, but he was sure he could use it to suggest that the villa needn't be a victim of the enshrouding darkness but a light that could dispel it. The key was Cormac's baptism. He would leave with Aongus immediately after the Sunday Eucharist to effect that. Drichan felt confident in his divine mission. *My God is my helper, and in him will I put my trust.*

His fingers traced the words of the psalm as he continued to recite the verses in a low whisper. A line caught his attention:

> *There went up a smoke in his wrath: and a fire flamed from his face:*
> *coals were kindled by it.*

Smoke. A prickling unease stirred in him. Something he had seen earlier, something that had teased the edge of his awareness. Smoke. He closed the psalter and rose abruptly. He began to feel that his dulled mind hadn't registered something important. The flicker in the courtyard—he remembered it now. A tendril of smoke, faint but unmistakable, curling up from the barn.

Drichan leapt to his feet and stumbled out of the chapel. No longer a tendril, smoke now poured out of the barn's loft window, billowing into the sky in a great column flaked with the bright embers of drifting straw. Inside, the horses had now begun to neigh with a frantic terror that was terrible to hear.

"Fire," he said to himself as though he needed to hear the word to confirm what he saw. "Fire!" he cried out a second time and again "Fire! The barn is on fire! Awake! Awake!"

Cadfan and Armoricus appeared from their rooms. Cadfan was the quicker and immediately ran over to the villa's bell. He clanged it furiously as he and Armoricus joined in Drichan's cry: "Fire! Fire!"

Meurig and Cunicatus tumbled outside and charged over to the barn where they were met by a few men, including the one who had been asleep by the bathhouse. Shielding their faces in the crook of their arms, they disappeared through the smoke into the barn's doorway. Moments later, the horses burst out in a wild stampede, their eyes rolling white with fear.

One man was knocked down in their frenzy. Drichan ran over to him and dragged him safely away.

"It's no use," called Meurig as he and Cunicatus reappeared with faces blackened by soot. "The fire's too far gone. We need to protect the other buildings."

"Go and rouse the hamlet!" ordered Armoricus to a couple of women who were standing close to him with their mouths agape.

The courtyard became a hive of desperate activity. Buckets were fetched from the villa and bathhouse, and immersed in the rain-filled cistern. Corotica and Ancarat formed a line of people to pass the buckets, hand to hand, though it was clear even then that their efforts would be dwarfed by the fire's fury. Smoke thickened the air, stinging eyes and choking lungs. Drichan could feel its heat against his skin, relentless and searing.

Then, a sharp sound—a whistling, almost musical like a skylark—cut through the chaos. Drichan ducked instinctively and at that same moment saw Cunicatus drop backwards to the ground as though he'd slipped on ice. Drichan was just about to step over to help him back up when to his horror a pool of crimson, dark against the pale dirt, began spreading beneath his head and around a small stone that lay by his cheek. The warrior's eyes stared blankly at the sky above. As Drichan stooped down to sign Cunicatus's forehead with a cross, a verse from Psalm XVII sprang to mind:

> *The Lord bowed the heavens, and came down:*
> *and darkness was under his feet.*

It was then that Drichan understood how sorely mistaken he had been. God would not restrain his wrath.

—

"We're under attack!" came voices from the far side of the chapel followed by the guttural cries that reminded Publius of dogs scrapping over their kill. He leapt out of bed, pulled on his tunica, and crossed over to his window.

What he saw froze him where he stood. A group of men—a score at least—were surging across the fields towards the villa. They carried clubs, axes, spears, and long knives glinting faintly in the pale light. Their movements were wild, their faces twisted with rage, their cries guttural and strange.

For a moment, he could do nothing but stare. His small body felt paralyzed by fear. Where could he go? What could he do? The room that had always seemed safe now felt like a trap, its walls closing in around him. He thought of hiding under the bed, but the space was too narrow. His limbs trembled, and his breath came shallow and quick.

From somewhere outside, he heard Meurig's voice rise above the din: "To arms! To arms!" The villa came alive with the sound of struggling men and screaming women while in the background roared the dreadful sound of the inferno. The clamour of it was too terrible for Publius to endure.

He was on the verge of collapsing in a flood of tears when he heard the unmistakable sound of his sister screaming. At once, he knew what was required of him. Whatever the danger, he was her brother, her protector, and she needed him to be brave. He knew he must also be swift and canny. If the assailants were ravenous wolves, then he would be the stag: too fierce and free for them to catch or harm.

Summoning the image of the forest's guardian to give him courage, he threw open the door and ran out onto the veranda, ducking past people he didn't even stop to recognize. He sensed the violence around him without ever actually seeing it. He kept his head low, his focus sharp, as blind to the scenes of battle and broken bodies as he was to his own peril. It was as if he were sprinting through a dense forest, skirting and skipping around trees and eluding the entangling clutch of briars. He found his sister huddled in the corner of the dining room next to a man lying face down on the floor. For a terrible moment, he thought her dead. But when he reached for her, she looked up with such relief that he knew he could not fail her.

"To the bathhouse, Rusticella," he cried. "Take my hand and follow me."

She obeyed wordlessly as Publius dragged her through the melee and out onto the veranda where they were greeted by an apocalyptic vision. To their right, the heat of the barn, now utterly consumed by fire, seared them with such fury that they were forced back towards the chapel and the heart of the battle. In the courtyard men and women fought in a desperate struggle amidst the smoke, the scattered dead and grievously wounded. Publius saw his parents protected by Meurig and a few other men, fighting with their backs to the old fountain. Others were resisting with whatever was at hand.

Publius never stopped. He was the stag, fearless and uncatchable. Holding tightly to Rusticella's hand, he skipped along the edge of the veranda, drawing as close as he could bear to the burning barn. Here, the heat was too intense for any combatants, and so their way was clear. Ignoring Rusticella's screams and his own burning skin, he ran along the barn and past the fiery maw of the barn's door. They passed Cunicatus's corpse, sizzling repulsively in the heat of the fire, without even recognizing him.

The struggle had not yet reached the bathhouse. Publius hesitated, considering hiding among the clutter piled against the walls. But he knew they needed a place where no one would think to look. The attackers would search everywhere above ground. They had to go below.

"The hypocaust," he said, more to himself than to Rusticella.

They were just about to continue when a sound stopped him—a faint whimper, barely audible over the noise outside. He turned and saw a small girl crouched behind a pile of grain sacks, clutching a doll to her chest. Her face was streaked with tears.

"Ceridwen?" he gently inquired. She nodded, her sobs subsiding at the sound of his voice. "It's me, Publius. Come on. We're going to a safe place. We must hurry."

She hesitated but then reached for his hand. He pulled her out from behind the sacks and led both girls towards the hypocaust. They passed through the carpenter's workshop, where Riderch and Rhodri and half a dozen men were fending off attackers with hammers and chisels. The master carpenter saw them and barked, "You know where to hide, lad! And don't come out until you know it's safe!"

Publius kept moving with the two girls, stopping only at the door briefly to let through Owain the smith and half a dozen men armed with the tools of their trade. Then they bustled into the gloomy chamber where their ancestors once luxuriated in hot water. Quickly reaching the hidden entrance into the hypocaust, they slipped unseen and unheard into the safety of the cavity. This time, Rusticella did not hesitate to enter and nor did Ceridwen, who was simply following his lead. Publius ushered the two of them through and pulled the crate back in front of the opening before following. They moved deeper into the space, feeling their way until they reached the supplies Cadfan had stored during the winter.

Publius pulled Rusticella and Ceridwen into his arms and held them tightly as the muffled sounds of battle echoed above and around them. In the terror of the darkness, they exchanged not a single word as they trembled with fear.

—

"Gather what you can but hurry," called Ancarat to Ria and Ceridwen as the bell outside rang.

As Ria began throwing a random assortment of belongings into a bag, she chanced to glance out of the back window. What she saw turned her blood to ice. Through the haze of heat and smoke, she made out the forms of men emerging from the southern woods. They carried weapons— makeshift clubs, axes, even spears—and their pace was relentless. Her breath caught, and the bag fell from her hands. *They don't know*, she thought wildly. The others—their minds focused on fighting the fire— hadn't yet noticed the approaching danger.

"Take my hand," she said to Ceridwen, reaching for her.

"But my dolls!" she complained, her voice trembling as she pulled away to gather her treasures.

Ria frantically rushed over and swept Ceridwen into her arms while grabbing the doll that Ancarat had made for her. Ceridwen cried out in protest, kicking and squealing, but Ria shoved the doll into her hands and hurried out onto the veranda.

"To arms! To arms!" shouted Meurig as Ria watched another group of attackers sweep around the chapel into the courtyard. Ancarat and

Corotica were organizing the bucket line, but the moment the attackers appeared, it dissolved into a scattering of screams and confusion. Through the inferno's shimmering heat, Ria glimpsed Cunicatus lying prone and Drichan signing his forehead with his thumb. But it was too much for her to comprehend.

The heat from the barn was too intense for her to enter the courtyard, and so she turned into the hallway that led to the orchard behind the villa. All she wanted now was to get Ceridwen to safety. But then she heard feet fast approaching and only barely had time to slip into the kitchen and slam the door before she heard a group of men charge past. Whether friend or foe, she could not tell.

She put Ceridwen back down but held onto her hand tightly. Her heart was pounding, but she felt no fear—not for herself. All her terror was for her daughter. There wasn't room in her mind amidst the chaos and confusion for more than those two thoughts. The kitchen felt stifling, its stone walls confining. Her eyes darted to the cast iron pan on the table, and she grabbed it, testing its weight. A poor weapon, but it was something. She moved towards the dining room.

She found two men there, one leaving through the outer door while the other raised his weapon for a strike. To her horror, she saw Rusticella cowering at his feet. The girl screamed. Ria moved without thinking. Releasing Ceridwen's hand, she swung the pan with all the strength her arms could muster. It struck the man squarely on the side of his head with a sickening crack. He crumpled, his body folding like a sack of grain.

Ria turned quickly, reaching for Ceridwen, but her heart sank. The girl was gone.

Before she could call out, two more men burst through the kitchen door. They were broad and rough, their words unintelligible, but their intent was clear. Rusticella had crumpled in the corner of the room, too low for the attackers to notice her. Ria knew she needed to draw them off if there was any chance of her escaping. So, she did the hardest thing she'd ever done: she abandoned Rusticella.

She backed towards the living room, the pan still raised, her grip sweaty but firm. The men followed, circling the table like wolves around prey.

"You cowardly Irish bastards," she screamed at the two men more to keep their attention than out of anger. "Well, you'll have to catch me first." Only later did it occur to her that they probably didn't understand a word she said.

She darted through the door, colliding with an attacker. Instinctively, she raised the pan, but the figure stumbled backward, a sword slicing through him from behind. "Ria!" came a familiar voice. She looked up to see Aurelius, his blade slick with blood.

"Two more behind me," she warned, breathless.

The room seemed to explode with movement. Men poured in from every direction, the clash of steel and cries of pain filling the air. She darted out of the way of the two men behind her as Aurelius and another man moved to engage them. She was frantic to find Ceridwen. By now, the room was such a tangle of furniture and fighting men that she found it almost impossible to navigate her way onto the veranda. To her astonishment, she saw Publius enter the room and start to weave around the combatants as though he were taking part in an elaborate dance. She saw a man move to skewer him, but she was close enough to hit him hard in the ribs with her pan. He groaned and tried to turn, but her blow caused him to trip over an upturned table. A moment later, he lay dying with a spear jutting into his stomach. The old mosaic floor ran red with blood.

Finally Ria managed to escape from the dining room onto the veranda where she found herself amidst a horrendous struggle. There was no chance to stop and take it all in. She was simply aware of the aggression: clashing weapons, the deafening sound of the burning barn, the groans of the fallen and the shrieks of women. Such was the horror of it all that she found it impossible to think. Panic overtook her and now she sought only one thing: safety. So, she ran, unmindful of where her feet might take her.

—

It was a day of grievous wounds and of death. It was a day for grief. But for Aurelius it was also a christening day: the moment when the old man became the new. The man who emerged from the smouldering ruin of his home that afternoon was as different from the one who had risen that morning as any Christian reborn in the waters of baptism. In ways that nobody then could perceive, his transformation signified the changing of their world, the exact moment that Rome became nothing more than a story to tell youngsters.

Aurelius's catechism was the battle itself. Meurig's alarm "To arms! To arms!" came like an altar call to which he responded with all the fervour of a new convert. He'd been preparing for this moment ever since his return from Isca Augusta. His newfound love for the villa burned more fiercely with his growing hatred for any who threatened it. There was no need for a struggle with moral ambiguities, no reason to come to some deeper knowledge of himself. Reflection yielded to action, and in that pure action Aurelius at last found freedom.

The moment he understood they were under attack, he ran back into his room, where a gladius hung on the wall. The sword was old but sturdy, brought back by Meurig from the city. Heavier than a play sword, it at first felt awkward in his grasp. But its balance was true and his arm strong—just holding it filled him with a sense of his own strength. The intimation of violence reflected in the sheen of its blade gave him a confidence he had never known. By that tool forged for hatred, he would prove his love for his *familia* and his worth to his father.

Aurelius stepped out onto the veranda, the sword in his hand transforming fanciful dreams of valour into grim reality. He was met by a brigand, armed only with a knife. The fight was swift and brutal; the man fell beneath the blade, his blood wetting the stones. He stood over him, breath heaving, the first lesson of his catechism learned: life was now measured in survival, strength and the shedding of an enemy's blood. With each swing of the gladius, he moved beyond reason, fighting his foes as fiercely as any beast driven by a biting and clawing instinct.

Had his foes been better trained, Aurelius might have met his end quickly. But they were raiders, desperate and ill-prepared, and Aurelius was sturdy and strong and bitter in battle. The sword was his curriculum. No longer would he find virtue and greatness chiefly in the books he had read or through the school discipline he received. No longer would he measure success in denarii and the import of fine goods from foreign lands. No longer would civility be the measure of the man. In the precarious world that was dawning, greatness and renown required violence. To love was to defend; to survive was to kill.

Such was Aurelius's catechism as he faced down his foes. By his sword, Ria was saved from her pursuers; by his bravery Publius evaded the men who would have bludgeoned him to a pulp; and by his example the men rallied to hold off the attackers while the weak and wounded fled. Though at the time he was hardly aware of any of this, each moment became clear in his memory and in the later retellings of others. In the days and weeks ahead, he would feed on those stories in his heart and be strengthened by the glory he received, like Christians partaking of their sacrament.

And yet, for all his valour, he could not save them all.

His father's death seared itself into his memory. In the dark moments of the night, when his old self seemed to rise closest to the surface, he felt ashamed. Had he been swifter, had he been cannier, he might have saved his father. But he had not, and his failure to defend him was too much for him to bear. So, he learned to bury that shame beneath an enmity towards his foes so fierce it would guide him all his days.

His failure began with a choice. Like a Greek fury, Aurelius charged into the courtyard eager to face the next attacker. He saw his parents and Meurig beleaguered by a growing number of attackers, and he moved to help them. But, at the same moment, he spied Ria fleeing down the lane alongside the baths pursued by two men. Had he not also seen that one of those men was missing an arm, he probably would have chosen differently. His parents were closer and their need greater. But here Aurelius learned the bitterest lesson of all: that his hatred was more powerful than his love and his need for vengeance greater than his desire to protect.

His decision made, Aurelius charged across the courtyard, evading blows and slipping past his attackers, none of whom gave chase, their attention fixed on easier prey. He sprinted down the lane, the chaos of battle receding behind him like the muffled roar of a raucous festival. But this surreal calm lasted no longer than it took him to round the corner of the bathhouse.

At first, he couldn't make sense of the scene before him. Ria lay on the ground, her face a mask of horror. At her feet lay Muconius's body with his head so smashed to a pulp that Aurelius would not have known him except for his missing arm. Over him stood Rhodri with a hammer as red with gore as his face was white with shock. Around them, the clash of close combat raged as men grappled and struck in a tangled mass. Aurelius had barely a moment to take it all in before an attacker lunged at him. He dispatched him swiftly and stepped forward to ram his blade into the back of another.

Two more fell with arrows in their sides. Aurelius turned with relief to see a band of militia, many armed with bows, arriving from the village. He knew then they would survive.

"Follow me!" he cried, his voice hoarse but urgent.

Lost now in a stew of bloodlust, exhaustion and desperation, Aurelius hardly noticed or cared if any followed. He knew only that he needed to get back to the courtyard to save his parents. Now at last was the moment to prove his worth to his father. The boy who had continually disappointed his father by hating his home now sought to become the saviour of both.

———

Years later in the quiet of her monastic cell, the memories of that day would too regularly accompany Corotica's prayers. She would at first smell smoke and taste ash and then feel the sting in her eyes, the pain in her lungs and the scorching heat against her skin. Strangely, sensations always preceded the memories, as though the day had been etched into her body more deeply than her mind. But once she began to experience again the dreadful sensations of that day, she knew that not even her desperate prayers could save her from returning to that morning when her beloved husband was killed.

Her memories surrounding the moment when Armoricus fell came only as fragments: the burning barn, the rush and growl of attackers, a brief and frustrating glimpse of her children, Ria's flight, and Aurelius's pursuit. These stood out vividly from the whirlwind of violence that her mind tried to bury. Later, she was reminded that the moment Meurig had sounded the alarm, she had helped Ancarat lead as many women and children to safety as possible. When they mentioned that, it would trigger a memory of Cunicatus dead on the ground with Drichan praying at his side. That was the moment when she realized the horror that day would bring. She vaguely recalled herding people along the eastern wall of the baths, past the remains of the bonfire, and onto the lane leading to the village. Survivors of that day often assured her that her prompt action had saved them from even greater carnage. But her hazy memories left her unsure if what they said were true or just words to soothe her.

And then the terrible moment came, an instant that she never had trouble recalling, that haunted her thoughts and nightmares for the rest of her life. The stench of men all around her as Armoricus, Meurig, Quercus and a dwindling number of others fought more desperately than valiantly against the brigands. The unbearable sounds: grunts and growls, the screams of the wounded, and guttural oaths in Brythonic and Irish. Amid it all, she struggled to stay clear of the attackers while looking desperately for Publius, Rusticella and Aurelius. She felt relief when Aurelius appeared with reinforcements, their cries announcing a turn in the fight. But even as hope flickered, she saw the archer—his arrow poised to strike her son. In that instant, she shouted the four words that she would never, as a mother, be free to regret.

"Armoricus! The archer! Aurelius!"

Armoricus did not hesitate for a moment. He must have known as he leapt into the fray to tackle the bowman to the ground that it would mean his death. She saw him only briefly as he slammed into the Irishman, knocking the arrow away as the two crashed onto the ground. But then he was gone, hidden beneath the feet of the attackers who were turning now to meet the new threat.

What made Armoricus' death even harder to bear was the knowledge that it almost needn't have happened. A few seconds later and the archer would have been swept away with his compatriots as they retreated from the flanking attack. They left their dead and the dying like strandlines in the wake of a receding tide. Among them, his body pierced all over, lay Armoricus dead on cobblestones that were slick with the slime of blood.

Then it began to rain.

Corotica knelt in the downpour, her husband's head cradled in her lap. As the water drenched her, memories came unbidden, vivid and overwhelming: his first admiring smile, their first fumbling caresses as each began to explore the only bodies they would ever know intimately, the glow of Armoricus's face at the arrival of each of their children, the quiet afternoons they spent together in the garden. The memories came fast and free—they could no more be restrained than the rain that was now soaking her through. But her mind held onto one image beyond them all, as if it were the set and stage where each recollection played its part: Armoricus in the fields, his silly straw hat askew, rake in hand, his face a picture of unguarded contentment. It was when she finally came to focus on that image that the flood of memories ceased and her emotions broke. Her tears were washed away by the cleansing rain.

—

Baglan's journey along the Roman road that Midsummer's night had been long and arduous. Fearful of pursuit when Gwas's absence was discovered, he did not stop until he felt that his weary legs could go no further. He had found a small clearing in the woods, far enough away from the road not to be seen or for his donkey to be heard, and there he had gently laid Gwas down to sleep.

In truth, his fears were unfounded. No one had come after them. Gwas was, to the world, a discarded thing—a sack of bones not good enough to miss, let alone pursue. Baglan had done the foremen a service by taking away the human refuse they would have only had to bury themselves. Only to Baglan did Gwas count as a man. Gwas's act of kindness on that bleak and friendless moor had bound them together as unbreakably as any bond of human love. He wrapped Gwas in wool blankets, blindly gave him some water, and then settled down beside him to sleep. In the darkness of that Midsummer's night, he could never tell if his eyes were open or shut.

But the deep quiet of the woods wrapped him up as securely as Gwas's blankets. He eventually fell into a long and restorative sleep.

Warm sunlight dappling through the leafy canopy brought him serenely out of his sleep the next morning. He rose and quietly searched his bags for provisions and was pleased to find a veritable trove of food. He started a fire and prepared fortifying porridge that would sustain them both through the morning.

The daylight gave him a chance to look at Gwas properly. He was gaunt to the point of translucence, his flesh stretched thin over a frail frame. His eyes were opened but seemed to register nothing of the world around him. Not once did he speak. It was as though the Ancestors were barring his exit from this life into theirs. Yet when Baglan fed him the porridge, he ate; when offered water, he drank. The small signs gave Baglan hope that Gwas might not yet be ready to die. Gwas might not yet be ready to die. He resolved to stay by his side until he either recovered or gave up his struggle.

As it turned out, their journey that morning under soft sunshine and surrounded by birdsong was not arduous. He estimated about a ten-mile journey lay before them, a long way for someone in Gwas's condition, but short enough for them to end their journey by the afternoon if the weather held. But by mid-morning, the sky darkened and clouds rolled in swiftly from the west. Torrential rain followed, drenching them and the earth, reducing visibility to mere paces. He was reminded of the last time he had approached the sacred grounds of the standing stone, when the heavens had similarly opened and washed away any chance that he had of finding his family. Perhaps the gods still deemed him unworthy of the Stone. If so, he would defy them with each step forward.

His cynicism proved unfounded. Though the storm was violent, it blew through quickly, clearing the air and leaving it cool and fragrant. As they rounded the northern slope and caught sight of the broad, peaty moors, the sun appeared and quickly dispersed the clouds left in the storm's wake.

They reached the standing Stone an hour later. Baglan stopped and looked at the ancient monolith. Rain had darkened its surface, giving it a sombre, solitary air, like a sentinel forgotten and impotent in the vast expanse of the moor. It stirred no awe in him this time, only a strange pity. He wondered who had originally raised it on that forlorn spot and why.

He lowered Gwas to the ground, propping him up against the Stone. He felt it was necessary, though he could not say why. Then he started rummaging through his bags for a little food. They couldn't stay long because he needed to build their camp before nightfall, but it felt right to be there at that moment. In that silent landscape, the world seemed as tranquil and empty as it was wide.

Gwas stirred, his voice a faint whisper. "Shadow."

"Shadow?" echoed Baglan, leaning closer. But he knew what Gwas wanted almost as soon as he asked. "Let me just shift you."

He gently moved Gwas around to the other side of the Stone, perching him in a place that still benefitted from the heat and light of the sun but where he could see the Stone's shadow stretching increasingly farther out as the sun set.

"We must go soon," said Baglan. "But take what strength you can from the Stone."

Gwas shook his head. "Must stay."

"What are you trying to tell me, Gwas? Why must we stay?"

"Shadow," Gwas repeated, weaker now.

Baglan remembered that uncanny sunset at the autumn equinox all those months before. The Stone's power had not arisen until that precise moment when, with the sun's final rays, its shadow had stretched out to the stream for a drink. Although they were a day late, he wondered if that would happen again. Was that the moment that Gwas needed?

Baglan wrapped Gwas in blankets and left him to rest while he prepared a camp in the grove where they first met. As twilight approached, he returned to the Stone. Gwas sat as he had left him, his face serene, his breathing shallow but steady. A faint smile graced his lips, as though he dreamed of something sweet.

"It's almost time," Baglan whispered, touching his shoulder. The old man opened his eyes, looked down towards the stream and smiled weakly. "The Stone. It drinks!"

Baglan turned to look, half expecting to see that the Stone had magically moved down to the stream. But, of course, no such thing had happened. It was only a trick of the light: the rays of the sun striking the Stone at an angle that made its shadow reach down to touch the stream.

"Yes," Baglan said softly. "The Stone drinks."

But his voice went unheard. As the sun dipped beneath the western hills, Gwas's spirit followed the shadow, leaving his body to grow as cold as the Stone behind it. Baglan knew then that this was why he had been drawn here, that this was where Gwas needed to be to pass over into the welcoming company of the Ancestors. The blissful peace present on his skeletal face left no doubt that he had been received with joy.

The gods had not been punishing Baglan after all. They had led him to this spot at this time for this final act of kindness towards a man who had never known kindness. In the benediction of that beautiful moment, he knew what he must now do.

He would go home.

XXXII

The days and weeks following the attack by the brigands were the hardest that Ria ever endured.

A time for grief.

The rains came too late to save the villa, which burned until nothing was left but the charred skeleton of what had once been their home. The barn, the servants' wing, even Ria's own quarters—all gone, smouldering in the ash-stained wind. The villa itself stood as a hollowed ruin, its blackened walls silent and still, like a body stripped of its breath. Only the chapel and its neighbouring bedrooms were spared, as though the perpetual flame within had held the consuming fire without at bay.

At first, Ria thought it wrong to grieve for bricks and mortar when so many lives had been taken or broken. Yet as days stretched into weeks, she came to see that her sorrow for the villa was more than a yearning for its painted mosaics, its familiar creaks and its warm hearths. Yes, she had adored the old building, but it was those who dwelled there, with their laughter, labour and love, who had infused the villa with life. Without them, it was no more than a husk. Home, she came to understand, was not made of stone walls but of the life that filled them—a life that Armoricus had tended as faithfully as he had his fields.

Ria now understood better how much the villa's life had depended on the Dominus who had loved his home with all his heart. His devotion to the villa, as touching as a man's tender fidelity to his wife, formed the rich loam in which all the other loves Ria knew took root and blossomed. Another metaphor came to mind: Armoricus's care had supported an intricate web of connections—families, friends, neighbours—that had given the villa its vitality. But he was gone, and now the web was unravelling, thread by fragile thread. Had the villa remained untouched by the fire, it would have become no less derelict. It was Armoricus's love, steadfast as the earth itself, that had kept the shadows at bay. Now that he was buried among his ancestors, Ria saw clearly how much they had been living on borrowed time. The brightness of their days had been a gift, fleeting and precious, like the brief flowering of a summer's meadow. They would never see its like again.

For a time, this grief was masked by others that pressed more forcefully on her worn-out heart. Chief of these was Armoricus's death itself. His burial rite capped a week of funerals that saw over thirty men, women and children interred amidst such wailing that no evil spirit could have endured it. By the time they assembled into their funeral procession to guard Armoricus's coffin on its final journey from the wrecked villa to the bedchamber of his ancestors, their voices were hoarse and their eyes as dry as used-up wells. Even Corotica was impassive during that woeful walk, displaying her grief only through the aching dignity of her bearing.

Yet even amid sorrow, there were small mercies to count. Despite their grievous losses, the *familia* had survived. Her own parents were spared, though Cadfan's wrist had been broken by a blow meant for his head. Her sweet Ceridwen had been saved by the bravery and quick thinking of Publius, a boy who seemed to find heroism as natural as breathing. Ria would never forget what she owed him, holding him henceforth in a reverence softened by a sisterly kind of affection. Publius himself seemed oblivious to the fact that he had done anything remarkable. Even old Quercus had stood his ground once again like an indomitable oak. Yet he was left a shell of his former impish self until time and the loving attention of his daughter-in-law worked their healing balm into his old soul. From time to time, he could be seen shaking his stick at the bathhouse as if to say, "I'll be damned if you're going to outlast me."

Life gradually crept back in through the cracks. Some who had been near death began to recover, a couple of babies were born, and Rhodri and Gwen were married a few weeks later. The festivities that marked that happy occasion taught Ria another lesson: that the rays of joy that pierced the dark clouds of their sorrow would eventually guide them back towards purposeful life. Though their lives had been stripped bare, there remained something rich, something vital, in the soil of their hearts. It was a goodness that could not be burned away.

About a month after the attack, Prince Cormac and his warriors, including Tewdrig, Meurig and now Aurelius, came to visit the remains of the villa. By then, the men had cleared away the debris while Ancarat and Ria had overseen the clean-up of what remained. The old and useless bathhouse now seemed even more imposing and out of place next to the ruins—no longer a workshop, it had become the makeshift home for those, like Ria's own family, who had lost theirs. Now, they were all refugees within their own lands.

Cormac came as an open-hearted lord. He brought food for them to eat and supplies for them to begin rebuilding. Though Corotica and Quercus welcomed him graciously, Ria shared the opinion of most that this jumped-up prince was more like the enemy they'd defeated than a friend to be honoured. But necessity bent their pride, and they took what was offered. Only out of earshot did they mutter darkly about the Irish prince and Meurig and Aurelius by whom they felt betrayed.

It was at this moment that Drichan performed a miracle. On Loaf Day, when the harvest was blessed and the first fruits of labour celebrated, the entire household was asked to gather down by the banks of the Isca. The promise of food and wine outweighed their reluctance enough for them to walk the two miles to the river without much grumbling. There, by the rushing waters, they found brightly coloured tents containing tables laden with food and drink. Aongus, clad in plain robes instead of his usual vibrant garb, greeted them with songs that lifted their spirits. For the first time in weeks, laughter rippled through the crowd, tentative but genuine.

After the elderly and the infirm had finally arrived, Aongus fell silent. Soon afterwards, Prince Cormac emerged from a tent similarly dressed in an undyed robe. At his side walked Drichan, his Gospel book in hand, with a gravity that immediately hushed the astonished crowd. Aongus fell in beside them as they strode wordlessly past the crowd and down the steep bank towards the shallow waters of the Isca to stand next to Quercus and two other men. Only later did Ria find out that one was the master of the estate on the other side of the river and the other the father-in-law of Tewdrig, who was said to have a magnificent hall on the banks of a nearby lake.

To everyone's astonishment and snickering delight, both Aongus and Cormac stripped off their robes and followed Drichan into the river as naked as on the day they were born. There, with Quercus and the two lords as their sponsors, Aongus and Prince Cormac, lord now of all Garthmadrun, were baptized. As they re-emerged from the Isca, each was clothed in white robes signifying their rebirth and then led by Drichan back up the bank. There, beneath the blue skies of heaven, two peoples long at odds worshipped one God and partook of one Body together. Watching it all, Ria felt something shift within her. The old world was gone. What lay ahead was unknown, but it was theirs to shape together.

In this new world, Ria found herself stepping into roles she had not imagined. Her mother, once the unshakable stewardess, seemed unable to adapt to the changes. The routines of the old villa had been her anchor, and without them she drifted. She was happy for Ria to take up her mantle, serving Corotica and caring for her children alongside Ceridwen. Waiting on Aurelius, however, was another matter. The new Dominus of the household was nothing like his father. He loved their home, of that there could be little doubt, but he did so with an angry possessiveness that contained nothing of his father's husbandly love. He was less like a farmer cultivating his fields and flocks than a miser protecting his possessions from both real and imagined thieves. In time Ria learned to navigate Aurelius's love for his home that seemed to her much more like hatred for a world that had failed him.

One of the first things Aurelius did was demolish what remained of the villa. He would have preferred to rebuild it—everybody knew that— but he lacked skilled craftsmen. So, the material was repurposed for a new hall down by the village that looked more like Tewdrig's hall than anything built by the Romans. One of the clearest signs of their changed circumstances was that the new hall contained no colourful mosaics and no plastered walls painted with pleasant scenes or office lined with books. All but one scroll had been lost in the fire. The survivor, fittingly, was Virgil's *Georgics*, which had been found by the side of Armoricus's bed.

The bathhouse was simply abandoned and left to decay.

Meanwhile, in the months that followed Armoricus's death, Corotica underwent her own transformation. Under Drichan's tender guidance and care, she became a holy woman, devoted to her Lord now as she once was to her husband. There was nothing pitiable in her new holy love—her devotion was not a clinging to the past but a reaching towards something eternal. She became the true mistress of their new life, balancing her son's bitterness with her own steady grace. Ria, watching her, saw in Corotica a reflection of the earth itself: scarred but enduring, yielding new growth from old wounds.

Life went on as life always does. New stories about Armoricus and the wonder that was his villa were added to older stories told by the fire on cold nights or recounted on long walks or shared with affection when out in the fields. What they had lost was absorbed into all that remained, like dead foliage into the rich loam of the earth, eventually nurturing the lives of those yet born. In this way, Ria came to learn that though their world had changed beyond all recognition, nothing really had changed at all.

———

Unlike his leaving, Baglan's journey home was made with a spring in his step. Though it would have been quicker to take the road, it felt more fitting to return by the way he had come, keeping to the hills and drovers' paths that lay above the encircling woods.

His heart was strangely light following Gwas's death. However much the old man may have been touched by the gods or attuned to the Ancestors, his life must have been arduous and lonesome. Baglan wondered about Gwas's past—his origins, his path to that desolate place, and the sorrows that might have unravelled his mind. Perhaps some tragedy in his past had opened his soul to the gods, like Potitus's conversion had to Christ. Perhaps there was something about pain that made people more sensitive to the gods. Perhaps it was just madness.

Baglan buried Gwas in the shadow of the Stone, where the two had long kept company. It seemed fitting that they remain together in death. When he had finished covering over the slight body with the black earth, he stepped back over to the Stone and placed his palm against it. For a fleeting moment, he felt a terrifying urge to take Gwas's place as its guardian. It hurt him to abandon it to that desolate landscape. But the thought passed.

The Stone would now be a burial marker as well as a sentinel, and Gwas's fidelity to it would endure for as long as his bones remained. Baglan had no right to impose on their company. So he gave the Stone a friendly pat and started for home.

Only once did he glimpse another soul on his way back—a solitary figure silhouetted on a high ridge, ascending towards the flat peak of a distant mountain. The figure was little more than a shadow against the sky, and Baglan wondered who it might be and what call had led him so far.

The emotions began to well as he reached the far side of the valley from his old home. He had expected by now to see sheep grazing, tended by his successor, but the hill lay empty. He clambered down the steep slope, crossed the river flecked with low falls, and ascended the far side, retracing steps he had made countless times before. Memories of Awen, Brochfael and Ceridwen, and of the happy life he had once known, accompanied every step. He found his *hafod* much as he had left it, which meant that no one had brought the flocks here for their summer grazing. Indeed, dry bones now marked the spot where many of his sheep had died. How had the *hafod* been allowed to remain derelict? Where was his flock?

That people had come to the place since his departure became obvious when he went to visit the spot where he had hastily buried Brochfael. Shame struck him like a blow; he had buried Brochfael in haste, without the proper rites to guide his spirit. The boy deserved the lamentations of his kin, the protection of their funereal songs to shepherd him to the Ancestors. How foolish he had been to go after his wife and daughter. How irresponsible he had been to abandon his son.

"Baglan?" The voice startled him. A tall, armed man emerged from the woods, his sword glinting faintly in the afternoon light. "Is it really you?"

It was Meurig. Just to see him filled Baglan with a sudden longing to be among his own again. "Yes," he replied. "I've made it back."

Without hesitation, Meurig sheathed his sword and embraced Baglan with an intensity that surprised him. "To see you alive is a miracle. Where have you been?"

The soldier and the shepherd sat together on a rough-hewn bench outside the *hafod* recounting all that had happened during the previous year. The sun hung low over the mountains when they were finally done. Empty of words, the two watched its rays trace the contours of the land and ignite an orange and red sky above the western horizon.

"A shepherd's sky, my friend," observed Meurig. "What will you do now?"

Baglan almost didn't hear the question, so lost was he in pondering Meurig's tragedy. He now knew what he had long suspected: that his wife was dead. He had mourned her so long that he could now only feel the release of that knowledge and the relief that she was now safe with their Ancestors. The rest of Meurig's story about his family brought him peace. Brochfael had been given the funeral he deserved, even if it was a Christian one, and Baglan felt assured that his spirit had also found a haven among the Ancestors. But to know that Ceridwen, precious and dear Ceridwen, had survived was the most momentous news of all. He longed to see her, to hold her once again in his arms, to have her sitting on his lap as he told her old stories.

He at last answered Meurig, but with a question. "You truly say that Ceridwen is happy?"

Meurig nodded. "It was something to behold, even for a warrior like me. When I found her and brought her back, I feared for her—thought her spirit might be broken, that perhaps she had been enthralled to evil spirits. But Ria took her in, cared for her as if she were her own. Did Ria have some tie to your family?"

"None that I know of," replied Baglan.

"Then it was a generous act, indeed," concluded Meurig. "People speak of power as wealth, status or the point of a sword. But I'll tell you something. I've never seen anything in this world like the power of unmerited generosity. I think Ria took in your daughter because she had to, because generosity was the lifeblood of our old *familia*. Ria's patient love was how that generosity could restore Ceridwen to health."

Baglan smiled warmly at that thought before replying, "Your words ring truer with me than you can possibly imagine. I would be dead or worse if not for the generosity of others. But what of evil? While my story ends well, your own seems to end in ashes. And our world seems to be growing too evil even to think about."

Meurig shrugged. "Such philosophy is beyond me." Then he smiled, as though struck by a sudden thought. "Perhaps the lesson found in each of our tales is simply this: that whatever goodness remains in our world will be preserved by the kind of generosity you and I have experienced."

"High sentiments for a warrior," laughed Baglan.

Meurig stood up and held out his hand to Baglan. "Perhaps that's because not enough people think this way. Until they do, they will need bastards like me. Now, I must get back. I will tell no one of this meeting. What comes next is for you to decide. Go well."

Baglan clasped Meurig's hand firmly and watched him disappear into the woods. The path forward was uncertain, but one thing was clear: Ceridwen had found happiness in a new life, and he would not disrupt it. His heart ached to see her and to visit his son's grave. But the gods had brought him here for the gift he had just received from Meurig. It would be greedy to demand more.

Yet one last duty remained; one friend he couldn't neglect. Just after dawn, as the morning sunshine glistened through the dew-drenched leaves of the woods, he made his way into the small grove where Empress Oak stood untouched by any of the previous year's troubles. The moment he came into her presence, he felt young again, as though the Baglan who had visited her in his childhood, the Baglan who had rollicked with his wife and children beneath her boughs, and the Baglan who came now to bid farewell became one. He recalled the acorn that had dropped into his hands, the small token of hope on the day his world collapsed. That had been the first act of kindness, the blessing that had grown into the others that came later. Like a tender mother, she had looked after him. And like a wise mother, she would now let him go.

He placed his hand on her trunk, a final gesture of gratitude. The tree, steadfast and enduring, seemed to bless him in return. Leading his donkey, Baglan turned away from the rising sun and began his return journey, ready to embrace the new life awaiting him.

—

The young stag ran like the wind through the woods. He skipped around trees, ducked under fallen branches, leapt over streams and shrubs with a grace as natural as he was free. He went towards no destination, though he ran from a place of death and danger. He sought nothing, wanted nothing but simply to run, to feel the wind on his face, his muscles straining as he climbed the slope, and to breathe in the rich aroma of a woodland in midsummer. He was wild and free and yet compelled never to stop, never to rest, but only to press forward in a frenzy of flight.

At last, the stag reached the place where he had been only once before: the edge of the woods that marked the boundary between hill and mountain. There he stopped, breathing hard, filling his lungs with the humid air. Behind him the woods stretched down towards the Isca, to where he had become trapped and almost domesticated, where pain and sorrow had threatened to smother his fierce freedom. In those woods lay shelter and liberty: safety from the evil of men and escape from their power, which he now knew to be unopposable. That is why wild animals run: to be free. Alone in the woods, he could also run—in the running lay his liberty.

Beyond him rose the terrifying heights of the mountains and the pinnacle where no stag had ever gone. And further beyond those heights lay a new world, one far removed from the men who had attacked and destroyed his home. Fierce and free though his spirit was, he now desperately wanted to flee that world. He wanted to be safe and secure in a place where no wolves prowled.

And so he pressed onwards. As he summoned the courage to step away from the shadow of the woods and begin his ascent up the turfed slopes of the mountain ridge, he ceased to be a stag. He became what he always had been: a mere boy.

Publius had fled the ruined villa on the morning after the attack. He had not planned to. He had not given the idea the slightest thought, which is why he had left without provisions. But the weight of the sadness inside him and of that which surrounded him were more than he could bear.

He felt as though he were being suffocated from the inside out. He was also gripped by the burning shame that he had cowered in the dark, trembling like a little girl rather than standing up against his family's enemies, like Meurig or his elder brother. When he awoke that morning with the stabbing knowledge that his father was dead, he no longer wanted to be Publius.

And so he became a stag. But as he ran through the woods with legs as fresh and free as his heart was heavy and his mind confused, his attention kept being drawn towards the four mountainous summits that lay to the south. If he could but stand atop the highest peak, he would finally see the wide world as it was and know then too what he must do. Perhaps from that height he might also glimpse his father's spirit in heaven. Surely he would be close enough to see it.

He passed the spot where he had watched the kite swoop down on its prey on the day that he saved Ria. This time, he didn't stop but pressed onward up the steep climb where bracken closed in around him, brushing against his chest, scratching his skin like a coarse, unshaven face. His legs strained as the incline carried him higher, his heart pounding hard in his chest, until the ground finally levelled out and he could take in the views around him.

Although Publius was still far from the most easterly of the summits, already the world to the north lay before him as though he were a god surveying a kingdom. He could see now how the mountains to the west were in fact a series of ridges, each capped by a peak like a head joined to two outstretched arms. Although the peaks and ridges continued to the west as far as his eyes could see, to the east he could now see the wide gap formed by the Isca valley and another range of mountains in the distance that stood like a wall above the hills beneath it. Then his eyes were drawn to a much closer movement: the smoke that still was rising from the wreck of his home. Publius frowned and turned away.

The climb continued, and soon he reached the summit of the first peak. The final approach was a scramble, his hands and knees smudged with clay as he clambered up the rocky slope. At the top, he stood braced against the wind, letting it pull at his hair and tug his clothes. From there, the view opened southward, revealing a broad valley cradled within a vast horseshoe of stone and turf. The ridge curved like an arm encircling the valley, each bend marked by a craggy peak. For the first time, he realized how high they were and how hard it would be to climb them.

But Publius was undaunted. As he started down the steep western slope of the first summit, dropping down to a high gap through which, to his astonishment, ran a narrow road, he was buoyed by an equally unexpected sense of elation. Despite all that had happened during the previous day, he was swept up by a delight that allowed no space for pain or a troubled mind. He more danced than scrambled down the slope, with such a light heart that he felt almost as if he could fly. He shed the freedom he had known as a stag and imagined himself now like a red kite, flying freely above the earth, impervious to the evil and sorrow that lay far below.

As he climbed up to the next pinnacle, physical weariness and thirst began to check his elation. Alone on the ridge, he began to grow aware of his solitude. There were no enemies here, no beasts or men to threaten him. Yet he was exposed, his isolation made stark by the wide emptiness around him. If he were to stumble, if misfortune found him here, there would be no one to help or rescue him. He slowed his descent into the final gap that separated him from the highest of the four peaks.

The climb to its flat peak of wind-blasted rock was the hardest yet. Near the top, he had to use his hands and knees to scramble over a jumble of rocks. When at last he reached the summit, he found a cairn of ancient stones stacked at the far edge. It was a marker left by those who had come before, their purpose as mysterious as the wind that swept across the high ground. Publius wondered about those long-gone hands, about their lives and what had drawn them to this place. The cairn seemed old beyond reckoning, though for all he knew it might have been raised only days ago.

Exhausted and thirsty, he rested there, perching on the cairn as his gaze travelled south and west. The mountains unfurled before him, great rolling waves of stone and green, their edges softening into the southern hills and hidden valleys. The hill country stretched as far as his eyes could see. But then as he began to make better sense out of the scenery's features, he saw a light blue horizontal line, mostly hidden by the hills, stretched across his horizon.

The sea!

He knew that it must be the channel that led out into the vast ocean, even though it was too distant to see it as anything other than a streak of aquamarine. But that was enough. He tried to imagine himself travelling by ship on it to the strange lands that lay beyond the ocean. That would be freedom, indeed! Then he recalled that it was along that same sea that the Irish had come and that the world he now saw contained as much savagery and sorrow as the lands to his north.

And so, at last, he turned to look on the woodlands, meadows and hills in which his own home lay. The sun, once harsh, was now softened by a veil of thin clouds, its heat gentled. For the first time, he grasped the immensity of the world. He knew that in every direction he could see for miles and miles, and yet in each direction the land stretched far beyond his vision. He imagined that everything he could see around him was unchanging—that within the eternal hills and woodlands and valleys, all the tragedies he'd experienced were as nothing. He now knew why stories could be forgotten and how the people who told them could disappear. He could see how inconsequential they all were in such a wide world. Yet the world was not merely vast; it was beautiful beyond words. All the evil that had been inflicted on his family and on so many people living in his part of Britannia could not touch that beauty.

And then, all at once, he knew that all would be well. His people had been living here since time out of mind. And even if some couldn't remember their ancient stories, and even if their own lives and stories might one day be equally forgotten, they would survive these dark days just as they had all the others. What he had to do—what anyone had to do—was to try to live a life equal to the world's beauty. That is what his father had done. He could see that now. The virtues that had made him admirable were precisely like the beauty that made the wide world breathtaking. Publius now knew what it really meant to be good.

He clambered down the cairn, brushed the dirt off the seat of his tunic, and started back the way he had come. He now understood that his place didn't lie somewhere out there in the world but here amongst his own. It was time for him to go home and start a new life in which he was neither a stag nor a red kite, but simply Publius, son of Gaius Rusticelius Armoricus, the best man he had ever known. He didn't know if he'd ever measure up to his father. But he also didn't feel the need to try. He had seen with his own eyes the immensity of the world and understood now that within it he was only a small boy.

Chorus

"*Let us now praise famous men,*" began Drichan as he faced the curia in Isca Augusta three weeks after the death of Armoricus. The moment he had decided to travel to the city to address the curia, he had known that he would begin with that verse. "*Let us now praise famous men, and our fathers in their generation.* That, most excellent fathers of this city, is what we read in *Ecclesiasticus*, a book full of wisdom and understanding. *Let us now praise famous men.*

"But I will risk blasphemy by saying this: that command, on its own, is fatuous. What is easier than to praise famous men? Don't the great seek fame precisely that they may be praised? Each of you knows fame well. You are the pillars of Isca Augusta, scions of venerable families. You can look back on your lineage with pride. You can say with Sirach, the author of *Ecclesiasticus*, 'We have among our ancestors, *Such as have borne rule in their dominions, men of great power, endued with great wisdom.*' Perhaps some of you even pour out your libations to your family gods, thanking the figurine wrought by a seller of trinkets for the fame you inherited. Some of you may even thank God."

As Drichan had predicted, these last two lines drew the first murmurings from the council. But he was confident enough in his oration not to be daunted by their sharp looks. No one yet sought to interrupt him. He looked again at the empty seat where the Bishop had sat during Aurelius's appeal on his father's behalf. Drichan had not been surprised to learn of the Bishop's death, apparently within a couple of weeks of their departure. He had just enough time to bequeath all his possessions to the poor, so earning him their blessing as St Martin had foretold in his dream. The grateful prayers of the poor would now benefit him before the Judgement Seat.

Drichan returned to his oration. "I left this place nearly a year ago, hardly more than a boy. I may have been a man young in years, I may have even gained wisdom through my studies and prayers, but I can now see that I was only a child. I still sought to praise famous men—if not my own ancestors or even the great men of Rome, then holy men such as St

Anthony, whom I admired more for his life than the holiness he received from God."

Drichan's voice softened as he recalled those days, a lifetime ago. "I had not yet grown in love. *When I was a child, I spoke as a child, I understood as a child, I thought as a child.* I had not then known what it means to love and be loved, to truly belong. *But, when I became a man, I put away the things of a child.* This past year has shown me the cost of love, its power to expose the heart to grief and loss. Love makes martyrs of us all because it insists that we die to ourselves, as Christ taught. Nothing is more painful than dying."

He let the silence speak before continuing. "Still, what is more precious than love? The wise value it far more than fame and glory. And yet, I've learned that for all its power, love stands naked against the evils of this world. *Love conquers all,* says the great poet Ovid. But it doesn't. It can't. Conquest is not within its remit. As the Apostle says, *love is not ambitious, seeks not her own, is not provoked to anger, thinks no evil.* Love lies completely exposed to the ill-will of those who seek fame, who care nothing for virtue, who desire only to impose their will on others.

"What then is love's strength? What I have learned during my ministry to Armoricus's *familia* is that love's strength lies not in conquest but in kindness. I've experienced kindness during the past year such that would break any man's heart. The kindness of a *familia* who welcomed me, a self-doubting young man, as its priest and pastor. The kindness of a Dominus and Domina who looked beyond my childish fancies to see what I needed to be a man. The kindness of a household who received the lost and the suffering and made them their own. The kindness of a woman who gave a little girl a second chance at life. The kindness of neighbours pouring out their grief for the sake of their dead. We think such loving-kindness is rare and precious. But I wonder. I begin to think that it's more common than we know. But because we're obsessed with praising the famous, we're blind to it."

Drichan paused again to gather moral strength for the next part of the oration. He could feel around him the presence of the fallen. He could even see their faces, as though they were waiting outside his old chapel to receive Christ's Body from him. He now understood that in feeding them he had himself been fed.

"I have not come here to praise famous men. I leave that to you who have chosen fame over love, hatred over kindness—a greedy man over one abounding in virtue. No, no!" Drichan exclaimed as a few of the magistrates began to object vocally. "I will speak. I will say my piece. And then I will go. Now that Crassula has faced the consequences of his own depravity, you cannot deny my words."

When Drichan had arrived in Isca Augusta, he had been given news of the tax agent's murder. The perpetrator was the lover of a woman whom Crassula had blackmailed into becoming his own mistress. With Crassula dead, others came forward with tales of his wickedness. Crassula's corruption had been exceeded only by his depravity. Had Muconius not attacked the villa, they might well have been spared the tax. That was Drichan's first thought at the news of Crassula's death. But it was no good dwelling on it since it only compounded the tragedy of Armoricus's death.

"*The days of men are like grass; like the flower of the field so does he flourish. For his spirit shall pass away from him, and he shall not be: he shall know his place no more.* That, my friends, is what I've learned during the past year. Each of us would have it otherwise. We would escape death, even conquer it, if only we could. But these are only deceptions, as are fame and glory. Is the hope of being remembered not the root of ambition? Yet we all fade, and the memory of us, too."

He leaned forward, his voice earnest. "Consider this lesson: Armoricus and Crassula are dead. One was virtuous, the other venal. The first dedicated his life to serving his people, his lands, and his *familia*. The second served only himself. Yet, both now moulder in the ground. And so, the question: what makes them different? Answer me that riddle.

"If fame and glory are your guiding stars, then both lives are alike. Virtue or vice, each ends in death. Soon, no one will remember Armoricus or Crassula. Whatever meaning Armoricus found in serving others and whatever debased satisfaction Crassula found in serving himself lasted not one moment longer than their final breath. I could say that the difference lies in their destination—that Armoricus, by God's mercy, is now in heaven while Crassula writhes in hell. I believe that such may well be the case. But that isn't the main difference.

"*Ecclesiasticus* again: *There are some, of whom there is no memorial: who are perished, as if they had never been: and are become as if they had never been born, and their children with them. But these were men of mercy, whose godly deeds have not failed.* Armoricus and Crassula—both are dead, both will soon be utterly forgotten as undoubtedly will we all. But Armoricus was a man of mercy, a man of kindness, and a man of love. Because of his complete dedication to his people, his deeds haven't failed. As long as his family remains, they can never fail. Armoricus will be remembered in the conduct of their lives. His virtues have produced a bountiful crop in those he loved, like wheat whose seed scatters in a winnowing wind. I've learned that we live most fully through the kindness we show others. To love and be forgotten—is that not the highest ambition?

"I speak as a fool. I came to praise Armoricus so that you, at least, will not soon forget him. But I now see that Armoricus isn't the subject of my oration at all. That person is someone else entirely. Someone, without whom not even Armoricus could have achieved the virtues that made him great. That person should now be mourned above all others, for her loss is grievous beyond words.

"I speak, of course, of the villa: the household and *familia* of Corotica and Armoricus. *Like the flower of the field*, she once flourished. The villa's life sustained all who called her home. She welcomed the stranger in the guise of refugees. She knew no ambition other than to be bountiful; she sought nothing more than to know her own place. She was copious not just in the crops she produced but also in the goodness she cultivated among those who cultivated her. And I grieve for her deeply. I am the priest I am now because of the privilege I was given to rest in her bosom for a brief space of time. The life of the villa was never her bricks and mortar. It was the life of all who called her home.

"I leave you now, great men of Isca Augusta, to your fame and glory. I leave you to the decaying ruin of your city, the rubble of your vain ambitions. Like Christ's disciples, I shake the dust off my feet to the vainglory even of Rome herself. The pride of man never endures. I see that clearly now. But kindness? Kindness is its own reward."

293

Historical note

A month after the American Revolution ended, a gang of workmen outside Brecon in mid-Wales came upon a surprising discovery: the foundations of a massive Roman bathhouse. According to the contemporary historian Theophilus Jones, they eventually uncovered a 45 by 65-foot building with several rooms containing elaborate mosaics. They also found slag, probably from ironworking, which may indicate that the baths were at some point used as a workshop. Sadly, the workmen then destroyed much of what they found.

There have been no subsequent archaeological excavations of the site. Why such an enormous bathhouse was built on the northern slopes of the Brecon Beacons in what was then the backwater of Roman Britain remains a mystery. The best guess is that it may have been part of a villa complex, possibly built or owned by a tax collector or a commander of the local auxiliary. Really, no one has the slightest idea.

Much the same can be said about Wales during this time (then part of the Roman province of Britannia Prima). What later would be known as Brycheiniog, and later still as Brecknockshire, was then on the northern border of the tribal lands of the fierce Silures. Although Rome had conquered the area during the late first century, it probably was never seriously Romanized. The nearest cities were Isca Augusta (Caerleon) and Glevum (Gloucester), though there was also a substantial tribal capital at Venta Silurum (Caerwent). But each of these lay several days' travel away. The primary local reminders of Roman rule would have been various forts, roads, and a series of lead, silver, and gold mines. To speak anachronistically, it must have felt like a colony exploited and heavily taxed by imperial agents but otherwise left much as it always had been.

The end of Roman Britain itself is traditionally dated to AD 409 when the last legions evacuated the province. For decades, Saxon, Irish and Pictish marauders had been raiding Britannia, destroying trade and threatening towns and cities enough for them to build walls, such as can still be seen at Caerwent. It would have been a terrible time to be alive in Britain: a person who lived from, say, AD 380–460, would have seen their entire world collapse. While scholars debate the scale of violence, socio-economic collapse and migration, the fact remains that by the end of the fifth century, Britain contained no cities and was described by writers at the time as cut off from civilization. The parallels with the American withdrawal from Afghanistan give some indication of what this might have been like.

According to much later Welsh annals and genealogies, by the fifth century, much of southern and western Wales had been either conquered by the Irish or else devolved into petty kingdoms based roughly along old tribal boundaries. The short-lived kingdom of Garthmadrun may have been a client sub-kingdom of the Irish based in Demetae (Dyfed in west Wales) or else an independent kingdom with strong links with the Irish. By the mid-fifth century, the kingdom was called Brycheiniog after its eponymous leader King Brychan, who produced twenty-four children, most of whom were later considered saints.

But as with so much of Welsh history during this time, it's impossible to say much about anything with confidence. As the whole corpus of early Arthurian literature bears witness, this period is so enshrouded in legend and folklore that it's impossible now to distinguish fact from make-believe. The only textual evidence written remotely close to this period are the great jeremiad by Gildas entitled *The Ruin of Britain* and St Patrick's *Confession*. For almost everything else, we must rely on legends, annals, poetry and genealogies written more than five centuries later, or on archaeology. Essentially, historians know something about Britain before the fourth century and after the seventh century, but they must rely on their imagination, guided by whatever evidence they think dependable, to fill in the space in between. Hence, the much lamented but entirely reasonable description: the Dark Ages.

That being the case, I could say that all the characters in my novel are fictional. That doesn't mean that none of them is historical. Characters who certainly lived are Patricius, who would later be better known as St Patrick, and Calpurnius and Potitus (respectively his father and grandfather). While Patrick's birthplace remains much debated, the village of Banwen, north of Swansea, is a possible contender.

Other characters are also mentioned in the historical documents. Drichan was supposedly a blind hermit who taught Brychan when he was a small boy. Tudwal and Tewdrig are mentioned as being Brychan's grandfather and great grandfather (Tewdrig is the later Welsh version of Theoderic, a German name, and so I back-formed Tudwal as Theodwald to make him a German auxiliary who settled in the area). Finally, Cormac mac Urb appears in several Irish genealogies as a local sub-king, whose son would become Brychan's father. He strikes me as being a key transitional figure for this period. Everyone else shares the misfortune of having been entirely conjured up by my own imagination.

Despite this being a work of fiction, I have sought throughout to be as historically plausible as possible. I tried to be chronologically accurate, though I quickly gave up on squaring the dates derived from various lineages and annals for the historical figures. Patrick was probably born a generation later than in my novel. The most ahistorical aspect of the book is the speed of social collapse—but I wanted the whole narrative to occur in a single year and so for dramatic effect I accelerated the rate at which everything falls apart.

One final historical note: Drichan's description of the effect of St Anthony's life on him is inspired by St Augustine's account in his *Confessions*. Similarly, his funeral oration for Brochfael draws heavily from one that Augustine delivered, and his sermon about Eden includes parts of Augustine's wonderful description of Eden in his commentary on Genesis entitled *De Genesi ad litteram*.

You can visit several of the sites that appear in my novel. A footpath outside of the village of Llanfrynach, a couple of miles east of Brecon, takes you across fields where a farm now stands on the site of the bathhouse and possible villa. You can follow this along the Nant Menasgin up into a secluded valley that's dominated by the summit Fan y Big. If you know where to look, you can wander the woods where Empress Oak presided and see the place where Baglan's hut would have stood. The old Roman fort, now called Y Gaer, is also worth a visit, especially if you follow the old Roman road from the Promenade in Brecon. Across from it, the small church in Aberyscir is where Drichan's hermitage would have stood. Gwas's standing stone is Maen Llia, located in a landscape as remote and desolate today as it was then. Go there, and you can read for yourself about the legend of the stone drinking from the nearby stream, as it has done for more than four thousand years.

EU GPSR Authorized Representative:

LOGOS EUROPE, 9 rue Nicolas Poussin, 17000 La Rochelle, France

contact@logoseurope.eu

www.ingramcontent.com/pod-product-compliance
Lightning Source LLC
Chambersburg PA
CBHW071856020726
47502CB00003B/773